THE FLOOD

THE FLOOD

David Hewson

This first world edition published 2015
in Great Britain and the USA by
SEVERN HOUSE PUBLISHERS LTD of
19 Cedar Road, Sutton, Surrey, England, SM2 5DA.
An earlier version of this book was published in audio format
only in Great Britain 2013 by Whole Story Audio.
Trade paperback edition first published 2015
in Great Britain and the USA by
SEVERN HOUSE PUBLISHERS LTD.

British Library Cataloguing in Publication Data

Hewson, David, 1953- author.
  The flood.
  1. Florence (Italy)–Fiction. 2. Suspense fiction.
  I. Title
  823.9'2-dc23

ISBN-13: 978-0-7278-8525-8 (cased)
ISBN-13: 978-1-84751-625-1 (trade paper)
ISBN-13: 978-1-78010-678-6 (e-book)

All Severn House titles are printed on acid-free paper.

Severn House Publishers support the Forest Stewardship Council™ [FSC™],
the leading international forest certification organisation. All our titles that
are printed on FSC certified paper carry the FSC logo.

Typeset by Palimpsest Book Production Ltd.,
Falkirk, Stirlingshire, Scotland.
Printed and bound in Great Britain by
TJ International, Padstow, Cornwall.

The water you touch in a river is the last of that which has passed, and the first of that which is coming. Thus it is with time present.

Leonardo da Vinci, 1174

Friday, 30 October 1942

Rome

The boy was four, a pretty child, slim, dark-haired with bright and thoughtful eyes. On this cold, wet day he stood by the bridge to the Castel Sant'Angelo, the city side, not far from home, staring at the stone angels and the vast brown shape across the river. They said it was once the tomb of an emperor, one of the greatest Rome had ever known. But he was a child, so it reminded him of nothing more than the little drum he had in their cramped one-room apartment in the ghetto, the only toy he owned.

Down the Lungotevere soldiers marched in dark uniforms, rifles to their shoulders, gleaming bayonets pointing at a sky so flat and lacking in colour he might have drawn it with a soft pencil and a sheet of paper. He wondered if these serious, frightening men thought their blades could pierce the clouds themselves, slashing their leaden bellies, bringing the heavens down to earth.

His father said the soldiers could do anything they wanted now. The boy didn't understand what that meant. But in the morning warplanes had flown over the city, their low and threatening engines bellowing like the voice of a great mechanical storm. From the windows of the great palace in the Piazza Venezia the man they called 'Il Duce' had spoken to a vast, adoring crowd.

Best not go, his mother told him. We're not welcome there.

And all the time it rained. He stared at the river, swollen to a torrent, muddy brown, with branches and debris floating on the surface as it raced through Rome. He'd heard there'd been floods before, times when the Tiber burst its banks and brought its freezing, dank presence into the crowded city itself. An inquisitive, curious child, he wondered what a flood might be like. Did people take to boats? Was there a new danger brought into a world that already seemed fragile and perilous? He couldn't swim, had never learned. It wasn't a good idea to go to the baths, they said. Best to stay home, in the ghetto, safe among those who were like you.

Which meant . . . he wasn't sure. The other families had habits, rituals, a certain style of dress. On the day called Sabbath they turned more stony-faced than usual and went to the synagogue. But not so much of late, and never in his case. The three of them – father, mother, son – were 'secular', whatever that meant. One day he'd ask. Not now.

Across the bridge, life was different. Bigger, brighter, bolder, more colourful. Safer too. The Vatican was there, another country, one ruled by the Pope, a man from a different religion, another life. That place was set apart from his world in a way the boy couldn't begin to comprehend. St Peter's, the Pope's beautiful basilica, with its vast, bright dome, stood on a hill, apart from ordinary Romans. The flood, if it came, would never reach there. Those severe men in their bright robes, cardinals and bishops, the ones he'd seen from time to time scuttling about Rome looking miserable and worried, would hide behind their pale brick walls and let the world outside go any way it wanted, or so his father said.

'What's troubling you, child?'

The man holding his hand had a warm and kindly voice. He was a priest of the Pope, in a long black robe and strange circular hat. In his left hand was a vast umbrella, one broad enough to keep the rain off both of them. His name was Peter and he came from a place called Ireland. That must have been why he spoke with a funny accent. Not that this mattered. He was a good man, or so the boy's father said, and he wasn't someone who gave out praise easily.

'Why are we here?'

Something was happening and it frightened him.

'Your mother and father have to go away for a little while.'

'What for?'

'They'll be gone soon. This morning.' The child noticed he was watching the troops milling along the riverside as he spoke. 'That's what I understand.'

'Why can't I go with them?'

'It's a long way. These are awkward times. They need you to be brave.'

The boy thought of their little apartment. His few belongings there. When the priest came for him just after nine his mother had cried, held him in her arms, hugging so hard it hurt. His father watched, grim-faced, pale, then patted him once on the back as if to say: on with it. The child hadn't known what to do, what words to utter. So he simply stood there, stiff and cold and frightened, then left with Peter, the priest in black, when they said it was time to go.

'Will the soldiers kill them?'

The priest's face changed. It became stiff, wracked with an emotion unreadable to a scared four-year-old child standing by the swollen Tiber, holding the hand of a stranger.

Peter bent down and gazed into his face. 'Of course not. What makes you say that?'

'I think things. I dream them.'

'That's called your imagination, which is a blessing in many ways. A kind of pet. And, like a pet, you need to keep it firmly on a lead. Remember: those dreams aren't real. They never will be.'

The boy wondered whether to say what was in his head: he'd never had a pet. There wasn't room or money for one.

Instead he closed his eyes and in his mind saw the muddy brown waters of the Tiber rising like the ocean, pouring over the stone walls that ran beside the river, roaring into the ghetto and the city beyond, sweeping away everything: men and women and children; cars and soldiers; tanks and all the guard posts set up on the street corners. There were bodies on the surging waves, skeletons and corpses, and all their faces turned to him and asked a single question: why?

Shaken by this interior sight, he opened his eyes to look at the wet, grey day again and saw the bridge, the drum-like Castel Sant'Angelo, and the stone angels, with faces that seemed both happy and sad at the same time.

'There's a game we must play,' Peter said.

'Not good at games . . .'

'It goes like this,' the priest continued. 'When we walk across the river we will go to see a friend of mine outside the Vatican. There we'll get in a car and you'll leave the city for a little while. Until things are better for you and for your mother and father. Which won't be long.'

'How long?'

The child could hear the surging tones of the torrent below. They seemed to be getting louder all the time.

'Be brave, be patient,' the priest went on. 'Here is the game.'

'Not good at games.'

The figure in black bent down and his pale and whiskery face came close to the child's. There was a strong smell on his breath, both pleasant and offensive. His eyes were watery and pink. Even though this man knew God, was one of His servants, he was not content.

'You must be good, child,' the priest said firmly. 'For all our sakes. These terrible times may . . .' He shook his head and tried to smile. 'May yet get worse if the Germans take the place of that man.' His placid face became stiff with anger. 'Mussolini. Please . . . try.'

'What game?'

Peter, the Irishman, pointed at the footbridge with the frozen figures, eyes turned to heaven.

'When you cross the Ponte Sant'Angelo,' he said, 'those angels will take your name. Your real name. They'll keep it safe for as long as they need to. So you'll never forget it. Never lose it. Till things get better, your name will stay a secret. Between you and them.' His finger touched the boy's nose lightly and he beamed, happy once more, or so he seemed to say. 'And me.'

'What will I be called then?'

'Giuseppe, I think. You like it?'

'I hate it.'

The priest's long black arm pointed to the angels on the bridge. 'But everyone will call you Pino. And it won't be for long. A few months, a year at most. Then you can return and cross that bridge, and speak to those sweet creatures with their wings. And say, "I'm home again. I'm me. Thank you for saving this part of who I am. But you don't need it any more. Our world is back the way it was. I'll take it now. It's mine."'

The boy was silent. Then the priest in the long black robes led him gently across the road, past a group of surly soldiers who watched them every step of the way.

Halfway along the bridge, the child felt something slip from him and wondered: did an angel subtly remove it as he walked, head spinning, fearful of the future, beset by shapeless doubts and nightmares?

Or did his small and shapeless identity steal away from him of its own accord, race over the grey stone handrail of the Ponte Sant'Angelo, and drown itself in the rushing swampy waters that sang in a constant, wordless chorus beneath their feet?

Friday, 4 November 1966

Florence

Monsters and demons. Wild beasts and crazed animals. When he came to, they were leering at him, frozen in the walls of the cave. Dead eyes, grinning mouths. Laughing, taunting, mocking.

He knew why, too.

They *saw.*

His name was Aldo Pontecorvo and he was seventeen years old; tall but skinny, half naked, his long, dank hair ruffled and greasy, face smeared with lipstick.

Belongings.

He had a bag, a woman's leather purse, and found himself clutching for it, scrabbling across the floor even though he hated the thing, couldn't understand why he'd gone along with this at all. Hard rock bit at his bare limbs. The ground was strewn with food and discarded wine bottles. The mush stuck to his hands and knees as he crawled across the damp, freezing stone.

This was what the world looked like once the party was over. Shattered glasses, spilled wine.

Some of these dishes he'd helped prepare, carefully, to recipes handed down, generation to generation. It was not food for commoners like him. A servant. A slave, there to do the bidding of grand and imperious hosts.

But all this happened *before.* The food was why he came. The rest . . .

Memories came creeping back. Some of the chaos around him was part of the ceremony. And so was he.

Drink this now, boy, and everything will be fine.

Seventeen and never been with a woman. Never had a father to take him to one of the whores who hung around the station of Santa Maria Novella or with the bums in the square of Santo Spirito. Never had the courage or the money to do it himself. The other kids at school laughed at him constantly. He was tall enough to punch them out if he wanted. But Aldo Pontecorvo was different; had been so long he wanted to stay that way.

And now his virginity, his precious innocence, had been snatched from him. Roughly, in the midst of a riot he only half understood.

His mouth felt dry, his head hurt. He got the bag, scrambled to his feet and tried to walk straight, think straight.

He was in a cave somewhere in a hill behind the Pitti Palace, the vast grey rusticated hulk from which the Medici once ruled Florence, meting out justice from a distance, never reaching down to touch the common, stinking humanity in the streets.

People like him.

'Like me!' the boy cried in a sudden, bold burst of angry despair.

His shrill voice echoed off the strange, fantastic walls around him. The fountain at the end of the chamber made a noise, as if disgusted by his outburst. He stared at the thing. Four demons set around a marble bowl, evil leers on their faces, spouts between their teeth. Above them a woman was trapped in the arms of a creature that was half-man, half-goat. The satyr's bearded face rose up to laugh at her fear and pain. The two were joined, him inside her, in a way that was more brutal, more physical than the young Pontecorvo had ever seen in any of the many statues and paintings that ornamented his native city.

Naked things were bad.

They were there in the Brancacci Chapel of his parish church of Santa Maria del Carmine in the quiet, local neighbourhood of Oltrarno where he lived. Adam and Eve, before and after the Fall. Happy figures on one wall, tragic on the opposing column.

He wondered: have I crossed the Brancacci now? From one wall to the other?

The satyrs answered with a chorus of belches. As he watched they spat brown, muddy water out of their mouths into the beautiful bowl. It came with a force that stained the naked ankles of the woman in the clutches of the lascivious beast who raped her.

'What are you doing, boy?' a brusque, coarse voice barked at him from the back of the room.

He turned and clutched the bag to his chest. No words.

It was Bertorelli, the man who organized the food. His employer, after a fashion. The only one who'd give him a job. A hard, brutal butcher from Scandicci, an old man with a violent temper and no time for fools. In spite of his crude character, he had a business catering for the aristocracy and the upper classes who owned and ruled the city of Florence as if they were natural heirs to the Medici themselves. Weddings and funerals. Civic gatherings in the Palazzo Vecchio and private functions on the Accademia. Bertorelli had provided for them all, and hired Aldo Pontecorvo when no one else would. The old farmer was a good cook, using ancient techniques and recipes that he was sometimes willing to share. Pontecorvo was grateful to him. And frightened of him too.

Then, the day before, he had taken Pontecorvo to one side and told him there would be a special occasion. A privileged one. The first Thursday of the month, every month. Be a success, Bertorelli said, and this is yours forever.

'If they like you,' he'd added with a wink.

'They like me?'

'One of them does already,' Bertorelli had muttered, then ordered him back to the stoves.

Now it was Friday, the early hours of the morning, and Aldo Pontecorvo was standing stupid, drugged, in a cold, damp underground cavern, watching four stone demons spew muddy water at a semi-naked nymph who was being raped by a man who was half goat.

The night was over. The deed done.

'Get your clothes on,' Bertorelli barked. 'For God's sake.'

He looked a little put out by something, the boy thought. Which was odd because all the shame was surely his.

The stone demons vomited up more brown bile.

'Jesus,' Bertorelli cried. 'It's pissing it down out there.'

The brute butcher glowered at him, his face contorted with disgust. 'Go home,' he said. 'I feel sick just looking at you.'

Fifteen minutes later, Aldo Pontecorvo ventured out into the cold night. He'd never known weather like this. The rain had been falling on Florence for days. It felt as if it might never stop. Torrents of muddy water ran down the hill, flooded the steps and walkways of the Boboli Gardens, roaring in a muddy spate out into the Via dei Guicciardini as it led towards the Ponte Vecchio and the Arno river itself.

Home was a hovel on the sprawling Boboli estate.

How did he face that? How did he face *her?* Not now.

There was a place near Santo Spirito. Stayed open all night. Illegal, naturally. The kids at school had told him about it. They dared go there. He didn't, couldn't. But now he was different, and it was this new Aldo Pontecorvo who stumbled through the drenching rain trying not to cry. He still had the woman's purse they'd given him. There were things in it. Lipstick. A tube of cream. Some lire bills. A way of saying . . . what? Thanks? Sorry? Know your place, little boy?

All the other kids had fathers. Men who played football with them in the streets. All he had was her. The woman with the belt and boot. A severe, judgemental mother, who dragged him to Santa Maria del Carmine three times a week, threw him in the confessional booth just for catching a glint in his eye.

Two weeks before she'd caught him in his tiny room.

'Touch your cock and you'll burn in hell!' she'd screamed, and then came the belt and a trip to see the sour old priest.

Hell was everywhere in Florence, staring at him from the walls of the Duomo, inside and out.

Hell was here, with him on this cold, soaking night, a vile soreness that got worse as he walked, awkwardly, like an infant who'd peed his pants. He wondered if that pain would ever go away. If he was destined forever to be the chattel of the people who'd used him that night.

Men with polished, aristocratic accents. Sleazy women in shiny silk dresses and garish make-up.

Drink this now, boy, and everything will be fine.

And so he had. Because you did what these people told you. That's why you were born.

Head hurting, lost for where to turn, Aldo stumbled on, full of grief and guilt and shame, though he'd done nothing to deserve it. Except obey.

There was a light in the square of Santo Spirito, a group of men outside the bar. More than there should have been, but this was no ordinary night, not for anyone. The rain seemed so persistent it might have been a punishment, like the flood God sent to cleanse the world. Not that there was a Noah in Florence that night. Just a new Aldo Pontecorvo, born somewhere beneath the dank, soaked earth of the Boboli Gardens, locked in the embrace of a man . . . more than one . . . a gang of them . . .

He stopped, choking at the memory, stumbled against a rusting Fiat 500, bent down and gagged, the sour acid bile rising in his mouth. Then, like the stone demons beneath the ravished nymph, he began to retch in forced and painful gasps.

The sky seemed to resonate to the rhythm of his agony, sending showers of gusting rain to wash away his spewing on the black, shining cobblestones of Santo Spirito. After a while there was nothing more to vomit, no dregs of the strange, rich meal they'd let him taste in the cave before the cup of tainted wine came his way.

He stayed in the gutter, drenched and mindless, wishing the downpour might wash away his agony, knowing in himself this was the daydream of a child, a creature he could never be again.

Five, ten, thirty minutes later, with the street now turning into a river, he splashed and staggered towards the light ahead.

The voices made him stop in sudden dread.

There was someone here he knew. A shape, happy and drunk, sated with wine and victory. Tall and erect in the clothes of a gentleman. No, two of them he saw, sheltering under an umbrella.

They walked down the street, towards Santa Maria della Carmine.

He took the woman's purse out of his jacket and looked at the lire notes. More money there than he could earn with Bertorelli in a month. The price of his acquiescence. The cost of his silence.

Drink this, boy, and everything will be fine.

But it wasn't and never would be. So he followed them, like the peasant he was, into the narrow lanes of Oltrarno. Watched, blood frozen, as they came upon her. Watched and knew he was lost.

Monday, 3 November 1986

Florence

Pino Fratelli, *maresciallo ordinario* of the Florence Carabinieri, was a lean, diminutive man of forty-eight; he was still shivering visibly, though he was dressed for this cold day in an ankle-length winter wool coat with a scarlet scarf at his delicate neck. When his leather gloves were not gesticulating at the vivid and spellbinding paintings in front of him, they fumbled with each other like tubby wrestlers fighting for domination. His face was more that of a musician than a Carabinieri officer: thoughtful and dignified, the prepossessing features combining melancholy and intelligence in equal measure. Beneath a deep-lined forehead, the round brown eyes seemed bright and alert; those of a younger man, heavy-lidded yet restless. Then there was the hair, a full and wayward head of it, pure white, the colour of hoar frost, flowing down over his collar. In the thick, heavy overcoat he had the appearance of a solitary and lugubrious artist of meagre means, stranded on the pale, unbounded beach of life, seeking amusement or enlightenment and finding neither.

By his side sat a serious-looking woman called Julia Wellbeloved, twenty-eight, intense and academic. She had a long and pleasant northern face, skin so pale it seemed translucent under the bright arc lights. These searing lamps were attached to the scaffolding that, with heavy sackcloth sheeting, separated the alcove of the chapel from the larger, darker nave behind. Her fair hair was pulled back behind a sharply angular head and tied in a severe bun held in place by a single elastic band – practical, if scarcely elegant. Sharp and icy blue, her eyes followed every move ahead. She possessed a calm, ascetic face, neither beautiful nor unattractive, yet striking: that of a Botticelli handmaiden staring querulously out of the side of the canvas; pretty enough to be visible, yet insufficiently distinctive to hold the painting.

A bystander watching these two – as they talked in low and earnest tones next to one another on a narrow church pew – might have thought they looked like minor politician and pretty young mistress, lecturer and attentive student. The truth was more mundane. They were landlord and tenant, drawn together by mutual interests and strange circumstances, puzzling over the curious sight that had closed the famous basilica of Santa Maria del Carmine and would keep its doors firmly shut to all but the Carabinieri and officials of the city cultural department for some time to come.

It was three days now since Julia Wellbeloved had arrived in Florence, seven months since she'd left her well-paid job with a City of London law firm and chosen instead the semi-poverty of being a postgraduate student. Money was tight, but not short. The sale of the flat in Islington, part of an ill-fated marriage that had lasted a too-long year and a half, saw to that. Now she was through with the law; through with men, too – for a while, anyway. All she wanted was to exercise her intellect, and that through a specific task: a dissertation so arcane it had taken an Italian cultural association to find the means to fund it.

Or perhaps the Florentines had more reason than most to help. The academic paper she was writing, one that would, she vaguely hoped, lead to an academic career, was entitled 'Why Murder Culture?' It would seek to document, investigate and hope to explain the infrequent but troubling attacks by members of the public on works of art, paintings and statues principally, some famous, some obscure, and a few, perhaps the understandable ones, wrapped in notoriety.

Funding apart, it made sense to start her work in Florence, a place that was in some ways a living exhibition itself; both inside its galleries and outside in the teeming streets and lanes where, with Dante and Machiavelli, Michelangelo and da Vinci, and many others now mostly forgotten, the Renaissance began. Was there another city in the world that stood to suffer more from such bizarre and seemingly inexplicable acts?

No. And now it was the third of November, 1986. There was blood on the walls of the Brancacci Chapel, the most famous corner of Santa Maria del Carmine, the 'Sistine Chapel of Tuscany', or so the guidebooks said. Thanks to Fratelli, a charming, intense man, she could see the subject of her studies at first hand.

'Signora,' the man next to her said, indicating two officers with more arc lamps, struggling through the jungle of ladders, paint pots and toolboxes strewn across the stone chapel floor. 'The officers need to pass.'

She pulled her slim legs underneath the pew and said, 'They should be careful of strong light. Old pigment may be affected.'

'I'm puzzled,' Fratelli replied, peering into her eyes with friendly interest. 'Which are you? An artist or a criminologist?'

She'd seen little of her landlord since her arrival. Inconclusive and unsatisfactory meetings at the Uffizi and with the cultural authorities had occupied her time until that afternoon, when Fratelli had knocked excitedly on her door and announced that there was an incident close by that might prove of interest to her work. The Uffizi had arranged accommodation: a separate studio in Fratelli's small terraced house three streets from Santa Maria del Carmine. This side of the city was known as Oltrarno – the quarter 'beyond the Arno', the broad and powerful river that swept through the centre beneath a line of fine bridges and was now a swirling, forceful flume thanks to recent constant rain. The Ponte Vecchio was only a ten-minute walk away. It was easy to reach the tourist quarters – the

Duomo, the Piazza della Repubblica – across the nearby Ponte Santa Trinita. And the Uffizi, with its constant crowds and close by the inchoate architectural mess that was the Piazza della Signoria.

But she hadn't found herself in the Florence of picture postcards, of tourists posing in front of the statue of David, and endless queues for the stairs to Brunelleschi's great dome. Fratelli lived in the city the Italians knew as Firenze: close and local, shabby in places, a muddle of dark and secretive alleys.

'Neither really,' she confessed. 'I'm a student.'

Fratelli frowned at the inadequacy of her answer.

'I'd love to paint but I can't,' she added. 'So if I can't create art I thought perhaps . . .' She shrugged her slender shoulders. 'I might at least try to save it.'

'What an honourable aspiration,' he said in a light and pleasant voice.

'For a policeman you seem very familiar with art yourself. If you don't mind my saying.'

He gestured at the chapel and said, 'Not really. History perhaps and this' – he glanced at the Brancacci Chapel – 'is history. A little of mine, too. When church was a place I favoured, I came here. I grew up with these faces. They were a part of my childhood. Better to stare at dead and pretty people than listen to a tedious sermon that takes half an hour to express a sentiment which might be said in a single minute. Oh . . .'

A stern and stony-faced priest close to the officers in the chapel turned and glowered at them.

'*In nomine Patris, et Filii, et Spiritus Sancti,*' Fratelli declared in a lilting singsong voice, then made the sign of the cross.

The priest shook his head and barked, 'Pino! Behave or I will throw you out of here myself! Show some respect. How . . .'

He was a somewhat older man than Fratelli. Burly, with a wrinkled, flushed face – once handsome, she guessed. He looked utterly distraught, as if this act of vandalism was a personal affront, which perhaps was how it seemed.

'I consider myself admonished, Father Bruno.' He winked at Julia Wellbeloved. 'We're old friends. Don't worry.'

'You're a very mischievous man,' Julia said, not altogether seriously. She was grateful he'd knocked on her door that afternoon, inviting her round to the church to see the chapel, even if she hadn't known the reason. In other circumstances she would have had to seek permission: the Brancacci was closed off from the transept and undergoing restoration. So much of Florence was in the same condition. Twenty years on from the great flood of 1966, the city still seemed to be half complete. Only those directly involved had access to its many partly closed galleries and precious monuments. Fratelli appeared glad of the opportunity too. He looked like a man in search of a puzzle, something to exercise his obvious intelligence.

'That may be true,' the Italian agreed. 'However, I approach my work with deadly seriousness. As to Pino Fratelli the man . . .' He frowned. 'It's difficult, when you've known yourself so long. Marco!'

One of the Carabinieri officers, a man in a flowing dark blue cloak, turned and fetched him an ill-tempered stare.

'You should listen to what my young English friend says about the lamps,' Fratelli ordered. 'Wait for the people from the Uffizi to turn up. They'll get here once they've finished their afternoon nap. Shine the wrong light on our lady on the wall and you may find they throw *you* in jail, not the beast who first assaulted her.'

The *carabiniere* uttered a single foul epithet and went back to work.

'Violence and this place are no strangers,' Fratelli continued, as if speaking to himself. 'What am I saying? Violence and art are bedfellows and always have been. You know the story about Michelangelo?'

She shook her head.

Fratelli swept his gloved hand across the space in front of them. 'He loved this place, one painting above all others. *The Expulsion.*' His eyes flickered towards the left wall. 'When he was young he was set the task of copying some of the portraits as an exercise. With other pupils, naturally. Michelangelo was an honest man with a wicked tongue. He told one of his peers, a sculptor, Torrigiano, exactly what he thought of his work. The opinion was not put kindly.'

He pointed towards the area before the small altar.

'Somewhere there, Torrigiano attacked him, breaking Michelangelo's nose like a biscuit, or so Benvenuto Cellini records. Look at any picture or statue of him and you see that wound. Disfigured for life, a nose that belongs on a boxer or a thug. Not a genius. Over nothing but a student drawing.' He scanned the walls. 'Not that Cellini was an angel. How many murders did he confess to in those scandalous memoirs? I don't recall. The point . . .'

There were more people arriving by the main door. Loud,

important voices. The word 'Uffizi' was spoken as if it were a magical incantation.

'The point,' Fratelli said forcefully, 'is that what we see here is supposed to take us through the cycle of our earthly lives. From the moment of the first temptation' – he indicated the fresco high on the right wall: Adam and Eve, beautiful and serene, a writhing serpent behind them bearing the face of a woman – 'to our expulsion from Eden. Our inevitable fall from grace.'

He turned to the counterpart fresco on the left wall, an image of heartbreaking force. The same couple in despair, expelled from Paradise, Adam burying his face in his fingers, Eve shrieking in agony, hiding her shame with her hands, above them a vengeful scarlet angel driving both out of Paradise with a fearsome blade.

'These two, Michelangelo did adore,' he said. 'They stayed with him throughout a long and dramatic life. You know the words?'

'Sorry?'

'Therefore the Lord God sent him forth from the garden of Eden, to till the ground from whence he was taken,' Fratelli continued, resurrecting his sermon tones. 'So he drove out the man; and he placed at the east of the Garden of Eden cherubim and a flaming sword which turned every way, to keep out the way of the tree of life.'

The priest was staring at the pair of them.

'Genesis is such an unforgiving book,' Fratelli said, returning the man's anger with a smile. 'I am honoured to be beyond its reach.'

He turned and glanced at the group approaching through the nave.

'Tell me what you see, Julia Wellbeloved,' he demanded. 'Swiftly, if you please.'

The priest, the man on the ladder by the first fresco, and the Carabinieri officers around them stopped to listen.

'I see a damaged painting.'

He gestured for more with his gloved hands.

'I see,' she added hesitantly, 'a ladder, I assume for the restoration, which was used to inflict the damage. A dead brown hen on the altar, its head removed. Blood on the fresco.'

'Where precisely?'

'On Eve, as she's tempted.'

'The purpose being?' Fratelli continued.

'I don't know!'

'Oh come on,' he cried. 'You have eyes!'

He pointed at the fresco on the left, the expelled couple. Michelangelo's favourite was by Masaccio, an unfortunate artist of brilliance who died young, perhaps poisoned by a rival, his great promise unfulfilled. The gentler, placid image of *The Temptation*, the one that the intruder had spoiled with chicken's blood, was by a more conventional, less adventurous artist.

Julia Wellbeloved felt as if she were an undergraduate again, being examined. She glanced at the visitor's sheet on her knee. The name was there.

Then she looked at the faces on both pillars.

'The purpose being to make Eve's expression by Masolino, which is graceful, beatific, at one with God, resemble that of her painted by Masaccio,' she said. 'After the Fall.'

'After the Fall,' he repeated, staring at the altar. 'In pain and despair. Expelled from Eden. Deprived of the gift of the tree of life. Immortality.'

Then, more loudly, so that the priest and the officers around him turned to stare, he added, 'You hear?'

Fratelli got to his feet, a little unsteadily, and brushed his too-long white hair away from his artist's face. 'This is not the vandalism you believe,' he muttered. 'Nor some childish prank of witchcraft. There's a purpose. A deliberate intent. Exactly as our observant English expert says.'

He looked at the disfigured Eve. The bird's blood was smeared over her delicate mouth, turning it into an empty scarlet chasm, the gore stretching in diagonal lines across her eyes, just as Masaccio had painted on the countervailing fresco.

'And then,' Fratelli said, sounding a little puzzled, 'there's this.'

He pointed in turn at two garlands of cardboard vine leaves, surely from a supermarket or gift shop, plastered across the hips of both women – Masolino's serene, eternal Eve and Masaccio's wretched mortal exile. They were held in place by nothing more than black electrical tape.

'That,' Fratelli declared, 'may be the single most important fact we have. Although . . .' Something else had caught his eye.

'Pino!' roared a deep male voice through the gloom. 'What in God's name are you doing here?'

A tall, formidable figure in a dark blue uniform, cap beneath his arm, marched in front of them. He had a ruddy, thunderous face.

When no response came he folded his arms, glared at Fratelli and bellowed, 'I am waiting for an answer.'

'This is my local church,' Fratelli objected. 'What am I supposed to do when I hear there's trouble? Stay at home and watch TV?'

'You go to church now, do you? Is this what sick leave entails?'

'Walter . . .'

'Capitano to you!'

'Now I am truly confused,' Fratelli cried, throwing his arms out wide. 'Am I on duty or not?'

'Not,' the uniformed man declared. 'I want—'

'Expel me the way God expelled Adam and Eve if you wish. But for your own sake, hear out my friend.' He gestured at Julia Wellbeloved. 'She's come all the way from England and is an expert in such matters. Attacks upon works of art. It is her speciality.'

'Well I'm starting to study it . . .' the Englishwoman added weakly. 'I wouldn't call myself an expert really . . .'

'Signora,' the captain said, nodding his head. 'This is a crime scene. I require you and Fratelli to allow us to examine it without further intrusion. Please leave, the pair of you . . .'

He beckoned to the open door of the church and the failing day outside.

'Walter,' Fratelli began, taking the man's blue serge arm.

'Get out!' the Carabinieri captain ordered.

Fratelli shook his head and stared at the plain grey stones of Santa Maria del Carmine.

'So be it,' he said with a sigh. Then he winked at the woman next to him and offered her a wry, apologetic smile.

The man was fifteen years younger than Pino Fratelli but no less striking in appearance. Six feet tall, with the physique of an athlete, wrapped inside the cowl of a black duffel coat that made him resemble an ascetic mountain monk, he stood in the square of Santa Croce staring at the marquee of the olive fair blowing in the squally rain. For one moment he removed the ample hood to see the activity ahead of him more clearly. A passing street cleaner paused from sweeping rubbish and stared. He saw a man who seemed conspicuous in his anonymity, his features a plain and featureless mask, without movement, without apparent life. A long nose curved like the beak of a cruel bird of prey, eyes grey and bulbous, fierce under dark eyebrows that ran together as one. In the white expanse of flesh that was his face, only the full grey, sensuous lips seemed to carry a hint of blood. There was not a single hair on his head, only a gleaming and flawless scalp soon covered up once more by black fabric, like a demonic tortoise retreating inside his shell.

He pulled back the cowl, turned on the cleaner and said in a low and vehement voice, 'Do not stare at me. I bite.'

The worker with the broom turned his eyes to the cobbles, apologized and pushed his cart further down the square.

The piazza was empty in the sleeting rain. Few tourists. No customers for the sellers of overpriced new-season olive oil straight from the press.

Beneath the ankle-length coat he wore heavy moleskin trousers stained with flour, a cheap blue shirt, a warm black sweater from a country clothing shop. The cockerel's blood stayed sticky on his fingers, hidden now inside old woollen gloves. How many times had he washed them? Countless. It stood there as a reminder of his inaction. His cowardice. His reluctance to play the part he knew, in his heart, was his own.

In the Carmine church, hurriedly splashing the bird's blood on the wall, covering up the obscene nakedness of her vile body, he'd felt alive. Four minutes he'd allotted himself. A blink of an eye; less than that, in the endless stretch of time.

The relief, the pride he'd felt, lasted no longer. A slaughtered cockerel, a point – the point – made upon the figures on the wall.

And then he'd wandered the city, feeling the excitement and the pleasure leach away inside him. By the Arno, in the park near San Niccolò, he'd watched the brown waters of the river fighting, roaring as they raced across the weir. Rain and wind had brought down foliage from the countryside, trees and branches floating furiously on the ceaseless swell. Swans and ducks wandered in the shallows at the river's edge, over the grass fields where only weeks earlier children had played in the last warm breath of autumn.

And what had he done?

Killed a cockerel, smeared blood on paint, fastened some decoration about their wicked loins with tape.

'I'm as weak as a child,' he murmured. 'Without its innocence.'

He knew why he'd hesitated too.

Fear.

Vengeance never dug a single grave. It was always two, and one of them was his.

An icy shower swept from behind the towering basilica of Santa Croce and chased away the few rash visitors who still loitered on the cobbles.

He began to walk back towards the Ponte Vecchio. Halfway across the square, the leaden sky burst forth, despatching its contents over Florence in gusty blasts of sleet so forceful they made the bravest dash for shelter.

There was nothing else to do but dart into the marquee of the olive-oil producers. The place was half full with reluctant shoppers, stamping their feet to stay warm, eyeing one another as if to say, 'No, I don't want to be here either.'

Some walked around the stalls, made small talk, tried the oil and bread. Since it was the new season's crop from individual farms, it fetched twice the price of the commercial product. Twice the quality, said the posters.

The man felt hungry so, without a word or a glance at the huddled figures seated behind the trestle tables, he went from one to the next, taking lumps of coarse white bread, dipping it in saucers of oil, moving on, not saying a single word.

Some were mediocre, some superb. He knew his food. That was why he never lacked for kitchen work whenever it was on offer. One job in particular, his for twenty long years, the first Thursday of each month. An unusual, private event. It was Monday now. By Thursday he'd be expected back in the kitchen, preparing the strange, exotic dishes once again. He didn't dare avoid that appointment. Splashing the blood of a bird on the walls of the chapel did nothing to lessen his hatred of the duty, or his pain at its past memories. He needed money. Somewhere to live.

When he got to the end of the line, he found himself staring into the eyes of an exotic-looking woman with ringlets of dark hair, gold on her wrists and around her neck.

'It's not raining in here,' she said. 'You can take your hood down if you like.'

'Still cold,' he murmured.

The woman cocked her head to one side and said in a heavy accent he couldn't place, 'You look familiar.'

'I don't think so.'

She shrugged, held up a bottle of green fluid, so bright and fresh it looked more like alcoholic spirit than oil. There were photos on the table. The woman half naked in the countryside, harvesting olives.

Just this side of thirty; short but sturdy, forceful. Beside her was a tall, strong young man with a black beard and a knowing face. A few words about a tiny estate the two of them ran alone. One that followed the latest trend, being '*biologico*'.

Organic. A fad copied from the Americans.

He looked at their names, examined her face again, recognized it, placed it. Looked at the man pictured with her, and remembered him too.

It was the end of the afternoon. The weather had turned bitterly cold. A gusty rain had begun to fall two days before, with such persistence and force that older Florentines, who could recall the great flood of twenty years before, watched the sluggish, muddy waters of the Arno rising and shivered, remembering.

Fratelli put a gloved finger to his lips and said, 'Ice cream.'

'Ice cream? What's ice cream got to do with it?'

'With what?'

She glanced back at the dark hulk of Santa Maria del Carmine.

'With the paintings?' Julia Wellbeloved was confused. She'd read Fratelli incorrectly, and felt a little foolish for doing so. 'I thought you were the police officer here. In the church.'

'Carabinieri officer please. I was just such in the church. I still am.'

'I meant the one in charge.'

'I never said such a thing,' he replied, baffled. 'Nor does the ice cream have anything to do with the paintings. How can it?'

'I . . .'

He tapped his watch.

'We're wasting time. The Grassi dragon cleans the house today. We dare not return while she's dancing round with the vacuum cleaner. I'd rather go back into the chapel and joust with the captain.'

It was Julia Wellbeloved's turn to fold her arms and stare at Pino Fratelli.

'Every Thursday, when Signora Grassi does the cleaning, I go for ice cream,' he said, as if the explanation were obvious. 'There's a place in Santo Spirito. They make it themselves.' He smiled. 'Want some?'

'It's freezing.'

'Not inside it isn't.'

He beamed at her and looked very like an expectant child.

'With regard to the painting . . . you study well,' Fratelli added.
'Even if you're not an expert. I exaggerated. Still, you have the
skills.'

'Thank you.'

'That was not a hen, of course. There were long claws on the back
of the legs. Old claws.'

Fratelli tugged a hank of white hair to his mouth and chewed at
it for a moment.

'The bird's severed head was beneath the painting. The comb
would have been long and stiff. Except, of course, there was no
comb. It had been cut off for some reason. Also . . .' He looked
embarrassed. 'Trust me. It was a cockerel. A mature bird. The kind
you find on a farm or a smallholding. Not a shop. Never a shop.'

'Pino,' she said delicately. 'There wasn't much blood and what
there was will wash off. The fig leaves were cardboard stuck on
with tape. It's terrible the paintings should have been attacked. But
in all honesty . . . the damage is minor. The chapel's in the middle
of restoration. They'll fix it. No one will know.'

'I know.' He nodded at her. 'You too, and I would have thought
this might have been of interest. Given your paper.'

'But I don't have any answers. It may just be a vandal. Someone
who broke in overnight.'

'Of course you don't have any answers. You haven't started
looking.'

She glanced back at the church.

'They should have better security.'

'What? You mean cameras? Invisible alarms? Devices that discern
our intentions, good or bad, before we're allowed to enter?'

'Cameras and alarms. Yes, of course.'

Fratelli pushed out his bottom lip in a very Italian gesture of
disgust, then briefly stuck a finger in his ear and jiggled it around.

'God was God and still he couldn't stop his own creations stealing
from the tree. We focus on mechanisms far too much. Better to hunt
for motivations, intentions, their sources. To analyse what information we possess, instead of counting off possibilities.'

'Security . . .'

'They have alarms. And one day they'll have cameras, I'm sure.
This is the habit of the modern world, I think. To invent a new toy
for every problem, while meekly peering at the facts themselves
through horrified fingers.' His gloved hands went to his face and

he briefly peeked from behind them, a child once again. 'The bell went off. But the man was ready. Perhaps he knew no one was working in the Brancacci today. He was so quick – the bird was dead already, the fig leaves in hand – and gone by the time anyone arrived.'

He gazed at her and the intensity of his bright brown eyes was a little disconcerting.

'One of our patrol people arrived twenty minutes after the alarm was triggered. That was all it took. Our culprit was swift and prepared. Unlike Capitano Walter Marrone of the Carabinieri and our friends from the Uffizi who only now have come to see. They probably heard on the way out to lunch. No point in interrupting one's social calendar, eh? You're right. It's minor damage and they know it.'

'Quite.'

'But this was not an idle case of vandalism. This is obvious. It was about saying something.'

'What?'

Fratelli shrugged and said, 'Search me.'

'Well, at least the paintings got off lightly,' she noted.

He put a hand to his chest and breathed in the damp air with care. She watched him and thought: this man is ill and doesn't want to show it.

'You never saw them before today, did you?' he asked.

'Not that I recall. Perhaps in a book . . .'

'Then you have an excuse. Ice cream,' he said, tapping her arm and pointing in the direction of Santo Spirito. Fratelli sniffed the darkening day. 'Quick, before they close.'

'I can do you a deal,' said the woman from the olive *fattoria*. 'Try some. We made it ourselves.'

She poured a spoonful into a tiny paper cup, as if she were serving wine, and handed it over. The woman wasn't scared of him. Maybe his appearance wasn't so bad. He didn't look like one of the Santa Spirito bums, the *barboni* who hung around the piazza begging for coins. Not yet.

He swigged it back in one. The taste was peppery and fresh. And behind it . . . nothing. All good Tuscan oil had that fire in it but he knew the kinds he liked, even the commercial ones. All were better than this. It was poor stuff, the work of a hopeless amateur unable to pay for an expert press to turn their second-rate fruit into something worthwhile.

Five thousand lire for a half-litre bottle. The most expensive he'd ever seen. He looked at her, the cheap clothes, the gold, the dead, strained eyes.

'A husband and wife can't run an estate on their own,' he said. 'Too much labour.'

The card read: Aristide and Chavah Greco. There was a hand-drawn map on the back to a place in the hills, an offer to buy direct from the farm at special prices. He thought of offering his help. But she looked penniless too. Had to be, from what he knew . . .

'I do other things,' she said very quietly.

'Like what?'

'First crop.' She held up a bottle and looked a little awkward. She didn't want to answer the question. 'I'm hoping' – she shrugged her sturdy shoulders at the cardboard cases of bottles of oil piled high behind her – 'I won't have to lug every one of these back to Fiesole when this party's over.'

She smiled a weak smile. He guessed she hadn't sold much at all. The tourists might fall for this trick, but not the Florentines. They never spent a cent without good reason.

'You're Greek,' he said, thinking of the surname.

'No. Greco's my husband's name. He's from Calabria. I'm Chavah Efron and I come from Newark, New Jersey. Via Kathmandu, Morocco, and several places I'd best not mention.' That smile again. 'Efron.'

She made a tweeting sound. Trying so hard to sell something. The oil. Herself.

'My mom came from Tel Aviv. In Hebrew Efron means lark.'

He picked up a leaflet from the stack on their table. It was a big pile. Not many people were interested in paying a fortune for fresh green olive oil that had never been near insecticide. The words and pictures told a kind of story, a myth about a couple trying to find their way back to the Garden. A couple of hippies. Took over a rundown estate five years before. Had to wait that long to get organic accreditation. They even had short profiles of themselves. Chavah left America to 'travel' when she was just sixteen. Asia, Africa, Europe. Ari, a big, unsmiling thug, clean-shaven; none too bright by the looks of the photo. Son of a 'businessman' from Reggio in Calabria, the very toe of Italy. A world away from here. Ari was a good head taller than her, though looking at the photos he guessed she wore the trousers.

'Chavah Efron,' he said when they went back for the last two cases.

'That's my name.' She looked tired and a little puzzled. But grateful somebody was talking to her. No one else came near.

'Why Florence?'

She scowled and said, 'Life beats you up sometimes. I'm bouncing back.'

'Efron means lark?'

'Like I said.'

'And Chavah?'

He didn't know why he asked that.

'It's Jewish. In the Torah it means the mother of all life.'

'What the hell's the Torah?'

She laughed. 'The Book of Moses. The Jewish Bible, if you like. Don't ask me to explain. Not my thing.'

His head was hurting. He kept seeing the blood-smeared paintings on the wall. And something else too: another memory of her, that time almost a month before.

The first Thursday of the month. A little piece of hell come down to earth.

'What kind of name's that?' he asked, almost to himself.

'My name.' She seemed bemused by this conversation. 'The mother of all life, of everything . . . Sounds pretty good to me.'

'I meant . . .' he began. 'As a name.'

She folded her arms across her chest. He tried not to stare.

'I guess you're a Catholic. Don't get me wrong. Doesn't bother me. I got a Jewish mom. Doesn't make me one. Worked that out when I tried the kibbutz thing and a little . . .' She looked guarded. 'Other stuff. I got too much going on in the present to worry about tomorrow. God . . .' The woman glanced at the marquee door, back to the severe black and white facade of Santa Croce. 'You got that bastard coming out of your ears.'

She waited. When he didn't speak she said, 'Chavah. Eva. See the connection?'

He couldn't move. Couldn't think.

'Eve! That's where it comes from,' she said, as if it were nothing. She held out her hands and did a little dance. The snaking, sinuous movements brought back more memories. 'Eve!'

He stood there, shaking, seeing her in his head, another time, naked, laughing, twisting, crying, in a room full of lascivious men bawling for more.

When he calmed himself he thought of the husband. The stories he'd read in the papers.

First Thursday of every month.

However much they pressed, she wouldn't go back. She couldn't. It was unthinkable.

'What other things?' he asked.

'Is this a job interview or something?'

'Maybe. I've got friends who could use this stuff. Thursday. You're here in the market? I know someone who runs a restaurant.'

She looked suspicious. 'Give me his number. I'll call.'

'Thursday evening. Not the day . . .'

A moment of hesitation, a scared look on her face, then she said, 'Thursday evening I'm busy.'

'Eve . . .'

'I said it meant Eve. My name's Chavah.'

All things happened for a reason.

'My friend with the restaurant. He's got big money. Only night he closes is Thursday. You could cancel.'

She sighed. 'What do you mean, I can cancel? I told you. Thursday's taken.'

And so, he thought, are you. 'How much for a case?' he asked.

She put a grubby finger to his fleshy lips, thinking. 'Sixty thousand, list. But I think you'd have a nice face if you let me see it. To you, forty.'

'I'll take one . . .' he said, and didn't move.

'Two for sixty. You can sell it to your restaurant friend.'

'Two it is,' he answered, and didn't move.

She waited, tilting her head from side to side, soft black locks shifting, golden earrings alive with light. 'When you're ready . . .'

'For two I have to bring my car. And the money. I don't have either with me now. When the market closes.'

'Fine,' she said, and handed him a card, sighing as if to say: you're just a time-wasting lunatic. You won't show and we both know it.

And Thursday I'll be back in the same place, whatever happens, because I need the money. I've got to be there.

'Six thirty. Signor . . .?'

'I'll help you, Chavah,' he said. The thin, unsmiling mouth broke just a little. 'With your van.'

She raised a glass of olive oil as if it were a toast. Chartreuse, the French liqueur. That, he realized, was what it looked like.

'Six thirty,' he repeated, then walked out into the cold and rain.

The direct way was not that of Pino Fratelli. Five minutes after setting off for Santo Spirito, he diverted to his terraced house with the admonition, 'A book. We need a book. The Grassi dragon will be on guard. Stay behind, smile and keep silent.'

The cause of his apprehension turned out to be a large woman in a threadbare dress who was sweeping the stone stairs with great vigour as the two of them arrived. Home was an ancient terrace, the ground floor two storerooms, one full of cardboard boxes of junk, the other occupied by the skeletons of old bicycles and several motor scooters in pieces. At the top of the staircase the place divided into two separate apartments, his on the right, the rented studio that Julia Wellbeloved was using to the left. He never locked his door. Most of the time it was half open, with the strains of old jazz drifting through.

'What, may I ask, is this?' Signora Grassi demanded the moment they came in. 'You know I wish to clean alone.' Her beady eyes fell on Julia. 'And who . . .?'

'My latest guest,' Fratelli announced. Then, as if it explained everything, 'She's English.'

'Have you taken your tablets?' she asked, eyes narrowing. 'I've counted those in the bathroom and it would seem so. But I know your dark and sneaky nature by now, Fratelli. If you wash them down the sink . . .'

'I took them!' he said quickly, scuttling past her. 'A book if you please. Then we're gone.'

The woman held her broom like a weapon as Fratelli led Julia up the stairs and, for the first time, beyond his front door into the flat beyond. The place was rather more ordered than she expected, with a polished pine floor and a window on to the narrow street that led to Santa Maria del Carmine. A small table with dinner plates was tucked into an alcove. Shelves of books covered every wall. Between the history and art titles was an expensive-looking record player with a set of classical albums neatly lined beneath. Opposite was a single leather chair. This was a room for one person only.

Fratelli marched over to the rows of titles above the hi-fi system, chose the one he wanted, then led her back past the glowering figure on the staircase.

'She didn't seem much of a dragon,' Julia observed once they were back in the street and out of earshot.

'The woman was in a better mood than usual. Take my word: Grassi is a she-devil. Though I love her dearly. Come.'

They walked round the corner into the tree-lined piazza of Santo Spirito. In the dark November drizzle, the square of one of Florence's oldest churches looked a little worse for wear. Stray cats scavenged the rubbish bins, sorry tramps begged for money as they sheltered in doorways. The city changed as it crossed the river. This was not pretty or fey, but real and grim. Mean, even, a word she could never have applied to the elegant streets around the Duomo and the Piazza della Signoria.

The ice-cream parlour turned out to be a tiny, narrow room, little more than a corridor, one side lined with gleaming silver tubs full of ice cream, and what looked like a disused domed pizza oven at the rear. A cheery man of some size perched on a stool behind the counter. He knew Fratelli. Perhaps everyone in Oltrarno did. They were the only customers, seated at a rickety table by the window, watching the rain and the tramps. He picked at a pistachio cone while Julia stirred the *crema* of a very fine cappuccino. The idea of eating ice cream on a dark November evening was a step too far.

'Wellbeloved,' Fratelli said with a sudden, bright smile. 'What a beautiful name. *Beneamato*. So, are you?'

'Am I what?'

'Beloved? Family. Boyfriends. Girlfriends. Who knows? I'm across the hallway from you. It's important we should be frank with one another during your stay. To avoid any embarrassing moments. I have no restrictions on what you may do in my house. Provided it is as close to legal as a generous morality such as mine allows. No' – he made a gesture of rolling a cigarette and then putting it between his lips – 'magic puff, puff. This isn't London.'

Her face flushed. 'That's a lot of very personal questions, if you don't mind my saying so. Nor do I indulge in' – her slender fingers mimicked his gestures – 'magic puff, puff.'

His tidy silver brows furrowed in bafflement. 'This last I believe,' Fratelli said. 'So why the reticence on the rest?'

'Because you don't know me!'

He licked the cone, shaking his head. 'This is why I ask. The English . . . Sometimes you're very obtuse. How are we to become better acquainted if you tell me nothing about yourself?'

'In England—'

'You're in Florence.'

'In England,' she repeated, 'we get to know one another gradually.'

'Bah!' A gob of green ice cream flew from his cone as his hand gestured at the air. 'Patience is for idle fools. Do you really have time for such games? The world's a fragile place. Who knows what tomorrow may bring? I ask you these things, Julia Wellbeloved, so that we may put such small matters out of the way and discuss the mystery of our tarnished Eve.'

'In England!' she repeated again, more loudly.

'Oh. I understand. You behave as if you're trapped inside the pages of that writer who came here. Forster. What was the book called?'

She had to think quickly. This man seemed to demand it. 'A Room With a View?'

'Correct. Well, I am not running the Pensione Bertolini. Nor do you look much like a lost and insipid young thing who goes by the name of Lucy.' His face darkened for a moment. 'Though there was a murder in that book, if I recall correctly. So it cannot have been entirely without interest.'

'It was about repression, I think,' she suggested.

'How very like your race. My point exactly. So, Julia Wellbeloved. Who are you?'

What was there to say? Not much, so she told him – some, anyway. Twenty-eight years old. A recently enrolled postgraduate student at University College, London. Daughter to a widowed general practitioner from Berkhamsted in Hertfordshire. Not poor; certainly not rich. Blessed with a limited talent with a paintbrush but not a scintilla of originality, though this never affected her love of art, that of the Italian Renaissance in particular. The rest, her private view of herself, she withheld, though it occurred to her that a perceptive man like Fratelli could probably guess for himself.

Not unattractive, yet insufficiently striking to turn a head. Able to acquire a husband when the curiosity took her, but not for long. The determination and the conviction were lacking. The same might be said of her brief career as a commercial lawyer, straining at the lead, with no success, to find some criminal work to keep her mind alert. That was at an end now, too, which meant she came to Florence without ties of any kind, would be here for a month, no more, then return to London to finish her postgraduate studies in the same uncertain condition.

'And after you have unravelled the motives of the murderers of art?' Fratelli asked.

Julia finished her coffee and found herself lost for an answer. He waited, just long enough, then said, 'Sometimes we're defined as much by what we're not as what we are. There's nothing wrong in this, I think. The sin is to allow ourselves to be fixed by the opinions and the desires of others. Whether through fear or laziness. Better to be a shapeless creature flitting through the dark than a trapped bird in an ugly cage, crammed into a pre-formed mould that the world wishes filled for no other reason than because it's there. Which is the sad fate of most, let's face it.'

'You'd make a terrible careers advisor.'

'I'd make a terrible anything. Except a detective. I was good at that.' A flash of fierceness crossed his gentle face. 'I still am. Given the opportunity.'

'Why don't you have it?'

'They deny it to me on the grounds I'm sick.' He put a finger to his white hair and twirled it. 'Here. *Matto*. Crazy. What's that word you have? I know. I studied English once. Ah, yes.' He leaned forward and whispered, as if it were a secret, 'Bonkers! I am bonkers as a mole.'

'Do you say that in Italian? Mad as a mole?'

'*Sì*. A mole. Also I'm a liar and an impostor. Your own frankness demands candour on my part also.' He licked the last blob of green *gelato* from his cone, stared at her and said, 'I am not who I seem.'

'You mean . . .?'

She couldn't imagine what.

'Pino Fratelli,' the man in the thick coat said very forcefully, 'is a fraud. Strictly speaking, he doesn't exist.'

He twirled the finger at his ear again and added, 'Bonkers. See?'

'As a mole,' she murmured.

'Exactly. Also . . .' His gentle, pleasant face turned serious and grim. 'I have an intuition. I can feel when bad things are going to happen. They say this is a part of the illness. The madness.' He drained his glass. 'But I tell them . . . no, it was always like this. When I was a child . . .' His voice fell to a whisper. 'Later.'

'You mean . . . premonitions?' she asked in a quiet, worried voice.

'No. I don't know what I mean. If I did . . .' There was the faintest of smiles now. 'I wouldn't be mad now, would I?'

The ice cream was gone. Her cappuccino finished.

'The book?' she asked, anxious to change the subject, and concerned that Fratelli seemed to have forgotten why they braved the Grassi dragon.

He thought for a moment, then a light came on in his eyes. He dragged from the depths of his overcoat a thin volume on the Brancacci Chapel. On the cover was a photograph of Masaccio's Adam and Eve, banished from Paradise, their faces racked with grief and shame.

'This is a proof copy of the guide they intend to sell to tourists once the Brancacci is reopened. You can see the frescoes before and after restoration. Here is how they were when the Arno swept into that place twenty years ago.'

Fratelli placed a page in front of her.

She gazed at the tragic couple, expelled from immortality and perpetual joy by the scarlet angel brandishing a sword above them. Away from the chapel she felt some distance from these figures, a sense of useful perspective. What she saw now was both intriguing and bewildering.

'Eve's different when she leaves Eden,' she said. 'She's fatter. Her body is more corpulent, more . . . physical.'

'Well observed. The serpent has done her work. She now exists for the purpose of sex. Of bearing children – not as a solitary beauty, an intellectual mate for her man in Paradise. While Adam, even in his humiliation, seems little changed physically. This is a male world. And?'

It seemed impossible to believe. But there was the proof, on the page.

'The fig leaves were there before,' Julia said, staring at the vine that wound round the torsos of the agonized couple. This was no cardboard ornament from a tourist shop. It was real, painted on both frescoes around the lower regions of all four figures. Yet it was wrong too, somehow. 'I thought the vandal was just being prudish. But he wasn't. He was recreating something . . . something old and lost. He wasn't the first to object to their nakedness.'

Pino Fratelli looked at her. He seemed fascinated.

'I have a career for you, Miss Wellbeloved. Once you have purged these academic ambitions from your system. You must be a detective. Not only are you observant, but you interpret what you see very judiciously. This is rare in one so young. Though . . .' He breathed on his fingernails, then brushed the front of his coat. 'I possessed it in spades from an early age.'

'When . . .?' she began.

'When I was younger than you. Oh! You mean the frescoes? The fig leaves were plastered on our beautiful couple, before and after the Fall, in the seventeenth century, by one more prudish barbarian of the Medici. Twenty years ago there was the great flood of Florence. An event of' – his eyes turned black and sorrowful – 'biblical magnitude, the papers will always say. For once they do not lie. The Brancacci Chapel was damaged. Not as badly as some places. But still sufficient to warrant restoration.'

Fratelli stopped. The man behind the counter of the ice-cream parlour had come over to collect the coffee cup and the half-eaten cone.

'We're closing,' he said, eyeing them as if half expecting trouble. 'Some of us have homes to go to.'

'We all do, apart from our bearded friends outside in the street,' Fratelli replied.

He watched the man go, then leaned across the table.

'Even now, two decades on, there's much work to be done. In the case of the Brancacci, the city authorities undertook to remove the Medici's ham-fisted ornamentation and return our pair of lovers to their original nakedness. Which is exceptionally frank, I might add. See. Our couple in Paradise here . . .'

He flipped to another page and then a close-up. Her eyes widened in amazement. In the Brancacci she'd focused on the blood and the damaged face of Eve in *The Temptation*. Now she could see the subjects in greater, more candid detail. She was used to nakedness in classical Italian art, familiar with the way it was toned down too. Pubic hair was mostly unknown, and only seen when male genitalia were displayed quite frankly. The female form though . . .

'Am I seeing what I think?' she asked.

Fratelli threw his arms wide open and said nothing.

It was unmistakable. Masolino's original depicted Eve almost naturally. No hair, but there was the distinct line of a vagina depicted on her torso. It seemed, too, that the female head of the serpent was gazing down directly towards it.

'That's new,' she said. Her fingers ran across the book and the image there. Julia Wellbeloved felt excited, enthused, thrilled by the prospect of the mystery that Pino Fratelli seemed to be placing in front of her.

'It's shocking, I agree,' Fratelli replied. 'To some sensitive souls, at least. To depict a woman the way she really is, in her nakedness . . .'

'Whoever damaged the paintings must have come from the congregation,' she said confidently.

He demurred.

'Too far,' Fratelli said. 'Think again.'

'I can't see any other possibility.'

'Why do you assume the congregation is familiar with our newly naked Eves?'

She cursed herself. The entire chapel was closed for work. Heavy sheets and scaffolding set it apart from the main transept of the church.

'Stupid of me. The only people who got to see it would be those involved in the restoration.'

'Only?' he asked. 'A multitude, I would think. Visitors, workmen, art officials, experts in the dubious field of restoration. The lesser souls who must feed and serve them during their working day.'

His eyes gleamed.

'Curious students with a mission. Still, it's a start, and a start is all we need . . .'

'Pino!' barked the man behind the counter, tapping the watch on his wrist.

'After ice cream comes Negroni,' Fratelli said. 'There's only one place for that. Drink and a little food.'

'I've things to do,' she said, not entirely truthfully. 'Tomorrow morning I meet the mayor.'

This news interested him. Fratelli placed a thoughtful finger on his cheek and murmured, 'Sandro Soderini? I'm impressed.'

'You know him?'

'Everyone does, in theory anyway. He's a Soderini. The closest we have to a Medici these days. I'm a little man from Oltrarno. I don't move in such circles. But I know of him. An intelligent, educated man. His namesake was an aristocrat, uncle to the vile

Lorenzino Medici, who murdered an even more vile Medici despot, another Alessandro, in a house not far from here. Lorenzino was later assassinated in Venice by Cosimo the First, the man who sits on the horse in the Piazza della Signoria with pigeons pooping on his head. Soderini can confirm all this for you. He was a professor of history before his elevation to that office of the Pope's he now occupies in the Palazzo Vecchio. He'll give you five minutes of his time then pass you to some pretty minion. Ask him to get you into the Vasari Corridor.'

'The what?'

He wrote down the name on a napkin and passed it over. 'He'll know. It's in his gift. Not many receive that favour. Only great statesmen and . . .' He winked. 'Pretty young women who catch Soderini's eye.'

'Oh,' she whispered. 'Thank you.'

He toyed with another napkin on the table. 'After ice cream comes two Negroni, no more. I'm a man of habit, Julia Wellbeloved, solitary but not lonely. I like to know my guests a little, and always make this offer, whoever they may be. Hospitality is a duty for a host. You are my guest. But truly . . . I do not wish to foist myself upon you.'

'I didn't think that for one minute.'

'Of course you did,' he said, getting up and throwing some money on the counter. 'Tomorrow you must meet the mayor of Florence. Why waste your time on a sick old Carabinieri *maresciallo*? I apologize. Come. I'll see you home.'

Outside the rain had diminished to fine drizzle. The cobbled pavements shone beneath the street lights. A couple of tramps started making begging noises the moment the two of them emerged.

'Don't walk here on your own after dark,' Fratelli advised. 'Around my street it is safe enough. The piazza is best avoided except in daylight . . .'

'Where are you going?'

'I said. Negroni. The drink of Florence. I catch a bus round the corner. There's a place I frequent. I no longer drive.'

He waved the finger at his ear and mouthed the word '*matto*'.

'I've never tried a Negroni.'

'You're twenty-eight,' Fratelli replied. 'You've all the time in the world.'

Julia looked at this peculiar man, with his heavy coat, his white hair, the face that was both young and old.

Then she glanced back at the clock on the wall of the ice-cream parlour: six thirty. As she watched, the owner turned the sign on the door so it read, '*Chiuso*'.

Time moved strangely in this city. Early and late seemed to swap places at will.

'I thought patience was for idle fools,' she said, as much to herself as him.

Fratelli shuffled in his heavy coat. 'You shouldn't take me too seriously. It's not necessary. Or wise.'

'I can spare an hour,' she said.

He spent the time staring at the grey waters of the Arno. The river looked angry. As if it wanted to belch the renegade priest Savonarola's ashes back into the city that had dumped them into its midst five centuries before.

Then a bell somewhere chimed six thirty. He walked back into the Piazza Santa Croce. The rain had turned steady and settled. The olive growers' marquee was closed, its main doors secured by heavy ropes and locks.

The woman called Chavah Efron stood outside at the back, huddled in a khaki anorak, looking around, bedraggled, wondering, he guessed: did this strange man keep his promises?

Yes. Always, in the end.

He strode over, nodded. Her entire stock seemed to be piled next to the tent, covered with plastic sheeting to protect it from the rain. She looked younger than he remembered. Vulnerable when the hard mask dropped.

'So I didn't get stood up.' She tried to peer into the cowl. 'Are you sure we haven't met before?'

'I'm sure,' he said, and looked at the pile of cardboard boxes. 'You want two?'

A few night people were wandering into the bars and restaurants. She'd parked her VW on the corner of the Via de' Benci, the busy road that led down to the river and the Ponte alle Grazie across to San Niccolò. Fiesole lay in the other direction, a short drive away in the hills overlooking Florence.

'My restaurant friend . . .'

'Don't ask about Thursday again. I told you.'

In the sharp street light her hands looked like leather. Marked with cuts and rough skin.

'The thing is,' he went on, 'I can't carry more than two cases. Are you here tomorrow?'

'Tuesday's not Thursday,' she said straight away, running a finger at her curly black hair, keeping it out of her face. 'What do you think?'

Chavah Efron was both beautiful and fallen, like the woman on the wall. He looked at the black night around them and could feel her slipping away.

'Do you have any money?' she asked.

'I'll give you what I have now,' he said. 'You keep all the cases. I'll come back in the morning and get four.'

He took out the crumpled wad of small denomination notes. She stuffed the money into a zipped pocket on her jacket, anxious for anything.

He picked up the two cases again. 'Open the doors. I'll pass them to you.'

She climbed into the back of the rusty Volkswagen and held out her dirty hands, beckoning. 'Give,' Chavah Efron said.

He pulled back the cowl, felt the chill night on his bald head. The way the van was parked blocked any view of them from the pavement on the other side of the Via de' Benci. No one close by.

She was crouching in the back, staring at him. 'I do know you. I've seen you before. I . . .' Her grimy fingers went to her mouth. 'Oh shit . . .'

By then he was on her, hands round her cold damp mouth. Pushing her back on to the pile of cardboard boxes, dragging the length of rag out of his pocket. He held her firmly, not tightly, never went near the soft curve of the belly. This was about rescue, not harm.

The gag went round her mouth, met her teeth, stifled her screams. Then he yanked off the bulky, filthy Afghan jacket, bound her hands in front of her, tightly, not cruelly. After that, he closed both doors behind him. The only light in the rear compartment came from a street lamp drifting through the front window. He could just make out the crumpled form lying on the filthy floor of the van, mumbling what sounded like obscenities. Her hands were to her face. Her head was a mess of black, curly hair, shaking with surprise. She wasn't sobbing. More furious than angry.

'I won't harm you, Chavah Efron,' he said as loudly as he dared. 'I know who you are. I know what's happened. I wish . . .'

Her legs were apart and kicking, rough farm boots against the tinny van floor.

A breathless silence. A sensation of control, of power, and the ecstasy of shame. He looked at the woman, her eyes blazing with fury, and he thought of the creatures on the wall in Santa Maria del Carmine. One perfect, one sullied. And a third, crippled with the body of a serpent, triumphant.

'I can save you,' he said.

She stared at him with bright, furious eyes. Not like the Eve on the wall, not much.

All things happened for a reason.

He picked up the sheepskin jacket. It stank of animals. Sifting through the tissues and coins, the little tinfoil tabs of dope, he found a set of keys. Then, ignoring the writhing of her limbs, he clambered over into the front seat, took out the business card, worked out the hand-drawn map in his head. Stabbed the puny engine in to life, and gingerly edged the VW out of the city until he found the winding Via Salviatino towards Fiesole, ignoring the angry, mumbled cries, the thrashing of the body in the back.

'My name . . . my true name is Ariel Montefiore,' Fratelli told her as the bus chugged along the choking streets that led to the Ponte Vecchio and beyond, following the southern bank of the Arno. They had the back bench to themselves, watching the city stagger past beyond the rainy windows.

'That sounds lovely,' she observed.

'I was born in the Roman ghetto in 1938. And you?'

'Hemel Hempstead General Hospital, 1958.'

'Twenty years apart. Yet different worlds. Mine was about to fall bloodily apart. You opened your eyes to a place that was a little gentler, I feel.'

'A little,' she mused. 'There always seems to be a war somewhere. And bombs.'

The bus lurched into the busy piazza at the end of the Ponte Vecchio. Pedestrians everywhere swarming into the street, carrying shopping bags, pulling heavy hats over their heads.

'No,' Fratelli insisted. 'They were different. My parents ran a bakery in the ghetto. Not far from the Piazza Mattei. You know it?'

She shook her head.

He was smiling, remembering something.

'A beautiful, modest part of that marvellous city. There's a fountain with tortoises. I fool myself I recall the place. In my mind's eye' – he tapped his white-haired head – 'I can see it. But this must be a false memory, from a later visit. It's impossible.'

Finally the bus broke free of the crowds. She could see the river running through the centre of the city, a watery spine that reflected the street lights from both banks. Across the torrent stood the grand, severe arches of the Uffizi stretching back towards the Piazza della Signoria. Somewhere there, tomorrow morning in an office in the Palazzo Vecchio, she would meet the mayor, Alessandro Soderini, an aristocrat whose family was important here four centuries before. That was the grand face of Florence. On this more modest side of the Arno there was just a straggly line of traffic working through the rain.

She'd walked along the riverside road the day before on a long trudge to the Piazza Michelangelo, the hillside viewpoint which was so popular with visitors. The area at the foot, by the Arno, was old and undistinguished, yet likeable somehow, a pleasant place to stop for a solitary coffee. San Niccolò. It seemed to be their destination.

Fratelli couldn't take his eyes off the vast building across the river and the heavy tower of the Palazzo Vecchio behind.

'I'm still a Roman really. I like it there. Most everything exists for beauty, for pride, for love. The city manifests that warmth, that affection to everyone it meets. Florence,' his eyes were fixed on the Uffizi, 'is a bloody place. Everything kept hidden except for those judged fit to enjoy it. A monument to the power and majesty of its rulers.' His right index finger went up in a gesture much like a schoolteacher's. 'Which is why you see so much rustication in our buildings. They're meant to resemble fortresses; domestic castles which hide their secrets behind thick, impenetrable walls. I detest rustication. Compare the exquisite Quirinale with the brutal Pitti Palace behind us . . .'

'Why couldn't you remember the tortoises?' she asked.

He turned to her with a quick and self-effacing smile. 'Because when I was four years old a brave and kindly Catholic priest took to smuggling Jewish children out of Rome and spirited me here. A few years later he was shot by the Germans in the Ardeatine Massacre in retribution for a partisan attack. Three hundred and thirty-five men murdered by the Nazis on one bleak day. I knew none of this, of course; nor that I'd been secretly delivered to an equally brave and kindly spinster in Oltrarno. She owned the house where you're staying. Until I was fifteen years old, I thought she was my mother and I the most conspicuous bastard in Florence. Then she told me the truth.'

Julia looked at him and struggled for words. The Second World War happened to other people, older people. Not someone like this man next to her, who seemed in some ways so young, full of life and a curious kind of juvenile enthusiasm.

'Mussolini,' Fratelli continued. 'They speak of him now and say he wasn't so bad to the Jews. It depends on your point of view. He didn't kill them outright, so if a failure to commit mass murder is kindness, then perhaps he was a benevolent man. Many were deported from Rome, though. In the case of my parents, they were rounded up and sent to a place called Porto Re in Yugoslavia. Porto Re was a camp. Not Belsen. Not Auschwitz. But a prison for Jews and anyone else he hated or feared or both.'

'I never realized.'

They were past the Uffizi. On both banks the houses grew more modest; ancient terraces with the odd patch of open grass or pavement.

'Me neither,' Fratelli replied. 'When I was very young, a good Catholic with a brave unmarried mother here in Florence, Mussolini was warring with his peers. They ejected him, but then an infuriated Hitler placed the idiotic little tyrant back on his golden throne.' He tapped the side of his nose. 'With conditions. Those Jews he was hiding in Yugoslavia among them. Eight thousand in all, shipped north in trains like cattle.'

He turned and pointed back to the Ponte Vecchio.

'See those windows in the middle at the top?'

Julia squinted back at the strange, medieval bridge, made up entirely of shops.

'That,' Fratelli went on, 'is the Vasari Corridor, the place I mentioned. A private walkway between the Pitti Palace on this side of the Arno and the Palazzo Vecchio a kilometre away in the Piazza della Signoria.'

'A secret passage?'

'Not at all,' he said with a shrug. 'The Medici didn't want to mix with the hoi polloi. They didn't mind who knew it. But those windows in the centre . . .' His face was, for a moment, quite bleak. 'Mussolini invited Hitler round for tea when the war was going well. As I said, the corridor is a place for statesmen. So they met there, and in order for his German friend to enjoy a better view, the

little marionette had those ugly modern windows inserted into
the Medici's private escape route from the filthy, stinking masses.'

He took one more look and then turned to face the front of the
bus. 'Ask Soderini to let you walk the length of it, one side of
the Arno to the other, and see it for yourself. Florence always sucks
up to dictators, anyone with power. It makes us feel privileged.'

There were vessels on the river. Fast, slender rowing boats with
five or six men sculling frantically against the heavy swell.

'My father's name was Gideon,' Fratelli said. 'My mother's
Esther. As I said, they were communists. Internationalists, which is
why I imagine they chose names that weren't as Italian as one might
expect. Like Ariel for their son.'

His sudden sadness was so real she felt she could touch it.

Have you taken your pills?

The Grassi dragon asked that. Walter, the austere, ruddy-faced
Carabinieri captain, had sounded just as solicitous that afternoon in
the Brancacci Chapel when, beneath his anger, he'd inquired, 'Pino.
What in God's name are you doing here?'

'Communist and Jewish. Twice damned. They died in Auschwitz.
I went there once. I don't know why.'

She placed her hand on his arm, squeezed the thick coat briefly.
'I'm sorry, Pino.'

He stared at her, puzzled. 'Why? I never knew them. I never
found a surviving relative in Rome who might help me colour in a
little of who I was. Help me dispel my ignorance. To all intents and
purposes, I am Pino Fratelli, son of an unmarried woman from
Oltrarno; a beautiful, caring mother, one I loved dearly all the days
of her life. But . . .'

His brown eyes grew misty. This habit of a sudden distraction
was one she was coming to recognize.

'There's a certain Hebrew gloom about me at times. I can't avoid
it. The thing's passed on in the blood, I suppose. Along with much
else. Generation to generation. Not that there'll be any passing on
from me.'

He looked up, abruptly alert.

'We're almost there. So that's out of the way. I apologize I felt
the need to burden you with this knowledge. Please, dismiss it now.
I don't know why I told you really. It's just that . . .' He pushed
the bell for the next stop. 'You seem a very attentive listener for
some reason.'

They got off and stepped out into the rain again. His house was a mile away or more, she guessed, and in between lay the square of Santo Spirito, a place to be avoided after dark by a woman on her own. It was too late to change her mind. Besides, she liked this man. He intrigued her.

'Negroni!' Fratelli said again, and pointed across the road to the bright lights of a deserted bar. 'The best there is in Florence!' He grinned. 'The best there is in the world.'

It was a rundown farmhouse reached by a dead-end farm track a good ten minutes by car outside Fiesole. No near neighbours. No lights. No sign of anyone inside. Nothing to get in the way.

He drove the VW slowly over the rutted lane until the gravel ran out at a small square of disintegrating concrete. A howling dog came and barked at him when he climbed out, then gave up when it reached the length of its chain. There was a chicken coop, the sound of gentle, alarmed clucking coming from inside. The sky had cleared to ragged strips of cloud. In the dim moonlight he could make out rows of low grey olive trees, ancient and crooked like an army of wizened crones stretching down the hillside. A rusty tractor stood outside a corrugated-iron barn that looked ready to collapse. Beside it was a rickety stack of wooden crates. The place smelled of rotting fruit, a nearby cesspit, and poverty.

Five years to tell the world not a drop of chemical had touched your precious bright-green oil on its way into the bottle. And still the stuff tasted like cheap crap. They were crazy. Except that wasn't the whole story, and he knew it.

A hefty key from her ring worked with the front door. He turned on the lights and walked into a low living room, sparsely furnished and smelling of damp. A wood-burning stove close to death leaked weak smoke. He walked over and put some more fuel behind the doors, watching the flames rise. There were brightly coloured bean bags for chairs, an old hi-fi system, posters on the wall. Che Guevara and Trotsky, Jim Morrison and Hendrix. Bare bulbs dangling from wires. A kitchen with a gas ring and some pots and pans drying over the sink.

One plate, one knife, one fork, one mug. The rest were still in a bright orange cabinet by the window.

The woman was screaming and banging on the van walls outside. He didn't mind. No one would hear.

An open staircase led to the first floor. He turned on more lights and walked up. One room full of boxes of bills, invoices and tax documents, books on olive growing and agriculture, old newspapers. A couple of albums of photos. Golden temples and smiling Buddhist monks in saffron. A postcard of a square in Marrakech labelled Jemaa el-Fna. Not many of the man, and all of them by the look of it in Italy.

He walked to the window and looked back outside. The van was there, not moving much. He'd kept the back door closed. She was quiet now, shuffling around, trying to get free, he guessed. Pointless. He'd bound her tight and the nearest lights were half a valley away, down towards Fiesole.

There was a small, black lacquered box beneath the ledge. It looked oriental, covered in exotic decorations. He opened the lid, stared at the plastic bags full of marijuana.

Beneath his feet the floorboards squeaked and moved as he walked across them. He bent down, got the large door key in the gap between the planks, lifted what looked like a loose one.

Small sacks of white powder, more grass, heavy lumps of resin. Dope was another of their sins. And weapons. Three handguns. A semi-automatic rifle of the kind he'd only seen in movies. A sawn-off shotgun and next to it boxes and boxes of shells. And, in plastic bags, a hard, dark substance he first thought to be a kind of drug. Then he picked it up, smelled it.

Chemicals, noxious and strong.

Explosive?

Things didn't add up.

Like waiting five years for the poison to leach out of the land. They had to make money somehow. The husband came from Calabria. The crime organization there, the 'Ndrangheta, had been quietly making inroads into Tuscany. Or so he'd read in the papers. They'd need foot soldiers, a lowly advance guard. A couple posing as hippies pushing dope while they waited for the paperwork to come through for their oh-so-clean olives. The woman was American, from New Jersey. A place the Mafia liked. He'd read they had some Jewish gangs there; big men who thought of themselves as *compari* to the Sicilians.

Fallen. So many times, he guessed. Just like him. And the more you fell, the more you ached to go back home, to that green place without pain or death or sin. Whores and drug peddlers, thieves and usurers. Little people. Insects running in between the cobbled cracks of Florence, scuttling from one grubby corner to the next. They were always the first to be saved.

He walked into the other room and looked at the double bed. It was black cast iron, with an oversized mattress, crumpled sheets and a livid orange duvet. Even from this distance, he could hear Chavah Efron back to kicking hard and repeatedly at the walls of the van.

He walked outside, went to the van, threw open the doors. She lay in a crumpled heap among the boxes, glaring at him.

'Why do you make this noise?' he asked, shaking his head. 'This is your home. You know no one's here.'

He climbed in, crawled over on his knees, untied the gag. She didn't try to kick him. That he found surprising. Her cheeks were wet with tears. He took out a handkerchief and wiped away the stains as best he could.

'Answer me truthfully. When does your man come back?'

'Any minute now, asshole. And when he does—'

'Don't lie!'

Chavah Efron fell quiet. But she didn't weep. Just stared at him with those sharp and knowing eyes.

'He's coming,' she whispered. 'He's a good man and he'll kill you . . .'

'A good man gives you dope? A good man makes you whore yourself for him? Sell his drugs and warm his bed?'

There was hatred in her face. No fear at all.

'What do you want?' she shrieked.

'To be washed clean,' he said, and it was close to a whisper. 'Just the same as you.'

He picked her up in his arms, holding her so tightly she couldn't struggle, though she kicked and fought as best she could, screaming all the while.

The dog barked and leapt against the chain. He heard the flapping of frightened wings in the chicken coops. From the grey, crippled shapes of the olive trees, he thought he heard the cry of a fox. He carried her up the stairs, placed her on the bed, then one by one undid her hands and tied each, outstretched, to the iron bars at the top. Not too tight. Room to move. No more.

After that he went back down the steps, walked outside, closed the van, locked the front door of the farmhouse behind him and turned off the ground-floor lights.

When he returned to the bedroom she didn't try to kick out any more. He was a big man. She was small, unable to harm him. She lay there on the bed, tiny body on the orange duvet, legs apart. Looking at him in a way he didn't like to see.

'Do it then,' she said.

'Do what?'

'What you want. You're just like all the others, aren't you? Just like . . .'

'No, I'm not,' he said, and sat on the bed.

'Why would someone cut off the comb of a cockerel?' Fratelli stirred his drink with a lurid red plastic straw. 'Leave the head and neck but gut the thing? Take out its insides and leave the meat?'

Their destination turned out to be one street back from the river in the Via de' Renai, a sloping cobbled lane with a handful of cafés and restaurants. The place Fratelli chose was a long narrow bar full of mirrors. The elegant woman behind the counter nodded in recognition as they entered and didn't look at Julia for one moment. The room was full of cigarette smoke emanating from a handful of customers. She was pleased to see Fratelli try to wave it away with a scowl. He seemed to be one of the few Italian men who didn't have a cigarette to his lips every minute of the day. There wasn't an English voice around.

'The comb?' she asked, relieved that the story about his childhood now seemed to be behind them, as if it were a necessary hurdle he wanted her to cross before returning to more direct affairs.

Fratelli had ordered food and two glasses of the cocktail he'd mentioned. A Florentine speciality, invented in the city, he said. Red vermouth, gin and Campari. An odd combination, sweet and strong, yet somehow well suited to the chilly weather. He sat admiring his ruby-coloured tumbler full of drink and ice, lost in thought.

'What about the comb, Pino?'

He stroked his white hair and said immediately, 'Nowhere to be seen. Removed completely. Sharp knife. Scalpel even. Why?'

'He wanted the blood?' she suggested. 'To smear it on the walls.'

A long, lugubrious stare. 'He removed the head for that. Used the neck as if it was a paintbrush. He'd no need to remove the comb or to gut the bird. Why? And why was it a cockerel? An old one you wouldn't normally eat?'

Julia pushed away the salami and bread Fratelli had ordered. She wasn't feeling hungry.

'Where would you get something like that?' she asked.

'In the countryside,' he said with a shrug. 'Where else? A farmer. Or a worker there. I'll tell Walter. In the morning. When his mood has recovered. A decent man but he has a terrible temper.' He smiled for a moment, looking a little guilty. 'At least, he has with me.'

'What will he do?'

'Same as always,' Fratelli grumbled. 'Mutter *grazie* then go his own sweet way. A farm. He should crosscheck with known offenders. Do the kind of thing he's good at. Menial work. Walter's a clerk at heart. Not an artist.'

She had to laugh.

'And you are?'

'Of course! Why do you think they never promoted me beyond *maresciallo ordinario*? I have a creative temperament which offends them. I am Brunelleschi, dreaming of new ways to build my dome. They are the mealy-mouthed, penny-pinching paper-pushers of the Signoria, bidding me to dream up a miracle before ungraciously shoving a few lire across the table and saying, "Make it happen with that."'

The straw made one more round of the glass, then Fratelli took a sip of the strong cocktail and briefly closed his eyes, delighted.

'Credit where credit's due. Genius requires patronage, since it's rarely possessed of a pecuniary mind. I need them as much as they need me.'

His keen eyes fixed on her then, Fratelli leaned forward, lightly punched her knuckles with his and said, 'I was joking. I'm an idiot. A holy idiot sometimes, but that still leaves me an idiot. Walter's damned good at minutiae. Better than I could ever be. If only the man would do as I say!'

It seemed futile to point out that Walter Marrone appeared to be Fratelli's boss.

'Perhaps our vandal was simply deranged.'

Fratelli stared at her and said nothing.

'Crazy. Unbalanced,' she added.

'Is that the intended conclusion of your report? Why do people attack works of art? Because they're lunatics. If so, it will surely be the shortest academic paper in history.'

'Of course I want to find reasons . . .'

'Reasons are all we have. Without them everything is reduced to chaos. To folly and irrationality. You know the kind of people who commit crimes like that? Crimes that make no sense, have no source, no connection with any prudent purpose?'

'Lunatics,' she said firmly.

'No. Ordinary, boring, middle-class men and women. The people you see on the bus and the train. Who think themselves the most normal and law-abiding citizens of all. Then go out one day, get drunk, get mad, get furious with the world around them, or simply see an opportunity for mischief when no one else is looking.'

He stared at the cocktail, swilled it once round the glass and ordered another.

'Then commit a feat of idiocy – an act of violence, of murder, of gross cruelty; some cowardly, disgraceful sin of omission – simply because they can. Once it's done they're horrified by it, by themselves, and shrink back into their little shells, hoping no one will notice their brief lapse into wickedness. While secretly praying for it to happen again because in that moment . . .' The straw came out of the glass and described a 360-degree circle over the Negroni. 'In that very moment, they feel more alive than they've ever known before.'

He shook his head and she realized she was becoming mesmerized by this man. By his strange, bohemian appearance: the clothes; the wild, white hair. And the languid yet unremitting energy inside him, as furious and relentless as the churning waters of the Arno.

'We should be grateful for that sense of guilt. It makes the job of the Carabinieri so much simpler.' He scowled at the gleaming counter. 'But a man who smears a priceless painting with the bloody neck of a cockerel . . .'

Fratelli's sad eyes roamed around the bar. There were just five or six other people: a woman staring at a glass that appeared to have a carrot and a stick of celery in it, and a few men, all like Fratelli, looking a little lonely.

'He has a reason. There's a line from an occurrence, a thought, perhaps an offence against him in the past. That line runs directly to the present. Without guilt, without that averted look in the face of a man one suspects, the discovery of that line becomes the principal challenge any investigator must face. The one you must deal with in your paper. A criminal who possesses a sense of guilt is a case half solved. It's the ones who burn with self-righteousness, who know that what they do is both justified and logical . . . they're the challenge. Hitler, listening to that pusillanimous dwarf

Mussolini in those garish windows of the Ponte Vecchio, never thought himself a criminal for one moment. He was a liberator, a hero to his people, a man of the most refined and sensitive morals. Morals that allowed him to murder mankind by the million.'

The glass of Negroni rose in a toast.

'It's bastards like that we've got to worry about.'

'Because?' she asked.

'Isn't it obvious? Had you sat and listened to Hitler and Mussolini at their little tête-à-tête forty-odd years ago, you would have heard the most genteel of conversations, by two men who saw themselves as dignified masters of their respective worlds. Monsters, and they didn't even know it.'

He glanced at his watch. She caught the clock on the wall. It was eight.

'I'm sorry, Pino. I need to eat.'

'You can eat here! They'll make anything you want. A panino? Some pasta?'

She didn't rise to the offer.

'Be my guest,' he pleaded. 'I won't pester you after this, Julia Wellbeloved. You'll go back to your studies tomorrow. I'll nag Walter for as long as his patience lasts. With luck our culprit shall be found. And after that we'll meet on the stairs and nod politely at one another. Not a word of what I say will be of the slightest practical use to you in your work.' He grinned. 'See? An artist. I told you. For amusement only.'

'A sandwich,' she agreed. 'Cheese. No more meat.'

'You don't like *finocchiona*?' he asked. 'I'm shocked. This is a Florentine speciality. Meat from the Cinta Senese pig with fennel seeds. Beautiful. This' – he picked up a slice of the pink and fatty sausage, dangled it in front of her – 'is the best. From Greve. We call it *sbriciolona*. Crumbly. See?'

'Too strong for me.'

He called out to the woman behind the bar for more plates.

'In Florence we like exaggeration. Everything bigger, tastier, more powerful, more . . . gross. You must tell us when we overstep your mark. This' – he tore off more of the raw *sbriciolona* – 'I buy down the Sant'Ambrogio market for a pittance an *etto* and—'

His eyes closed, as if he felt a sharp pain. Fratelli rocked on his bar stool, looking for a moment as if he might tumble to the floor. Her hand shot out to steady him.

'Are you all right?'

'What? What?'

'You nearly fell.'

'Ridiculous! I was thinking. That's all.' He beamed at her. 'I told you I was an idiot. And you . . .!'

He reached over quickly, took her hands and kissed her briefly on each cheek.

'. . . Are a genius, my new English friend!'

She was blushing and could feel the heat in her face. Fratelli, a sensitive man caught by his own enthusiasm, saw this and let go of her fingers, refused to meet her eye.

'I apologize,' he said. 'Italians have strange habits for you. I understand this but sometimes I forget. What we view as everyday warmth you see as an unwanted intrusion . . .'

'It's all right,' she replied, amused by his embarrassment. 'I'm not a stranger to Italy or Italians.'

'No?' he asked.

'Why am I a genius?'

He nodded, as if thinking this through for himself. Food arrived. Cheese and bread, olives and other antipasti.

'Because you asked the right question. Where would one buy an old cockerel? Like a fool I said . . . a farm. Which is possible, of course. But if I wanted one I wouldn't dream of going there. I'd go to the market. The real one, not that tourist trap in the *centro storico*. To Sant'Ambrogio. If it moves, if it's edible, they'll sell it.'

Fratelli raised his glass again.

'*Salute*,' he said, and took a hefty swig.

'And the comb?'

'Haven't a clue,' he replied. 'You?'

Julia Wellbeloved shook her head and found herself laughing. His meandering way of thinking and sudden, sharp, unpredictable intelligence intrigued her. She was also struck by the idiosyncratic nature of his conversation. Threads and questions entered it and never reached a resolution, unless his companion asked for one. Was this because Fratelli was using her as a sounding board? Or did his illness – whatever it was – make him forgetful at times?

'You said something,' she pointed out, 'when we left the church. About how I had an excuse.'

'For what?' he asked, seemingly baffled.

'For not seeing everything you did. About the paintings, I imagine.'

Fratelli thought for a long moment, chewed on some more of the fatty, half-raw meat and then prodded a stubby forefinger in the air.

He retrieved the book for which they'd braved the Grassi dragon, opened it, found the right page, thrust the photograph before her and said, 'It was this.'

His finger indicated the serpent behind the beautiful Eve. The creature possessed a woman's face, one that was very much like Eve's own; lovely, with blonde hair, though tied back behind the creature's neck.

'Think,' Fratelli urged. 'Remember.'

She felt tired, not least from this man's intense presence. Yet still he tempted her with his mysteries.

'I do!' she cried, recalling what she'd seen in the Brancacci Chapel, beyond the blood and the strange defiled frescoes on the wall.

This serpent was unadorned. Slyly triumphant, as it led the original Adam and Eve away from Paradise, into the world of flawed and mortal humanity.

'Today it had something over its head . . .' she whispered.

'What?' Fratelli demanded.

The memory and the reality were both so faint she wondered whether either could be real.

'An oval. Lightly drawn in blood. Not blatant, like Eve's face. More like a . . .'

She hesitated. She was no more religious than Pino Fratelli. Still the idea seemed sacrilegious in the extreme.

'Like a halo perhaps.'

'A halo, exactly. Executed with a glove I think,' he said, indicating his own index finger, scrawling an ellipse in the water left on the bar by his icy glass. 'He didn't simply wish to punish Eve for her nakedness. But also to reward the serpent, the female viper, a hellish, womanly Satan, for dragging her down from the heights of Heaven in the first place. An intellectual point, I imagine; one he made while ensuring he left no fingerprints behind. So he's a practical man too.'

Fratelli raised his glass and said, 'Congratulations. You get better by the hour.'

'What can it mean?'

'A guess? It's the best I can do.'

'I think your guesses are probably good ones.'

'My guess is that what we've seen is not the end but the beginning. Of what,' he added quickly, before she asked, 'I cannot know.'

He looked at his watch.

'One hour, you said. I've taken enough of your time. Too much. I'm sorry. Sometimes I don't know when to stop.'

'Don't worry. It was an interesting day.'

She meant it, too. More interesting, if she was honest with herself, than waiting hours for dry Uffizi officials to grant her interviews in which they did little except keep glancing at the clock.

'Home,' he said, with a self-deprecating smile. 'Tomorrow you go to meet a true Florentine, one with centuries of history in his blood. And I shall nag Walter with my crackpot ideas.'

'They don't sound crackpot to me,' she said.

'They should,' he insisted. He shook his white-haired head. 'Really. And I hope – I'd pray if I could – they are.'

The blue sweater had ridden up as she struggled. He could see the pale, smooth skin of her stomach. By the tight, disordered bundle of flesh that was Chavah Efron's navel lay a butterfly, a tattoo in red and blue, small and a little amateurish. As he stared at it she murmured something in a language he couldn't understand. The words were strange, exotic, like an incantation. A prayer, perhaps.

I'm not what you'd call a good Jew either.

They all found God in the end. If they didn't, God came to you, one way or another.

He climbed half over her, put his hand to her throat, peered into her face, wondering at how calm she looked. As if she expected this, had brought it on herself.

'Get on with it then,' she said. 'I'll lie here and not move a muscle. I won't even notice. Promise.'

'You don't understand,' he muttered, wary of her.

'Ari will kill you . . .'

He closed his eyes and shook his head.

'When he gets back . . .'

His hands gripped hers, his face came close.

'Don't lie to me. Your man's dead,' he said. He looked into Chavah Efron's bright, alert eyes and said, 'Shot in Rovezzano two weeks ago. I saw his photo in the paper. Same man.' He tapped his bald head. 'I remember things.'

Wished he didn't sometimes.

There was no emotion on her face at all now. Except, perhaps, curiosity.

After a while he stared at the tattoo again and said, 'This dream of yours . . .'

'You don't know anything about my dreams.'

He nodded towards the door. 'When I came here I saw the dope and the guns. Your man was a Calabrian crook who got what he asked for. What you get for pushing poison to suckers who know no better.'

He thought about this ramshackle, falling-down farmhouse, set alone on a hill outside Fiesole.

'Good place to hide. He was smart that way. The cops wouldn't come looking here.'

'Smart?' She glared at him. 'He's dead. How smart is that?'

She drew back her head and spat in his face.

He wiped the saliva from his cheeks.

'I need to go,' she said.

'Go where?'

'*Where do you think? Idiot!*'

He walked into the room with the dope and the guns, picked the best he could find, a recent East European pistol, loaded it, came back, showed her the thing, untied her hands, waved her to the bathroom. He left the door half open and kept his eyes on her as she squatted. To make sure she didn't try to get out of the window. That was why, or so he told himself.

'Now what?' she asked, reaching for the toilet roll. He led her back to the bed, bound her hands again, then her feet at the ankles. Legs tight together. It had to be that way.

Then watched her struggling on the duvet. He could run again now. Take the weapons and the dope and the van and go back to the city to turn them into cash. After what he'd seen she wouldn't do a thing. Couldn't have the police sniffing round this place, asking searching questions. Listening to her plead, 'But it's all for the farm, you see. *Biologico.* Macrobiotic or something. What's a little dope and gun-running, a dead Calabrian hood for a husband, next to that?'

'What the hell do you want?' she asked.

'Thursday.'

'What about Thursday?'

'You'd do it all over again?'

'I need the money. One more time and I'm gone. What's it to you?'

'That's what the kids said when your husband sold them dope.'

'One more time! Why throw this at me? You're one of their slaves too.'

He thought of the dead cockerel, stolen from the kitchen, and its blood on the wall. It seemed like a weak and childish prank.

She laughed at his silence. Then said, 'See? We're no different.'

'Not true.' He picked up the duvet, dragged it out from underneath her, watched the way she stiffened at his closeness. He placed the coverlet over her small body. It wasn't so cold in the room for him. A woman . . . He didn't know.

'Go to sleep,' he ordered.

Ignoring her squawking he went downstairs, drank some bottled water and stretched out on the sofa, big hands behind his big, bald head, counting the options, the possibilities. After a while she shut up and so did the dog on the chain by the barn.

He waited an hour. The farm was silent throughout. Not a sound from upstairs. Only, through the grimy glass of the cracked windows, the distant call of owls and the blood-chilling shrieks of a nearby vixen.

At ten o'clock he went to the kitchen then rifled through the cupboards: not bad. Some decent food there and a few vegetables. He opened a pack of dried fava beans from Puglia, held them to his nose. The bitter stink made his stomach ache with hunger so he seized a lump of pecorino and munched on that. Half the beans went into a saucepan filled with cold water. It was important to think about the time ahead. To prepare.

After that he found the two biggest, sharpest knives they had, picked up a butcher's cleaver and a meat saw too, then walked upstairs and looked at her.

Chavah Efron was, to his relief, asleep. Or pretending to be.

All for the best, he thought.

Ten o'clock in the house in Oltrarno. Rain spattering the windows, nothing beyond them but a single street light swaying in the blustery wind. She'd asked Fratelli for some of his favourite books on Florence and walked away with her arms full. No guides to art and architecture, no lists of local restaurants. Instead a collection of obscure titles in Italian and English. The strange and disturbing autobiography of Benvenuto Cellini, Machiavelli's *The Prince*, Francesco Guiccardini's *History of Florence*, another work from the sixteenth century, thankfully in translation. A life of the monk

Savonarola by Roberto Ridolfi – a modern author, not the Florentine nobleman who plotted against Elizabeth I, hoped to marry Mary Queen of Scots, and later returned to his native city to become a senator. And a copy of *A Room with a View* if, Fratelli said, she fancied 'something light'.

She carried them back to her own small, tidy and rather overheated room, then lay on her single bed to browse through each. The tortuous birth of the Renaissance was part of her degree. But that was an academic exercise, conducted dispassionately through books and paintings, not people, not life. Now she was beginning to feel a part of the canvas of that astonishing drama, drowning in the feverish burst of violent creativity, beauty and inspiration that began just beyond her window.

And such players among its vivid cast. Cellini was a Florentine through and through, soldier, artist, sculptor, goldsmith and, as Fratelli had said earlier, a self-confessed murderer and necromancer who, in his autobiography, boasted of his affairs and killings, of conjuring up a legion of devils one night in the Colosseum. Machiavelli lived through the turmoil of the expulsion of the Medici and then the Savonarola years, rising to become a senior civil servant after the monk's execution in 1498. He wrote his most famous work *The Prince* while exiled from the city, suspected of conspiracy for which he was tortured in the Bargello, the grim city prison near the Piazza della Signoria. Guiccardini was the consummate politician, working for the Vatican or the Medici, depending on the prevailing political climate. He saw the rise of Savonarola as a youth, knew Machiavelli personally, and, according to rumour, was fatally poisoned by the godfather to one of Cellini's children.

Flitting through the dog-eared, annotated, well-thumbed pages of the books Fratelli owned, she found herself transfixed by the contrast between the city's sumptuous visual beauty and the cruelty and degradation of those who created it. Assassination – by poison, by public sword fight, with a stealthy dagger in the dark – was commonplace. Sexual hypocrisy was rife. Both Cellini and Machiavelli stood accused of sodomy, a capital offence at the time, as did Savonarola when pilloried by his enemies. In the struggle between the working classes, the merchants, the noble families and the Medici (the latter a kind of royal family), loyalties shifted like desert sands, marooning the unfortunate, turning yesterday's heroes into the next day's decapitated traitors. And that was just within the city walls. Beyond, in the ragged patchwork of individual states that preceded modern Italy, lurked the scheming Vatican and rival states like Venice and Milan, bristling with arms and ambition, covetous of one of the most prosperous and financially astute cities in Europe.

For those with ambition, the journey from glory to destruction could be shocking in its savage brevity. When 1497 began, Savonarola was ruler of Florence in all but name, with sufficient power and influence over the city to persuade thousands of its citizens to burn their paintings, finest clothes, mirrors and 'immoral' books in the bonfire of the vanities. By the following Christmas the friar's enemies were openly taunting him and his supporters in the street, driving a donkey into the Duomo during a church service and slaughtering it before the altar. In May 1498 Savonarola and his two closest priests were hanged then cremated on a pyre in front of cheering crowds before the Palazzo Vecchio, on the very spot of the bonfire of the vanities. As the priest approached the pyre, one of his executioners whispered into his ear, 'The man who wanted to burn me is now himself put to the flames.'

The friar's great enemy, the Borgia Pope Alexander VI, applauded from Rome before returning to the simony, debauchery and corruption which Savonarola had so loudly condemned. In the crowd, watching the fiery spectacle, stood Machiavelli, already marshalling the political theories that would one day, in sorry exile, turn into *The Prince*.

Drawn into these distant stories, Julia found herself seeing these men – and all were men – walking the streets she was coming to know. Politics in the rival gangs fighting for control of the fortress-like civic headquarters, the Palazzo Vecchio. Misery in the Bargello where Savonarola and thousands of others were suspended from the ceiling, hands behind their back, then jerked and dropped using the cruel torture known as the *strappado*. The violence of the monk's fall saw the siege and sacking of his great Dominican monastery of San Marco and the persecution and occasional slaughter of his acolytes. None of this took place in that remote, imaginary terrain that carried the easy label of 'the past'. The city those lost souls all knew and fought for, the Duomo, the Baptistery and the austere black and white facade of Santa Croce; they still stood today, little changed on the outside, a testament to their stories.

The Florence of the Medici, of Benvenuto Cellini, Machiavelli and the unfortunate friar was a hothouse of fervent, apocalyptic religion and its darker twin, a desperate, sweaty sensuality. The venal and the venerated walked those same cobbled streets together, changing sides on a whim or through some sudden threat, struggling on occasion to tell the difference between the two. Sacred mixed with profane. The highest, most devotional art emerged from the hands of the most bloodthirsty and profane of individuals.

She closed the last book that had gripped her, Cellini's autobiography, written with a repugnant sense of self-justification and not an iota of shame. In the section she'd opened by accident Cellini told how, while separated from his wife, he'd fallen in love with a man, a rival goldsmith, only to return home and find the object of his lust meeting his estranged spouse. He'd stabbed both to death as they stood on the threshold, and dismissed their murders as 'a justifiable accident during a heated argument'.

The casual brutishness from a man lauded as one of Florence's greatest sons, honoured with a bronze bust in the centre of the Ponte Vecchio, appalled her.

It was now close to midnight. Julia wondered whether she could sleep, and if she did what dreams might come, of dark shapes flitting through the alleys of Florence, of the beautiful Eve smeared with blood, and her counterpart on the opposite wall of the Brancacci Chapel howling while she and Adam fled Paradise in ignominy and despair. Of the strange serpent with a beautiful female face, newly crowned with a bloody halo by an intruder spurred on by uncertain motives.

With those frescoes, many believed, the artistic Renaissance – informed by perspective, by an accurate depiction of the human body, of light and the physical world – began. In fifteenth-century Florence, humanity started to take its first, faltering steps out of the dark age of superstition and feudalism towards a rationalist conscience and a world of equality and justice.

Or so, she whispered to herself, we like to think.

Faint strains of atonal modern jazz were drifting through from Fratelli's rooms opposite. She went to the door and saw his was open, with a light on.

Gingerly she tiptoed across. He was fast asleep in the solitary chair, a book in his lap. He looked younger like that, as if all the many troublesome ghosts that seemed to haunt him had been briefly exorcized.

Sleeping in a chair couldn't be comfortable, or good for a man who was not, she had come to realize, well at all.

She walked over and gently shook him awake. It took a few moments for him to come round. Then he stared at her, frowned and said, 'Yes?'

'It's late, Pino,' she said. 'You should sleep in a bed. Not a chair.'

He looked at the clock on the wall.

'True,' Fratelli said sleepily. 'This worries me. I don't need two dragons in my life.'

'Bed,' she insisted. 'There's nothing you can do now.'

He peered at her, still half asleep.

'Well, is there?' she added quickly. 'Nothing happened today really. An idiot smeared blood on some beautiful paintings. I bet we never hear anything else about it again.'

'A lot happened today,' he said. 'It's just that we don't know it yet.'

Then he started to stand, sending the book he was reading clattering to the polished wooden floor.

Julia picked it up and handed it to him. He gave a little salute in return then disappeared without another word through the door by the front window.

She was sorry they couldn't talk any longer, but he looked exhausted. It was for the best. All the same, books were her second love, after paintings. Pino Fratelli owned so many, in English and Italian. He must have adored them as much as she did. Unusual books, too, indicative of a wandering, restless and highly unusual mind.

The one he'd been reading, a hefty title he'd taken off to bed, was to do with Hebrew myth and a name she vaguely recalled, though not in any great detail.

The title on the cover was *Lilith*.

Tuesday, 4 November 1986

The following morning Julia Wellbeloved woke at seven, Cellini's bloody life story still open on her sheets, still rolling around her imagination. The bells of Santa Maria del Carmine clattered in a sonorous tumult beyond the window. She got dressed and threw open the curtains.

The weather had changed completely. A bright winter sun cast the street outside in contrasting tones: one side deep black, the other a bright, chilly white. Men and women in heavy clothing shuffled up and down the pavement, many led by small dogs trudging along in front of them. There were lights in the tiny café a few doors away on the opposite side of the street, and wafts of either steam or cigarette smoke curled out of the half-open door. As she watched, a rusty Fiat estate car came to a halt outside the place, blocking the entire narrow street. A man got out and headed into the café, carrying several trays of pastries. Meanwhile a small, very old bus, lurching towards Carmine, dispatching a fog of diesel fumes in its wake, was forced to a halt behind the Fiat.

The delivery man emerged, and a brief argument of gestures and words that she could just about hear ensued. The language of Florence seemed to her very . . . florid. Full of words she could only guess at; terms that, judging by the vehement tone with which they were delivered, were unlikely to grace any A-level Italian examination back in England.

The appointment at the Palazzo Vecchio was for nine thirty. For some reason she wanted to get out of the house without seeing Pino Fratelli. So she tiptoed out on to the landing. His door was still open but there was no light and no music. Still sleeping, she thought. All the same, she went down the stone steps as lightly as a mouse and closed the door quietly as she let herself into the cobbled street.

A short dash through the crawl of morning traffic, once again blocked by a stationary car further along the street, took her to the tiny café. She breezed in and, in her best Italian, asked for a cappuccino and a *cornetto alla crema*.

Signora Grassi, who seemed rather larger and more formidable than she had the day before, glared back at her from the till, a cigarette dangling from her lower lip, almost half of it ash.

'*Buongiorno*,' Julia added quickly.

'*Buongiorno*,' the woman grunted with a nod that sent the ash tumbling down on to the shiny red plastic counter top.

A middle-aged man, slight, with a brown toothbrush moustache, burst into action at her behest, handing her a pastry in a paper napkin, then setting to work on the shiny Gaggia machine.

There was no one else in the place. The attention of the woman at the counter, dressed in a garish pink nylon jacket embroidered with the name of a coffee company, was focused entirely on her single customer.

'*Inglese?*' Signora Grassi said.

'Yes.'

The woman nodded across the road. 'Fratelli's . . . guest?'

The last word was spoken with such a suspicious intonation that Julia felt her temper start to rise.

'I'm a postgraduate student here on assignment. The Uffizi arranged the accommodation.'

'The Uffizi!' said the man at the coffee machine brightly.

'I'm researching an academic paper,' Julia added. Then, out of nothing more than a sense of pure mischief, threw in, 'I have an appointment with Signor Soderini, the mayor, in a little while to discuss my work.'

The barista's eyebrows rose in admiration. Signora Grassi, who had to be his wife, puffed on her cigarette and squinted through hooded eyes. The coffee arrived, creamy and welcome. Julia tasted it, wiped the froth from her lip, and told him, truthfully, it was delicious.

She gazed around the little place, which was not unfriendly, merely suspicious of strangers. The walls seemed to be entirely devoted to Fiorentina, the local football team. There were violet banners, photographs of players and managers, some signed, going back decades, and several flags bearing the city's coat of arms, the red giglio lily. The colours were so bright and vivid they reminded her of the figures in the other frescoes of the Brancacci Chapel, those dedicated to the story of Saint Peter. The scarlet spears of the ornamental lily were an emblem Machiavelli and Cellini would have recognized.

'The mayor,' the Grassi woman murmured. 'And Fratelli comes with you?'

'No. I think he has work of his own.'

'What work? He's supposed to rest.'

The ferocity of the woman's reply shook her.

'I don't know,' Julia said. 'He's my landlord. I barely met him until yesterday. He asked me to look at some vandalism in the chapel—'

'The best detective Florence ever had,' her husband chipped in, braving a caustic look from the woman at the till. 'If anyone could get to the bottom of that outrage—'

'Fratelli's on sick leave,' his wife broke in. 'He's not allowed to work and he knows it. If he—'

'The best detective in Florence,' the man added under his breath.

'What's wrong with Pino?' Julia asked outright.

'Ask him,' Signora Grassi suggested.

'I did. He said . . .' She made the twirling finger at her ear, just as Fratelli had done. 'He told me he was mad. As a mole.'

'As a mole?' the man demanded.

'That's what he said.'

'I've never heard such nonsense. A mole? What talk is this? Pino's a decent man. A cheery man for the most part, especially given that life's not been kind in many respects. His wife—'

'Beppe!' the Grassi woman roared. 'There's beer out back to be moved.'

'I'd like another cappuccino, please,' Julia interrupted, smiling at him.

Beppe took her empty cup, placed it in the sink and went back to the shiny Gaggia.

'Fratelli is one of the sanest men I know,' he said, fixing his wife with a rebellious stare. 'Though what my wife tells you is the truth. You should ask him these questions yourself. This is Pino's business, not ours. Not unless he asks it. In Florence we do not gossip.'

'With strangers,' the woman added.

'And if he won't tell me?'

The man frowned, puzzled. He handed over a fresh cappuccino, one she didn't really want. 'Then you won't know, will you?' he said.

Fratelli had a nine-thirty appointment with his consultant, not far from his old office in the street known as the Borgo Ognissanti. This was the other side of the river from Oltrarno, an area beyond the usual tourist crowds. So he loved the place, after a fashion.

In Ambra Neri's consultation room, he was more than a little surprised to see Father Bruno Lazzaro, smug in his black priest's robes, beaming beatifically like a saint in waiting.

Lazzaro was a fixture in Oltrarno. He'd joined Carmine from the neighbourhood seminary in the Piazza di Cestello around the time the adolescent Fratelli was rebelling against his Catholic upbringing. The arguments that minor fury prompted brought about the only serious disagreement Fratelli had ever had with his mother; one that was mended, with many tears, when she told him the truth about his birth and race.

The young Pino revealed none of this to the priest and simply argued his own case for atheism, doggedly, with great conviction. It was an infuriating exercise. Lazzaro was a priest of the old school, one who smiled constantly, listened with great care, nodding sagely at each point made. Then closed, as he always would, with the simple question: but if there's no God, what can possibly explain Florence?

How could such geniuses as Michelangelo, da Vinci, Botticelli and Brunelleschi be fooled into devoting their lives to works of art glorying a deity who did not exist? Was an Oltrarno teenager wiser than them?

After which he would smile more gracefully and await an answer. He was a very handsome man, with a clean-shaven face, perfect white teeth, peaceful blue eyes, a full head of light brown hair. There were those who said he administered to some of the women of the parish privately, in ways of which the Pope might not approve. Fratelli knew little of this and cared less, reminding himself that there were plenty in the Vatican for whom such behaviour appeared no sin at all.

But he had no good answer to Lazzaro's perpetual question – if Michelangelo believed in the existence of an unseen deity, what did the scepticism of an ordinary mortal matter? Which was why the infuriating man found such pleasure in asking it.

And now, more than thirty years later, he sat in the office of Ambra Neri wearing that same, smug smile.

Fratelli found it impossible not to reward his charming consultant with a scowl for such treachery. He'd known this woman for a good decade, long before her interest in him became professional. She was beautiful, sympathetic, pragmatic and – to him – unimaginative in her outlook towards the mysterious and the unknown. He would, he knew from experience, be wasting his breath if he spoke of his ideas about the Brancacci incident, something she would regard as idle speculation, an extravagance deserving of condemnation. Though, given Lazzaro's presence . . .

'I thought this was a private consultation,' Fratelli said, trying not to sound too surly.

'It is. But we must take your behaviour into account, Pino. How do you feel?'

'I feel fine!' Fratelli protested. 'How do I look?'

'You look well. I'm pleased. You're a very good patient.'

'Oh for pity's sake. How am I supposed to feel? I wake, I read, I talk to anyone who'll talk to me. Then I sleep. What else is a man supposed to do?'

She smiled at him.

'And, while I wish no disrespect, why is Father Lazzaro here?'

'You're one of my parishioners,' the priest said with a generous wave of his hand. 'Whether you like it or not. You were baptized in my church. You're a part of us. We care for you. Given the spiritual trial ahead we want you to know we welcome you back, with open arms.'

'What I want,' Fratelli retorted, 'is my job. Ambra. Fix it, please.'

'You know I can't do that. I'm a doctor, not an officer of the Carabinieri.'

'The minor incident in the chapel yesterday,' Lazzaro went on. 'Your response was quite out of proportion. This is evidence of the stress you feel. Ambra here agrees with me. We need to bring you into our pastoral care and—'

'The incident in the Brancacci's just the kind of thing for my talents. Not too onerous. Not so taxing. Nor, in terms of the Carabinieri, too important, I imagine.'

A copy of the morning paper, *La Nazione*, lay on the desk in front of them. The attack on the frescoes headed the front page. Fratelli had read the story already, frustrated by the lacunae in the narrative, the lack of meaningful detail; even – and this seemed odd – any photos of the actual damage. The attack was being treated as if it were one more act of vandalism, akin to a hoodlum spraying graffiti on the walls of the Pitti Palace. There was no attempt to understand the context, and for him context was everything.

'What an obscene act,' Ambra Neri said, trying to cool things a little. 'Why on earth would anyone break into a beautiful place like that and do such a thing?'

'Give me the chance,' Fratelli declared, 'and I'll tell you.'

'It's a matter for the officers next door,' Lazzaro broke in, his voice no longer so warm and cheerful. 'I would prefer you leave it that way. We've much work to do in the Brancacci. You had no right to be there yesterday.'

'I thought I was a parishioner.'

'The chapel is closed. Even the parishioners have no access. Not during restoration. And you bring along this foreign woman . . .'

'An expert on vandalism, no less!'

'I don't care, Pino. What you did was wrong and must not be repeated. I've no desire to ban anyone from God's house. But if you disobey the rules you shall leave me with no choice.'

'I thought God only had ten rules, and for the life of me, Father, even as an atheist, I doubt I've broken one of them. Much, anyway.'

'This is irrelevant . . .' the man in black persisted.

'May we speak alone?' Fratelli asked, staring at the worried woman in front of him. 'I came here for a medical appointment. Not a sermon.'

'I'm supposed to help you,' she said. 'It's not easy.'

He folded his arms and said nothing, merely gazed at the priest. Eventually Lazzaro grunted and got up. At the door he turned and said, 'You know where I am if you need me. Any time. You only have to ask.'

When he was gone, Fratelli repeated his demand. 'I want something to do. And by that I do not mean putting flowers on the altar.'

'You can be very awkward at times.' She looked at the papers on her desk. 'If you want to go to Marrone again and ask for reinstatement, I won't object.'

'You could tell him it would be good for me. Help my fragile mental state.'

'Fragile?' she cried. 'You're the least fragile patient I have.' She thought for a moment and added, 'Because, I suspect, you don't care much. For yourself, that is. You have friends, Pino. Many. Professionals like Father Lazzaro . . .'

'A priest is a professional now?'

'Don't be so caustic. Think of others for once in your life.'

'To hell with them. What about me? I feel fine. My mind is not so disordered mostly. I'm twice as bright and energetic as some of those fat slugs Marrone keeps around him . . .'

'Now, now!' She wagged a scolding finger at him. 'I'll pretend I didn't hear that.'

'What if I were to tell you I think this Brancacci Chapel matter is more serious than they appreciate. That I have good reason to believe it may well be the beginning of something far more threatening. Perhaps dangerous.'

'Then I'd ask you why you thought that.'

'Can't say. Not yet. You think I'm crazy already. I'm not supplying more evidence to damn myself. Maybe if they let me into the case . . .' He nodded at her desk and the pen and notebook there. 'A simple, short letter. I'll dictate. "It is my expert opinion that Maresciallo Ordinario Fratelli's condition would be greatly ameliorated if he were given some small task to occupy his overactive mind. An insignificant case involving cerebral investigation, nothing more. No physical activity."' He kept his eyes on her. "'No call for access to firearms. A simple act of vandalism, say. Such as this incident in the Brancacci."'

The doctor kept on smiling at him and said nothing.

'Please,' Fratelli added.

'Marrone and I have discussed your condition. More than once. Lord knows you've begged me to talk to him often enough. The answer was always no.'

'This,' he pointed at the paper, 'gives us a firm and good reason to ask again.'

'They won't have you back in the Carabinieri. Nothing I can do will change that, Pino.' She looked through the window at the bright day. The Italian flag was fluttering in the breeze outside the Carabinieri station a few doors away; a red, white and green banner moving lazily with the wind. 'Nothing out there will either. You have to learn to live with that. If you like . . .'

Ambra Neri reached over, picked up her pen and grabbed the prescription sheet he knew so well.

'There are other medications we can try. Ones that may be more effective. Let's see . . .'

'No!' Fratelli cried, and found his right fist slamming down on the desk. The gesture was too violent, his voice too loud. He was immediately ashamed of himself and apologized. She was a good, decent woman. Doing the best she could.

'If you don't wish . . . of course I respect that,' Ambra Neri said with the matter-of-fact disdain of a consultant used to dealing with recalcitrant patients.

'Help me get back to work. I want to think. To look beneath stones and see what lurks there. That' – Fratelli's mournful head rose and he gazed at the woman across the shiny, professional desk – 'is what I do.'

'Not any more,' she answered. 'I'm sorry. I can't write to Marrone. I won't speak to him again. What's the point? You accept your condition so easily, so bravely. Why can you not accept the consequences?'

'Because they're far worse,' Fratelli grumbled and gathered up his things. '*Buongiorno*, Ambra.'

'Next week?' she asked as he rose to leave. 'We could go for a coffee. For lunch.'

'I'm your patient now. We can't . . .' He turned and looked at her, sorry that he was the reason for the evident pain in her face. 'Even if it was a good idea.'

'Don't spend too much time on your own,' she told him. 'Find a hobby. Volunteer for something. Be occupied. Go and talk to Lazzaro. He's a good man. It doesn't need to be about religion.'

'Lazzaro believes in fairy stories.'

Her eyes were shiny – close to tears, he thought – and that only made him feel worse.

'Lots of people do. If it helps . . .'

'I'm not in the mood for a placebo, certainly not one offered by a priest.' He blinked and stammered, 'You make me sound like an invalid. Or a pensioner eking out his days.'

'You're not a well man,' she said gently.

'I know what I am. Thank you.'

That was a victory, he thought, watching the way she took those last few words. And now I might make a doctor cry.

Fratelli did his best to smile at her.

'I meant that. Thank you. You've more important patients than this one. We should keep these meetings to a minimum. Unless there's a point . . .'

He had no more words.

Outside, Fratelli wrapped himself in his coat and scarf, then walked round the corner for a coffee, choosing a bar where he knew it was unlikely he'd find anyone from the station. He didn't want to experience their sympathy or see the way they struggled for something to say.

The same newspaper was on the bar there. He reread the story on the Brancacci Chapel again. The conviction – that this was not just wrong, but deeply wrong – had locked itself inside him now and would not leave.

'Dammit, Walter,' he said, as he threw back his macchiato. 'You will see me.'

A few minutes earlier, Julia Wellbeloved had met Piero Soderini's descendant, Sandro, an elegant and talkative man who looked in his early fifties, olive skinned with finely chiselled aristocratic features and dark hair, perhaps dyed.

The mayor of Florence sat at a desk in an elegant study on the first floor of the Palazzo Vecchio, an area cordoned off from tourists trekking towards the grand Salone dei Cinquecento. Half palace, half crenellated fortress, this curious building overlooking the Piazza della Signoria had been the town hall of Florence for more than six hundred years. Kings and princes had been welcomed here, politicians murdered, traitors defenestrated, suspects – Savonarola and the first Cosimo de' Medici among them – held prisoner before being marched to the nearby Bargello to endure the *strappado* and the inquisition of the torturers. The harsh facade apart (Julia was beginning to appreciate Fratelli's opinions on rustication), she found it difficult to associate such a vivid and violent history with the serenely beautiful interior of today.

The office Soderini occupied, behind a desk bearing a large sign that read 'Sindaco di Firenze', was part of the quarters once allotted to Pope Leo X, decorated for the Medici by the industrious Vasari, whose corridor she had mentioned at the outset of her conversation with Soderini, as Fratelli suggested. There were canvases on the walls and ceilings, so many she didn't know where to look. He did, though. Straight at her, with a frankness and interest that was so open she found it hard not to laugh.

Soderini, a powerful, striking man who didn't mind who knew it, clearly relished the sound of his own voice and his position at the historic heart of Florence. Fratelli had predicted Julia would get five minutes of his time. He was wrong. At ten o'clock, as the former detective was marching towards his old Carabinieri *stazione*, muttering darkly with each step, she was still sitting on an ornate gilt chair opposite Sandro Soderini, listening to him talk history – that of his own line, mainly – and complain heatedly about the lack of funding that made the protection of the art of Florence – 'the most precious in the world' – from vandals, the elements, and the constant ravages of time, so difficult.

'Everyone wants beauty,' Soderini said. 'Few realize it comes with a price. Does that help?'

'It's the psychology that interests me. Why people would wish to damage something wonderful. The attack in the Brancacci Chapel—'

'That's obvious, isn't it? Envy. Ugliness hates its opposite. Wishes to damage it, if it can. In a way . . .' He stroked his chin and stared at her across his desk. 'It's perfectly understandable. As for the Brancacci . . .' He waved away this subject with the back of his hand, as if it were beneath him. 'From what I understand, the damage is slight and easily rectified. They will redouble the security on that place, trawl the bars of Oltrarno for misfits and drunks, and pick a likely suspect from the dross they recover there.'

'There may be more to the case than simple vandalism.'

'I doubt it. I'm aware of your paper. I was merely trying to give you a little perspective on its subject.'

Julia smiled and said nothing.

Soderini broke the brief moment of discomfort.

'I've arranged for you to meet Vanni Tornabuoni. He's my arts commissioner. Another old name, though' – he grinned at her – 'one that has not prospered quite so much over the centuries.'

He passed over a note with a time, an address and a name on it.

'On Thursday you will talk to my people in the Convent of San Marco. Savonarola's old home. They are reworking much of the place and security is, I imagine, much on their mind.'

A thought came to Sandro Soderini. 'So you want to see the Vasari Corridor?'

'A friend suggested . . . It was just an idea.'

'An excellent one, in the circumstances. The corridor begins a little way beyond that door. It reaches the Uffizi by a small bridge, then continues all the way along the riverfront, across the Arno, across the top of the shops on the Ponte Vecchio to the Pitti Palace.'

The smile turned into a broad, flashing beam.

'Most people don't know it's there. Even if they did, they'd have no way of getting in.' His tanned face broke into a vulpine smile. 'We don't show all our jewels to everyone.'

He reached into the desk drawer and pulled out a heavy set of very ancient keys.

'But to a visiting English academic . . . In return for your being my guest for dinner, I will grant you access. Tornabuoni's office is at the far end. In the Pitti. Faster than ploughing through sweaty tourists on the Ponte Vecchio.'

She couldn't stop herself laughing. 'I'm sorry . . .'

'Dinner,' he repeated. 'The English do eat, don't they?'

'I don't . . .'

Nothing more.

'Ah,' Soderini sighed. 'You mistake my purpose. Or at least my invitation. We have a small supper club in Florence. Men, mainly. The first Thursday of each month. We ask along a select number of guests. It seemed to me you might be interested. A little light entertainment after the sterile gloom of San Marco.'

Julia was blushing. 'I thought . . .'

'I know what you thought. Perhaps another night for that. This is a select gathering. Twelve men and a few lady guests. A very private occasion. An old tradition that dates back to the thirteenth century. You can find it mentioned in Dante, in Boccaccio and Cavalcanti too.'

'A tradition . . .?'

'La Brigata Spendereccia. The Spendthrift Brigade, as you'd say in English. We eat what Dante might have eaten. We drink the rarest of Tuscan wines. We sing songs. We behave as if we are the most irresponsible, the richest, the most privileged men on earth – for one evening, anyway. And the next morning we trudge back to the office with aching heads. Childish, but for a single night only, and in something of a special place.'

'Where?' she asked immediately.

He held up the set of keys and chose one. It was long and old fashioned, the kind a jailer might use.

'Later. If you wish. To walk down the Vasari Corridor is a privilege shown usually to statesmen and the most senior figures in the world of art. And the odd Florentine civil servant in the know who wishes to avoid the crowds.' Soderini's twinkling eye caught hers. 'To pass an evening with La Brigata Spendereccia . . . That is something quite different. It's also a secret society of a kind, so you must mention it to no one. That is an absolute condition. Agreed?'

He stood up and held out his hand. She nodded and took it.

Julia said. 'Are you coming with me, Mr Mayor?'

'Sandro. Please. For the Brigata I will be your guide. Be here on Thursday night at seven o'clock, please. Now . . .' He frowned. 'I have more boring work to do.'

He picked up the slim modern phone.

'Fiorella will take you. I trust you'll find Tornabuoni entertaining.'

'Ambra Neri is adamant it would be good for my condition if I were involved in some kind of intellectual activity,' Fratelli insisted. 'I'm not asking for much, Walter. A desk even. Just the chance to see some files, knock on a few doors, stick my nose in where it's not wanted . . .'

'I rather thought you were doing that already.'

Marrone had eyed him suspiciously from the moment Fratelli walked through the door. The captain had the best office in the

Carabinieri headquarters on the narrow Borgo Ognissanti, one with long windows looking out towards the church. This two-storey ochre building had been the focus of Fratelli's life for two and a half decades, until he was dispatched to the exile of sick leave. He felt he knew every brick, each corner, every last noise, from the howl of frustrated officers struggling with a case to the complaints of the iron pipework that made up the ancient central heating system now groaning against the winter cold.

'I don't know what you mean.'

'Rushing round to the Brancacci like that. Upsetting that pompous priest. With your pretty English girlfriend in tow . . .'

Fratelli threw up his hands. 'Don't be ridiculous. She's young enough to be my daughter. A lodger sent by the Uffizi.' He leaned across the desk and pointed at the man in the blue serge suit. 'A very intelligent and perceptive young woman. She used to be a lawyer.'

Marrone frowned and said, 'Who in God's name gives up the law to be a student? Where's the money in that?'

'Not everything's about money. I don't pretend to understand her reasons.' It occurred to him he should have asked. 'All the same, I feel we may come to be grateful for her presence.'

'We?' Marrone cried. 'There isn't a "we" any more. You're off the force.'

'Strictly speaking I'm on sick leave—'

'You're off the force! And kindly don't call me by my first name.'

Fratelli's arms spread out even more in exasperation.

'Here we go again. With one breath you tell me I'm gone from the Carabinieri for good. With the next you try to pull rank. How is an invalid like me supposed to follow . . .?'

'It's a question of respect. Even civilians call me *capitano*.'

'Respect, respect.' Fratelli toyed with his heavy winter coat. 'How long have we known one another? No. Let me tell you. Since we were raw cadets, shivering in our uniforms at the age of seventeen. If I had no respect for you, would I be here now? After all this time? In these circumstances?'

Marrone leaned across the desk and growled, 'I know that look. You've got a bee in your bonnet, and you're not letting on what it is. The days when you could pull those tricks are over.'

'All I want is to help! To track down the deeply disturbed human being who attacked those paintings in the Brancacci yesterday. Before he does something worse.' Fratelli paused to let that sink in. 'Which he will, I think. As night follows day. We may be too late to stop him already.'

The captain slumped forward on to the desk, head briefly in his hands. Fratelli had spoken the truth. These two had known each other for thirty years. One soaring through the ranks, a good, obedient servant of the state. The second clawing his way upwards until he reached the middling position of *maresciallo ordinario*. Only to find himself trapped there, mostly by his own penchant for free speech and thought, accompanied by the occasional act of blatant insubordination.

'I'm telling you, Walter,' Fratelli persisted. 'Remember that monstrous old butcher from Scandicci who was none too picky about what went into his *finocchiona*? Without me—'

'Without you we would have sent the wrong man to jail and left that bloodthirsty bastard out there to kill yet more of his neighbours. Yes, Pino. I know. How often have you reminded me of this?'

'Let's not forget the charming widow Bartolini from Bel Riposo either.'

Marrone refused to look up, staring at the desk with a stony resolution.

'Did anyone else think to check on the chihuahuas? Well? Did they?'

'No,' the captain said grumpily.

'Quite,' Fratelli replied and folded his arms.

Marrone glared at him.

'Pino! I meant no! To you! To whatever hare-brained idea you've come up with. Listen to me.'

'I always listen to you,' Fratelli objected. 'There's no need to take that tone.'

'Listen to me! You're on permanent sick leave for a reason. We both know that. Ambra Neri and I have discussed this at great length. If either of us thought it would be for the best—'

'Best for you,' Fratelli broke in. 'Not me. I'm the one who's doing the favours here. I could sit at home, listen to Beethoven and read books if I wanted.'

'You're sick!' Marrone cried.

The captain's long, sallow face fell. He looked, Fratelli thought, deeply miserable. This was a shame. They were close when they were cadets. Friends; warriors in a constant and difficult struggle for some kind of justice. Along the way came girls and drinking and the odd bout of fisticuffs with a few nocturnal rogues. He admired and liked this man.

'You're sick and you won't be coming back,' the captain added quickly. 'No one's more sorry about that than I am. Pino . . .'

'Ten minutes,' he pleaded. 'Listen to what I have to say. After that, if you want to kick me out of the door . . .'

'I don't want to. I have to—'

'Twenty years. An anniversary. Do you remember?' Fratelli demanded.

Marrone didn't answer for a while. Then he said, 'Of course I remember. How could I forget?'

'Twenty years,' Fratelli repeated. 'Please listen to me, Walter. Ten minutes. It's not much to ask now. Is it?'

A severe middle-aged woman in a dark blue uniform bearing the scarlet lily of Florence took over when Julia Wellbeloved left Soderini's office. More by grunts than spoken instructions, she guided Julia to the second floor through a succession of halls and chambers devoted to the elements, brushing past groups of tourists as if they didn't exist. They passed quickly through a room with a bust of Machiavelli, a place Julia felt sure, from her reading, must have been the man's private office itself when he worked here as an important servant of the state. There were paintings and globes and maps and . . . so much that she could only watch it whisk by in a bright, gilded haze. The woman in the blue uniform was in a hurry; not best pleased, it seemed, by this sudden mission.

They turned one more sharp corner. Then she found the key she wanted and set about opening the plain door that led, by various secrets turns, all the way from the seat of power of the Florentine republic, through the Uffizi, across the Arno and the Ponte Vecchio, all the way to the Pitti Palace, once home to the House of Medici, rulers of this small and rancorous state off and on from the middle of the fifteenth century until its collapse in bankruptcy, despair and bitter internal division three hundred years later.

As the two of them crossed the bridge over the narrow street beneath and entered the Uffizi, unseen to the milling visitors in its overfull galleries, Julia felt assaulted by the past. The famous gallery she'd seen already several times, amazed by the richness of its collections, the way some of the greatest canvases in the world seemed to be fighting for space to breathe on its miles of walls. In the confined space of the Vasari Corridor, the weight of the centuries seemed even heavier. A kilometre long, it was a practical construction, a way for the Medici to stroll from their palace home to the offices of state without having to meet the grubby and occasionally violent proletariat along the way. Even so, there was scarcely a stretch of bare plaster anywhere along the way. Self-portraits covered the walls mostly – some recent, some five hundred years old. A sea of dead faces with glittering eyes following the lucky few allowed to cross by the corridor.

Halfway across the river, they stopped by two sets of large windows on each side of the corridor.

'Mussolini,' the woman in the blue uniform said. 'And Hitler. You know the story?'

Julia remembered what Pino had told her.

She walked to the window facing away from the city and admired the low, elegant shape of the next bridge along, the Ponte Santa Trinita, not far from Fratelli's home. Hers too, for a little while.

The views from the other side, out towards the viewpoint of the Piazzale Michelangelo, above Fratelli's Negroni bar, were equally exquisite in the pale winter sun. The river, the lines of tall houses, church spires and, in the distance, verdant hills.

'Hitler liked to sit here and take tea,' the woman said. 'That saved the Ponte Vecchio.'

No it didn't, Julia thought. She was with Pino Fratelli there. That morning, on her way to see Soderini, she'd crossed the old bridge and watched the jewellers starting to open shops full of garish baubles, well beyond the reach of an impoverished postgraduate student. She'd stopped by the grand statue of Benvenuto Cellini, directly below these windows on the western side, midway along the span. Already tourists were taking photos. Cellini was a consummate artist, sculptor, writer, painter and musician. His terrifying image of *Perseus with the Head of Medusa* stole the breath from all who saw it standing in the Loggia dei Lanzi in front of the Palazzo Vecchio. And he was as vile a murderer and villain as the city had seen, one who confessed his crimes – boasted of them – in the memoirs Fratelli had given her the night before.

Evil was evil, she thought. It saved nothing. Simply existed alongside beauty, sucking the life from it.

'First,' Fratelli declared, 'something our English friend spotted straight away. The fig leaves.'

'Christmas decorations,' Marrone interrupted.

'Do you put up fig leaves for Christmas?'

'Well, no. But . . .'

'My intuition is they have something to do with catering.'

'Fine, fine,' the captain agreed.

'More importantly, and again I'm grateful to Julia Wellbeloved for prompting this realization, there's the question of why? What's the point of covering up the supposed shame of some 500-year-old frescoes? Who could possibly object to their nakedness being revealed, and the removal of the prudish, ugly additions of whichever damned Medici put them there to begin with?'

Marrone's head went from side to side, a sign of faint agreement.

'I can see there's something sexual here. I'm not as stupid as you think.'

'I don't think you're stupid for one moment, Walter. You're the most clinical and precise investigative officer it's ever been my privilege to work with.'

The captain looked surprised and said, 'You mean that?'

'Of course I do! In ninety-nine per cent of cases you're king, and my small and unpredictable talents are quite unnecessary.' He hesitated then added, 'But this is the one per cent. I'm sure of it. Of course we can assume that whoever daubed chicken blood on these frescoes was motivated by fury at what he perceived to be their obscenity. That's obvious. But we're missing a more important and informative question.'

Marrone blinked. 'Which is?'

'Who knew our beautiful couple would soon be revealed in all their naked glory? Not the general congregation of Carmine, that's for sure. The chapel's been sheeted off ever since restoration work began. There's been no announcement in the papers. Nothing in the art magazines. I've looked.'

'Interesting,' Marrone observed.

'Who knew?' Fratelli repeated. 'The restorers themselves. The officials of the Uffizi, the city art institutions, the writers and photographers preparing the tourist guides.'

'Bleeding-heart atheist liberals, all of them,' the captain noted. 'They'd love the fact there was a bit of nudity on the walls. No point looking among that bunch . . .'

'Very probably. So we must think about the small people, the invisible people. The ones they never notice. Builders and scaffolders. Suppliers of paint and materials, food and drink. Church wardens.

That stolid proletarian stock from which this city was built. The Medici's cannon fodder. The hoi polloi.'

'You're starting to sound like a bleeding-heart liberal yourself.'

'Politics have nothing to do with it. That's where we start looking. The little people.'

The captain sniffed. 'I have a report on my desk saying the damage was insignificant. Chicken blood is easily washed off, apparently. It will be back the way it was by the end of the week. In any case, even supposing we could drag some lunatic vandal to court, he'd get a suspended sentence and an appointment with a psychiatrist. There are no obvious suspects. If we happen to bump into one—'

'I haven't finished!'

There it was again. The sudden anger. The flash of violence. Ambra Neri had seen this same strange and uncontrollable emotion earlier that morning. Where did it come from? This was all so foreign. Unlike the man he thought himself to be.

Marrone sat sullen and silent.

'I apologize,' Fratelli told him. 'But you must hear me out. The daubs on Adam and Eve were what we all saw. They weren't everything. Over the serpent. The beast with a woman's head. There he painted something else. A bloody halo.'

The captain's right eyebrow rose in disbelief.

'Bear with me,' Fratelli begged, and seized some books from his carrier-bag collection, turning the pages on two titles about Hebrew mythology and ancient biblical lore. 'Who was the first woman, Walter? Do tell me.'

'Eve, of course.'

'You think?'

Marrone looked at his watch and scowled.

'Jewish folklore,' Fratelli said, bringing out a book. '*The Alphabet of Ben Sira*. Probably eighth century. According to this, the first woman was called Lilith. She wasn't drawn from Adam's rib. She was his equal. Made from dirt and dust like him. Like us.'

'And?'

'And she refused to mate with him the way he wanted. Lying down, him dominant, on top. Lilith believed herself as good as any man. If there was sex to be had, she wished to control it.'

'Pino, Pino . . .'

'Bear with me! Lilith abandoned him and went to live with the demons, bearing their children, dominating them, not him. It was then God made Eve. The second woman. The obedient, servile wife. That's why Masolino's serpent has a woman's head. A beautiful one. She's Lilith, come back to take her revenge on the man who failed her, and the woman who took her place in Paradise.'

Walter Marrone was a literal-minded man. Not slow, certainly not dense.

'This is an interesting idea,' he said. 'You're saying that, by painting a halo on the woman of the snake, this Lilith, our vandal is somehow worshipping an ancient Hebrew myth?'

'I don't know what I'm saying,' Fratelli admitted.

'That he's Jewish? How many Jews are there in Florence?'

Fratelli shuffled on his chair. 'Well, there's one here, if you remember.'

'Oh, come on. That was an accident of birth. You're as Florentine as any man I know.'

'It was not an accident! I was taken!'

Marrone looked a little shame-faced.

'I'm sorry,' Fratelli added, his voice losing some of its volume. 'My antecedents are irrelevant. I wasn't saying he was Jewish. Just that the inspiration came from there. We get ideas from everywhere. Painters, writers, dreamers, mystics, all kinds of people, Catholic, Jew, Protestant, atheists even . . . they all got obsessed with Lilith one way or another. You should look at some of the things the English were doing during the nineteenth century . . .'

'The English now! You said we were looking for a builder. Or a caterer. One of the hoi polloi.'

'An educated man too,' Fratelli replied. 'Self-educated, perhaps. Obsessive. There. See. We're narrowing it down already.'

'Pino . . .'

'Think about this, Walter. Someone breaks into the Brancacci Chapel with a dead rooster. He smears blood on two sets of precious frescoes and covers up the nakedness of the figures with some cheap decorations from a restaurant. After that he paints . . . very carefully I think, look at the pictures you must have . . . he paints a halo over the beautiful head of the serpent, the female demon who tempted Eve and brought about our expulsion from Paradise.'

Marrone did think about it. Then he said one word. 'And?'

'Does that feel finished to you? Does any of this leave you thinking: we're done now? He's had his fun? He'll return to putting plaster on walls rather than the blood of a slaughtered bird. Doling out *lampredotto* or selling pizza. Our man will go off the rails just this once, and never again feel the need to walk to that feverish, sexual place he visited in the Brancacci when he stood there, wiping the bare flesh of those beautiful creatures with the neck of a dead chicken?'

He tugged at his white hair and shook his head.

'Though I still wish to God I knew why that rooster had no comb.'

'Are you sure you're telling me everything?' Marrone asked. 'You seem very confident of yourself, I must say.'

'In this I'm confident,' Fratelli replied, and didn't look him in the eye. 'Don't ask for reasons. You wouldn't understand them.'

'I could try . . .'

'No. They're irrelevant and you don't have the time. I want to see the files. The detailed reports. I want access to criminal records. I want to be able to ask questions of people who'll come running to you to complain afterwards, and when they do I need you to tell them to go shove their heads up their arses.'

'I can't. You know that. You're not a serving officer. You never will be.'

'And when the next call comes?' Fratelli roared.

His voice was so loud it bounced off the white walls of Marrone's room and carried through to the adjoining office where the plain-clothes officers worked, ten or more crammed tightly together on desks that hadn't changed in four decades.

'I'm sorry, Pino,' Marrone said, eyes on his pens and notepad again. 'Find your own way out, please. I've got a lot to do.'

'Give me a boy, Walter. The stupidest, most useless cadet you have. The one no one wants to work with. The idiot you want out of your hair even more than you wish it of me.'

'You are out of my hair,' Marrone retorted.

Fratelli sat there, arms folded, waiting. There was always a failure in the *stazione*. A mistake who'd slipped through personnel for some reason. The runt of the litter. The accident in waiting.

'I'll be gentle, Walter, I promise. He can look at the records, wave his card at people. I'll merely pull the strings.'

'What did I do to deserve you as a friend?' the captain asked with a mournful sigh.

'You gave me rope to hang myself. And profited rather well from that, I think. Remember the *finocchiona* in Scandicci. And the widow

Bartolini's chihuahuas. Come on. One useless cadet is all I ask. You won't miss him. Not for a minute.'

Marrone's lined and dignified face darkened.

'You always know my weak spot,' the captain grumbled.

'An occasional capacity for original thought is actually one of your many strengths,' Fratelli said, and crossed his fingers beneath his heavy coat.

'If I were to agree to this,' Marrone muttered in a low, cold tone. 'Do you promise you won't break any rules? Or get the infant into so much trouble I have to fire him? And if you find out anything – anything – I want to know first and decide what to do with it.'

This small victory brought a smile to Fratelli's face. He shook back his head of white hair and beamed, then untwined his fingers and held out his hand across the desk.

'Agreed!' he declared, and pumped Marrone's fingers before the man had the chance to change his mind.

'And don't look so damned pleased with yourself,' the captain added. 'You haven't met him yet.'

The corridor twisted and angled through buildings, across streets, finally, to a set of steps that led out into a chilly bright day. She'd been here before, on an earlier visit as a student. The vast behemoth of the Pitti Palace lay ahead.

Her guide seemed anxious to pass her charge on to the next link in the chain. She ushered Julia into the back of the Pitti and found an office with a sign bearing the name 'Giovanni Tornabuoni'.

There was a secretary inside wearing an identical blue suit. She was filing her nails and reading a glossy magazine.

'Tornabuoni isn't here,' this new woman said.

The attendant from the Palazzo Vecchio shrugged and walked out without a word.

'I do have an appointment,' Julia said.

'I am aware of this,' the secretary replied, as if the statement was idiotic.

'Will Signor Tornabuoni be back soon?'

'Who knows?'

'Shall I wait?'

She frowned and said nothing.

'Did he leave a message?'

'No.'

Then a thought. 'But someone did. Soderini's office passed it on.' The note was sitting on the desk in front of her. 'Here.'

It was from Pino Fratelli and read, 'I have uncovered matters which may interest you. Please meet me at the market in the Sant'Ambrogio at twelve thirty. We will eat *lampredotto*. Pino.'

'Dammit, Fratelli,' she swore. 'I am not yours to summon.'

Except she was. Men who missed appointments never deserved a second chance. Not after she'd married one. Vanni Tornabuoni could live with Sandro Soderini's displeasure over this particular missed date. She felt it might be considerable.

Besides, Julia had come to feel that Fratelli was the most interesting person she'd met in Florence. Spot on about the mayor with the wandering eyes, and probably a few other things, too.

That left her at a loose end. There was no one to interview and time to kill.

'Can I look round the paintings?' she asked.

'The ticket office,' the woman said, scraping her nails once more, 'is round the corner.'

Fratelli stood at the counter of I'Trippaio, his favourite *lampredotto* stall in the Sant'Ambrogio market hall, watching Luca Cassini, Walter Marrone's boy, feed. There was no other word for it. Cassini was twenty-two, a good head taller than Fratelli, broad-shouldered and huge, with a blank, childish face that looked forever lost. He played for the Florence rugby team in his spare time. Seemed more interested in that than Carabinieri work, as far as Fratelli could work out. In the space of fifteen minutes he'd downed two panini from the stall, one stuffed with *lampredotto* and broth, the other oozing tripe.

In spite of his true lineage, Fratelli thought himself a Florentine mostly. This meant that, especially in winter, he found it difficult to get through the day without stopping at one of the *lampredotto* stalls in the city for a snack. He'd grown up with the stuff. He didn't mind that it was the fourth stomach of a cow, stewed until it resembled a dirty dishcloth, then sliced, drenched in cooking juice and handed over steaming in bread for a pittance. Tripe he could take or leave, but *lampredotto* . . . They were eating it here when Brunelleschi was bossing around his builders. It was as much a part of the city as the Duomo itself.

But one was all he could take. Not so the giant, blank-faced Luca Cassini. The young man was now on to dessert with a large, cheap chocolate bar. Fratelli felt his own appetite would remain absent at least until the evening snacks that came with a Negroni. He was glad they'd arrived early and that Julia Wellbeloved, if she were to answer his call, had not witnessed this pasty-faced giant in a cheap grey suit chomping on guts, patiently pulling out bits of fat and gristle and dumping them on the cement market floor without a second thought. Foreigners could be funny about *lampredotto*.

'Are you full?' he asked when Cassini finished the chocolate bar and whisked the wrapper over his shoulder.

The young man thought about this for a moment, glanced at the steaming tubs of offal in front of him and, to Fratelli's relief, said, 'For now.'

'Didn't I know your father? Used to be a *carabiniere* too?' Fratelli thought for a moment and added, 'He was big as well.'

'You mean granddad?'

'Right,' Fratelli said, nodding. Sometimes he lost track of time.

Cassini seemed a willing enough kid. Perhaps the low brow and slightly piggy eyes were deceptive. It was possible his manner, so slow and ponderous, represented nothing more than a personal trait, not the sign of dim-wittedness it appeared. Luca's father was a Florence councillor, a trader with a shop selling expensive tourist tat, ceramics and leather, near Santa Croce. The kind of man who could exert a modicum of influence, pull a public job for a son who had no obvious qualifications for anything else. The family connections with the Carabinieri one generation back helped too.

Fratelli always made an effort to try to like the people he worked with, hard as that was on occasion. Not now. Cassini possessed none of the sarcastic surliness that marred some other young officers. Besides, he could recall his own too-smart self at that age in their caustic comments and sly glances. If this kid could do the job . . .

'Let's go over those notes we made, Luca,' he said. 'Tell me what you're going to do when I send you back to the station.'

'Check criminal records to see if they know any of the workmen at the Brancacci Chapel,' Cassini began, reading slowly from his notepad.

'Good,' Fratelli said.

'Check with catering companies to see if they've any record of stolen decorations with . . .' He leaned down and peered at his own handwriting, struggling with it. Fratelli's heart began to sink. 'Er . . .'

'Fig leaves. Fig leaves. Write it down properly. Capital letters if you need to.'

'I was never good at writing,' Cassini admitted. 'Not my field.'

'What is?'

The big youngster grinned, balled a massive fist and said, 'Trouble. Bit of a fight? I'm your man.'

Fratelli sighed. 'Don't let them do that to you.'

'Do what?'

'Use you as a punch bag.'

'I can handle myself.'

'And one of these days you'll walk in with that big grin and that big fist and the man you're looking at will be carrying a knife. Or a gun.'

'Not happened yet.'

'You only need it once. The records. The catering suppliers. Take a look at any sex crimes in Oltrarno too. See if there's something recent.'

'Like what?'

'I don't know!'

And it's probably not a sex crime either, Fratelli thought. That would be too obvious.

Having some kind of line into the station seemed a good idea when it occurred to him in Marrone's office. Now he wasn't so sure. The records department was a lair of filing cabinets and paper going back decades, the staff both inefficient and – on occasion – downright surly. They would devour this callow young man as easily as he'd swallowed down his *lampredotto* and tripe. There was supposed to be computerization coming along soon, and with it the ability to track down suspects in an instant and cross-reference known crimes with possibilities too. Sometime there would be radios that worked as well, not just when they felt like it, and a central control centre that could take and dispatch messages in seconds. Peace and happiness would break out all over the world, probably on the same day.

He was never going to see any of that, and he knew it.

'Take a look at the sexual assault files outside the city. Go back a few years. Murder cases, even. Look to see if you've any record of women being found with . . .'

His blood chilled as he tried to say the words; his voice failed him.

'Found with what?' Luca Cassini asked.

'Marks on their faces. On their mouths.' Fratelli opened up his coat to get some air. It suddenly seemed hot in the market. 'Lipstick or blood or something red. Daubed on them.'

The big young cop just stared at him. 'How do I find that out?' he asked.

'You read the files.'

'Which files?'

Fratelli took a deep breath. How did he explain this? Sometimes he'd spend days in records, going up and down the shelves, looking for links that eluded him. It was an obsessive, time-consuming task, one that frequently ended in disappointment. The Carabinieri didn't work that way any more. They wanted quick results. Not people spending weeks poring over ancient scraps of paper.

'Never mind. Just stick to the recent stuff. Ask whoever's running records these days if something rings a bell.'

'Why did we come here?' Cassini asked.

Fratelli was watching the side entrance of the market. She'd turn up. He was sure of it.

'Couple of reasons,' he said, without taking his eyes off the door. 'When did you join up?'

'Been an officer eight months.'

'You won't understand then. Over there . . .' He nodded towards the southern door. 'Two streets away, no more, you'll find a building site. Until a year or so ago that was the Murate prison. Not a nice place.'

'Heard of that,' Cassini said.

'You should have done. For a couple of hundred years it was where we locked up anyone we didn't like. So did the Germans during the war. If there's such a thing as ghosts . . .'

Cassini was laughing. It sounded as if someone had told a bear a joke.

Fratelli glowered at him and the kid shut up.

'If there were such a thing,' the older man continued, 'we wouldn't be able to hear ourselves think for the sound of their screams. I used to deal with prisoners there sometimes. You know those paintings of the Virgin, the little shrines along the Via Ghibellina?'

Cassini was putting gum in his mouth. He hadn't a clue.

'They were there to give men a glimpse of the hereafter just before they went to meet it. On the scaffold.'

Not a flicker of emotion. The young, Fratelli thought. And then he saw her marching in through the open doors, looking furious, scanning the crowds hunting for fish and meat and vegetables. And *lampredotto*.

'I still don't know why we're here,' the young *carabiniere* repeated.

'Because it reminds me of things. It helps me think.'

No one removed a rooster's comb without a reason. Finding that was on his own to-do list, and he damned near forgot it too. His head wasn't right sometimes . . .

'Also,' Fratelli added, 'because this place serves the finest *lampre-dotto* in Florence. And I am a man of taste. I'll catch a bus across town for the best, the most memorable of anything. A Negroni. A glass of good Chianti or Montepulciano. The right cheese. A piece of perfect stomach. An intriguing conversation. Such as this.'

'You've got a lot of time on your hands.' A pause. 'From what I hear.'

'What you . . . hear?'

But it was too late by then. Julia Wellbeloved was with them.

'That bastard in the Pitti Palace stood me up,' she cried. 'I had an appointment . . .'

'This is Italy,' Fratelli pointed out. 'Time tends to be more flexible than you're used to.'

'An appointment made by Sandro Soderini.'

The two men blinked and stared at her, then Fratelli asked, 'What bastard?'

'Some ass called Giovanni Tornabuoni.'

For a moment they were lost for words.

'You move in such grand circles,' Fratelli said finally.

'Not when they don't turn up I don't. My work! How am I to do it if no one speaks to me?'

'The mayor spoke to you, didn't he?'

'I know that look,' she said darkly.

His eye caught hers, and he nodded slyly at the giant next to him.

'A fine man,' Fratelli declared. 'A credit to the city. Your work will be done. And done brilliantly.' He took the young *carabiniere*'s arm. 'Julia Wellbeloved, meet my young colleague Luca Cassini. He's here to help us.'

Cassini nodded and blushed and stuttered. Didn't meet women much, Fratelli guessed.

'Buy your new English friend something to eat, Luca,' Fratelli ordered, handing over some money. 'I must leave you for a moment. Julia . . .'

'Where are you going?' she asked.

'Nature calls,' he lied.

She was leaning over the glass counter of I'Trippaio, sniffing the tubs of *lampredotto* and tripe.

'You don't have to eat that,' Fratelli said quickly. 'Really. It's for us locals. Pretty disgusting . . .'

'It's the guts thing I've heard about?' Julia's lively, attractive face broke into a grin. 'I'll try some. Why not?' She leaned and stared at the offal swilling around the silver pots. 'Which bit is which?'

'Best not ask,' Fratelli said, then gave a little salute and pottered off down the aisles towards the butchers' stalls.

Fratelli was gone for much longer than she expected. He'd lied about his purpose. She could see it so easily in his face. So Julia was forced to talk to the young *carabiniere* Luca Cassini, a task she didn't find easy.

Eventually she decided it was time to deal with the question that had been nagging her since the previous day.

'What's wrong with Pino?' she asked Cassini straight out.

He shuffled uncomfortably on his massive feet and stared around at the stalls, the people, the porters heaving crates around. Anywhere but in her direction. Cassini was chewing gum, a little too vigorously.

'Luca?'

'What do you mean, what's wrong with him?'

'He's off sick,' she went on. 'I don't know who he leaned on to get you. But it doesn't change things. There's something wrong . . .'

'Have you asked him?'

'Yes! He said he's mad.' A pause. It had to be said. 'As a mole.'

His broad blank face wrinkled in bafflement.

'A mole?'

'Precisely.'

'Doesn't seem mad to me,' Cassini said. 'Bit forgetful. Bit out of it sometimes. Only to be expected in the circumstances . . .'

He knew he shouldn't have said the words the moment they left his mouth.

'What circumstances?'

'Well . . . he's . . .'

'What?'

'He's dying, isn't he?' Cassini said, so loudly the man behind the counter stared at him in shock.

Julia put down the panino. It was disgusting anyway. Luca Cassini shuffled even more awkwardly on his big feet and gazed at the grey cement floor.

She felt cold and stupid and guilty for dragging this out of him. Aggrieved that she'd made him share such a confidence with a stranger. That pained him, obviously.

'Dying?' she repeated.

'It's not as if it's a secret. I'm sorry. I thought you two were friends. You must have known.'

'Then why would I have asked? Oh bugger . . .'

'The captain told me to humour him. Everyone in the station knows. He's been off duty for a year or more. Before I started work there. They reckon it's a miracle he's not in hospital by now.'

'What is it?' she asked, and wished she didn't have to hear the answer.

'Head,' Cassini replied, and put a finger to his own pale temple as if to make this clear. 'Got something wrong inside it. Tumour, they said. My gran had one. Lot older than him, though. Horrible thing. Makes them seem stupid, mad sometimes, and they don't even know it. Don't realize they're acting oddly at all. We had to have her put away . . .'

'He's the smartest, nicest man I've met since I came to Florence! He doesn't need putting away.'

Cassini looked hurt by the vehemence of her outburst.

'No, he doesn't. And I never said he did. Everybody likes Pino. Everybody feels sorry for him. I'll do what I can to help. With whatever this obsession is.'

'Obsession . . .?'

'That's what the captain said. His words, not mine.'

Walter Marrone was fond of Fratelli. She'd seen that for herself. Perhaps he was right. This strange attack on the Brancacci Chapel was a fixation. A mania related to his condition.

'I'm sorry, Luca. I didn't mean to force you to say something you didn't want.'

'Oh, didn't you?' Cassini retorted.

He nodded down the lines of stalls. She followed the line of his gaze. Fratelli was coming back towards them, tugging at his white hair, thinking. He looked absent-minded, a little lost. But he walked like a fit and active man.

'Pino's good at that trick too, apparently,' Cassini said. 'Getting stuff out of you when you'd rather keep it quiet. Known for it.' He looked at her. 'You two make a pair if you ask me.'

'I said I'm sorry.'

'Yeah well.' He seemed downcast, a little upset. 'Horrible thing to have. You think there's nothing wrong with you. Then one day . . .' He took out his gum and stuck it underneath the counter, as if that made it disappear. 'My gran never knew when it was going to happen either. After a while she forgot it was on the way altogether. Next thing she's gone in the head. Not long after that she's gone altogether . . .'

Fratelli strode up to the pair of them, beaming. 'Well,' he said, rather dryly. 'It looks as if you two are getting on.'

Julia felt she was rather too close to tears.

'How was the *lampredotto*?' Fratelli asked, trying to look into her face.

'Vile,' she muttered. 'I'm sorry. I have to go. Another appointment . . .'

'But I thought . . .' She was leaving already, head down, eyes damp. 'Julia?'

The briefest of glances back in his direction, but enough to give him pause for thought.

'I have some . . . information.'

'Not now . . .'

'Negroni,' he said. 'The usual place? Six thirty?'

'Possibly,' she murmured, then turned on her heels and left.

Fratelli glared at the young *carabiniere*. 'Luca . . .?'

'Yes?'

'What did you say?'

'I didn't say anything!'

Fratelli tapped his feet.

'Women,' the young man added. 'You know what they're like. Can I go back to the station now, boss? Look up those records? The ones you want.'

'Very well,' Fratelli said, with a nod to the door.

He watched Julia Wellbeloved march out of the market, head down, clearly upset about something.

'When you meet my English friend again, Luca . . . go easy on her,' he told the young *carabiniere*.

'Tell her to go easy on me then,' Cassini grumbled, and looked just like his grandfather then: mutinous and trouble.

*   *   *

It was cold on the ragged little farm outside Fiesole and there was something thrashing in the old VW van again.

In the kitchen he checked the fava beans he'd soaked the night before. At four in the morning, hearing the sounds from outside, he'd peeled a potato, skinned an onion, chopped them, heated some water in an ancient pot, mixed them with the soaked beans and some water. That was eight hours ago now, and still the dish sat in the alcove by the fire, its base just in the embers. This was the way the peasants cooked. Basic. Ancient. Beans and vegetables simmering all day while a man went about his work.

He tested the white bodies with a fork. Drained them, fed the dog from some tins in the refrigerator, coming to an accommodation with the animal. It no longer growled at him. That was all it required. Care.

Stupid.

His mother called him that from the start. It was, he thought, the first word he'd ever heard, uttered from her curled lips as she bent over him in the crib.

Stupid.

An idiot servant born to obey, to waste away his meagre life doing what others wanted. And, for all the secret reading, for the many furtive, wrestling thoughts inside his head, maybe they were right. When hard decisions came along, he avoided them. Sought other things on which to waste his time.

Like cooking, idly, easily, letting the knives do the talking for him.

The dried beans were soft now, ready. So he picked some wild chicory from outside – plenty there, not far from a small greenhouse with a few marijuana plants in it. After that he mashed the messy contents of the battered pan into a rough puree, chopped the chicory and mixed in some of their low-grade olive oil. With the half-stale bread from the kitchen, there was a meal.

Savonarola himself probably ate something similar, day in, day out, while the Medici and the lords of the Signoria feasted on peacock and wild boar. Food was about sustenance, nourishment. Not lavish displays of excess, ostentation and boasting. A careful, timid man could live on nothing if he so chose. Then dip into their world, take what he wanted, and retreat back into the shadows.

He gave the mashed beans a stir in the earthenware pot, piled some on a lump of bread. The beat-up van was moving again. A body trussed up in the back, struggling, terrified, expectant.

Why had he waited?

Because he was weak and frightened.

He gazed at the fire, listened to the muffled shouts from beyond the door, watched the VW lurching from side to side.

Twenty years before, down a dark, drenched Oltrarno street, he'd met the Devil. Seen him and his cronies at their work. Joined them, after a fashion.

That night he'd felt something planted in himself; a poisonous seed, a cancer that would grow steadily over the years, whispering in his head, demanding he find the courage one day to cut it out.

And when that day came . . .

He went over to the sink and picked up the two knives he'd taken with him the night before, trying to stifle the thought: this would have been so much easier if he'd got it over and done with then.

Outside.

The dog didn't bark. The birds didn't sing. No voice rose in objection. No fiery angels fell from heaven shrieking at him to stop.

The only witnesses were the spindly, wizened shapes of the olive trees clinging to the steep hillsides.

Something still didn't feel right, though. The story the woman had told him the night before . . .

She was supposed to be weak, defenceless. It hadn't felt that way.

He found himself wondering about her, questioning how truthful she was when she spoke about the olive oil that was supposed to save them. *Biologico*. A magic wand that might mean they could one day give up selling dope and coke and heroin. How much bright green oil would be needed to fill the gap that junk left?

An ocean. And, in the end, nothing changed. She was still lost but alone now. Stranded. Dancing for self-made princes, whoring herself to their whims.

Dead before long, like him. That was the way it always went.

He stuffed some bread and beans and wild chicory into his mouth, watched the van shake in front of him.

When he'd finished with the food he raised the largest, shiniest, sharpest knife to his mouth and licked the edge of the blade with his tongue. It cut into the soft flesh. He tasted the warm saltiness of his own blood, felt the welcome steely sting of pain.

This will do.

The dog sat quietly on the bare earth, watching him.

It knew what was coming.

Beneath the pale uncaring sun he walked towards the van, tramping through the thick brown mud, staring at his hands and the implements they carried, trying not to shake.

Julia spent the afternoon in the Bargello, trying not to wonder whereabouts in the sprawling, high-walled Florence fortress they'd tortured prisoners for century upon century. Now the place was one more gallery full of beautiful objects – statues mainly, with little sign of its grim past. Savonarola and his fellow friars were forced into confessions inside these walls with the liberal use of the *strappado*, presumably in one of the elegant rooms that now contained the beautiful works of Donatello, Michelangelo and the ubiquitous Benvenuto Cellini. Had time erased their screams and the brutality of their tormentors? Did the past still live behind a closed door or trapped inside a glass case, waiting on the amusement of passing visitors?

That depended on the individual imagination, or a willingness to render oneself blind to the deeds that haunted the stones she found herself walking every day. The night before, in one of Pino Fratelli's books, she'd read about the controversial executions that preceded the fall of Savonarola, when five of Florence's leading citizens were convicted of secret correspondence with the exiled Piero de' Medici. These men were treated to the *strappado* inside the Bargello too, then hurriedly led into the cold, square courtyard and beheaded one by one. Ever practical, the civic leaders of the time had liberally scattered straw across the cobblestones to make it easier to remove the stains. Now she stood on the first floor of the museum, amidst the beautiful statues, looking down at the scene of their bloody end. Bored tourists meandered over the unmarked paving stones, unconscious of history, blind to the pain of those who went before. Yet, she noticed, she felt the faint and ancient patina of their agony. And so, she thought, would Fratelli in this place, for reasons she couldn't yet understand.

Her motives for coming to Florence seemed to be growing more tentative – illusory, even. There was only one more research appointment in her diary for this week: two days hence, in the convent of San Marco, a little out of the centre, once the seat of Savonarola himself. She'd read copiously about that place and couldn't wait to get inside, though the letter confirming the meeting warned that some parts of the building were closed '*per lavori*'. Works. What the Americans liked to call 'refurbishment'. Florence seemed to be in a constant state of repair, much of it from the dreadful flood of twenty years before. Fratelli had referred to that event in passing, and when he did she'd noticed a brief creasing of his benign face, as if the memory caused him pain.

Or else it was the illness. Mad as a mole. Another game of his; a riddle, a trick. There was no such saying in Italian. It was part of the man's disguise, an effort to hide his true malady, a terminal one, just as Florence concealed her own past with a show of bright magnificence and marvellous statues over the bloodstained cobblestones. What kind of illness might it be? Was it terminal because the Italian doctors didn't know how to treat it? Would an English physician feel the same way?

She'd thought of medicine as a career before choosing the law, rejecting it only because her own father was a general practitioner in Berkhamsted, one with more wealthy and influential medical friends working in Harley Street and the great London hospitals. Julia wanted independence as much as she craved a profession. This, she knew full well, was why her marriage had failed so rapidly. She'd refused to become Mrs Benjamin Vine. There seemed no point. Not in the 1980s. The modern world. And besides, in Italy, and many other parts of Europe, married women held on to their maiden names after they took those wordy and rather meaningless vows. What difference did it make anyway? For Benjamin, a crucial one, or so it turned out. He felt she'd rejected him. Or rather failed to embrace him, to fall in with his ways, to love him as much as his self-esteem merited.

The whole business was doomed from the beginning and she remained baffled as to why she'd never noticed till the crockery was flying round their little flat in Islington, amidst the tears and shouts.

Wandering round the Bargello, watched by the serene statues, she thought of her ex-husband and her failed career as a lawyer; thought of Pino Fratelli, an intelligent, charming man, dying quietly, slowly, day by day, from an illness so subtle and insidious it was scarcely visible at all. It was entirely possible Florence was the wrong place for her to be at that moment. That her dreams of academic offers stemming from a brilliant dissertation were fantasies, never to be achieved. She'd split with Benjamin only six months before, left her job not long after. Everything had happened in a rush, against her naturally cautious English nature. If she wished, she could quickly return to Oltrarno, pack in a hurry – hopefully before Pino Fratelli got home from his investigative peregrinations around the city. Then walk to the station of Santa Maria Novella, catch a train north, be in Paris the following day. After that she would change lire to francs, meander slowly to the coast, eking out her dwindling money along the way, take a ferry across the Channel, and be home in chill, grey Hertfordshire, penniless, before the week was out.

Her loving father would always take her back, say a few kind and gentle words, offer support, moral and financial. Twenty-eight and as lost as a child. It seemed pathetic, selfish, and she wasn't like that, not at all.

The close, high walls of the fortress museum began to oppress her. She walked out into the street, went into a nearby café for a macchiato, sat alone on a stool at the counter idly watching the TV. The core of her planned essay – to try to fathom the reason behind inexplicable, insane attacks against works of art – seemed to be growing more distant by the hour. Someone committed this very act almost in front of her yesterday in the Brancacci Chapel, and her immediate instinct had been to shrink from the deed. To seek an explanation for it from books or interviews with dry city officials, not the obvious sources: the police and the people they hunted. That was why she was still no closer to understanding the riddle she sought to solve. A lack of effort, of determination, of curiosity. Of courage. Though, if she were honest, even Fratelli – who possessed all those in spades – was wrestling with those strange bloody daubs on the Brancacci's walls.

She remembered him wandering off in the Sant'Ambrogio market, leaving her with the nervous young *carabiniere* who'd blurted out the truth about his illness. He was looking for something there. From the expression on his face, she suspected he'd found it. Or a kind of answer anyway. And here she was, waiting on Sandro Soderini and the feckless Tornabuoni, begging for appointments that might never be kept, instead of attempting what the sick Fratelli did as second nature: hunting for direct answers; sifting for clues in the narrow, grubby streets of Florence, among the detritus of the centuries.

There was no excuse. No good reason to drift back to England, a failure twice over in less than a year. On Thursday, she thought. In San Marco. That's where I begin. In the meantime . . .

Time to kill, and her head too full of paintings and statues. More than anything all those smug dead faces that lined the Vasari Corridor, staring mutely back at her as if accusing her of complicity in the unsolved crime of being alive for no good purpose.

She needed an escape. Julia walked back into the centre of the city, found a cinema and sat in an almost-empty theatre watching a harmless American comedy new to Italy, *Ferris Bueller's Day Off*, laughing infrequently, mostly at the strange way the subtitles translated High School American English into Italian.

It was dark by the time she came out. She felt better. A Negroni with Fratelli, some news of what he'd found, would be welcome. Could she sit and listen to him, be charmed by him, without mentioning she now saw behind his mask? She'd no idea. But he was the only man in Florence she'd warmed to, and his presence and pyrotechnic conversation, forever leaping in unexpected directions, amused her. The man appreciated her company too, she thought. It was an agreeable bargain on both sides.

There were few tourists in the Piazza della Signora when she walked across the square towards the river. Lights still burned in the offices of the Palazzo Vecchio. She wondered what Sandro Soderini, the slyly lascivious mayor was up to. Working? Plotting? Bawling out Vanni Tornabuoni for missing an appointment with a woman Soderini wished to impress? Or fixing a date with a girlfriend? She doubted he had just the one.

She stopped and stared at the bronze circular plaque set in the cobblestones in front of Michelangelo's *David*. The inscription said this was the exact spot where Savonarola and his two fellow priests were hanged and burned almost five centuries before. The place too, she realized, where the friar himself had organized the famous bonfire of the vanities in which paintings by Botticelli and perhaps Michelangelo had perished in the flames. A few yards away, in the shadows of the Loggia dei Lanzi, stood another reminder of the past's ubiquitous presence around her. Benvenuto Cellini's brutal bronze of Perseus, holding the head of the slaughtered Medusa.

Julia strolled over to look more closely at this fierce figure on its plinth at the edge of the loggia platform. Even under the weak lights, the intentional savagery was evident, in the muscular stance of the warrior, the severed head gripped in his fingers, its realistic tendons, sinews and cortex dangling beneath, seeming to drip real blood on to the stones of Florence. It wasn't hard to see there was a shocking facility for violence in the artist who made this ferocious scene real. Not that this was obvious in his majestic bearded statue, which she'd seen midway on the Ponte Vecchio that morning, and from Hitler's window in the Vasari Corridor. There was a hidden side to the Florentines, as there was to their city. Both concealed their interior nature with a fluent, casual ease.

The light from the street lamps was poor and forced her to get nearer. Close up the nature of the statue changed. Now she could see that Medusa was no monster at all. Her naked body, on which the victorious Perseus stepped in triumph, appeared voluptuous, a middle-aged sculptor's sexual fantasy. Her dead face, frozen in the severed head held aloft in Perseus' left hand, which gripped her snaking hair, was guileless and bewitching. Medusa's features were not unlike those of Perseus himself: young and preternaturally sensual. Some struggle was going on here, between male and female, oppressor and oppressed, and it seemed to her that Cellini was hinting that there was precious little to divide victor and victim. Julia thought again of the couple on the walls of the Brancacci Chapel, naked and innocent on one pillar, shamed and made all-too-human on the other. Florence appreciated such a war of opposites, liked watching this struggle between dark and light, and with it the opportunity to dive into the swimming, grey ocean of moral and sexual uncertainty that lay between the two.

A memory from a guidebook. She stepped on to the loggia itself and walked to the rear of the statue. There, sculpted on the back of Perseus's helmet, like a death mask reproduced in bronze, was Cellini's own face, bearded and strangely contorted. She shivered and checked herself. So much art, so much of the past . . . so much blood.

A voice came out of the darkness at the back of the loggia. It was coarse and aggressive and a little unsound and it said, 'What are you looking at?'

She staggered against the Medusa statue in shock, reeled round and saw – just – a shape in the shadows.

'Nothing,' she said loudly. Then in Italian, '*Niente. Niente.*'

A man came out of the gloom and for the first time since she'd arrived in Italy, Julia Wellbeloved felt afraid. He was tall and strong. Around his powerful shoulders was a full black cloak with a hood that rose to cover most of his features, giving him the appearance of a violent, fanatical monk. What she could see of his face was pale and hairless, with a prominent nose and sunken eyes that gleamed in the light of the loggia's lamps. She felt she ought to know him for some reason, though the idea seemed ridiculous.

'Nothing,' she murmured in English again, retreating to the steps down to the square.

He had what looked like a boathook in his right hand and a huge canvas bag, weighed down by something heavy, in his left.

As she watched, a little more of the face came out from the hood and his large, canine mouth opened and shut, with a snapping noise.

She turned and strode quickly away, down towards the arches of the Uffizi and the river. It was dark and empty in the gap between the galleries on both sides and she wondered whether he would follow. At the end there were a few hawkers' stalls on the raised pavement by the river, beneath the Vasari Corridor. Julia hurried over, stood in the lights of the nearest, and then, only then, turned to look behind her.

There was nothing. She was shaking like a leaf. The man with the stall, cheap jewellery and souvenirs, looked at her and asked, 'Are you all right?'

'I'm fine,' she whispered without thinking, fighting for control of herself, perplexed by this extreme reaction to nothing more than an itinerant lunatic, the kind of down-and-out she met in London all the time.

Why did she run away like that? Why was she so hesitant, so weak sometimes? Pino Fratelli didn't fear a thing and he was dying. Waiting for her in the little bar across the river now. It was six thirty already. She'd lost track of the time.

A taxi tottered across the hump of the Ponte Vecchio towards her. She waved it down and told him to take her to the bar in San Niccolò.

The man turned to her and looked impressed.

'Negroni,' he said.

'Excuse me?'

'They do the best in Florence, Signora,' he said. 'You should try one.'

Then they bumped along the Lungarno, past the arches of the Uffizi. She couldn't help but look back towards the piazza, though there was nothing there to see.

'The cock's comb,' Fratelli declared with obvious pride. 'I should have guessed.' He raised his tumbler of Negroni and toasted her. 'I never would have spotted this without your prompting. *Salute!*'

The little bar was empty except for the two of them. Fratelli had bagged a table at the back. It was now laden with food; among the dishes a platter of vegetables with olive-oil dressing which he called '*pinzimonio*' and said was especially for her. Raw fennel, carrot, celery, peppers . . . an odd thing to eat on a wet and chilly November night. But with some cheese and the strong cocktail, which she was starting to appreciate, she was beginning to feel happier after the odd encounter by Cellini's *Perseus with the Head of Medusa*.

'You seem shaken,' Fratelli noted. 'Are you OK?'

She wished he could be a little less observant at times.

'I met a beggar. Outside the Palazzo Vecchio. He was hiding in the loggia. I think I disturbed him.'

'We have too many *barboni*,' he said. 'Though honestly it's not their fault. If you fall through the cracks in Italy there are few people to drag you back.'

'*Barboni?*'

'The ones with beards. It's what we call tramps.' He shrugged and picked at some *finocchiona*. 'I always feel guilty when I see them, for some reason. Going home to a warm bed. Some food. A little peace and privacy. They mean no harm, usually, though the druggies in Santo Spirito are best avoided, as I warned you.'

'I can deal with tramps,' she told him. 'What about your cock's comb?'

He was quiet for a moment, gazing at her, then he picked up one more piece of the fatty pink sausage and held it for a moment.

'Food,' Fratelli said. 'We've always been obsessed with our stomachs. There are things we eat today that the Medici would have regarded as commonplace. You might have seen them in Sant'Ambrogio. Stuffed chicken necks, the head still on. Tripe. Intestines. *Lampredotto* itself.'

She found herself laughing. 'Who on earth would eat a cockerel's crest?'

'And his balls too,' he added. 'Don't forget that. I told you there were some curious cuts on the poor bird's body. He must have wanted them and couldn't be bothered to split the thing open to take anything else. Or else the meat was too tough to be used. It was an old cockerel. I'm no cook. I don't know. But he was.'

She folded her arms and stared at him.

'It's a very old recipe,' Fratelli said. 'One they used to serve at some of the dining clubs that the aristocratic . . . ahem, gentlemen . . . patronized in the old days.'

Julia immediately recalled Soderini's invitation and felt a little cold.

'Dining clubs?' she whispered.

The man with the bright white hair opposite her waved his hand dismissively.

'The rich aren't like us. It was the same when Dante walked these streets. They would take themselves to private places, drink and gorge and whore themselves stupid. Then, when that venal side of their nature had been exercised, return to governing the gracious republic of Florence before popping into the Duomo to confess their sins to a priest who might have been at the very same table.' He scratched his cheek. 'At least we've come on a little since then . . .'

'You think?'

'I do,' he said emphatically. 'But that doesn't stop a few aficionados trying to recreate the glory days of the past, does it? And here's the dish, made a few days in advance usually.'

He retrieved his notebook. It still had the logo of the Carabinieri on it.

'*Cibreo*,' Fratelli announced. 'My butcher friend from Sant'Ambrogio is an amateur cook of some skill. He has these ancient recipe books. He's never tried it himself, principally because he's never found anyone willing to share the dish with him. There are several versions. One demands . . .' He scanned the page. 'Chicken combs and testicles cooked in butter with sage, then mixed with broth from a calf's head, some unborn eggs, candied fruits, chopped biscuits, celery, cabbage, saffron, cloves, all thickened with beaten egg and lemon juice . . .'

'Stop! Stop!' she cried, pushing the plate of vegetables away from her.

'I said it wasn't popular. I've never heard of anyone eating anything like that. Why would you? Most of Florence lives on pizza and pasta, *finocchiona* and *lampredotto*, which seems a well-balanced diet to me. Particularly . . .' He pushed the food back towards her. 'With some *pinzimonio*.'

She couldn't get Soderini's face out of her head. That sly grin when he invited her to dine with the Brigata Spendereccia, the Spendthrift Brigade. And his words . . . *We behave as if we are the most irresponsible, the richest, the most privileged men on earth – for one evening, anyway. And the next morning we trudge back to the office with aching heads.*

'Even I wouldn't eat that muck,' Fratelli said, and shook his head.

To pass an evening with La Brigata Spendereccia . . . That is something quite different. It's also a secret society of a kind, so you must mention it to no one. That is an absolute condition. Agreed?

'Definitely,' she murmured.

'Pardon?'

'What does this mean, Pino?'

He reached up and tugged at his long white hair. She so wanted to reach out and stop that particular habit.

'It means we have one more way to narrow down the possible identity of our intruder in the Brancacci Chapel. We may surmise he has some connection with the Carmine. As a worker, perhaps; even a parishioner close enough to see behind those thick sheets that hide the chapel from the nave. Maybe a supplier of food or something. Those fig leaves he plastered on to Adam and Eve . . . they were from a restaurant or a catering company. I'm sure of it.'

'And how many of those are there in Florence?'

'Hundreds,' he said with a frown. 'Perhaps thousands. I don't know. But one that makes *cibreo* . . .' Fratelli shook his head. 'That's unusual. Unique, I'd guess. I've never heard of such an establishment. Everyone wants fancy food these days. We're too rich for the old muck. We want steak and guinea fowl and lobster. Not five-hundred-year-old offal. Nor has my butcher friend a clue who might cook *cibreo* any more, though anyone can buy a cockerel, of course. Or pick up the rest very easily. I can't see this going on a restaurant menu.'

'I may be able to help there,' Julia said quietly.

Fratelli smiled. Such a genial, pleasant man. 'You can?'

'Possibly.'

'Well . . .' He grinned at her and waited.

'There's a price.'

'Name it.'

She didn't take her eyes off him. 'The price is the truth. About your illness. No nonsense about . . .' Julia twiddled her finger at her ear. 'Madness and moles.'

Fratelli's face fell at that. He thought for a moment. 'Ah. Luca Cassini. I wondered what was eating at that callow young man. He seemed intimidated by you. I should have guessed he wouldn't keep his mouth shut. Walter said he was giving me the office idiot, though to be frank I feel he was uncharacteristically unjust there. Luca's just young and a little frightened by the large and complex world in which he finds himself. As are we all, if we have any sense.'

She'd finished her Negroni before him. Fratelli turned and spoke to the woman behind the bar, who made two more.

'Very well,' he said. 'If that's what you wish.'

'I do.'

'May I ask why? This curious matter of the Brancacci apart . . . we're strangers. Foreigners. When you finish your dissertation and return to academic glory in Great Britain, we will write perhaps, from time to time. And then . . . nothing. Why?'

'Because I can't deal with lies. I can't take that from someone. I . . .'

The woman was bringing over the drinks. Julia was surprised by how welcome this conversation felt.

'There will be a reason,' he said, 'but I don't need to hear it.'

'My husband. Ex-husband. He's gone. He lied to me and . . .'

Fratelli shuffled uncomfortably on the plush bar seating. 'You don't have to tell me, Julia,' he said quietly. 'Truly.'

She let him finish squirming. 'What if I want to?'

'Then . . .'

'I never thought I'd get divorced. That kind of thing happens to other people.'

'Bad things are supposed to be like that.'

'But they don't. They happen to you. To me. I never really talked about it. To Ben. To my father. To anyone.'

'You don't need—'

'I do, Pino. Please listen. I thought things were just . . . wrong. A little cold and awkward. Then I found out there was someone else. His business meetings. His nights away from the office. It all started not long after we married. Perhaps before. I was never enough for him. I was wrong somehow.'

'He must have been a very blind and stupid man,' Fratelli said as he clutched his drink to his jacket.

'No. He was a bastard. I've always had an eye for them somehow. I'll never know why. The worse they treat you . . . The more you forgive them. I hated myself more than I hated him for that very reason.'

'This is ridiculous,' he said straight out. 'He was the one who deceived you.'

'You deceived me too. About . . .' Another twirl of the finger at her ear. 'Madness and moles.'

'You were a stranger then. It was a white lie. I'm not a . . . a . . .'

'A bastard,' she said, and felt the uneasiness between them. 'I realize that.'

He stared out of the long window at the front of the bar. It was raining again, steady drizzle that made the cobbles in the street outside shine like black mirrors.

'I can't stomach lies,' she said. 'I want the truth. Then I'll tell you what I know. If it's any use . . .'

He smiled. Such a calm man. Easy in himself. Resigned to whatever future lay ahead. She'd never met anyone quite like Pino Fratelli before.

'But you don't have to if you don't want . . .'

'There's no need for a bargain, my dear. You asked, so I'll answer.'

He spent hours hidden in the chilly shadows at the back of the Loggia dei Lanzi, waiting for the square to clear. It was stupid to have approached the woman earlier. She was English. A tourist, probably. With any luck she'd be gone in the morning, his one witness vanished to the next destination on the Grand Tour: Venice or Rome, Pompeii or Capri. They fluttered through the city like transient insects blown on the wind; temporary minor nuisances, nothing more.

But she spoke Italian, he thought. Easily, confidently. And the way she looked at him . . .

There was no point in wasting time or effort on what he could not change. To her he was a tramp in a hood, nothing more.

A set of nearby bells was striking the half-hour. Eight thirty. The steady rain had driven all but a few stragglers from the Piazza della Signoria. Those that did emerge from the darkness of the Uffizi or the adjoining streets scurried across the cobbles hoods up, heads down, or struggling beneath copious umbrellas billowing in the stiff breeze.

Wait for the moment. Do this well. Nothing would be the same hereafter. An endgame was in motion, one he could shape a little, direct to some extent, but never control. That was impossible, for anyone; even the great dignitaries whose lights no longer burned in the municipal offices of the Palazzo Vecchio to the right of this small and curious alcove on the square. His life was a series of distinct events, each magnificent in its horror, separated by long stretches of boredom and insignificance. Now the period between each occurrence was shortening. Or he was hastening the arrival of the next. He was unsure which. Something moved, an unseen impetus, shuffling him on, as the angel with the sword hastened the fallen couple from the garden in Masaccio's fresco.

All that mattered was the immediate act ahead and he knew full well what that was.

When the square was as clear as it was likely to be at this time of night – scarcely a soul nearby, no one emerging any more from the Palazzo Vecchio; no cars, no bicycles – he strode out from the gloom at the back of the Loggia dei Lanzi. In his gloved right hand he held the boathook he'd stolen that evening from the rowing club on the city bank of the Arno. In his left was the object he'd kept in the bag. It proved heavier than he expected.

Walking towards Cellini's *Perseus*, he attached the thing to the boathook. Then, very quickly and purposefully, he shone a torch on the bronze of the warrior, aiming it at the left hand that held the Gorgon's severed head.

The face was beautiful and sensuous, her body naked and beguiling with its bronze gouts of blood and fleshy sinews. But this Medusa was an exaggerated, theatrical creature too, her severed head dripping with a snakelike cortex and a profusion of torn and dangling veins and muscles.

Artistic licence. Or a point about the woman. That serpents were a part of her, just as they were with Lilith in the Brancacci. Everyone knew that carnal trio on the Carmine walls.

The truth, as any butcher understood, was more mundane. A sharp knife did swift work, on beast or man. Reality was less dramatic. Both cleaner and more messy.

Still, this curious creative fancy helped his purpose. He secured his gift to the Piazza della Signoria more tightly on the boathook, then lifted it high until the hair met the shining head of Medusa glittering in the rain. There, in the prominent prow of snakes, above her closed and peaceful eyes, he moved it carefully to entangle new with old and keep the thing in place for all to see.

For one tense moment he stood back and surveyed his work.

A noise. A group of tourists cackling like teenagers on the far side of the piazza. Drunk, probably. Students from the language schools; young Americans discovering what it was like to enjoy cheap and plentiful alcohol in the place they called 'Yurrup'.

He moved the hook, untangling it from the thing above him. Dampness was seeping through his gloves. Rain, or something else. He'd no idea. No witnesses, no fingerprints, no easy lines to join him to this deed.

A job well done, he thought, then lobbed the pole into the shadows and hurried off through the rain, back to the little van parked in a lane close to Santa Croce, and then the green silence outside Fiesole.

'I told you no lies,' Fratelli objected. He pointed at his head, his pale finger prodding the thick white hair there. 'I'm mad.'

'As a mole?'

'That's how I think of it. Something dark with sharp teeth. Beneath the surface. Moving. Growing. Something I can't see or touch. Or feel much any more, thanks to the drugs the kind and careful doctor prescribes. But something which' – that very Italian frown once more, brief – 'will one day break surface, look around and wish for a life of its own. Which will be my death, of course. And its, too. Not that the mole is to know. It's an innocent creature. Entirely blameless. Such things happen.'

She sipped at her drink and watched him recounting all this as if it were the most natural sequence of events in the world.

'When?' Julia asked.

That shrug again.

'Tonight. Tomorrow. Next week. Next month. Next year. Probably not beyond that. Or so all the specialists say. In the meantime I must be patient. I can't drive. I can't work. I mustn't indulge in anything which may be stressful – the drugs are supposed to help there. I must wait for death and twiddle my fingers in the meantime. The twiddling is the grimmest part. Far worse than the sickness or the prospect of my . . . disappearance.'

He leaned forward and touched the sleeve of her coat, gazing intently into her eyes.

'I'm no different to anyone else really. Each life winds down a day at a time. Mine travels at the same speed as yours. All that's different is the duration, not the pace. Which, since I'm almost twenty years older than you in the first place, is only natural. Don't feel sorry for me. Pity is the most debilitating of sentiments. Spare me that.'

'My father's a doctor,' she said briskly. 'He knows specialists in London . . .'

'I've seen specialists in Florence, Rome, Milan, Turin. You think they're somehow inferior?'

'Of course not! But medicine's not . . . fixed.'

'It's science with a little art on the side,' he replied with a smile.

'I had a friend who was a doctor once. Briefly. The relationship that is.'

'Pino . . .'

'You asked. I answered. I'm one more human being afflicted with an incurable disease. A kindly ailment in some ways. Most people never know. I can walk . . .' He raised his glass. 'I can drink, in moderation, naturally. I can play with puzzles.' A broad and genuine smile. 'And discuss them with my charming English lodger. People say they're frightened of death. But really . . . I think it's life that scares them the most. Mine's not so bad. I just wish . . .' A flash of anger. 'I wish Walter would let me back in the *stazione* one more time. That boy Cassini's no substitute. I have a feel for cases. For index cards and ancient records. I like the smell of old paper; the way you can pick it up, read the words, store them, make some connection elsewhere . . .'

A quick sip of Negroni.

'That art's dying faster than I am. Youngsters like Luca Cassini think machines should do this for them. In twenty years' time original thought will be deemed heresy within the Carabinieri, and every other law-enforcement system in the world. Instead detectives will wait for computers and scientists to give them answers, and shriek in agony when those simple solutions aren't forthcoming. I was never made for such a world. I need to think. And when I think, I live.'

'Why?' she asked.

Fratelli blinked at her, puzzled. 'Why what?'

'Why did you get it? This illness? What happened, to give it to you and not someone else?'

It seemed to her a simple question. She expected an equally straightforward answer. Asbestos in the office. Some hereditary factor, though given Fratelli's curious background it seemed unlikely he would know about that. Or an accident. A blow. An admission that it was nothing more than bad luck. A dreadful twist of fate.

Instead he looked a little uncomfortable, shuffling on his chair at the back of the bar, fiddling with his fingers.

'No one knows the cause,' Fratelli said eventually. 'They happen. Like the weather.'

'Pino . . .'

'No . . .' He waved his hand at her. 'I have strange ideas. Strange theories sometimes. You must have noticed.' He brightened instantly, the way he did. 'And I have fulfilled my obligation to you, Miss Wellbeloved! A frank confession of my previous lack of candour. Which was not so much a lie as an obfuscation of the truth, as I hope you'll accept.'

'Up to a point,' she muttered, still dissatisfied.

'Now.' He was all smiles again. 'It's your turn. The mystery of the cock's comb and *cibreo*. You have news for me?'

Just before nine, two Japanese tourists – a woman of twenty-one and her boyfriend – tottered into the square after an extortionate meal in the Borgo dei Greci. The rain was coming down steadily, sloping thirty degrees to the black shiny cobbles on the icy northern wind. The woman clutched a copy of a tourist guide, trying to scan the pages. The Piazza della Signoria was deserted on this bleak wet November night. She didn't have much idea of the way back to the hotel. There was no one to ask in her shaky English.

'That way,' the boyfriend cried, pointing at the Ponte Vecchio. 'That way!'

She was getting sick of him. Every night it was the same. Food, then drink, then sex. They could have been back in Tokyo, hunting for a cheap hotel in Roppongi. Why come to Italy for this?

'I want to see something,' she said, and walked into the centre of the square, peering at the damp, flapping pages of the book.

Statues, she thought. Paintings. Beauty. That's why they came here. It had taken all her persuasion to get him into the Uffizi, where she'd marvelled at Botticelli's swan-necked Venus while he sighed and grumbled about not being able to use his shiny new Canon SLR. But it was night now, and everything that Florence had to see lived inside, behind those stern, dark exteriors. She'd expected beauty everywhere: flower-filled piazzas, men with guitars and accordions, warmth and colour and life. The city wasn't like that. It was cold, dour and severe as a hated maiden aunt.

'I want to see . . .'

There was *David* ahead of them, illuminated in front of the Palazzo Vecchio, shining in the steady drizzle. Michelangelo, she thought. That was a name on the list.

Still clutching the book to her, glancing at the page, she crossed the empty piazza and stood in front of the tower of the palace. It looked like something out of Disneyland, she thought. There should have been knights in armour. Elegant, pale, blonde-haired ladies in

medieval dress. Perhaps they were there sometimes. Just not on a
night like this.

'Seen it,' he grumbled behind her. 'Let's go to bed.'

'Bed can wait. Let's see it again,' she said, and stood in front of
the tall, handsome nude whose eyes were set towards the river,
aimed south at Rome, the book said, a warning to the Pope to heed
Florence's independence.

He looked strong and beautiful. A nice young man, her mother
would have said. The kind of foreigner every Tokyo girl wanted
to meet. But there was a slingshot over his shoulder and something
in his eyes that said: don't mess with me. I'm not just pretty. I'm
tough too.

She could hear her boyfriend coughing and choking on the
cobbles. Maybe he'd throw up again. She didn't get why he had to
drink so much. Especially the grappa which she hated.

'There are more statues,' she said, and liked the way he reacted,
shaking his head as if in disgust, too frightened to argue. 'Over
there the book says. You can get dry.'

And you'd better not puke, she thought. That would be the end.

She strode over to the odd alcove by the entrance to the Uffizi,
still wondering at the way the reality of Florence so contrasted with
the image she'd built of the place when she read the guidebooks
and histories back home. There was supposed to be magnificence
everywhere, a visible show of all Europe's grandeur. Not lowering
fortresses hiding their riches behind windows cloaked in iron bars.
The loggia was, she realized as she walked towards it, one of the
few free displays of art anywhere they'd seen. A collection of statues
set in a small enclosed area, the front open to view so that you
could walk round them, feel close to the past.

'What the hell's that?' the boyfriend asked, coming close and
staring at the flapping, damp pages. He looked interested finally.

'*Perseus*,' she said, '*with the Head of Medusa*.'

'Who?'

Something from mythology, she thought. Quite what . . . It was
late. She was tired and a little woozy from cheap red Chianti.
Another day . . .

He walked to the front of the statue and stared up at the warrior
with the sword and the strange severed head in his hand. Then,
like an idiot, he put a foot on the bottom ledge of the plinth,
reached up and slapped the figure hard on the leg, yelling some

stupid cry, the kind he copied from all the dumb Samurai TV shows he loved.

'That's the way!' the boyfriend barked at the still figure above him. As he spoke a bead of something thick and dark dropped from the dangling head, landed on his face, spattered his eyes and lips.

Rain, she thought. Except rain didn't move like that, slowly, in big, gouty gobs that looked too physical, too real to come from the sky.

She watched him start screaming. Watched him begin to gag and then puke. Then she looked at the statue again and, as her eyes adjusted to the faint lights of the Loggia dei Lanzi, saw the thing there, the staring eyes, the matted hair, the mouth open in terror.

Real, she thought. It looks so real, and then her legs buckled, her breath came in short, agonizing gasps and she fell on to the stones in the Piazza della Signoria as a black fog of nothing came to swim around her.

'The Brigata Spendereccia,' Fratelli said. 'Who would have thought . . .?'

'You've heard of it?'

A tug at the hair. She was learning to ignore this.

'Dimly. Florence is drowning in history, in case you hadn't noticed. Even I can't recall every single detail. Dante, Boccaccio, the Guelphs, the Ghibellines. Civil war. The Medici. Art and philosophy. Then that brief and strange interlude with Savonarola. Such busy times . . .'

She smiled and tapped his jacket. 'Soderini's made me an appointment at San Marco for Thursday,' she said brightly. 'I'm going to see the monk's cell.'

'Lucky thing. Our mayor does seem inclined to open every door he can find. I wonder why.'

'No prizes for guessing that. We've got wandering eyes in England. Wandering hands too.'

'Soderini's a politician,' he said with a shrug. 'What do you expect? They have strange habits, and even stranger ideas about their own importance. But the Brigata Spendereccia . . .'

'What is it?'

'What was it?' Fratelli replied.

He picked up some *finocchiona* and dangled it in front of her. Julia shook her head.

'No, thank you.'

'You'd best not be so picky when it comes to Thursday night. The Brigata is . . . *was* about excess. A group of twelve men, if I recall correctly. I think the idea was imported from Siena, which is odd given that the Sienese were our greatest enemies in those days. Anyway . . . imagine your prime minister and his fellow deputies—'

'Cabinet ministers,' she corrected him.

'I stand corrected. Imagine that they feel they're owed some favour in return for all the long hours they expend on behalf of the state. The collection of taxes, which they skim for themselves, naturally. The formation of foreign policy. Who to fight and who to back. In return for a consideration, of course.'

'Cynicism does not become you,' she scolded him.

'I'm a practical man. Not a cynic. In Italy we accept these things for what they are, part of the natural order. In England you pretend such peccadilloes do not exist, or at least only in foreigners. You're mistaken, and will one day realize it. But I digress . . .'

'They want a party,' Julia suggested. 'A break from the tedium of governing.'

'The party to end all parties. One in which they may lose themselves for a while. In the most exotic and luxurious of foods. The most expensive drink.' He looked her in the eye. 'In engaging and beautiful company.'

'A Roman orgy.'

'Certainly not! A Florentine one. Far more refined. And discreet too, I'll bet. We love our secrets. You believe our friend Sandro has been organizing these things for a while?'

She thought back to the way Soderini spoke about his invitation.

'I got the impression they've been going on forever.'

Fratelli sighed. 'Well then. There's something I never knew about the ruling classes. What a furtive little bunch they are.'

'*Cibreo*,' she said.

'Sounds very much like the kind of thing they might eat.'

'Pino. Are you sure they wouldn't serve it in a restaurant? If you think your man's in the catering business, surely that's the place to look.'

He shook his head, adamant to the last. 'No. My Sant'Ambrogio butcher supplies the finest and most expensive establishments in the city. If anyone knew, it would be him. No one eats that kind of thing these days. Imagine it on the menu!'

'You eat *lampredotto*, which is the umpteenth stomach of a cow or something.'

'Fourth,' Fratelli corrected her. 'And that's tradition. Boiling cocks' combs isn't. Not since the fifteenth century or so. Detection depends greatly on the question of probabilities. Remember this, Julia. It may prove useful in your studies.'

'Oh, them . . .' she whispered.

'*Cibreo*'s a dish for a feast, a banquet. Hardly a TV dinner for two. If it's not on the menu of a restaurant, then a private occasion such as Soderini's would seem the prime candidate here.'

Fratelli shook his head and frowned. 'For the life of me I never knew that kind of thing still went on. You hear of squalid parties in the hills. In the villas of the rich. We occasionally had to deal discreetly with a drugs overdose. But the Brigata Spendereccia . . .'

There were people coming into the bar now. A couple had occupied a table within earshot.

'There's something old and aristocratic about the idea,' Fratelli continued, sotto voce. 'One can imagine it would appeal to those obsessed with their birth.'

'Like a Soderini? Or a Tornabuoni?'

'Plenty of others too,' he said softly, casting an eye at the adjoining table. 'And their cronies. So I doubt *cibreo*'s on many menus. Which, if we're lucky, may mean our man works for whatever catering institution supplies our friend with his peculiar specialities. Do you know where it takes place?'

'I meet Soderini at the Palazzo Vecchio at seven. That's as much as he's told me.'

He waited.

'It could be anywhere, couldn't it?' she asked. 'How many palaces do you have in Florence?'

'This is a city of rusticated monstrosities. I believed I'd made that clear.'

'Well then.'

'Are you going to go?' he asked gingerly.

'To an orgy? No thanks. I'd rather sit here and talk to you.'

'I'm flattered I suppose. But then what would we find out? Discovery comes from action, not idle discussion. We can exchange our theories endlessly, but where will that get us? Even if Walter listened to me, he wouldn't approach Soderini and ask for the menu. Not if this is meant to be secret. If you have a location for these

events then I can find out more. Who handles the catering. Luca
can quietly check the files and see if there are any workers involved
with a criminal record. We have an entrance point into proceedings.
A way in. I . . .'

She was staring at him, outraged.

'Why are you looking at me like that?' Fratelli asked.

'You want me to go to an orgy just so you can find out what
kind of lunatic swipes chicken blood on precious paintings? Commits
so little damage that even your own Carabinieri colleagues don't
seem much interested?'

He seemed a touch put out by this remark.

'You don't need to participate, do you? Just watch, have a drink
and a bite to eat. Then make an excuse and get out of there when
the entertainment turns a little risqué.'

'I noticed you said when, not if. All this for the sake of a chicken?'

His intelligent face turned stony and serious.

'I thought you wanted to know why bad things happened. I was
under the impression that was the purpose of your dissertation.'

'It is . . . I suppose . . . Oh, dammit.'

Fratelli finished his Negroni, staring at the glass, then said perhaps
it was time they caught the bus.

'I don't want to catch the bus yet,' she complained.

'You seem upset. And I'm just making it worse.'

No, you're not, she thought to herself. You're listening, patiently,
carefully. No one else has done that for a long while.

'I'm sorry, Pino. This degree idea seemed to make sense when
I was in London, looking for something new to do. Now I'm here
. . . I don't know. I thought I had the right questions. I thought I'd
understand what I'd hear in return.'

'A good detective never anticipates the answers. He – or she –
must focus on phrasing the correct inquiries. Nothing more. An
open mind is essential. A closed one takes you nowhere.'

'I'm not a detective.'

'That's not true. You're a very astute and curious young woman.
Perceptive and sharp at spotting the rhetorical flaws that provide an
opportunity to uncover the truth. You should focus on that skill more
than you do.'

'By going to Sandro Soderini's orgy?'

His eyes blazed for a moment as he shushed her across the table.
'Please. You never know who's listening in this city. Besides it's

not . . . what you claim. Not necessarily. Just a night out for him and his friends.'

'Why is this so important?' she demanded. 'A bunch of playboys? A dead bird? A meaningless act of vandalism?'

He finished his drink, looked at his watch and stayed silent.

'Why is it so important?' she persisted.

That's another story. I have strange ideas. Strange theories sometimes.

'Tell me, Pino,' Julia demanded. 'I need to know.'

The Carabinieri were first on the scene, followed by a squad car from the state police. They looked at the mess in front of the Loggia dei Lanzi: a couple of Japanese tourists, the woman unconscious on the soaking cobbles, the man screaming and weeping hysterically.

'Drunks,' the senior *carabiniere* said to the first state cop to join him.

'There's a surprise,' the cop agreed.

'You can have them if you want. I mean . . .'

Sometimes these two forces were rivals. Mostly they tried to get along.

'You mean it's a small enough thing for us to handle?' the cop replied.

'Not exactly . . .'

'Boss?' said the young cadet who'd been behind the wheel of the Carabinieri car.

He was out in front of the loggia, taking a look beyond the couple on the cobblestones.

'We could do it if you like,' the *carabiniere* continued to the cop. 'It's just that we cleaned the car earlier. And yours . . .' He cast a withering glance at the ancient pale blue Fiat the police came in. 'Let's face it . . .'

The crackle of a radio cut through the night. The young cadet was speaking into it, asking for assistance.

'We don't need help for foreign drunks,' the older officer barked.

Something stopped him after that.

The young *carabiniere* was beneath the Cellini statue, looking up at the figure of Perseus. His voice kept getting louder. He sounded scared.

The cop was staring in the same direction too, so the older *carabiniere*, a man who thought he'd seen it all, followed suit.

Statues didn't interest him much. Or paintings. He'd grown up in Florence, surrounded by this stuff. It was so familiar he never took any notice. Except when something was wrong.

The cops from the pale blue Fiat saloon were starting to look a little queasy themselves. One had his hand over his mouth. The other started mumbling something unintelligible that might have been a prayer.

'Tell you what,' the senior *carabiniere* said, going to stand closer to the Cellini bronze so that he could get a better view of what was suspended there in its raised bronze hand, pale and gory, dripping blood on to the steps of the loggia. 'I think we'll take this after all.'

The empty bus ran slowly along the Lungarno, dodging the pedestrians scurrying through swamped streets awash with water. As the vehicle drew level with the Uffizi across the river, she saw flashing blue lights at the head of the arches, close to the Palazzo Vecchio.

'Something's happening,' Julia said.

Fratelli was hunched and miserable in his coat.

'Something's always happening. Nothing's always happening,' he mumbled, staring at the black flume beside them. 'Life's like the river. Always moving. Always in the same place.'

'That's a bit enigmatic,' she said gently.

He seemed downcast, upset by something. The way she kept prodding him for more answers, she guessed. What else could it be? And why would he turn this way now? She'd already prised from him the perilous state of his health. That was a very private admission, particularly when it was offered to someone he barely knew. Not that she thought of him as a stranger any more. An odd intimacy had grown between the two of them. It was a surprise to both, yet she felt she understood why it had happened on her part. Pino Fratelli was such a gentle, easy, intelligent man. Full of interesting questions to which he had no answers, seeking them mostly from others. The fluent, call-and-response rhythm of their conversations happened so naturally, without any of the usual effort she found necessary with others. Yet there was still something unknown, a mystery yet to be revealed.

Fratelli pulled out of his hunch and squinted through the rain-soaked windows at the lights across the river. The Arno was lively and thrashing as it flowed swiftly towards the Ponte Vecchio. She recalled his brief mention of the terrible flood from twenty years before. Anyone who experienced that strange terror would surely look at a November night like this and find some unwanted memories returning.

'A lot of lights,' Fratelli said, a welcome note of professionalism in his voice. 'I'm sorry. I get down sometimes. Not often, but you must yell when it happens.'

'Act the policeman for me. I want to see what he looks like.'

'*Carabiniere*, please.'

'Be the *carabiniere* then. What might be going on over there?'

He frowned, thinking.

'A mugging maybe. A fight.' He stared at the lights. 'I'd guess there are three or four cars. That's a lot for a fight. Perhaps a dignitary is visiting the Uffizi in private. Wandering down your Vasari Corridor. The high and mighty always receive protection in Florence. They're valued so highly. We'll hear in the morning. On the radio. I listen first thing. Every day.'

He mumbled something that sounded like, 'Just in case.'

'Was there much for you to do here? When you were a *carabiniere*?'

'What do you think?'

She thought about it and said, 'Not a lot.'

'Theft and drugs. Wife-beating and the occasional assault. Murder very rarely. Malice domestic, usually, as I think the English describe it. Man against wife. Once and once only wife against husband. Florence is not a normal city in many ways, but humanity possesses some universal qualities.'

Fratelli took one last glance at the river, the Uffizi, the flashing blue lights beyond the arches. Then the bus went behind the line of buildings leading to the Ponte Vecchio and the narrow streets that meandered towards Carmine and home. Whatever was happening in the Piazza della Signoria, they'd see no more of it.

'You don't have to go to Soderini's squalid party,' he said. 'Not for my benefit. It was thoughtless of me to ask.'

'It wouldn't be for your benefit, would it? For ours. I want to write this study. I need to.'

A few hours earlier she'd considered going back to England, throwing herself on the mercy and bank account of her father. At the age of twenty-eight. The idea was unconscionable. Running away would be a cowardly, miserable act. And where would she find herself when she stopped? Alone again, in limbo.

'If I help you find this man it will make my paper better,' she said. 'Academia likes the odd small thrill too, you know. A theory proved by practical action. A guaranteed success. There. Self-interest. Your conscience is salved.'

He winced and she thought for a moment he was in pain.

'Are you all right?' Julia asked.

'Never better. And now? My last story?'

'Not if you don't want to.'

'I don't,' he said. 'And I do. The trouble is, I've never really told anyone before.'

She felt nervous at that. 'Why?'

'Because there was no one to listen. No one who'd believe me anyway. Or try to understand. I was mad for a while.' His eyes were glassy and blank. 'Truly. Before this present sickness. A long time ago. I didn't know who I was. Or what. Walter Marrone could have fired me then if he'd wanted. Perhaps that would have been the right thing to do.'

'Pino . . .'

'No, please.' He shook his head, then peered at her so directly, with such an earnest, pained honesty, she felt her breath catch. 'You ask such pertinent questions. Why? How is this? In twenty years I've never known anyone . . .' His voice fell to a whisper. 'In all that time.'

She took his gloved hand and looked him in the eye. 'It doesn't matter,' Julia told him. 'Let's forget all this. I'll go back to my paper. On Thursday I'll visit San Marco, then Soderini's party. You can chase your chicken-murderer . . .'

'I'm not chasing a murderer of chickens,' he muttered with an uncharacteristic sourness. 'I never have been . . .'

'You're starting to worry me.'

'Only now?' he asked, suddenly amused.

'Yes. Only now.'

'You asked what causes . . . this.' Fratelli pointed at his white hair and then his temple. 'Here is my theory. A lunatic's explanation for his madness. Treat it as such.'

The bus lurched through Santo Spirito. She could see tramps sheltering in the doorways and arches of the closed shops.

'On occasion a man or woman . . . a child . . . meets something dark and alien,' Fratelli said as he stared outside the window. 'A black, bad thing we label evil – for our own sake, mainly. Because we wish it to be separate from ourselves, not a wickedness that stems from the fragile creatures we are.'

She could see the piazza with the church of Carmine in the distance. So could he.

'Those painters in the Brancacci understood all that,' Fratelli went on. 'Why else did the serpent have the head of a beautiful woman? My belief . . .'

He scrubbed the misty window with the arm of his sleeve, checking for the bus stop.

'My feeling is that everyone meets the black thing some time. It's how we grow. How we survive. And most sensible people . . .' He turned and looked at her. 'Like you. They will recognize it, be afraid of it, reject it, let it go. Spit out the monster the way a child coughs up something nasty. Vomit all that black bile out of their systems and carry on with their lives.'

He reached for the rope that rang the driver's bell and got up. She followed him to the door. It was so stiff he had to force it open when the bus came to a halt.

The rain was falling steadily. He raised his umbrella briskly and held it over her as she joined him.

'I think I first met it when I was four years old,' Fratelli went on as they walked. 'When the Nazis pushed me out of Rome, seizing my parents, my real mother and father, as I fled. I swallowed down that grief. I let it live inside me. Like a malevolent foul bundle of hate that I clutched to my heart. Not that I knew. I was a child. I thought it was part of my imagination. Something that would go away . . .'

She wound her arm inside his without thinking. This was Italy. Not England. Even men walked together like this. Closeness, a sense of shared humanity, was normal.

Fratelli pointed to the pizza restaurant on the corner and asked her if she needed something else to eat. No, she said, trying to smile.

'Let's talk again in the morning, shall we?' Julia suggested as he opened the door to the little terraced house. 'It's been a long day for both of us.'

'I haven't finished,' Fratelli said, then strode up the stone steps, opened his door and ushered her in. 'I've barely started.'

The place was too warm. The lights were still burning. An LP sat on the hi-fi as if begging to be played.

He walked over to a plain white set of drawers and took out an old photo album, placed it on his untidy dining room table, next to the books and the record covers. Fratelli called her over and her heart sank as he flicked through the pages.

Julia recalled the odd conversation in the café that morning. The sympathy of the Grassi couple. The mention of a wife.

Here she was, in photos that looked as if they came from another era. Fading already. A lovely dark-haired woman, smiling, with bright, intelligent eyes. Beautiful in an elaborate white wedding gown next to a grinning, bashful Pino Fratelli, the two of them outside the church of Carmine along the road. Later, in the washed-out colours of a distant, lost summer; at the beach, in a rundown old car. Happy in a tiny, battered dinghy on a river, a fishing rod in Fratelli's hands.

'I didn't cough up the black thing,' he said, staring at the photos. He closed the album. 'So a part of it never left. After a while the rest came back, out in the open, released by something from the place I kept it captive. I think . . .'

Pino Fratelli tapped his hair again; longer than it was twenty years before; white, not black.

'If I'd spat it out of me the way I should, this never would have happened. And much else besides.'

'You can't blame yourself for things that—'

'How do you know?' he roared, eyes wild with fury, arms flailing. 'What do you know? Of me? Of this city? Of anything?'

His voice was so loud she scarcely recognized it. Or his face, which was torn by grief and anger.

'Oh, God . . .' Fratelli cried, his hands clawing at his face. 'Now I scream at the one person who listens to me. Jesus . . .'

There was a bottle of grappa on the shelf. He was going for it. She strode forward and stood in the way.

'I'm allowed just a small one,' he told her, calm again, his gentle face so full of grief and shame it tore at her heart. 'My doctor says so.'

'Is that a lie? I told you about those.'

'It never left me, Julia,' he murmured. 'I invited it back. Do you understand what I'm saying? This thing inside's been growing all these years. In a way I never understood, I've been nurturing it. Calling to it. Ever since Rome. Ever since the flood.'

'The flood . . .'

'And now I've introduced it to you.'

Fratelli reached round and grabbed the bottle anyway, then took down two small glasses off the shelf, filled them with the clear liquid. She could smell its strength even as he placed the drinks on the table.

'Sit down and listen,' he ordered. Then he nodded at the grappa. 'You'll need this. So will I.'

Friday, 4 November 1966

'Two in the morning. What time of day is this to leave me?'

'The time the roster says. A woman who's fool enough to wed a slave shouldn't complain about the hours he works.'

He kissed his wife, smiled at her, touched her soft auburn hair. They'd been married two years. Still no sign of children – not that they hadn't tried. Kids would come. His instincts, that small voice inside he'd had since childhood, told him so, and it was rarely wrong.

'Slaves have no choice. Fratelli does,' she told him. 'Here. I made you something to eat.'

He'd slept till one. Then Chiara roused him, put on her dressing gown and got up to make some coffee and a panino for him to take to the station. Tomorrow was her day off from the department store. She could sleep late. He felt guilty that she should work at all, but they needed her wages. His salary as a junior Carabinieri officer was so slight it almost seemed insulting. Even though he'd inherited his mother's house near the Carmine church, money was still in short supply. It wouldn't always be like this. Soon he'd climb on to the promotion ladder like Walter Marrone before him. Walter was smart when it came to internal politics, acting captain when no one else was around, which would doubtless be the case that very night. Fratelli wasn't in the same league and he knew it. But Walter could teach him the tricks. They could talk about it later: Walter the temporary boss, an officer on the up; Fratelli his lineman.

November on the dead man's watch. Perhaps someone would break the tedium and smash the window of a tourist's car. That was the most he could hope for. There'd be plenty of time to chat.

Fratelli looked at the food she'd prepared for him. Cheese and bread. He knew Walter would have brought along some *lampredotto* they could reheat in the station kitchen. Maybe even drink a beer or a glass of wine to get through the long and empty hours.

Chiara came close and kissed him.

'What was that for?' he asked.

'A wife can kiss her husband, can't she?'

She had dark, alluring eyes; a beautiful face that belonged on the walls of the Uffizi. Fratelli had no idea what he'd done to deserve this woman, and refused to give the matter a moment's consideration, believing that to do so might break whatever magic spell held her to him for no good reason whatsoever. Charming, funny, of a resolutely intelligent and independent inclination, Chiara Brunelli could steal the heart of any man she wanted. She chose his. It was the only dubious and irrational decision he'd ever known her make.

'Of course,' he said. 'But go to bed.'

She wasn't normally this affectionate late at night, when he was about to disappear for ten hours or more.

'Let me call Walter and tell him you're sick.'

'No!'

'You have your feelings. Your intuitions. Why can't I have mine?'

This mood of hers was so strange.

'Because you're the rational one. With your feet on the ground. I'm the moody creature. Leave that role to me.'

She shook her head and clung to the lapels of his coat. The rain beat heavily on the windows of their little terraced house.

'This weather!' Chiara whispered. 'Will it ever stop?'

'Yes,' he said patiently.

'I listened to the radio while you were snoring. It said the army and the police were going into the hills. There was flooding. People leaving their homes.'

Fratelli didn't follow the news much. He liked to look at whatever was in front of him at that moment, to peer hard and try to unravel its mysteries. Distant happenings in the hills didn't bother him. They were someone else's problem.

'Will you go?' she asked.

'If they wanted me, someone would have phoned by now. It's winter. It rains.'

She pulled at his tie, making the knot fit more snugly against his freshly pressed shirt. Fratelli wasn't a fastidious man. His clothes were cheap and well-worn, but Chiara liked him to look smart; worked hard with an iron and the antiquated washing machine in the ground-floor storeroom to keep him that way.

'Let me call Walter . . .'

'No,' he said and placed a single finger briefly on her nose.

'Don't play your condescending tricks with me, Fratelli,' she said in a comical voice. 'I don't appreciate them.'

He took her shoulders, felt her warmth and strength, and said, 'I have to work. And when that's done I'll come home. As I always do. I'll bring . . .'

'No flowers! We can't afford them.'

'Some food then. A pizza and some cheap red wine. Let's live the life.' His hand went to her soft, brown hair. 'One day, I promise . . .'

With a petulant sulk, Chiara pulled away and got his coat, put it on him. He could see in his mind's eye how she'd do the same so fondly with the child to come – a boy, he guessed, and then a girl.

'I can't sleep when you go out like this,' she grumbled. 'Maybe a little. Then in the middle of the night I'll do some washing. You need the shirts. This rain had better stop or it'll never dry.'

Fratelli didn't know what to say, so he kissed her once more and then, without another word, went out into the dreadful night.

The car was in the garage, broken down again. So he had to pull his collar around his face and walk through the constant rain across the bridge of Santa Trinita to the Carabinieri station in the Borgo Ognissanti. He stopped mid-span and looked in both directions. He'd never seen the river so high. It was approaching the foot of the bridge where he stood and wasn't far from the top of the arches on the Ponte Vecchio along the way. There were lights in the shops there. Night watchmen, he thought. And cars on both sides, with figures carrying boxes to them.

Clearing the shops of their jewellery. A wise precaution. The rains had been incessant for days. There were stories, old tales, of how Florence had flooded in the past, the river seeping into the city, filling cellars and the ground floors of homes, causing expensive havoc.

Fratelli suddenly felt he understood Chiara's qualms. This was strange. It felt outside the normal round of dismal winter weather Florence knew and expected any time from November onwards.

He strode across the bridge and turned left towards the station.

Ognissanti . . . all the saints. He didn't expect to bump into any that night. The street lights shone on empty streets where water ran across the black cobbles in snaking, writhing torrents. There was a siren from somewhere near Santa Maria Novella. No activity outside the station, though. If something did turn bad, they'd have to bring in more men.

He ought to get into the habit of listening to the radio. Walter Marrone surely did. People on the up ladder cultivated habits like that. For Fratelli it was always the same before night duty. He needed time to be alone with his wife, to talk to her, to feel free of the burden of work for a brief while before picking up his Carabinieri badge once more.

Chiara must have been glued to the set while he slept. What was it she'd told him? There were floods in the hills. People being moved out of their homes. It was foolish to believe his own colleagues weren't part of that effort too. He belonged to a proud and decent organisation. It wouldn't let others struggle alone against the vagaries of the elements.

Yet the phone never rang. Someone had to stay in the city. Twiddling their thumbs while the countryside was awash with rain and mud, displaced families and terrified animals. He wished it wasn't him. Fratelli liked thought, action, helping people. But that was someone else's decision.

Feet cold and wet, listening to the constant heavy patter of the rain, he walked briskly along the narrow street, past the hospital and the church, found the *stazione* and saw, through the glass door, a single uniformed officer on duty.

He wondered later why he'd turned back to see the way he came. Whether it was chance or instinct. That old inner eye he'd told himself he possessed, even when he was a child.

There was no knowing. Only the reality. Two weeks later, trying to come to terms with the greatest natural disaster he would ever experience, Fratelli learned it was around this time that the first victim came to die. Out in the hills, a fifty-two-year-old farmer in a tiny village had gone out to see the state of the land around his home. Along the way he met a group of neighbours and told them the area was a shambles, everything was going under. Then he went to try to reach his animals. Forty-eight hours later his corpse was found in a tunnel choked with mud; unrecognizable, twisted in pain and terror like an Egyptian mummy torn from its tomb.

One dead man in a far-off village. No one in Florence would

have believed at that moment that more than thirty others still
breathed in the city who would join him in the morgue in the painful
days to come.

As Pino Fratelli watched the long and narrow street of Borgo
Ognissanti, he heard something – a roaring animal voice beneath
his feet. The ground trembled. Then, back along the way he'd come,
a manhole by the church leapt out of the cobblestones as if thrown
into the air by some explosion. Beneath it was a violent plume of
filthy water, forcing the iron disc high into the air.

'Chiara . . .' he murmured, feeling the blood in his veins run cold.

A second manhole burst from the cobbles a little way along, and
then a third . . .

Something came back to him at that moment. A cold autumn day
long ago. A small boy standing on a beautiful bridge, stone angels
staring down at him as he listened to the rush of another muddy
torrent, one that took away something that was supposed to be
returned to him and never was.

'Chiara . . .' he said again, and began to run towards Santa Trinita.
But the water was ahead of him now, writhing and rushing like a
malevolent living creature. It was the best Fratelli could do to turn
and dash back into the station, flee for the stairs behind the terrified
uniformed officer running from his desk, and take shelter – breathless, mind racing – in the first-floor office where a pale-faced man
in uniform stood shocked and shaking, barking into a telephone that
seemed dead to the watery world beyond.

'Let me go!' Fratelli shouted, struggling in the arms of three
uniformed officers. 'For God's sake let me go!'

It had reached almost four in the morning. Marrone had only
then managed to reach Ognissanti, and that by boat. Shocked, out
of touch with headquarters, he was captain of a *stazione* marooned
in the bleak night. Fratelli had spent the past two hours fighting to
break free of the place and go home. No one would allow it.

And now, with a superior finally in place, he was denied again.

'Where the hell have you been anyway?' Fratelli demanded.

Marrone looked dreadful. He wouldn't talk about what he'd
seen out in the city. And still they were trapped on the first floor.
The lights were out. The phones and radios were dead. From
nearby came sounds that took Fratelli back to his childhood and
the war. The dreadful bloody close-quarters fighting during that

sweltering August in 1944 when the Allies battled their way into Florence, street by street, house by house. The hurt and angry screams of the wounded outside the terrace where he was a six-year-old living under a name he believed his own, though troubled at times by memories of a different boy, a different city, and a father and a mother who could only be the products of a childish dream.

Twenty-two years on the streets of the city rang once again to the rising shrieks of fear in the dread darkness that sat above the stinking river and all its dirt. They were Carabinieri and could do nothing, since beyond the door the torrent raged, growing higher and more powerful with every passing minute.

The massive, grizzled officer called Cassini relaxed a little of his bear grip.

'Pino,' he grunted. 'Don't be a fool. None of us can go out there. Even if we had some means . . . a boat. A light beyond these . . .'

Cassini nodded at the torches they'd set up by the first floor windows. There was no moon visible, thanks to the heavy clouds that brought this constant rain upon them. So all they could see was what lay in the beams of their standard-issue lanterns, the kind they saved for traffic accidents and – that rarest of Florentine events – a murder.

'Walter got here, didn't he?'

'And nearly died,' Marrone said. 'The boat's gone anyway. I couldn't tether it. I could barely manage to get to the stairs.'

'Let me try. I'll find a way . . .'

'You won't,' Marrone barked at him. 'That's an order.'

Pino Fratelli could scarcely believe his ears.

He managed to shake himself free of their arms and stood there, stiff and outraged.

'An order, Walter? Your precious world's broken, man. Look outside the window. If I could do a thing to help a soul out there I would. But I can't.' He glanced at the others. 'I want to be with my own. Don't you?'

Cassini, a senior, gruff *carabiniere*, old enough to remember the war as an adult, glowered at him and said, 'It's times like these we need to stick together. To keep the ranks. To do what we're told.'

'Like we did for the Germans?' Fratelli bellowed. 'You bastards sicken me. You think this precious city of yours is the finest there's ever been and never see the dirt and death between the glorious cracks. Thank God I'm not . . .'

One of you, Fratelli thought. Except, as far as they were concerned, he was. The truth about him was something he'd yet to share. That would take time. Years of trust that needed forging – rebuilding, in some cases.

'This is my life,' he bellowed at them. 'Mine! I'll find some way across the bridge. And stay there till you summon me.'

'Dammit, Pino,' Marrone replied, then dragged him to the window. The two of them stared at the gushing torrent outside. It was broader, higher, stronger than ever. 'How will you get there, then? Fly?'

'I don't . . .'

Pino Fratelli stared at the raging flood and wondered if this was how the world died, in a single driving wave of mud and water that kept on rising till it drowned them all. No ark, no Noah, no tidy evacuation for those who would be saved. Just a cold and dismal end to everything. The bleakness, the fearful sense of doom that had lurked within him since childhood was beginning to pulse now, like a painful vein in his forehead.

'Chiara . . .' he whispered.

'It can't go on much longer,' Cassini said. 'Give it half an hour. I've seen floods. They go as quickly as they come. Half an hour. Then we'll go out and do what we can.'

He seized Fratelli by his coat. 'If that means racing home to see your wife, then so be it.'

Marrone began to say something, getting between them.

'No!' the old *carabiniere* roared, pushing him back. 'I never liked this stuck-up little prick. He thinks he's better than us. Smarter than us. If he feels he's got the right to race over to his pretty little wife, then let him go. She'll be upstairs watching all this shit like the rest of us. Waiting . . .'

'I don't feel better,' Fratelli murmured, shaking himself free of Cassini's grip. 'Or smarter.'

But you're wrong about the flood, he thought. He knew that somehow. Felt it in the cold damp in his feet. Smelled it in the stinking, fetid reek from beyond the window.

It would be several weeks before the Tuscan authorities managed to assemble the first accurate chronology of the disaster that engulfed Florence that night. There were more important things to do. Count the dead. Reconnect power lines and telephone cables, water supplies and transport networks. Bring life back to a city that had briefly stepped outside the twentieth century and found itself thrust into a shapeless, primeval past. After a while, when the scale of the catastrophe was obvious, came the task of directing the influx of 'mud angels', volunteers who flew from around the globe to help rescue the priceless objects now buried beneath an ocean of stinking mire.

Yet, whatever Pino Fratelli's inner eye told him at times, this was a natural event, a chain of unfortunate incidents; each insignificant in itself, but turned into a terrible and devastating progression of violent physical disorder by their actions upon each other, like dominoes tipping over in an accidental chain.

The rains began three days before, heavy and constant. By the third of November the two dams that served the region, in Valdarno, south-east of the city, were already overflowing, dispatching two thousand square metres of water down the valley towards the city. Cellars in the lowest-lying area, Santa Croce, began to flood before midnight, cutting off power and mains water. Heating oil installations were swamped, garages found their underground storage tanks inundated. Sewerage systems were breached by the force of the current. Soon the Arno was a rank and noxious mix of rainwater, mud, raw sewage and black oil, rising all the time.

At two a.m., the slender Mugnone stream, a tributary that rose near Fiesole, burst its banks and flooded the Cascine Park on the right, northern bank of the Arno, beyond the densely populated centre. Though none in the heart of Florence knew it at the time, this single act sealed the city's fate, allowing the flood waters to encircle the entire population of the *centro storico*; almost seventy thousand people crammed into an area little more than eleven square kilometres in size.

As the downpour continued, engineers in the Valdarno began to fear for the integrity of the two dams there and took the fateful decision to release yet more water into the torrent headed northwards. Minutes later the Arno breached the entire length of the Lungarno Cellini by San Niccolò. An hour on, the flood burst over the right bank around the Lungarno Acciaioli on the opposite bank. Within ninety minutes the main arteries into the city were turbulent rivers, not roads any more. Cars and trucks floated on the thrashing current. Furniture, washing, prams and rubbish bins raced along the streets at speeds approaching forty kilometres an hour.

When day broke on a city that was largely unrecognizable even to those who'd spent their lives within its boundaries, Santa Croce found itself under three metres of water. In the famous basilica, filthy water lapped against the stone tombs of Michelangelo, Galileo and Machiavelli, despoiled Giotto's precious frescoes, the priceless crucifix of Cimabue, centuries of much-loved painting and statuary. Almost on the stroke of eight, waves the height of two men battered down the doors of the Museum of the History of Science in the Piazza dei Giudici by the river next to the Uffizi. Before the hour was out, the square around the Duomo itself was inundated, with such force that the water broke through the gates of the Baptistery and covered Ghiberti's beloved panels, the 'Gates of Paradise', in rank, corrosive mud and muck.

Still the flood grew, until at one point the Piazza della Signoria was six metres deep in swampy filth that lapped at the shins of the statue of David and ran over the ramp of the Loggia dei Lanzi. Cellini's terrifying bronze *Perseus* stood there, plinth submerged, like an avenging angel rising from a squalid quagmire.

All this time the city waited, knowing the monster that had invaded their sleepy winter idyll must at some stage begin to shrink back and start to die. Yet at four that afternoon, as night began to fall on a dreadful day that none who experienced it would forget, the Arno and its associated sewage was at its highest, turning vast swathes of the city into a brown and putrid lagoon.

By then the men of the Borgo Ognissanti Carabinieri station had been working slowly, patiently, in the streets, through all the daylight hours without pause, without direction much of the time. Mid-morning the handful of boats that were stored along the riverfront were coming into use. Marrone commandeered as many as his men could handle. Communication was still impossible. No phone, no electricity, no radio. All they could do was respond to the community around them, people who were scared for the most part and, in the case of the sick and elderly, in need of physical aid as well.

The arguments between Fratelli and his colleagues ceased the moment the scale of the catastrophe became fully visible. With the gradual acquisition of some means of local transport, the men in the station began to row down streets where they usually drove their squad cars, calling out to the houses, telling people to stay where they were. For the whole of that day Fratelli found himself partnered with a genial cadet, Ludovico Ducca, a determined young man full of energy and good cheer, even in the most exasperating of circumstances. The two of them formed an immediate bond as they patrolled the waterlogged city centre looking for those in trouble. In the Ognissanti Hospital Fratelli and the muscular Ducca helped elderly and infirm patients to safety on the higher floors. Two babies were born there that day, and the young *carabiniere* looked a little shocked when one mother, a woman he'd carried up the staircase in his arms, asked for his first name and promised to pass it on to her infant son.

When there was time they comforted the distraught, the terrified, the angry. Told a few that this was not the end of the world. Not a divine judgement on a wicked city, the kind of horror once foretold by Savonarola from the pulpit of the Duomo. It was just rain, a lot of it, and soon the waters would disperse, leaving Florence to recover its glories from the mud and filth, and one day welcome back the warmth of the sun.

Around three in the afternoon, Fratelli and Ludovico Ducca found an old man dead in his kitchen, floating on the brown tide, in a terraced house two streets from the station. A heart attack, they thought. Not that there was any chance to check. Fratelli gazed at this corpse, knowing there was precious little he could do except make it secure and decent. Ducca was silent, shaken, his pleasant face bloodless for the first time that day. Later Fratelli was to discover he'd only joined up two months before and this was the first dead body he'd seen. There was no time for such considerations then, though it did occur to Fratelli that at this moment Florence was, as he'd said in the heated argument with Marrone, quite without rule, without law, without any sense of formal order. The people they met astonished him in their humanity, their courage, their self-sacrifice, as did the relentless and seemingly inexhaustible Ducca. The healthy gave way to sick, the thirsty to the thirstier. Already teams were being assembled to make their way to the worst-affected areas when a route became clear and, if there were no more people to be helped, to put their shoulders to turning the city back towards some kind of secure normality.

All this came from a form of natural integrity, a sense of morality, of right and wrong that had been given them over the years, as part of the community to which they belonged. Cop or *carabiniere*, man or woman in the street, they needed no commands. This was how they were.

But Pino Fratelli was a detective at heart, and with a job like his came a certain kind of knowledge. He understood implicitly there were others in the world too, those who possessed no such compunctions, no sense of attachment to those around them. If someone wished to loot or rob, to murder or rape, there would be precious little even the most courageous and dedicated police officer or *carabiniere* could do to stop them. This bleak, distressed city possessed no fences, no barriers to keep out the wolves that lived on the periphery of society, their rapacity curtailed by a sensible fear of capture and justice that was now briefly absent. This, more than anything, more than the damage, the destruction and the occasional death, appalled him. Frightened him, if he were honest, because that nagging interior voice he'd heard since he saw the manhole fly towards the cloudy sky still whispered in his ear.

This was a day for monsters to roam, and something inside said they would. They were there already.

It wasn't till six o'clock that the waters finally began to recede. The rain had stopped by then. Perhaps the corner had been turned, and there would be some respite from the weather. Fratelli was back at the Carabinieri station in the Borgo Ognissanti, with Marrone and a team of other officers who'd come in to help. All thought of shifts and rosters and duty were gone. They would work till they could work no more, then sleep briefly and start again.

Someone had found a camping stove and heated up what was left of Marrone's cold *lampredotto*. There was still no electricity, no phones. Fratelli ate the grisly, strong meat in a bread bun and pulled on a beer that gruff old Cassini had given him.

Then Marrone came over and put a hand on his shoulder.

'They say the Trinita bridge is open again. I've got a boat heading into the centre soon. Why not go and see if you can reach Oltrarno? Ducca's trying to get home too.'

Fratelli, exhausted, so focused on what had occupied him since daybreak, blinked and felt ashamed. He'd not thought about Chiara at all. The flood had stolen every conscious thought and supplanted her in his head.

He nodded, lost for words.

'When you get to the other side,' Marrone added, 'be careful. I can't spare you a boat to take you over there. I wouldn't trust any to cross the river that way. You have to walk across the bridge then find your own way. Is that agreed?'

'Yes.' He smiled at his friend. 'Thanks, Walter. Sorry if I've been an idiot.'

'You've been a marvel.' He looked around them. 'They all have. I couldn't be more proud of any of you. Now go and see Chiara. Make

sure she's safe. This isn't a special case, you know. I'm offering it
to everyone now things are quietening down.'

Five minutes later, Fratelli got into a broad boat from one of the
rowing clubs, behind a soldier and state police officer he didn't
know, with Ducca by his side.

'Where are you going?' he asked the young cadet.

'I thought I'd take a look around Santa Croce. My nan lives there.
She's OK, I'm sure. Just want to see.'

Fratelli felt briefly lost for words. He leaned forward and held
the young officer in his arms for a moment. Ducca looked embarrassed as they were rowed through the night along a road that was
now a river.

The two men in front took the vessel down the street with their
steady strokes. Soon the low, elegant shape of the Ponte Santa
Trinita began to rise from a sea of black water. Pino Fratelli pinched
himself. Was he really in a boat gently sculling down the Borgo
Ognissanti? Could this all be just a ridiculous nightmare? Like a
strange childhood in Rome, one that seemed to have happened to
someone else. But hadn't.

The pavement on the closest side was just above the flood. The
two men steadied the canoe as they got there. Then Fratelli stepped
on to solid ground and felt the water resume its icy grip around his
ankles once again.

'Take care, Pino,' Ludovico Ducca called as the boat went on
its way.

The sky had cleared, a bright moon cast its cold and heartless light
on the tortured city. Fratelli barely recognized the neighbourhood
where he'd grown up. The high narrow streets, the grand buildings
of the Via Maggio as he left the bridge, the grubby square of Santo
Spirito, the meaner lanes beyond . . . he could never have imagined
them like this. The waters had, as Cassini predicted, receded with
great speed. When they retreated they left behind such devastation
. . . stretches of caking mud, wrecked cars and scooters, loose
branches and small trees, broken pottery, dislodged paving, TV sets,
chairs and sofas. It was as if the comforting minutiae of modern
life had been stripped from the homes of Florence and scattered
about by a peevish, gigantic child desperate to play in the swampy
muck and sludge the flood had left behind.

Along the Lungarno, men and women trudged warily around,

struggling in galoshes, greeting strangers in the street, asking questions that brought no easy answers.

Have you seen . . .?

No, Fratelli answered quickly. I'm a stupid, lowly *carabiniere* and I've been struggling to make sense of life on the other side of the Arno, in the Borgo Ognissanti, which is not my home and never will be, merely the place that work took me.

Do you have . . .?

No. I've nothing. Just a modest home, a beautiful wife, lots of debts and a head that hurts from thinking thoughts too dark to speak out loud.

Can you help me . . .?

He was a *carabiniere*. The badge stayed with him, off duty or on. Between the bridge of Santa Trinita and the back street he called home, Fratelli found himself asked that constantly – by strangers, by people he half knew, by friends, and by a few who loathed him. It was almost twenty hours since he'd slept. The day had been so strange and tiring he felt he might close his eyes and never wake afterwards. But he was a servant of these people, one they needed more than ever. So he helped everyone who asked, whether it was carrying or fetching, talking, comforting, or holding one tearful woman whose grandchild had gone missing for hours on end until the brat came back smirking as if this were all a stupid joke.

The reports of deaths were coming in by the time he left the station. Fratelli had no idea how many might have perished in this strange catastrophe. If someone said it was hundreds, thousands even, he wouldn't have called them foolish, though a sense of inner reason told him the toll was usually lower than one expected. This wasn't Hiroshima or Belsen. Only nature, which lacked the trained and tailored efficiency for death that human beings had refined so skilfully over the centuries.

Around ten he still found himself in the square of Santo Spirito, clearing debris and oozing sludge from the front door of an elderly man who was headed for hospital, short of breath, grey-faced, clutching his chest. When that was done, someone Fratelli recognized, a café owner in the square, called him over and dragged him into his narrow little bar. There were candles all round, people huddled together, chatting – laughing, even, at times. At the end of the bar was a lively fire inside a domed pizza oven. Fratelli could scarcely believe his eyes. The man was cooking, without power, handing out food for free to those who needed it.

He poured Fratelli a grappa, half a tumbler full, and pushed it over the counter.

'On the house,' the man said.

'Piero,' Fratelli murmured, remembering his name.

The grappa was cheap and fiery and welcome. He downed a good measure in one and saw the glass refilled in an instant.

'You're the cop,' the man said.

'*Carabiniere*. There's a difference.'

'Not to us,' Piero chuckled, and the men around him laughed too.

Someone asked the question Fratelli knew he'd hear for days to come. Was that it? Could they look to a world getting better? Cleaner? Safer? Or were they simply fools enjoying the eye of the storm? Trapped in a welcome lull before the maelstrom returned, determined to sweep away everything and turn the world back to how it was before the dreams of men had changed its face?

He thought before answering. Considered his own inner feelings. That instinct Chiara used to call his 'stupid third eye'. Stupid because it was so unreliable, seeing what wasn't there sometimes, missing the obvious on occasion. But hitting the spot too. That happened, and it was why he listened to it a little.

'I think the storm is over,' Fratelli answered. 'And now . . . or rather tomorrow, in the daylight . . . we must look at what it's left behind.'

'Go home,' Piero ordered. 'You're no use to anyone except your own.'

Fratelli wondered if the café owner, giving away his precious food and drink, had any idea how welcome those words were.

'I'd like some pizza,' he said. 'Just a margherita. And a bottle of Chianti.'

He placed some notes on the counter.

'I'm paying,' he added. 'I'm a *carabiniere*. I don't eat for free.'

The men around him laughed and one said, 'First cop I ever heard say that . . .'

'Not a cop,' Fratelli replied. And thought to himself: I'm not sure what I am. Who I am, even. Except when I'm at home. With her. When Chiara's love defines me, makes a place in her heart where I can live in peace and happiness.

Piero shrugged, took his money and came back a few minutes later with a bottle of red wine and a cardboard box with a plain pizza, just tomato and mozzarella. Fratelli stumbled outside and headed west. He needed to be away from people for a while. With his wife, the two of them shivering over food and cheap Chianti.

The area around Santa Maria del Carmine must have been lower lying than the rest of the quarter. The mud seemed deeper, stickier, more foul. There were lights on in the church as he trudged past. Fratelli found himself wondering what kind of damage the waters had wrought there. He admired the place, at least the Brancacci Chapel, with its beautiful figures on the walls: the story of Saint Peter, the historic depictions of Adam and Eve, before and after the Fall. Fratelli was not much fond of the awkward fig leaves painted on the orders of some prudish judgemental member of the Medici who didn't appreciate art, only power. The rest he loved with the detachment only an atheist could feel.

'Worry for yourself, Pino,' he murmured as he turned the corner into his own narrow street. 'You've done enough for one long day.'

The whitewashed walls of the houses carried a tidemark a good two metres high. Debris lay scattered among the ooze that spread almost knee-deep from pavement to pavement as if the level of the city itself had somehow risen with the flood. Now that he was in the place he'd called home for as long as he could remember, Fratelli found the catastrophe took on a personal aspect. Staggering through the mire, looking at these familiar houses, the cars and scooters and rubbish bins moved by the force of the inundation, the way the small and intimate landscape he knew so well had changed, he saw in his own bright imagination what must have happened, perhaps not long after daylight, when the mass of flood water came to occupy the rest of the *centro storico* on the other side of the Arno.

It was a moving, potent bore of icy sludge and rain, a surging wave at its head, racing in from the river carrying everything before it. Doors were off their hinges everywhere, cars lay upturned and useless, stuck in the greasy slime. The air smelled of water and sewage and fuel oil. A dry and bitter wind was starting to howl in from the north.

He saw his front door and Fratelli's heart quickened. There were no lights on upstairs. His instant fear was foolish. There were hardly any lights on anywhere. But a few places had flickering candles and oil lamps. And Chiara was so careful, so organized. She always kept a supply for when the electricity was out, knew how to get to them, place them carefully in saucers so she could navigate the narrow landing and reach the street if need be.

Fratelli's pace increased even though his freezing feet kept sticking in the dirt and clay.

Four doors away he called 'Chiara!' and didn't know why.

His cry echoed off the walls, with their tidemark higher than most men, then rose to the white, uncaring moon.

'Chiara! Where are you?'

Something caught him as he lurched forward, the pizza and the bottle in his hands. The edge of the pavement, hidden from view. An object dislodged by the force of the flood. He'd never know. He went down, face first, hands flailing. Piero's precious cardboard box was forced into the shitty brown filth where it took the weight of his fall and broke into pieces. The bottle of Chianti disappeared into the mire. But Fratelli's mind was racing with grim notions and so he barely noticed.

Hauling himself from the grasping mire, he stumbled to his feet, lurched on. Three doors, two . . .

He stopped, breathless, by his house. The black wooden door was half off its hinges, torn from the frame as if by a sledgehammer, but still blocking the view from the street. This seemed odd. He pushed at it with his shoulder and the wooden slab fell forward with a loud slap.

Fratelli stopped and stared into the pool of darkness that was the hallway of his home, turning the beam of his torch around, horrified by what he saw. The tide of mud had burst through the narrow entrance and now lay deep over the floor, up to the third or fourth step of the stone staircase.

They're all like that around here.

His heart beat like an overworked drum. He called her name again, heard his voice bounce around the narrow dark entrance hall, then race up the landing to the first floor where they lived, where she'd kissed him that morning, something in her mind that made her beg him, 'Don't go. Let me call Marrone. Say you're sick.'

But I'm the one who dreams those dreams, not you.

Pino Fratelli did his best to recover his breathing, then switched the torch beam ahead of him and took two uncertain steps forward, found himself stumbling over the washing basket, trapped in the quagmire at the foot of the stairs.

Something caught his eye. A naked, muddy foot emerging from

the mess that had travelled up the steps. The beam moved on. It found a familiar shape, one that broke his heart. Crying, half stumbling, he fell up the stone stairs, slipped to his knees, the torch trembling in his hands.

They'd visited Pompeii on honeymoon. She'd wept over the figures crouching there in the ancient ruins, caught by the cloud of volcanic dust that had trapped them, turned living men, women and children into statues, frozen in their death throes. And here was Chiara, much the same. Face and torso out of the muck, the rest of her caked in it, still wearing her dressing gown, head back at an awkward, unnatural angle. Her legs were forced apart, her thighs, mud reaching beyond the knee, bare and pale in the torchlight. He wiped his eyes then, with his right hand, moved the dressing gown across to cover her.

His fingers brushed her skin and then he took her hand in his. Cold, and so long gone. While he was carrying pensioners in Ognissanti, struggling to get food and drink to strangers on the other side of the river, his wife had died here.

How?

There were no words in his head – none he could recognize, anyway. No notion of what to do or say. Only reality: his beloved Chiara, broken on the stairs, taken from him, from everyone who loved her.

Imagination.

He thought in pictures from time to time and now that sly, unwanted facility returned with a sharp swiftness, reinforced by the automatic instincts of the detective inside.

She never slept well when he wasn't home. Some time early in the morning, probably close to dawn, she'd come downstairs to do the washing, only to be met by the flood and the shattered door, a city in chaos.

Pinioned between his grief and his need to understand, Fratelli didn't dare look at her face. Not yet. He had to think this through. To imagine. To see.

Someone, a passer-by, would notice her. Perhaps he called out for help. For shelter. Chiara would never refuse. If she'd known there was someone in trouble she'd have been the first to offer without a second thought.

This was a back street of Oltrarno. Not Santo Spirito, not quite. No danger here. Not usually. Except when the flood came and reduced this plain and ordinary world to its primal, elemental state.

The cop in him turned her hands in his. Blood beneath the fingernails. Scrapings of skin.

She fought.

'Of course she fought,' he murmured.

And what else?

There were two of him now. The first, the husband, imprisoned
inside the second, the *carabiniere*. It was the latter who played the
light around the hallway, saw no sign of footprints, only mud and
water. This was a murder without precedent. One in which the
elements themselves managed to remove all traces of the beast who
committed it.

An emotion inside began to work its way to the surface; a
choke, a cough, a cry, an arrhythmic tic that joined the two of them,
detective and spouse, in bleak and shapeless grief.

The sharp and brutal realization rose in his head and burned there
like a flare.

Fourteen hours or more had passed since someone killed his wife
here, on the stairs of their home. They would never find him now,
not in the sea of mud and muck that was Florence on the fourth of
November 1966. He couldn't even call the station. Summon a car.
Do anything but shout and scream to himself, perhaps for hours,
for all the long night.

Dead was dead. Gone was gone.

He shone his torch on her face finally and felt all sense of hope
and decency leave him; knew that if a man who looked culpable
had passed by in that instant, he'd tear him limb from limb and
never care about the consequences.

Chiara's blank and glassy eyes stared upwards towards the rooms
that were their home. Her hair was damp and messy, caked in mud,
set in hanks, as if her attacker had grabbed her there. Livid bruises
marked both sides of her throat where he'd choked the life out of her.

Pino Fratelli, twenty-eight years old, a good man mostly, stared
at what he saw and thought of another sight: the astonishing couple
in the Brancacci Chapel, Masaccio's Adam and Eve, newly expelled
from Paradise, the woman's mouth creased and contorted, corners
pointing downwards in a shriek of pain.

Chiara looked like this now and it took him a moment to understand why. Then he moved closer and saw. Perhaps it was lipstick.
Or something else. A stain, scarlet, smeared across her mouth and
lips, as if to make that same expression of agony, a clown-like cry

of despair, emphasized by the downturned smear of red at the edge of her mouth.

The husband in him took out a handkerchief from his pocket, dampened it with his tongue and cleaned the shameful smudges from her skin.

His tears fell on her filth-stained cheeks, his hands and the grubby handkerchief fought to clear this muck, this abomination, from her face.

Then he lay there with her, not moving, scarcely daring to breathe. There was no one to summon. No friend, no relative to reach on this strange and unreal night.

Pino Fratelli wept for his dead wife, whispered to her, said meaningless phrases, felt the rational, ordered part of his mind leave him.

Somewhere outside he heard a sound. An impossible one. The ebb and flow of the river, a familiar rhythm, constant and eternal. The ceaseless noise filled his head; the chill, dank waters swamped his imagination. When he closed his eyes he saw Chiara floating to her grave on its filthy surface, like Ophelia borne away by the flood.

It would be daylight, another ten hours, before a local police officer, checking the houses in the street, walked through the half-open door and found him there, still clutching the cold, stiff corpse of his wife on the drenched and dirty stairs. And another seventeen days before Pino Fratelli, finally waking to some kind of consciousness in a sanatorium by the coast outside Livorno, would speak again.

Not that he had much of substance to say.

Wednesday, 5 November 1986

Morning, just after eight in Fiesole. There was a portable TV in the kitchen. Black and white and old. He'd got some fresh eggs from the chickens and made frittata with tomatoes and onions bought from a store in Florence the night before. He got coffee, orange juice, some bread, took it all upstairs, the food on a tray, the TV in his left hand.

The room at the front, where they kept the dope and the guns, was bright in the morning light. Outside he could see lines of puffy grey rain clouds gathering across the watercolour-blue sky. The weather was going to be temperamental for the next few days. He'd heard that on the radio. The coming afternoon threatened a heavy downpour, one that would last for hours, until well after midnight.

Space to think. To plan. Time to flee.

He plugged the little TV into the wall, adjusted the circular wire aerial and played with the tuner. The best he could get was a crackly news channel, the face of the woman reading the bulletin distorted by the weakness of the signal. Her voice was tense and cracked. Clear enough, though.

He turned up the volume all the way and listened, nodding as he took in the details.

They weren't saying it but the Carabinieri knew nothing beyond the obvious. He wondered if his real name would ever be sufficiently notorious to find its way into the news. If anyone would know it, recognize it, understand who he really was. This seemed unlikely, whatever the outcome. Small people never mattered much in Florence. They were cannon fodder for the whims of their masters, who watched them bleed and die from the walls of their fortress homes.

He'd left half the frittata, cut neatly down the middle through the yellow egg. There was a second cup of coffee going cold and a half-glass of extra orange juice. He hadn't been in the other room since the night before. Something there frightened him. Was too close, too real.

Still, it had to be faced.

He unplugged the set, picked up the tray and walked in. Then he bent down to a power socket on the wall, got the TV going again, turned down the volume a touch and placed the food and drink on the bed. Got the saucepan he'd left by the bed the day before, walked it to the bathroom, emptied it, washed it like a servant.

Left it there and came back.

The signal was better near the back window. The TV newscast was still running. You'd think they had nothing else to talk about. Same old story, same old empty words, going round and round. One dead, that was all. So what?

She was watching, rapt. Couldn't take her eyes off the thing.

Finally he turned and looked at the bed and said, 'I did it for you.'

She was still tethered loosely to the iron posts, half naked beneath the coverlet.

'For your honour,' he insisted.

Her long curly hair was getting greasy. As he watched, it moved, and her face, sour and bossy, turned on him. Chavah Efron said, no warmth, no gratitude in her hard voice, 'You can't just leave me in here for hours on end.'

'Did you hear what I said?'

'I need the bathroom!'

Loud voice, woman's voice. That always made him cower.

He went back and got the gun from the other room, tucked it into his waistband.

She stared at him when he returned. 'Does that thing make you happy?'

'Maybe.'

'You don't even know how to use it.'

He didn't speak.

'Does it make you feel safe?'

'Safe as anyone.' He glanced at the window. 'Here. For a while.'

'You're a lousy liar.'

He wanted to argue. Wanted to shout at her. Control her. But she still wasn't scared of him and never would be.

'I need the bathroom,' she repeated.

He untied her wrists, watched as she got out of the bed, saw her nakedness, wondered about it. She kept the door closed. A long time. He heard running water. The shower.

To drown out the noise and the thoughts he sat on the bed and watched the TV again. After a while a kids' cartoon came on and he laughed at that, found himself briefly in another place, one that was warm and sunny, a long time ago. An empty hut in a hidden corner of the Boboli Gardens, no lone mother to shriek at him, to watch where his curious fingers might wander. A little space to himself, and an imagination that could run wild watching this funny couple, cat and mouse, beat the living hell out of one another.

Men and women did that too. All the time.

When she came out she wore nothing but a towel round her waist tucked in over her small breasts. Another was wrapped round her hair. The intimacy of the small, damp bedroom, too hot from the fire he'd stoked in the kitchen below, was disturbing. He'd never been this close to a woman like this, one who was confident with her nakedness, didn't mind him being there.

She reached up and took the towel off her head, then rubbed her hair vigorously.

'What are you looking at?' she asked.

He'd used those same words the night before in the Loggia dei
Lanzi. Same threatening tone. She might have been in his head,
doing the talking for him.

'Nothing,' he mumbled, and realized his voice sounded like that
of a kid, one caught watching Tom and Jerry when he was supposed
to be doing something else. Washing the dishes, bringing in the
coal from the heap outside. Being the slave.

'Does it turn you on?'

The TV was back with the news. The same story.

She pummelled her hair again, then threw the damp towel into
the space beneath the window. There was a fragrance about her.
Flowers and scent.

'I did it for you,' he said again.

He wasn't answering that question.

'Where did you kill him?' she asked.

'Outside.' He nodded at the window. 'In the barn.'

'Did you clean up afterwards? The Carabinieri will be here soon,
you idiot. You just gave them an invitation. They didn't give a shit
about Ari. Now . . .'

'I cleaned up. All the mess I made.'

'And the guns? The dope? The Semtex? Jesus . . .'

Damp hair on the pillow, she stretched her sturdy bronze legs
out over the sheet, closed her eyes, let out a long sigh.

Then, to his astonishment, she began to laugh. A light, soft, girlish
sound. It made his head spin.

'What's so funny?' he asked.

She stopped and looked at him directly. She had green eyes.
Dark green. The colour of the snake that wound itself round the
tree behind the couple in the Brancacci Chapel, not the cheap fig
leaves he used to cover the vile nakedness there.

Her hands went behind her head. He stared at the shape of
her.

'You're really not that bright, are you?'

'I killed that bastard. The one who . . .'

He didn't go on.

'Who what?'

'You know.'

'You watched, didn't you? In that place when I danced. I saw
you. I saw the look in your eyes.'

'He murdered Ari.'

'Because Ari got mad and went out there to kill him. Which was stupid. Never part of the plan . . .'

'He . . .' The words were hard. They had to be used. 'They took you. Raped you. I heard you screaming. I . . .'

He could still picture it in his head, and remember the way he'd watched from the shadows, fascinated, horrified. A part of him envious, too.

Those green eyes glittered at him.

'Didn't I ask for it? Dancing for them? Whoring myself . . .'

'I did it for you.'

'Did what?' she spat at him. 'Killed a single worm among many?'

'I'm just one man.'

'Not even that,' she said, and started drying her taut, muscular body through the bath towel round her torso. 'Show me your hands.'

He held them out. They were grubby. Stains beneath the fingernails.

'You're filthy. Take a shower. There's a towel by the bath. It was Ari's. Use that. Use his clothes. He was big and stupid too. Here . . .'

She went to a drawer and took out fresh jeans, a black shirt and sweater, some underclothes. He saw her nakedness as she moved. She knew it, and didn't mind.

'Put these on when you're done. You stink.'

She took a deep breath, rolled her head back against the wall.

'After that we need to talk.'

There was a new look in her eyes. He couldn't name it. Doubt? Surprise? Recognition?

'Maybe there's a reason you're here. Not that I believe in all that shit.'

He had the gun. He was bigger than her, stronger. Physically anyway. Yet somehow none of this mattered. She'd seen something in him. Recognized the weak tic of fear, of servitude.

Once that happened he always obeyed. Didn't know why. Didn't ask for a reason. Just couldn't find a way to say no.

She was playing with the towel, showing herself to him, grinning.

'Do as I tell you and maybe good things happen. That's what you want, isn't it?'

'No,' he answered, and heard the uncertainty in his own voice.

She waited. He put the gun on the bedside table and walked into the bathroom. It was spotless and smelled of her. The cracked shower unit had hanks of brown hair in the drain hole and on the neck of the rusty head. Long curly brown strands stuck to the broken white tiles.

In his head he could see the Brancacci again, what lay beneath the fig leaves. That was supposed to stay hidden but it wouldn't. It was with him, with her, always, bringing the itch of temptation, the offer of that red heat in the head that stopped you thinking about everything else there was in the world.

'Tornabuoni, Tornabuoni,' Pino Fratelli muttered as they sat outside the captain's office in the Ognissanti *stazione*. 'This can't be right.'

She sat by his side, silent, trying to come to terms with the news they'd both watched on the TV that morning. A man's severed head had been found attached to Cellini's statue of *Perseus* in the Loggia dei Lanzi, long hair wound into the bronze serpents of Medusa. It almost seemed like a bloody joke, real death superimposed upon the fictional.

The victim was Vanni Tornabuoni, the city art commissioner she was supposed to have met the previous morning in his office in the Pitti Palace. The TV said he was a bachelor, forty-two years old, though he looked younger: a handsome, slightly effeminate man. He had not been seen since leaving his office the previous evening. Officers had checked his secluded house in Bellosguardo, the exclusive green suburb behind Oltrarno. There were signs of a struggle. It seemed clear he'd been attacked at the property long before his severed head was found in the Piazza della Signoria. The Carabinieri, who had taken full control of the case, had yet to find any indication of where he was murdered.

'Why are you so sure this is connected with the Brancacci?' she asked.

Fratelli was lost in his own thoughts and didn't seem to hear. This obsessive certainty of his worried her. The confessions of the previous night – about his illness and then the death of his wife – had changed him. There was something intensely cathartic in his words, the way he unburdened himself of the past. If he was to be believed, these dreadful doubts and fears had been locked inside him for twenty years. So she was the first to hear the full story of how Chiara had died, since Fratelli had collapsed completely after her murder, the distraught husband in him defeating the *carabiniere*.

According to his story, he'd stayed with Chiara's body until discovered, and was so distressed and incapable of speech that, for a time, the investigators suspected he was responsible. Weeks in sedation, either silent or ranting, followed. The tone of blame in Fratelli's explanation told her he knew himself this was more than mere grief. There was something in him – a flaw; mental, physical perhaps. With hindsight, it might have been the tumour in its infancy or a disturbing remnant of his strange childhood history. Real or psychological, this wound healed only on the surface, remaining fragile and easily reopened. To the world he seemed such a calm, sane man. But another, wilder, more uncertain creature lived beneath, one that never spoke much in the months after Chiara's death, even to Walter Marrone, his friend and colleague, who took over what was to prove a fruitless murder investigation.

This was the flood inside him, Fratelli said, as she listened in the overheated living room, on a hard chair next to the record player, music playing softly in the background. Something that beckoned the muddy brown waters of death and uncertainty into Chiara's too-brief life, staining them both forever. There was no point in arguing against his certainties. The facts, in Fratelli's head, spoke for themselves. After her murder he was briefly insane, so the husband never thought to mention the small details that the *carabiniere* would have found so important. Those strange marks on his dead wife's face, the red smears making a downturned frown around her mouth, he never disclosed to Marrone. The overworked pathologists in the morgue failed to pick them up too, since they had other clients to deal with, and a rape victim, which Chiara clearly was, needed little in the way of explanation.

When Fratelli was released, he began to believe these visual images were all part of the madness, one more piece of delusional, psychic trauma left behind by that terrible night, like a tidemark inside his head, or that sign she'd noticed scattered around the city high up on the walls of houses, offices, churches . . . *on the fourth of November 1966 the waters of the Arno reached here.*

And, in the case of Pino Fratelli, never fully receded.

Julia remembered so clearly sitting next to him in the cold Brancacci Chapel two days before, wondering why he was shivering so much in his heavy winter coat as he stared at those paintings on the wall. He wasn't. He was trembling with shock and fear and the horror of a returning memory. The sight of the scarlet daub of chicken's blood on the mouths of the two Eves had taken him back to that night twenty years before. It was a miracle he'd kept his composure at all.

*   *   *

'They're connected,' Fratelli said, coming out of his shell with an abrupt nod.

'What . . .?'

It took a moment for Julia Wellbeloved to drag herself back to the bare, chilly anteroom of the Carabinieri station and the reasons they were there: to tell Marrone about what they'd seen in the Brancacci and to offer her possible glimpse of Tornabuoni's killer. To get Pino Fratelli back inside the Carabinieri. That was a part of his plan too. Not that he'd mentioned it.

'They're connected. But I thought he'd kill a woman. I felt it was women he hated and feared. That ought to be the case.'

'You talk as if you know him,' she said.

Fratelli smiled and tapped his head through the white hair. 'Mad as a mole.'

'No you're not. And there's no such turn of phrase in Italian. I checked.'

'See. You become more of a detective with each passing day. Yet I do know him. He's been in my head for twenty years, with the flood. Perhaps.' His eyes lost their focus for a moment. 'Perhaps it's in his head too and like me he refuses to listen. Wants it to be a bad dream. Part of the craziness. Things would be so much simpler that way. Life a lot more . . . acceptable.'

A fierce look of frustration gripped him.

'Then something surfaces to revive it. But what?'

After he'd spoken about his wife, Fratelli had shown her some of his books, the ones he'd taken to show Walter Marrone that afternoon. Told her about Lilith and some myths about the Fall. If she'd been able to pull herself out of that room, think rationally about all this, she knew she'd dismiss these ideas as nonsense, fantasies stretched out of a few old and flimsy facts: the memory of a scarlet stain on his dead wife's lips, the reappearance of something very similar on the walls of the chapel in the church of Santa Maria del Carmine.

Yet she crawled into bed at three that morning feeling the same unshakeable conviction that had gripped him from the moment he saw those smears on the face of the innocent Eve, and the halo above the serpent's golden hair. Fratelli had talked earlier about how he looked for links from the past to the present, from one act to another. It was exactly the kind of connection Julia hoped to make at some stage in her own work, the dissertation that was still hovering out of her reach. The unseen, elusive thread that ran from Chiara's death on the stone stairs of the house in Oltrarno to the daubs of chicken blood on the frescoes in the Brancacci Chapel was real. As real as Pino Fratelli himself, in all his perpetual, gentle confusion.

A few hours later she'd been woken by him hammering on her door. He'd been listening to the early morning news on the radio, something he did seven days a week since his wife's murder. Not long after, they set off for the Carabinieri station in Ognissanti. Julia found she could barely look at the plain stone steps of the house as she walked down them.

'It had to be a woman,' Fratelli repeated, shaking his head as he sat hunched on the bench outside Marrone's office. 'Not someone like Vanni Tornabuoni. A . . .'

He stopped short of saying it.

'A what?' she asked.

'Tornabuoni was a homosexual,' Fratelli said with a shrug. 'Gay, I think they call it these days. Or perhaps liked a little of both. So what? Everyone knew. No one minded. He was one of the aristocrats. The men who run this city. Even if they did mind, no one would say a thing. Could this be a part of his madness?'

He scratched his head.

'Our man is unforgiving, judgemental. He must hate homosexuals. This is not uncommon. Savonarola did. He wanted them executed . . .'

'I can't see a link. It may not be him—'

'Those answers exist,' Fratelli broke in. 'We simply fail to see them. Women, women . . . It must come back to them. That dreadful statue of Cellini's where he hung poor Tornabuoni's head. It's full of a hatred of femininity too. You see this? Perseus – and that madman Cellini – wishes to destroy Medusa because she's strong. Not the weak, submissive sexual toy he lusts after. Just like Lilith . . .'

'I see it,' she agreed and thought: *do I?*

The question needed to be asked again, even though she knew Fratelli had no answer.

'Do you think it was him, Pino? The man I saw? In the loggia last night. Did he kill Tornabuoni? Was he the same man in the Brancacci?'

He considered this idea, and when he did she could see the *carabiniere* surface; thoughtful, cunning, never saying anything he didn't wish to disclose.

'Who can know?' Fratelli answered in the end. 'But you must tell Walter when they finally have the sense to let us in there. Tell him everything.'

'What's there to say?'

'He frightened you.'

'Anyone would. Coming out of the dark like that.'

What are you looking at?

A figure in a cape and hood, with an aggressive, terrifying manner. Perhaps a murderer who'd decapitated a city councillor of Florence, a man of some wealth and position, not long before, and come to the heart of the city, carrying his severed head in a bag.

'I didn't see him,' she complained. 'Just a glimpse of a pale face. And a black hood.'

'He was carrying something. A pole. A bag. See? There are always other details a witness forgets. Perhaps important ones.'

Fratelli thought for a moment and said, 'You felt you recognized him. Didn't you say that?'

'Yes, but it's ridiculous. It was dark. I don't know what I saw really. I thought . . . I recognized something . . .'

But what it was she didn't know.

A tall, heavy young man was walking down the corridor towards them. It took a second or two for her to realize it was Luca Cassini, the station junior from the day before. That awkward, revelatory conversation by the *lampredotto* stall in Sant'Ambrogio market seemed very distant somehow.

Fratelli leaned over and whispered in her ear.

'I believe our time has come. Tell Walter everything, please. Except . . .' He winked at her and tapped his nose. 'Not the Brigata Spendereccia. That will only complicate matters.'

'But . . .'

She didn't have time to finish. Cassini was there, ushering them into Marrone's office.

'I don't think a few damaged paintings are on the captain's mind right now,' the young man said cheerily.

'We'll see about that, Luca,' Fratelli told him with a smile. 'I hope you're ready for a busy day.'

Walter Marrone was pale and drawn, staring at his unwelcome visitors with sad brown eyes. Papers lined his desk by the window overlooking Borgo Ognissanti. Two younger officers, Albani and Nucci, dressed in smart suits, sat next to him making notes. The phone cut into their conversation constantly. Fratelli fought to make his ideas heard against the constant flow of interruptions. It wasn't going to be easy.

The captain was one of Fratelli's oldest friends, but at that moment Marrone clearly wished them elsewhere, even when he was offered something Julia thought he would welcome: a witness.

'You saw what?' Marrone demanded gruffly.

'A man,' Julia said hesitantly. 'At the back of the loggia. He had a bag and what I thought was a boathook. He was tall. Bald, with a very striking pale face and a cloak, a robe. Almost like a monk's.'

'When?' asked one of the younger officers.

'Just after six, I think.'

The other man sighed and looked at his watch. 'You think?'

'Six fifteen or so. I took a taxi and met Pino for a drink at six thirty. So that's an accurate estimate.'

The officer glanced at his colleague, eyebrows raised.

'Tornabuoni's head didn't go up there until after nine o'clock,' he said. 'It can't have been him.'

'Your reasoning?' Fratelli wanted to know.

'Someone would stay there for three hours? In the loggia? With a head in a bag?'

Pino Fratelli shrugged his shoulders and glanced at Marrone. 'Why not? Who'd search him? November. A cold night. He had all the time in the world.' He glanced at the captain. 'It's a mistake to ascribe the motives and actions of a normal human being to a psychotic criminal. A man who inhabits a world that looks like ours but isn't. Walter? You know this as well as I do. They may not teach these things in detective school any more—'

'Don't start,' Marrone broke in with a scowl.

'Walter. You know—'

'A man with a severed head?' the captain interrupted. 'Hiding at the back of a public square? For three hours? For what possible reason?'

'Because he doesn't want to be seen. So he waits until there are no people. Or he has some magical connection with the number nine and wishes to hear it from the church bells. You're creating doubts out of thin air, with nothing to support them.'

'He was asleep,' Julia said suddenly. This conversation had made her think about the incident again. Fratelli was correct: there was more to be recalled, and perhaps there always was. One needed the prompt, the perspective that brought it into view. 'That's why he reacted so oddly. I thought he was a tramp, asleep there. Something I did woke him.'

Fratelli opened his arms as if to say . . . There.

'So a murderer with a head in a bag goes to sleep?' Albani or Nucci, one or the other, asked with a sarcastic side to his thin and weedy voice. 'Not once, but twice; more than that maybe.'

'Perhaps he was exhausted,' Fratelli said. 'Physically and mentally. I doubt he'd decapitated a man before.'

He glared at Marrone then waved a hand at the two young officers.

'Am I wasting my breath? Have these two not heard a word I've said? We're dealing with a psychotic individual here. One who feels he's outside our world. Any idea of logic, of rationality . . . some idea that we can comprehend his actions, predict them even . . . This is nonsense. The man can't manage that for himself. Why should others expect they can do it for him?'

'This is about the Brancacci, isn't it?' the captain asked wearily.

Fratelli folded his arms and took a deep breath. Then he said in a low voice that was close to breaking, 'No. It's not.' His right hand went to his forehead for a moment. 'Well, not entirely. It's about . . .' His head was shaking, a little too rapidly. 'Something I should have told you long ago.'

He stared at the younger officers.

'Something personal,' he added.

Marrone's face became a turn more miserable. He ordered Albani and Nucci out of the room. They left with a mutinous ill grace.

'Then tell me now,' the captain said patiently when they were gone. 'But I warn you, Pino. You're treading in unfamiliar territory. We already know a lot more about Vanni Tornabuoni than we did yesterday. His . . . friends and associates have been very forthcoming now he's dead. This has nothing to do with your frescoes in the Brancacci Chapel. Nothing at all. There's no need to hunt for complicated explanations; Hebrew myths and tales about serpents that are half snake, half woman. It's a mundane matter. A bloody and squalid affair, but murder often is. I'm sorry. Still, if you wish to speak . . .'

Fratelli seemed lost for words.

'The cockerel's part of the crest of the Tornabuoni family,' Julia said. 'I read that in one of Pino's history books.'

Fratelli and Marrone stared at her.

'So perhaps it was a message. Saying that somehow Tornabuoni was connected with the Brancacci. With—'

'It was no message,' Fratelli interrupted. 'Nothing as simple as that, anyway . . .'

It was his story to tell, she thought. No one else's.

'Then tell the captain,' Julia urged, jogging his elbow. 'Tell him what you told me.'

'What's going on?' Fratelli demanded of Marrone, scarcely seeming to hear her. 'I know you, Walter. I can read you like a book. There's some secret here. Something you don't wish to share.'

'Dammit, man!' the captain snapped. 'Don't try my patience.'

'Why not? You're trying mine.'

Walter Marrone took a deep breath and played with some of the papers on his desk. Then he stared gloomily at Fratelli and Julia Wellbeloved and said, 'If either of you breathes a word of this outside the station I will know and I will not be happy.' He folded his bulky arms. 'We have a man in custody for Tornabuoni's murder. A lover of his.' The captain scowled. 'One of many. Vanni Tornabuoni led a colourful life.'

'What does he look like?' Julia asked straight away.

Marrone watched her. 'Not tall. Not bald. He's a young man. Very disturbed. As one might expect.'

'How old?' Fratelli asked in a shaky, expectant voice.

The captain looked at a document in front of him, puzzled by the question.

'Twenty-six. He was Tornabuoni's gardener. Lived in a shack on his estate. Performed other duties, it seemed.'

'No,' Fratelli said. 'No, no, no. Twenty-six . . . is impossible. That would have made him a child. No, Walter!' He was on his feet now. 'I am telling you . . .'

'We found Tornabuoni's body outside his shack,' Marrone said gently. 'The gardener was with it when we went to the place. He was cradling it, for God's sake. I've kept this from the media for the moment. Until we have a confession from the man. Right now . . .'

His words drifted into silence.

'Right now, what?' Fratelli wanted to know.

'He's difficult to talk to. Upset. Psychotic, you'd say. Or so I imagine.'

Julia sat there, wondering what to think.

'Pino,' she said, rising to take his arm. 'You need to tell the captain. About Chiara . . .'

'What was that?' Marrone asked, not quite hearing.

'Sounds as if you don't need us then,' Fratelli grumbled.

'Tell him!' Julia shouted.

But Fratelli was leaving already, only turning to say, 'You heard the captain. He's a busy man. He has his suspect, who one day may even talk. Why should we waste his time?'

The most cursory of glances at Marrone followed.

'Do I still get to keep Luca Cassini? I assume your gardener is not under suspicion for what happened in the chapel. Given your low opinion of that young man, I imagine he is no use in a murder case, even one so quickly solved.'

'The boy's all yours,' the captain said, then answered the ringing phone.

In the bathroom he stepped out of his clothes with a rigorous, childlike precision, placed them in a tidy heap, then stepped inside the shower and ran the water.

He found a small bar of soap, rubbed it all over, ran it under his fingernails, did his best to get rid of the blood there. Smeared some of her sweet-smelling shampoo on his hair, put his head beneath the stream. The water was turning from lukewarm to cold but it didn't matter. He was hard, the kind of insane, uncontrollable hardness that stole away his mind. Then the cold turned icy and still the hardness stayed. So he got out, dried himself, kept the dead man's towel round him, and carried his pile of clothes back into the bedroom.

She was still on the mattress, looking as if she were sleeping. A hairdryer was beside the bed. He could smell the hot plastic. Smell her too – warm hair, perfume, skin, and something strong and physical he didn't want to think about.

Chavah had got dressed while he was in the bathroom. A long, flowing maroon skirt. A thick sweater, green covered with flowers, threadbare at the elbows.

'Get dressed.' She pointed to the black shirt, sweater and jeans at the foot of the bed. 'Don't worry. I won't watch.'

He snatched at the clothes, fought with them and the towel to maintain some modesty.

She didn't move. Just looked at him, hands behind her head, smirking, emerald eyes bright, amused.

'What's your real name?'

He didn't answer.

'Is this what you want? You go and kill someone. Then show me what you've done, like a cat bringing back a mouse?'

Eyes wide open, smart and incisive, as if they could see through everything. Green and old and knowing.

Her hand went out and touched him over the cheap cotton fabric of the towel. 'What are you then? A saint with a hard-on?'

'Just a man.'

'Man enough?' she asked.

'I killed that bastard, didn't I?'

'It's something, I guess,' Chavah Efron said, got up off the bed and pushed it back towards the window; one single, strong movement.

The floorboards beneath looked old and loose. He could make something out between the cracks. Glinting in the daylight.

'We've work to do, before they come,' she said. 'Things to hide. Stories to concoct . . .'

She opened the bottom clothes drawer, took out a crowbar, eased the edge beneath the nearest, loosest plank. Four more came up as she worked at them. The weapons and the dope in the next room were nothing next to this. Five machine guns. Ammunition belts full and ready to be used. Bayonets and military daggers. Long, black semi-automatics. More plastic bags full of dun brown material.

An armoury for war. And, rolled up in the corner, what looked like a crimson flag.

As he stood there, watching, trying to think, she reached in, took hold of the fabric, unfurled it.

'You hate them, just as we did. You want to do something too. I see it in your face. I hear it in your voice.'

She got up, came close.

'There are so many things I could teach you.'

That laugh again; he was starting to be fascinated by the strength and determination inside her hard, foreign voice.

'They never knew about me. I'm American. A hippie. A Jew. The rest they think are dead. Like Ari, who was rash and foolish and didn't do as he was told. Dead or safe in jail.'

The red flag rolled to the floor. He looked at the icon there, and the words.

'Just me left now. Struggling and alone.'

She was so close he could smell the sweetness of her breath.

'Brigate Rosse', the flag said, in crude, blocky writing, one word about a circle and a star, one word beneath.

The Red Brigades. They'd murdered politicians and industrialists up and down Italy for more than a decade. A force for chaos and violence and retribution. Death and vengeance inflicted on the idle rich and the corrupt political classes who supported them.

'Alone,' she said, her warm, damp breath in his ear. 'And then along you come.'

'I'm not—'

'You're what I make you,' she cut in. Then reached into the store of weapons, took out a shotgun and a belt full of shells. 'We'll move these to the wood now. The gear from the other room. Before they come—'

'I'm not . . .' he began again.

She marched up to him, thrust the weapon in his face.

Silence.

Closer again. She reached up and kissed him on his cold cheek. Damp lips against his skin. Then the slowest, gentlest touch.

'You're not a man who thrives on choices,' she whispered. 'I've saved you from that. Be grateful. Now do as you're told.'

'We can run,' he said, hoping.

She stood in front of him, reached up and stroked the black wool of his sweater.

'Not yet.'

Luca Cassini looked pleased he was still assigned to work with Fratelli and Julia. Less so when the older man told him what he wanted.

'You're trying to get me in trouble,' he complained as they stood huddled together in the station corridor, ignored by all who passed.

'No,' Fratelli insisted. 'I intend to salvage your career.'

Cassini folded his big arms and said, 'I'm not so sure about that . . .'

'Luca.' Fratelli gently took his elbow. Julia smiled at the tall, muscular young man. This made him blush. 'There's a murder case here. Are you a part of it?'

'You know the answer to that already.'

'And why?'

He didn't say a word.

'Because they don't want you around. They . . .' Fratelli shrugged. He didn't like saying this. 'They don't think you've got what it takes. Know something? Come April when those newfangled assessments they love so much arrive . . . you'll be out of here. Looking for a job. Do you doubt me?'

'I'll get something. They never gave me a chance.'

'That's their loss more than yours.' A pat on the arm, that seductive smile. 'But I'm giving you one now. Go back into the detectives' office. Find out what you can about the Tornabuoni case. Make a little small talk. Be inquisitive.' He smiled at the young man. 'Curiosity is the greater part of being an investigative officer, you know. Not rules and procedures, custom and practice. This!'

Fratelli tapped the side of his head. Cassini stared at the older man's white hair and looked downcast.

'What's wrong?' Fratelli asked.

'You, Pino. A lot wrong there, I reckon.'

Julia looked at the floor.

Fratelli laughed. 'A man who speaks his mind,' he declared, and slapped Cassini on the shoulder. 'If I was still running a team here you'd be on it and that's the truth. But I'm not. So the only friends you have are Julia and me, the mad *maresciallo*.'

'I didn't say you were mad. I said you were sick.'

'Whichever it is, I'm the only one making you an offer. Will you do it?'

Cassini shook his head. 'I don't deserve the sack.'

'You don't,' Julia agreed.

'How would you know?'

'Julia has friends in the English constabulary,' Fratelli chipped in. 'She's knowledgeable about these matters. Haven't you noticed?'

Cassini glared at them.

'And if anything's been typed up,' Fratelli added. 'Get a photocopy.'

'I can't do that.'

'Tell them it's for Marrone or something. Improvise, Luca. Be bold . . .'

'It's stealing.'

Fratelli tilted his head to one side and fixed him with a look that said: disappointed. 'This is why they don't want you. No spirit. No initiative.'

Cassini prodded him in the chest with a fat forefinger. 'My granddad told me about you. Last night. He said you were a shit-stirring troublemaker.'

'How is he? Mellowed in retirement, I gather.'

The young officer chuckled at that. 'He also said you were the best detective they ever had. Not that they appreciated it most of the time. Mainly because you were such a pain in the arse.'

'Very perceptive of him. I won't argue.'

'Luca,' Julia interrupted, taking the young officer's other arm.

'You mustn't do anything you don't want. If it bothers you at all
. . . about what might happen . . .'

Cassini shook his head. 'You two are a right pair, aren't you?
Him pushing me on. You making like I'm gutless if I don't do it.'

He glanced down the corridor, back to towards the incident room
where the murder case was being assembled.

Julia smiled at him and winked.

'And then?' Cassini asked.

'Then you meet us at the *lampredotto* stall in the central market
one hour from now. Where I will buy you as many panini as you
wish. Oh.' Fratelli scribbled something else on his pad and passed
it over. 'And check out one small detail too. It's an old record. No
one will argue there.'

The young officer nodded. *Lampredotto*. He seemed to like that
idea. 'Give me an hour,' he said, and walked back towards the offices.

Sandro Soderini sat at his desk in the Palazzo Vecchio listening to
the steady tramp of tourists work their way through the building. It
was approaching midday. Outside, in the corridors of the council
offices, the initial shock over Vanni Tornabuoni's murder was giving
way to a sense of grief and outrage. These things weren't supposed
to happen. Especially, thought Soderini, to someone in such an
elevated and privileged position.

After putting out a statement of condolence to Tornabuoni's
mother, an elderly widow living on Capri, he'd stopped all incoming
phone calls, pulled down the blinds, stayed in the dark trying to
think. In truth, he hadn't much liked the man. Tornabuoni was one
more aristocrat he'd inherited, a foppish pseudo-intellectual in need
of a job. He'd worn the right suits, made appropriate speeches, fawned
when demanded, crawled when told. Then wisely left the real work
in the culture department to the civil servants beneath him, most of
whom treated their director with quiet, unamused contempt.

Lightly informed delegation from on high. That was the way
things happened in Florence. Soderini possessed a detailed and
informed sense of history from his former profession as a lecturer
at the university. He appreciated all the many forms of government
that had been tried in the city over the centuries, from the Signoria
and the Twelve Good Men, the Sixteen Gonfaloniers and the Great
Council of his ancestor's day, to the *soi-disant* oligarchy of the
Medici, which was a monarchy in all but name. Then, much later,

came the brutal fascist tyranny of Mussolini. Life was simpler still in 1986. A form of benevolent dictatorship had quietly come to descend upon Florence; one founded through the certain knowledge the majority would vote a predictable way whatever the policies or name on the ballot paper. Once those crosses confirmed the status quo, power passed from broker to broker, through private meetings and conclaves, clubs and associations, mutual dependencies and the occasional exchange of hard cash.

It was a ritual, like much of life in Tuscany. A perpetual dance of money and influence, patronage and persuasion. Life and death. The seat of mayor had been handed on to him by a relative, a rich and corrupt uncle who, during the war, had quietly sided with the Fascists, secretly sitting behind Mussolini as he took tea with Hitler on the newly built lookout of the Ponte Vecchio while publicly proclaiming himself to be above politics, dedicated to the people of the city alone.

This masquerade was uncommon only in that it was opaque. Most such deceits were transparent, performed with a nod and a knowing wink. The Florentines were a proud and occasionally unruly people, too worldly wise to expect any direct, controlling voice in their own affairs. Nevertheless, it was important not to flaunt such impotence in the faces of the ordinary men and women who tramped the cobbled streets and went to work in offices and fashion houses, leather workshops and tourist restaurants. Soderini was groomed to be mayor by way of birth. So he too had found himself introduced at an early age into the clubs and secret societies, the brotherhoods and lodges through which an elite of aristocrats, industrialists, financiers, church officials and the occasional crook kept their fingers tight on the windpipe of the nation.

Most were tedious. The Brigata Spendereccia, when he found the time for it, rarely.

Now Vanni Tornabuoni, one of its most ardent supporters, was dead. Found murdered in the most extraordinary and public circumstances one day before the group was due to meet again. This was not simply wrong. It was offensive. Impudent.

Soderini stared at the paintings around him, the gilt furniture, the rich desk with its walnut veneer and the globe in the corner, commissioned by Lorenzo the Magnificent. He was mayor of Florence, duke in all but name. Heir to the Medici and those who went before, all of whom had walked down the Vasari Corridor for one reason or another, whether to find solace and protection behind the rusticated fortress walls of the Pitti Palace or, in recent times, for more pleasurable reasons.

This city belonged to him and he was not to be cowed.

Caution was in order, however. He picked up the phone, called Marrone's private number in the Carabinieri *stazione* in Ognissanti, and demanded the dour captain give him a report on the case.

It was brief and uninformative. No more than Soderini might have gleaned from the news.

'When will you charge the man? The gardener?' Soderini demanded.

There was a silence on the line. Then Marrone cleared his throat and said, 'This is a legal matter now. It's for the magistrate to judge how we proceed. Not me.' That pause again. 'Not you.'

'Don't tell me my job, Marrone,' Soderini barked back at him. 'I put you in that seat. What I give today I may take away tomorrow.'

The silence again then, 'I can tell you no more than I've said. Which went beyond what is proper, I might add.'

'This gardener? I hear he was Tornabuoni's lover.'

'That much is on the radio, I believe.'

'If everyone Tornabuoni slept with starts talking to the gutter press, we'll have a pretty picture soon. Put an end to this. Drag this sorry layabout into court and silence all speculation. I want no more adverse publicity. About this or that other matter.'

'What other matter might that be?'

'Rovezzano. Don't play clever with me. You're not up to it. We've got reporters from Rome sniffing at our door already. Don't give them dog shit to chase. They thrive on it. Feed them and they'll never leave.'

'Sir—'

'Florence is a piece of theatre, Marrone. I want nothing that detracts from the show. Those Americans with their dollars do not come here for this filth. If they find it they'll be gone, to Venice or Rome, and no one wants that.'

'I'm an officer of the Carabinieri,' Marrone replied. 'Not the tourist board. I have a man in custody suspected of murder. It may be we will charge him before the night is out.'

'Does he admit it?'

'No,' Marrone replied with some reluctance.

Soderini hesitated for a moment then asked, 'Did he do it?'

This brought the longest silence of all, one that Sandro Soderini found informative. It never came to a close, either. He was forced to continue himself.

'Your lack of cooperation in this matter is noted, Marrone. I find your intransigence offensive and ungrateful.'

'I'm an officer of the Carabinieri,' the man repeated. 'My duty is to the law, and to finding and prosecuting Tornabuoni's murderer.'

'Your duty is to the city and to me!'

These angry tones echoed around the room. The noise sounded strange to him. He was not a man given to shouting.

'Is there anything else?' Marrone wondered.

'As you know,' Soderini said, 'there's a meeting planned for tomorrow night.'

'Surely not now . . .'

'It's fixed.'

'Is that wise?'

'I judge it so. Vanni Tornabuoni was one of my kind. I knew the man and you didn't. This is what he would have wanted.'

Was that true? Soderini wondered. No. It was the kind of ridiculous nonsense politicians were forced to say in such circumstances. No one knew what the dead might say. Or desire. Such things were beyond them.

'I can't rule out the possibility that Tornabuoni's private life . . . his night-time activities contributed somehow to his death,' Marrone told him.

'We don't have gardeners at our gatherings. No fear on that score.'

'For the sake of decency—'

'I do not need lectures on that subject from a captain of the Carabinieri whose every step up the ladder has been dependent upon our patronage.'

'Out of common sense then!'

'You know what I require, Marrone. Keep your men away from our business the way you're supposed to. Throw this gardener of yours around the cell a little. Make him talk. He's your man. I'm confident of it. Then bury this story as surely as we'll bury Tornabuoni in a day or two.'

'And how are you sure, Mr Mayor?'

Soderini thought for a moment, then said, 'Vanni was a squalid little animal at heart. It was his idea of fun to dally with scum like that. He brought this end upon himself. We'll mourn him, then return to our business.' In his mind's eye he could see the cavern already; the lights, the food, the entertainment. A new guest too, from England. There would be a brief note of grief. And then the riotous wake. 'Make sure you go about yours.'

He put down the phone before the Carabinieri officer could say another word. The gardener. Tornabuoni would sleep with anything that moved, man or woman. He disappeared to Rome and Naples some weekends and came back drained, his face pale from whatever dope he'd consumed alongside the debaucheries. Sandro Soderini was above this kind of behaviour, such vile and physical company. This could not happen to him.

All the same . . . He got up and walked to the door of his office and turned the key. Then he went back to the desk and unlocked the private drawer at the bottom, the one with the reinforced metal lining, a kind of small, hidden safe.

The letters were there in cheap envelopes, the messages scrawled in blue biro. Each rising in hysterical tone. All addressed to the sprawling house in the Via Maggio in Oltrarno where he lived alone, equidistant between the goldsmiths of the Ponte Vecchio and the bums of Santo Spirito. It was a property that had been in the hands of the Soderini for three centuries; a handsome mansion, the exterior etched in dark, ornate frescoes that made it stand out among the plainer properties around.

His private fortress, his place of safety.

When the first envelope had dropped through the door he'd laughed. The words were so strange, so ridiculous. When the fourth arrived he'd sat brooding alone, wondering what these cryptic messages meant, what kind of man might have sent them.

The first read, 'The Signoria must make a law against the dreadful vice of sodomy. Make a law against it! One that shows no mercy, so that the beasts who behave so are stoned and burned.'

The next: 'You must ban games and taverns and public entertainments, the sordid nature of women's dress, everything harmful to the health of the soul. Everyone must live for God and not the world.'

The third: 'I cannot tell you everything I feel inside because you are too proud and indisposed to hear it. Oh! If you knew all you'd see that I am like a boiling vessel of liquid sealed up, bubbling but unable to escape! There are so many locked-up secrets behind our walls, Soderini, Florence would not believe them! Yet you know . . . You . . .'

The last was a threat, plain and forceful. He read it again and found it impossible to laugh, as he had when, the previous Saturday, it landed through his letterbox, delivered by hand, not the postal service.

'I shall spill flood waters upon the earth. You shall drown in them, and in that torrent shall flow your blood.'

All four were bastardized Savonarola. Most had been adapted from the Haggai sermons the fanatical friar had given from the pulpit of the Duomo in his Advent sermon of 14 December 1494, when the city was still in thrall to his theatrical power of speech, and working its way towards the purges that would lead, first, to the bonfire of the vanities, then, a few years later, to the violent downfall of the monk from San Marco himself.

'A lunatic,' Soderini murmured.

But did gardeners read the sermons of a fanatical fifteenth-century monk?

He reached further into the drawer and retrieved the compact Beretta semiautomatic pistol he'd got from Marrone, a spare in the Carabinieri armoury. It was thirty years since Soderini had done his national service, spending a year as a privileged, idle officer in the leisurely barracks in Sicily his mother had fixed for him – chasing women, mostly; building links with useful criminals and avoiding the odd irate husband.

He still knew how to use a gun.

The stall in the central market was called Nerbone. It had been there, the sign said, since 1874. Judging by some of the old men shuffling at the counter, getting stuck into panini of tripe and *lampredotto* and other mysterious pieces of meat, so had much of its clientele.

Cassini turned up on time, ordered a bowl of tomato and potato soup called Pappa al Pomodoro, a tripe panino and a can of Coke. He had a blue document folder underneath his arm and an air of happy release about him.

'Aren't you having something?' he asked, his mouth full.

'We're fine,' Fratelli responded immediately. 'Watching you eat, Luca, is like . . . eating yourself.'

'No argument there,' Julia declared, then retrieved the blue folder from beneath Cassini's arm.

Fratelli reached over and spread out the photocopied papers on the glass counter of the stall.

'Are they going to charge the gardener?' he asked Cassini.

'Not yet. The bloke isn't coughing to anything.' The young officer twirled a finger around his ear. 'Funny in the head, they said. Babbling mad stuff.'

'What kind of mad stuff?'

'Rubbish.'

Fratelli groaned. 'You must learn to be precise. Did the gardener see anyone?'

Cassini laughed out loud, the criticism bouncing off him as if it counted for nothing.

'He said he saw a monk hanging round the night old Vanni went missing. I ask you! A monk! How many of them do you get up in Bellosguardo?'

Julia Wellbeloved caught Fratelli's eye.

'A monk?' she repeated.

Fratelli went back to the documents and ran through them, a quick finger ticking off each line.

'As I thought,' he announced when he'd finished.

They waited. Nothing.

'As you thought, what?' Julia wanted to know.

Fratelli glanced around. They were out of earshot of Nerbone's customers. It was safe to talk. She thought he looked paler than usual this morning, strained and perhaps in pain. His tics – fiddling with his hair, scratching his cheek – were more marked.

'The gardener. It's ridiculous . . .' He took a sip of his glass of fizzy water. 'Walter must know this too. Why's he playing these games?'

'They're talking to the lawyers about charging him,' Cassini said. 'They don't think it's ridiculous.'

'Luca, Luca, Luca . . .' Fratelli sighed, shaking his head. 'Julia. You too. Listen to me. Think about this.'

They came closer.

'Tornabuoni was supposed to meet Julia in the Pitti Palace, yesterday morning. He never came in to work. So we may presume he was taken before that. Some time during the previous night. Last night his head appears in the Loggia dei Lanzi. It takes a long time to identify the man, naturally. A severed head does not look like a living one, I suppose. Tornabuoni is a bachelor. He has a bohemian lifestyle. No one seems much surprised when he fails to turn up at work, if one can consider what he did to be work. Some might argue—'

'Pino,' Julia began.

'Bear with me. He's taken two nights ago. Murdered. Decapitated.· Finally, we work our way round to his mansion in Bellosguardo in the early hours of this morning. And what do we find? The gardener. One of his several lovers. Weeping by the side of his body.'

Cassini polished off his sandwich. 'So?' the young officer wondered.

'So why would the gardener still be there if he killed Tornabuoni?' Julia said before Fratelli could speak. It was obvious when she thought about it. 'After all that time?' She stole a corner of Cassini's bread. 'Is that what a murderer would do? Cut off someone's head, drive into the city to hang it somewhere public, then go back to sob by the body?'

She shrugged. 'Doesn't sound right to me.'

Pino Fratelli beamed at her.

'Well?' she asked. 'Did I get something wrong?'

'Not a thing.' Fratelli turned to Cassini. 'Listen to me, Luca. I was the detective the *stazione* turned to when a murder case came in. I've talked to, joked with and jailed more homicidal brutes than you're likely to encounter in a lifetime.'

'Show-off,' Cassini threw back at him.

'No. I'm telling you something from experience, and experience is the way we learn in this business, not through classes in cadet school. Sooner or later, almost every murderer is appalled by what he or she has done. They wish to rationalize it. Excuse it. To bury it, more than anything. They don't want that reminder of their deeds around them, that bloody picture in their heads. Why do you think so many corpses end up in woods or rivers? Even the most hardened of killers is aware they've done something shameful, however much they seek to justify the act. They carry the guilt around with them, every waking moment. Why make it more real, more painful, by leaving the evidence so visible a day, a day and a half after they've killed?'

'Quite,' said Julia. 'It doesn't add up.'

'As you knew instinctively.' Fratelli raised his glass of water. '*Salute.*'

'They did find this chap with Tornabuoni's body, though,' Cassini pointed out. 'And he blurted out that they were . . .' The young man blushed. 'You know . . .'

'Were what?' Julia asked, determined to get him to say it.

'You know . . . Doing it,' he grumbled.

'Thanks to the Napoleonic Code, homosexuality hasn't been a crime in Italy since reunification more than one hundred and twenty years ago,' Fratelli pointed out. 'Except to the Catholic Church, and happily the Pope has finally found better things to occupy him than running our judicial system. The fact that Tornabuoni and his gardener are queer—'

'Is relevant,' Julia interrupted.

Fratelli stared at her, then raised a single grey eyebrow. 'How?' he demanded.

'I don't know. It has to be. You said yourself, the man who defaced those frescoes in the Brancacci feared women.'

Fratelli put a finger to his cheek and said, quietly, 'Actually, I said he hated them. But I prefer your word.'

'Well.' She shrugged. 'If you felt like that about women, perhaps you'd have the same loathing for someone who was gay. Both must have a reason, I imagine. Must stem from something . . .'

She couldn't get Fratelli's story about his wife out of her head.

'Something horrible,' Julia whispered, looking at him.

She wondered about that dreadful night two decades before when the chill and filthy waters of the Arno rose to swamp the city. In the river's icy embrace, Pino Fratelli's beloved wife died somehow. Fratelli said himself he felt the poison in his own head stemmed from burying the truth of that grim event deep inside himself. Was it possible the man they sought was shaped by a similar grief? Good and evil, right and wrong seemed difficult to discern sometimes. Life was not like those frescoes in the Brancacci, divided neatly and cleanly between light and dark. Most of us lived in the middle; in the grey, smudged area, swamped by a little of each. Fratelli more than most, and he knew it.

'I remain unconvinced,' he said, paying for Cassini's food, not returning her gaze. 'Something prompted this act. Something recent. There's also a very practical matter before us. A visible reason why this cannot be as simple as Marrone would have us believe.'

'Which is?' Cassini asked.

'The blood. Where is it?'

Fratelli placed on the counter a set of photocopied photographs. Even in black and white, rendered crude by the process, she found them so deeply disturbing she had to turn away. A stiff, headless corpse lay by a small greenhouse on a patch of lawn next to a neatly tended vegetable patch, arms outstretched, legs akimbo. He wore what appeared to be elegant pyjamas – silk, perhaps. Uniformed Carabinieri bustled round looking variously bored or disgusted. There was a trail of blood across the vegetables, spattered on the leaves of cabbage and leeks and cavolo nero.

The young officer came in close, interested suddenly. Luca Cassini so desperately wanted to learn.

'And where's the weapon?' Fratelli asked.

'Haven't found it yet,' Cassini said. 'Maybe he chucked it somewhere when he brought the head into town.'

Fratelli's right forefinger stabbed at the images. 'Why throw away something like that if you intend to stay with the body till you're found? It makes no sense.'

'Cutting someone's head off makes no sense, Pino,' Julia said gently.

'Vanni,' Fratelli went on. 'Giovanni, as he was christened.' He eyed Julia Wellbeloved. 'Who's the patron saint of Florence?'

'I've no idea,' she replied, astonished by the question.

'Everybody knows that!' Cassini cried, laughing.

'I'm not religious, Luca. I'm not from Florence. I've no—'

'San Giovanni Battista!' Cassini said.

John the Baptist. He was everywhere. On canvas in the Uffizi, carved from stone in the Duomo. San Giovanni Decollato. Murdered on the whim of Salome, his head brought to her on a silver platter.

'That's a stretch,' she complained. 'What about that cockerel and Tornabuoni's family crest? You don't like it when I see something you don't.'

'Nothing to see,' Fratelli said with a shrug. 'Merely an interesting coincidence. If it's our man from the Brancacci we're sure he knows his scriptures. Let's stick to the facts for the moment. Vanni Tornabuoni wasn't murdered in the garden where he was found. He was killed elsewhere and his body returned to his mansion in order to allow his killer to remain free. And a gardener . . .'

Fratelli stopped, frowning at something. Cassini, keen as ever, said, 'Well?'

'Men often murder according to their profession, Luca. When we have more time I will take you through the educational case of the butcher of Scandicci and his unusual recipe for *finocchiona*. I would expect a man who works the land to use the tools of his trade. A spade, a mallet. To bludgeon and then to bury. Not to decapitate. Besides, you read the initial autopsy. Julia, take a look.'

He picked up the photocopied sheet and handed it to her. 'Tell me what stands out,' he ordered.

They waited as she read through the document, line by line.

'Oh,' she whispered.

'Oh what?' Fratelli asked.

'He was shot.'

The older man stared at the younger. The expression in his eyes was clear: why didn't you mention this?

'I read that,' Cassini objected.

'And?' Fratelli said.

'And he was shot. Someone murdered him. I don't get . . .'

'Don't you normally behead people in order to kill them?' Julia said. 'I mean really, Luca. Isn't that very, very odd? Seems so to me. He's either rubbing it in. Or . . .'

'Or?' Fratelli wondered.

'Or frightened somehow. Ashamed.'

'Suppose,' Cassini grumbled.

'To behead a living man,' Fratelli added, 'is a dreadful thing. To defile the corpse of a murdered one is . . . quite extraordinary. Didn't he have the courage to kill him that way outright? Does this indicate some reticence – guilt, even – on his part?'

'You can't know that, Pino,' she said.

'Of course not. But we can make intelligent guesses. Also, we must ask ourselves what kind of man would possess the physical strength to commit such a terrible act. Most murders are simple, bloody affairs. A knife, a gun, a flurry of fists. Butchering a corpse like that requires . . .'

His eyes strayed behind the counter where another bowl of grey meat was being ladled on to a split panino.

'A farmer. A slaughterhouse worker. A man who works with meat.'

He was so sure of himself it seemed pointless to argue.

'To return to my original point,' Fratelli added. They waited. 'Blood. Tornabuoni was a tall man, of average build. I've seen him myself, at meetings. I would estimate his weight at perhaps seventy kilos. That's about . . .' He counted on his fingers. 'One hundred and sixty of your English pounds.'

'Wait a minute . . .' Julia began.

'Patience.' He waved her into silence. 'As any homicide detective worth his or her salt knows the volume of blood in a healthy person is around one eleventh of their body weight. Or something like four point seven litres, on average.'

He picked up the plastic bottle of water on the counter.

'That's almost five of these. To sever the neck involves cutting the carotid artery, not to mention much else. We've all seen Cellini's statue. That thug knew what a decapitated man looked like . . .'

He stabbed his finger on the photo from the garden and said, 'Well?'

Luca Cassini finished his panino and said, through a half-full mouth, 'Not enough, boss. Nowhere near.'

'Quite,' Fratelli agreed. 'That's why he waited until nine in the evening in the loggia. He had Tornabuoni's body in his vehicle and couldn't return it to the man's home until later for safety. Any arguments?'

Not a word.

Then Luca said, 'I suppose you're right about him being strong too.'

Fratelli waited. When there was nothing more he asked, 'Because?'

'He might have been a pansy, but he wasn't a pushover. He had form, that Tornabuoni. Kind of.'

Another mouthful of guts and bread. Still they waited.

'What do you mean?' Julia asked.

'I mean they only pulled him over that murder last week. Out in Rovezzano. The weirdo hippie we found shot. You remember, Pino? I know you're not on the job. But I mean . . . how many murders do we get? A couple in two weeks. It's like New York here. Quite exciting really . . .'

'What murder?' Fratelli asked, a little too loudly.

People were looking. He took Cassini's arm, dragged him towards the corner of the market, Julia close behind, and whispered, 'What murder?'

'Some hippie bloke called Aristide Greco. Came from Calabria. Sounds a bit dodgy if you ask me. Funny old business. Drugs, probably. Don't know why they pulled in Tornabuoni but he was out again like a shot. Mistaken identity. I mean, if it wasn't, they'd be sending someone out to the dead bloke's farm, wouldn't they?'

'And they're not?' Fratelli asked.

Cassini grinned. 'They've got their man, haven't they? Why bother?'

'I don't suppose,' Julia said, 'you'd happen to have the papers on that, would you?'

Luca chuckled. Then he reached into his blue folder and pulled out a few sheets of paper stapled together.

'I'm not daft, you know. I just wanted to see your faces . . .'

Fratelli snatched them from his hand. 'Three sheets? Is that it?'

'Hippie from Calabria,' Cassini repeated. 'Shot dead, left in a ditch. Murder squad seemed to think our dead mate Vanni had something to do with it. Then it turned out he didn't . . .'

'How do they know that?' Fratelli demanded. 'What cleared Tornabuoni?'

Cassini shuffled from one big foot to the other, uncomfortable.

'Search me. They thought they found something at the scene that was Tornabuoni's. Or supposed to be. And then he was out of the *stazione*, free as a bird.' A pause. 'Maybe he had an alibi.'

'Maybe?' Julia asked.

'I don't know, OK! I stuck my neck on the line for you, Pino. But I've got my limits. Sod this. I need a pee.'

He wandered off to the toilets, looking miserable.

'What was that about?' Julia asked when Luca was out of earshot.

'Probably nothing,' Fratelli said. 'There's an address for the dead man here. It said he lived on a farm with his American girlfriend. Out near Fiesole. Not far from Rovezzano where he was shot.'

She knew what he was thinking and it worried her. 'Marrone said you two could work on the vandalism in the Brancacci. Nothing more.'

Fratelli looked around the busy market hall. 'Do you see Walter here?'

'No, but . . .'

'Good. Let's get Luca to take us for a drive. You need some country air, young lady. You're looking terribly pale.'

The farm lay on a slope so steep the wizened olive trees clung to the rocky grass, rising at a diagonal from the dun earth. At the top of the hill lay a shallow indentation like a crater, full of thorny bushes and tangled weeds dying back for the winter. A narrow path led through the olives. She let the dog off the lead. The animal followed them there and back, a route it knew.

No words. No objections. He did what she said. Had no choice. So between them they spent the best part of two hours ferrying dope and guns, ammunition and explosives, boxes of fuses and things he didn't understand, up into the crater, followed by the happy, yapping dog, as if this was all a game. When everything was moved they covered the crates and dumps of weapons with blue plastic crop-gathering sheets from the barn, then threw broken branches across the top.

It wouldn't fool anyone if they looked hard. But there was so much. Enough for a small war. The last of the Red Brigades' weapons from Tuscany, she said.

When they had finished, they stood together on the rim of the indentation, looking at the broken branches and the blue plastic peeking underneath.

'What's your real name?' she asked.

He didn't answer. He was staring at his wrist. The brambles had caught him along the way. Deep scratches, blood, a sharp wound turning scabby. She looked at him, took out a tissue, wiped the dirt away.

'You need to wash that,' she said. 'You need a plaster on it. Come on . . .'

'We could run,' he said again.

She smiled at him, laughed. Not so unkindly this time.

'We could run,' he repeated. 'Get in the van. Go somewhere. Anywhere.'

She shook her head, then went down the hill, back into the farmhouse. He followed her into the bedroom. Chavah Efron put a hand to his head. Two days now without shaving. The stubble was returning. On his face. On his scalp.

In a drawer she found a cheap electric razor.

'Just your face,' she said. 'Not your head. I want you to look different. Why do that anyway?'

He didn't answer.

'For God's sake, talk to me.'

She ran her fingers across his scalp. His body was shaking.

'My name is Aldo Pontecorvo,' he said in a low, calm voice. 'I'm thirty-seven years old and I come from Oltrarno. No one left there any more.'

'Someone must have really screwed you up.'

He glared at her and said, 'Your excuse?'

Laughter again. 'I don't have one. I was born like this.'

Her fingers ran across his cheeks, his chin, working the razor.

'There's a man I read about,' he said. 'They hated him. Burned him in the Piazza della Signoria. Long time ago.'

'They don't burn the people they hate any more. They shoot them and leave them in ditches. Then shrug their shoulders and walk away. We want the same thing, Aldo. Don't we?'

'I shall spill flood waters upon the earth,' he recited. 'You shall drown in them, and in that torrent shall flow your blood.'

'My blood?'

'Everyone's. In the end.'

She leaned against him, her hips against his thighs. Hands on his chest.

'Then we should make the most of the time we've got left.'

Fingers reaching. Inside the black woollen sweater. Rising. Curling. Twisting. Tempting.

He didn't move.

Then there was a sound outside. Tyres and a car door opening. A voice. Male. Crying her name.

The smile disappeared from her pretty dark face in an instant. 'Damn,' she said.

She looked around. Walked back on to the landing, reached up and pulled on the lanyard for an opening into the roof space. A ladder there. Steps.

'Best I can do,' she said, then walked back into the spare room, got a handgun they'd kept back, gave him the weapon and a box of shells. 'Get up there. Stay silent as a mouse. If I need you, I'll yell.'

'What is this place?' Fratelli asked, climbing out of the car. They came crammed into Cassini's rusty white Fiat Cinquecento. The young officer was too junior to be allowed use of a Carabinieri vehicle.

A black mongrel ran to the length of its chain and barked at them wildly. Straight away Luca made cooing noises, walked over, pulled a packet of sweets from his pocket, calmed the animal with one.

'You have unexpected talents, Luca,' Fratelli observed.

'My uncle Silvio's got an olive farm. Big press, too. We go round picking up crops for other people. You've got to deal with dogs. Fact of life.'

Gingerly, he tried to pat the animal on its head, then thought better of the idea.

'Now this is a place run by people who know nothing about farming,' he said confidently, looking round the fields and the ramshackle, muddy yard.

'You're sure of that?'

'Dead right I am. You townies think farms are just shit and graft. But with olives, let me tell you: everything needs to be neat and spick and span. Specially when it comes to cropping.'

Cassini pointed at the ancient, rusty tractor. 'Uncle Silvio reckons you can always tell a farmer by his machines. If you're doing a good job you've got lots to harvest. Can't do that with a load of old junk, can you? Proper tools pay for themselves.'

Fratelli nodded, pleased with the answer.

'It's just olives,' Julia said, coming to join them. 'Can you live on that?'

Cassini checked his notes. 'Says they were doing this newfangled organic thing. Maybe what you save on pesticide you make up for on price. I dunno.' He scratched his head. 'Looks a dump to me. Just the sort of place a hippie would dream about. Nature don't grow of its own accord, you know. It's what we make of it. I mean . . .'

He stopped. A woman was marching towards them from the door of the two-storey house, little more than a tumbledown cottage with peeling white walls and a roof that looked as if it needed tending.

She was about thirty, attractive and gypsy-like, with wayward, curly black hair, fierce eyes and a lined, tanned face. In spite of the cold she wore a long maroon skirt and a green jumper and wellington boots as she tramped through the mire. A shotgun was broken over her right arm. She looked as if she knew how to use it.

'Signora . . .' Fratelli began. Then he waved at Cassini, who pulled out his Carabinieri ID card.

'What do you want?'

'About your husband . . .'

Her stare stopped Fratelli as he spoke. The woman was looking at Luca Cassini's decrepit white Fiat.

'Where's your ID?' she asked, then nodded at Julia Wellbeloved. 'And hers?'

'These are discreet inquiries,' Fratelli said carefully. 'We don't want to make a fuss. Please. If we could go inside for a moment. And talk . . .'

He took a step towards her. She moved back and in a single, swift movement closed the shotgun, held it in her hands, barrel to the ground.

'All this time you bastards have waited. You do nothing about Ari. And then you come to make . . .' Her face creased with sour anger. 'Discreet inquiries.'

'We interviewed you in the *stazione*, didn't we?' Cassini objected. 'You didn't say much there. I mean . . . if we had something to go on.'

'My husband goes out to work and then winds up dead in a ditch. You know more about this than I do.'

'I doubt that,' Fratelli intervened. 'Perhaps something's occurred to you since.'

'Such as what?'

'Such as did he know a man called Giovanni Tornabuoni?' Julia asked.

'Is he a farmer?'

'Not exactly.'

She shook her head.

'Ari never mentioned anyone like that. No. Who is he?'

Fratelli smiled at her. Kept looking round the yard.

'There's a nasty rumour abroad that your husband was involved in drugs, Signora. It would be very useful if we could take a look around. Disprove such a thing . . .'

'Did this Tornabuoni deal in drugs?'

'Maybe bought them,' Cassini grumbled.

She didn't move. 'Why are you here? Where are your papers? I see only one ID and that's for a junior officer.'

'We're trying to work out who killed him!' Cassini snapped.

'Here? I'm struggling to eke a living out of this place. On my own. I don't need this shit.'

Pino Fratelli took out a large, clean handkerchief and blew his nose, once again looked round the little farm with its crippled olive trees, its silent, watchful dog, the dilapidated cottage.

'Will you stay?' he asked. 'It's a lot of work for two people to run a farm. Even a little place. Just one of you . . .'

'What I do is my business. Not yours.'

The shotgun waved at him, then the car.

'If you've nothing to tell me,' she said, 'you'd best go.'

'Of course,' Fratelli agreed. He gestured to Julia and Luca Cassini, who seemed surprised that he deferred so easily. 'I'm sorry if we disturbed you. It's an unfortunate habit of ours, I'm afraid.'

He smiled, took Cassini's notes, looked at them. She seemed puzzled.

'Signora Efron. An unusual name. Is there anything you wish to ask us?'

A moment of uncertainty between them. No words.

'Get out of here,' she said.

Fratelli packed the notebook into his jacket. 'I apologize again. Good afternoon.'

Then he walked back to the car and waited for Cassini to get behind the wheel, Julia to climb into the back. They set off down the stony track, towards Fiesole.

'Your radio, Luca,' Fratelli said, holding out his hand.

Cassini passed it over. 'Useless round here. Won't get a signal until we're nearer home.'

'Stop at the first phone box we find, then.'

'Won't be till Fiesole. Is that a good idea? Should we hang around?'

Fratelli stared at him as the car bounced down the rough lane, then emerged on to the narrow single-track asphalt road towards the town.

'What makes you ask that?' he wanted to know.

'You spooked that woman, Pino. Julia?'

'You spooked him,' she agreed from the back.

'I reckon she's probably planning to scarper right now,' Cassini added.

'Possibly. Find me that phone box.'

'That woman's going to hop it!' Cassini cried.

'She didn't kill her husband, Luca. Or break into the Brancacci and deface those paintings. We seek a man for those things.'

'All the same . . .' Julia chipped in.

'She's a foreigner. No money. Only a beat-up van that doesn't look as if it would make it much beyond the autostrada. If she flees, even Walter's idiot detectives from this morning could find her. Chavah Efron in herself is of little importance . . .'

The two of them grumbled at that.

'Oh!' Fratelli cried. 'So now I must provide proof. No. You shall do it. I wish each of you to tell me one thing you learned during that exchange, please.'

'Are we on a bloody training course then?' Luca Cassini demanded.

'Yes. You first.'

'She'd no intention of letting us set foot in that house. I know that.'

Fratelli grunted, 'Pah!'

'What do you mean, "Pah"?'

'We could have got into the house if I'd pushed it. She just didn't want us there. Anywhere on the farm. Good place to hide things, by the way. Perfect, if you ask me. Julia!'

'That woman was lying through her teeth. It was quite obvious.'

Fratelli rubbed his eyes and sighed.

'Don't you dare say "pah" to me,' she added.

'I'll do my best but really . . . of course she lied to us. She's a criminal of some kind. We're the people who are supposed to apprehend her. What do you expect? An instant confession? Even the average innocent citizen lies to us as a matter of course. The fact someone is less than honest tells us absolutely nothing—'

'We should have insisted,' Cassini broke in.

'We couldn't!' Fratelli barked. 'You're a junior officer attached to a vandalism case. One that, for Walter Marrone, has nothing to do with a two-week-old murder. Indeed, so convinced is he of that fact, he expressly forbade me to go near anything remotely connected to it.'

'Oh, thanks for telling me that now!'

'As if you hadn't guessed. Don't play the fool with me, boy. I know that's nonsense. Had we barged in there and found nothing, Walter Marrone would have had your badge. And probably thrown Julia and me in jail for a day or two to boot. We'd no warrant, no accreditation, no legal right to question that woman at all. I think she knew.'

He patted Cassini's shoulder, then turned to look at Julia in the back seat. 'I don't intend to allow my personal obsessions to affect your lives or careers.'

'They have done already, thank you,' she observed.

He didn't respond to that. The car was winding down a steep hill back to the little town of Fiesole. There would surely be a phone box soon.

'So what should we have noticed?' Cassini wondered.

'Her husband was murdered two weeks ago,' Fratelli repeated. 'She's aware we've made no progress, have no clue as to who the perpetrator might be. Which is, one might add, very much the case.'

He glanced at both of them then asked, 'Well?'

'Why wouldn't she ask something?' Cassini said with a big, wide grin. 'I mean . . . his wife . . . why wouldn't she say . . . how are you doing? Why the bloody hell don't you have the bastard in a cell right now?'

'Because she knows who killed him,' Julia Wellbeloved said in a quiet, firm voice.

'The culprit being Tornabuoni,' Fratelli added, beaming at both of them. 'Very good. One other thing there was worthy of note too. Anyone?'

They were silent.

'Mud,' Fratelli declared, checking his watch. 'Words are all well and good, but you must learn to use your eyes too. Look at things. Consider the mud. Chavah Efron is a sturdy, active woman but small in stature. Even her boots were quite small. Say a size thirty-eight.'

He glanced at Julia, then at Cassini behind the wheel. 'She didn't object when I said she was on her own. Yet most of the recent footprints in that yard, including those that went to the dog, were much larger. A man's. Probably about a forty-seven, I'd guess.'

'Mud,' Cassini said and shook his head, laughing.

'Find me a telephone, Luca. I want to talk to your captain.'

The young officer looked worried suddenly.

'Don't fret,' Fratelli reassured him. 'All I have to offer is a small morsel of peripheral information picked up on our travels. I won't involve you. I promise.'

She walked back into the house, went upstairs, watched from the window. The lane to the farm was visible to the single-track road at the bottom. The white Fiat went all the way, then turned left towards Fiesole, disappearing out of sight.

They would need to call in help. She had some time – half an hour. More, perhaps. No room for hesitation.

The shotgun was still in her arms. There was no sound from the roof space. She wondered what to do.

Couldn't leave him. If they found him he'd talk. Couldn't take him far, either. He was slow, strange, unpredictable. A liability.

'Aldo!' she cried, then banged on the attic flap with the barrel of the gun.

She heard him scrabble across the timbers, then watched as he drew back the wooden covering. A querulous face. Not scared. Not anything, really. He needed to be told.

'We're leaving,' she said. 'You're coming with me. We're going to need some things.'

He didn't move.

'Now!' she shouted at him. 'They'll be back. More of them. With papers this time. They never wanted to look before. I don't know why . . .'

He ran down the folding ladder, took it step by ponderous step, stood next to her, tall, muscular, waiting.

'This is your doing,' she said. 'You brought them here. They'll be back. Maybe they think I killed him. Maybe . . .'

There was something about the old, silver-haired cop that

bothered her. It was as if he wasn't much interested in Ari or Tornabuoni at all. He was looking for something different altogether, and not seeing it.

That didn't mean he wasn't curious. 'I'll tell them what I did,' he said. 'You run. I'll stay. They can take me.'

She laughed. 'Oh, such a hero.'

His pale face, now beginning to grow stubble, become more human, watched her, puzzled, not knowing whether to be flattered or offended.

'The job's not done, is it?' she said. 'You know that. I thought I was alone. And now . . .'

Coincidences happened, and with them opportunities.

'I want you to help me collect some weapons and some ammunition. What money we have. Then we take the van into the city. Dump it.'

The ideas kept racing through her head, so quickly she couldn't possibly grasp all the flaws and lacunae.

'We need somewhere to stay. Just tonight. That's all. Where do you live?'

'Nowhere.'

He closed his eyes and she felt a sudden and unwanted pang of sympathy. This question pained him. It was the first time she'd seen that in his face.

'Aldo . . . Tomorrow. The first Thursday of the month.'

She stepped closer to him, touched his arm, not roughly, not possessively, but because she wanted to.

'Ari and I were supposed to do it then. Don't you understand? I didn't dance there for the money. I did it to get inside. To see them at their worst. To think. To plan . . .'

She sighed.

'And then the idiot goes and spoils it all through his stupid jealousy.'

Her hand reached out and touched his cheek.

'You understand now? What was it you said? I shall spill flood waters upon the earth?'

'You shall drown in them,' he murmured, picking up the refrain. 'And in that torrent shall flow your blood.'

'Their blood,' she said. 'Not ours. I was alone. And here you are.'

He looked around the landing, at the bare floorboards and the bedrooms. 'What weapons?' he asked.

'I'll deal with that. We need somewhere to hide. We can't stay in the van. They'll have the number.'

He didn't move, didn't speak.

'We've got to leave. You're from the city. Find us somewhere . . .'

'How long?' he asked.

'A night. That's all.'

'And then?'

She smiled. There never was an after. Not in any of their plans. Only a present, and an objective. 'And then . . . I don't know,' she said. 'We'll see.'

Cassini's radio stayed resolutely useless. They had to drive to the centre of Fiesole, the modest Piazza Mino, before they found a working phone box.

Fratelli rummaged through his pockets, then looked at them and said, '*Moneta, moneta!*'

Cassini held out a pocketful of change.

'I should have a squad car here with a radio that works,' Fratelli muttered, taking the coins without a word of thanks. 'And a team of men. Dogs. Specialists.'

'Civilians don't get them,' Cassini said patiently. 'Or have you forgotten?'

'For how much longer? We shall see! There's a café over there. Get yourselves something to drink. I'll join you.'

'If you're calling Walter Marrone, I'm the only serving Carabinieri officer here,' Cassini objected. 'I'm not being left out . . .'

'Would you let Julia buy her own coffee then? Off with you. There are no secrets. I'm merely briefing our friendly captain. I'll report back in a minute or two. A macchiato for me. It won't take long.'

A bright, broad grin and then he marched over to the phone, waving at them as they slunk off to the café.

It took a little persuasion with the switchboard before he was through.

'Walter!'

'Oh, wonderful,' Marrone grumbled.

'Don't sound so glum. I have news about the Tornabuoni murder! You must send me a squad car to the Piazza Mino in Fiesole immediately. No. Make that two. Armed officers please. And some men with spades and dogs I think . . .'

Silence. Then a small explosion occurred in the handset. Fratelli held it away from him.

'Tornabuoni!' Marrone roared. 'I gave you that boy so you and your English girlfriend could play detectives over that nonsense in the Brancacci. Not poke your noses into a murder case . . .'

'And if the two are linked?'

'They're not.'

'But if they are?'

'Where the hell are you? What are you doing with that fool Cassini?'

'Two weeks ago, a dubious hippie named Aristide Greco was found shot dead in Rovezzano. Our friend Tornabuoni was the preliminary suspect.'

Silence.

'I am, of course, telling you nothing you don't know,' Fratelli added. 'As you remind me constantly, you're captain of the *stazione* and nothing escapes your scrutiny.'

'So?' Marrone demanded.

'So I've paid Greco's widow a visit. Which is more than any of your officers have done . . .'

'The woman was interviewed here and told us nothing. Tornabuoni's connection to the case was entirely coincidental. A misunderstanding. He was released the moment that was apparent.'

Fratelli could picture Marrone speaking these words. He was such a terrible liar, the effort it cost him was even audible in his voice.

'What was misunderstood?' he asked.

'None of your damned business. Get back here. Bring me that boy. My generosity's over.'

'The widow's got something to hide, Walter. I believe she understands full well who killed her husband, doubtless over some drug deal. We both know Tornabuoni dabbled there.'

'I will not allow this . . .'

'Send me two cars. Take her into custody. Allow me to search her farmhouse and the surrounding land. An afternoon at most. At the end of it I will give you some answers.'

'Oh, for God's sake!'

'Don't get snappy with me. You were just as dubious over that bastard butcher in Scandicci. And the widow Bartolini's chihuahuas . . .'

'If you throw those bloody chihuahuas at me one more time, I swear—'

'A breakthrough, Walter! I'm offering you a lead, for God's sake.'

A pause. There was, he thought, perhaps a grim chuckle too.

'I don't need your lead, thank you very much. The Tornabuoni case is solved. The gardener confessed . . .'

Fratelli took a deep breath, then stamped his fist on the phone box wall. 'Oh! Oh! And can't I imagine what kind of interrogation that was? Your two monkeys from this morning, was it? What did they use this time? A hood? A few discreet punches . . .?'

'I would have thrown you out of the Carabinieri before long anyway, you know,' Marrone said in a low, cold voice. 'Whether you were dying or not. Your attitude towards your colleagues . . .'

'You're the one who gave me Luca Cassini because you thought he was an idiot. Don't play those games . . .'

'Tell Cassini to report back to the *stazione* immediately. You and your English mistress can go and play your games elsewhere . . .'

'Will you kindly stop saying that?'

'Stay out of my hair from now on. That's a warning. Every last favour I owed you has been spent. If I trip over you pretending to be an officer of the Carabinieri one more time, I will, I swear, lay charges. Against both of you, for interfering in our investigations, for . . .'

'Do you honestly think you can bury two murders?' Fratelli asked. 'Tornabuoni's of Aristide Greco? Then the man's own death at the hands of God knows who . . . because it certainly isn't the gardener. Who's pulling your strings on this one? Need I really guess . . .?'

'Enough!' Marrone cried. 'This conversation is at an end. As is whatever friendship we had. Goodbye.'

The phone went dead.

Pino Fratelli stared at it for a moment, shrugged, crossed the piazza and found them in the café.

'That took a while,' Cassini said.

'Walter and I are old friends. We rarely have brief conversations.'

Julia seemed worried. 'Is everything all right? You look pale.'

'It's a cold day. Winter on the way.'

The macchiato turned up. In three quick gulps it was gone.

'Everything's wonderful.'

'Marrone . . .' Cassini began.

'The captain's busy. He said we should go back and take a look at the farm for ourselves. He'll join us there presently.' He looked at Cassini. 'Do they give you a weapon, Luca?'

Luca Cassini laughed. 'If they won't give me a car, I'm hardly likely to be allowed a gun, am I? I'm the office boy, remember. That's why you've got me.'

'No problem,' Fratelli said. 'Let's go.'

Back on the outskirts of Florence, the old VW van belched diesel fumes into the dying afternoon.

'We've got to dump this thing,' she said. 'Somewhere a long way from where we're going. They're not that stupid.'

They had clothes, some food, a few weapons and ammunition. He'd never left a place in a hurry like that. Never thought of himself as pursued. It felt . . . good, for some reason. Exciting. Like being in the presence of something bigger, more important. The woman had that effect too.

'You do know where we're going, don't you?'

'I'll dump it. Don't nag.'

He drove on into Santa Croce, through the warren of narrow streets. History was etched into them, in the stones, in their names. Dead warriors, old tribes. Past the basilica itself and the white statue of the stiff Dante, skirting the square with the tents for the olive oil fair she'd never attend again. Down to the bridge and across the Arno into San Niccolò.

There he pulled into the side of the road, not far from the bars in the Via de' Renai, stopping the van next to a little patch of park between the low cobbled street and the busy riverside road.

'They don't have meters here. They won't notice it for a while.'

Chavah Efron picked up the two bags she'd brought. Weapons mainly. 'You're good at this,' she said.

'No. I'm not. I've never done . . .' He remembered Tornabuoni, the head beneath Cellini's statue. 'Never done anything before. Don't know why I started.'

'Because it was time,' she said. 'Because of me.'

'Maybe.'

'You're a natural. Ari wasn't. He was too . . . proud. He didn't listen. Didn't take orders. Didn't get it.'

He waited, said nothing.

'Where are we going?' she asked.

'Somewhere safe.'

'Nowhere's safe. Not any more.' She looked out of the window. The little bars were opening. Pleasant, comfy places for men and women of a certain age to drink themselves into a sleepy oblivion and forget what the world was like outside. 'Where are we going?'

He picked up the workman's canvas bag he'd brought from the farm, checked the crowbar there, prayed it would work.

'Home,' Aldo Pontecorvo said in a meek, low voice.

The rusty Cinquecento bounced its way up the narrow track to Chavah Efron's farm once more. The place was, as Pino Fratelli expected, now empty. Front door ajar, back door unlocked. Dog still on the chain, whining, afraid. VW van gone. Two sets of footprints through the mud in the yard. One small, one large.

'You were right there,' Luca said, looking at them. 'She hopped it swiftish, didn't she? With some bloke.'

'None of this should have happened,' Fratelli muttered caustically.

'I'm sorry . . .'

'It's not your fault, Luca. I wasn't trying to say it was. It's mine. It's Walter's. It's . . .' He wondered whether Cassini and Julia were ready to hear it. 'It's that damned city down there.'

Florence lay in the middle distance, Duomo and rusticated towers, campanili and basilicas, the grey form of the Arno worming through its centre.

'Shall we take a look around?' Julia asked quietly.

She was worried about something and he couldn't quite work out what. His head wasn't working right any more. It always focused ruthlessly on the task in hand. Now it lacked, on occasion, any peripheral vision whatsoever.

'Check your radio again, Luca,' Fratelli ordered. 'We're higher up here and . . . For the love of God, will you leave that dog alone?'

Cassini was with the black mongrel again, patting it on the head as the animal wagged its tail energetically.

'They left the dog,' the young officer said. 'What kind of people would abandon a dog? I ask you—'

'Your radio?'

Cassini looked at his handset. 'Sorry . . .'

Fratelli led the way into the house. Walked round the plain, cold ground floor, looked at the dirty plates, poked at the discarded rock albums and the magazines – political, most of them. Left wing.

'She was in a hurry,' he murmured. 'I should have done something . . .'

'Let's look upstairs, shall we?' Cassini said.

The front bedroom had some of the floorboards up. In the room opposite, the old iron-framed double bed had been pushed to one side. The floor was up there too.

'They've cleared something out,' Cassini said.

'I can see that.' Fratelli tried to think straight and found it a struggle. 'How long were we gone in Fiesole? Half an hour? Forty minutes?'

'Something like that,' Julia agreed.

'She was expecting a visit. Before we ever came. They got the things out of here beforehand. Maybe to the van.'

He walked to the front window, looked at the tracks in the yard outside. The dog was still there, staring up at them.

Fratelli looked at the space beneath the floorboards there, then came back to the other room, thought about what might have been hidden beneath the bed.

'I'm afraid,' he said, 'we're going to get a bit muddy.'

Julia Wellbeloved had found something in the corner. Fratelli looked, felt his blood chill. A red flag and a star in a circle. The words 'Brigate Rosse'.

Luca Cassini stared at it and said, 'Oh, bugger.'

'Do you read the orders every morning?' Fratelli asked.

''Course I do.'

'What's the status on terrorism at the moment?'

Cassini laughed. 'All that stuff's over! We put them in jail. There are no bombs and guns and stuff any more.'

'Just because something's stopped, doesn't mean it's gone away,' Fratelli said, his patience fraying. 'I haven't been allowed to see anything official in more than a year. What is the status today?'

Cassini frowned. 'There hasn't been any mention of it for months. Not since we got that woman of theirs and banged her up. They . . .'

He stopped. Went from one big foot to the other.

'What?' Julia asked.

'I remember peeking at her papers when they came in. They said something about . . . maybe there was a couple of them left. Unimportant people.'

'And weapons, Luca?' Fratelli asked. 'What did it say about them?'

Cassini shrugged. 'Nothing. We never found their weapons. We never do. I mean . . . if they're not out there, who cares where they've hidden their guns? Who—'

Fratelli marched downstairs. There was a spare pair of wellington boots by the front door. He told Julia Wellbeloved to put them on, then strode out into the yard, followed the line of old footprints, walked past the barn, into the low woodland, and picked his way up the hill.

'Keep checking the radio, Luca,' he ordered. 'We're getting higher. Maybe . . .'

Maybe I'm wrong, he thought. Maybe I *am* going mad.

But their tracks were recent and obvious. Up and down the hill. He had to follow.

They trudged along the Via Pisana towards the Ponte Vecchio for a while, then turned sharp left towards the rising mound of the Boboli Gardens. The private park of the Medici. A vast green paradise of follies and grottoes and groves, full of statues and surprises; so large that most locals had never visited every corner of its sprawling acreage.

A dead-end alley led to a high brick wall with a single door in the corner. A workman's entrance, little used. He walked to it, turned, looked round.

'You want somewhere to sleep, to hide,' Aldo Pontecorvo said confidently. 'This is it. The garden's a big place. There are things in there . . .'

Did he dare tell her? Was this a secret that could finally be shared?

He walked back to join her. Felt something slip from him as the words rose to his throat.

'I was born here. Thirty-seven years ago. To a woman who hated me. In a gardener's hovel in a corner they never bothered with.'

'You don't need to make excuses,' she said. 'We are who we are.'

She held the bag in her left arm, moved it up and down. He heard the weapons rattling inside. Then he went back to the door, took out the crowbar, put it in the crack between the frame and the wood and heaved hard.

Free in two goes. He helped her squeeze through the narrow door, closed it carefully when they were inside.

The police and the Carabinieri kept an eye on this place. It was part of the treasures of Florence, somewhere to protect, to keep from the hoi polloi on the street.

Ahead lay a narrow path strewn with autumn leaves.

The grey day was dying.

'Follow me,' he said, holding out his hand for her to take.

A picture in his head. The walls of the Brancacci. The magical, holy couple, inside the garden, expelled from its precious, immortal presence. He never knew which side he belonged to, never would. But this was a kind of home for him and soon she'd know it.

The woman followed him up the winding track beneath the walls of the Belvedere Fort as it meandered through crazily angled corridors formed by high conifers, past signs for grottoes and fountains, the Jupiter Garden, the Ladies' Garden, the palace itself. Finally they wound behind a low, artificial mound, walked half bent down a narrowing gap between shrubs and trees on either side.

Fruit lay on the ground. Apples and pears and oranges, starting to rot in the November rains.

In an archway of branches stood a tiny shack, brown brick leaning into the hill. A door, crooked, covered in cobwebs, grey and rotting in the wan daylight.

He turned the rusty handle, shone a torch inside.

No one came here any more.

The smell was the same. Smoke and dank earth. He felt he'd been breathing it every day of his life. Aldo Pontecorvo walked into the hovel built against the Boboli Hill, found candles where she'd left them, lit three, set them on the shaky wooden table. Slowly the light cast its dim yellow warmth into the shadows. Two rooms and a door to an outside privy. A washbasin, a gas stove fed from a cylinder beneath. Beyond the door the low double bed where she slept, and next to it the single mattress on the floor that was his.

Back in January she'd died in the hospital of Santa Maria Nuova, not far from the Duomo; the place, the plaques reminded everyone, founded by another Florentine noble, Folco Portinari, the father of Dante's beloved Beatrice. There was no love in the face of his mother. Had she owned the strength, he felt sure her dying words would have been a curse.

That was when they threw him out of the grim place on the hill and he found a single room in an Oltrarno boarding house at a price a casual cook could never afford. Coming back, his feelings veered from fear through hatred to a kind of awe. Every childhood had its share of innocence, even his. This lost corner of the Medici's orchard fed his simple imagination from the moment he could think. As a solitary, fanciful child, never forced to go to school, ignored mostly by his mother and his peers, he'd spent long days here, exploring every hidden inch, learning by heart the maze-like pathways that crisscrossed, from theatre to fountain, grotto to pavilion. At times the Boboli Gardens seemed a corner of paradise abandoned by the gods of the *palazzo* at the foot of the hill. It was all his, until one black night that would transform him from naive boy to knowing, broken man.

He held up the candle. 'We'll be fine here for the night. Two even. No one knows about this place. My mother . . .'

'You lived here?'

'Just the two of us.'

'Your father—?'

'I never knew,' he interrupted. 'She never talked about him. It was as if I was . . .'

He thought about the statues hidden in the garden; grinning gnomes and satyrs leering from beneath the bushes. One of these had sired him. Or so he'd always believed as a child.

'As if I came from nowhere.'

Chavah Efron placed her bag on the table. 'I'm hungry,' she said. 'Go fetch some food. And wine. Red.'

She looked around, pulled one of the two chairs up to the small wooden table, brushed away the dust with her arm.

'Red,' she said again.

They followed the muddy tracks through the bare trees in the wood, then marched to the brow of the hill. The day was failing, street lights coming on all over Florence as they watched; lines of illumination marching down the avenues, worming their way through the narrow alleys in the city centre, along the banks of the Arno.

'This isn't a job for two men and a girl,' Luca Cassini grumbled.

'Am I a girl now?' Julia Wellbeloved asked as she clambered through a thicket of brambles, following Fratelli who walked head down, eyes on the ground.

'Stop being picky, will you?' Cassini retorted. 'You know what I mean. We ought to have a team with some proper lanterns. And dogs.'

They said nothing.

'I'm not leaving that poor thing of theirs here, by the way,' he added. 'Whatever happens . . .'

'Kindly shut up about the dog and look around you,' Fratelli demanded.

He'd come to a halt by the side of a saucer-shaped crater. A little like the mouth of an ancient dwarf volcano, filled with the same ragged, untidy scrub they'd walked through most of the way. But when Fratelli turned his torch on the branches below them, flashes of blue were visible. Plastic, by the looks of it.

'What do you see, Luca?' he asked.

'Does teacher ever knock off for supper?'

'No. Talk to me.'

Cassini and Julia strode to the rim of the indentation.

'Muddy footprints,' the young officer said.

'Something's hidden there,' Julia added. 'Underneath sheets, or something. They put those branches over them. Judging by the footprints, they did it just this afternoon.'

Fratelli put one leg over the edge then scrambled down the side, staying clear of the slippery muddy tracks someone had left earlier. The two others followed. By the time they got there, he was throwing broken branches out of the way.

'They were in a hurry too,' Luca Cassini said, pushing to the front, then launching a whole line of twigs and leaves out of the way with his strong arms. 'What's this then?'

Fratelli extended a hand to Julia.

'Be my guest,' he said.

She lifted up the cold wet plastic sheeting, rolled it back a little. Something was covered in tape and bubble wrap at her feet. A familiar shape. It came off easily and revealed some kind of semiautomatic weapon.

Cassini watched and whistled, then kicked his foot over a few of the identical objects piled alongside. Row after row, box after box.

'Try your radio here, Luca,' Fratelli said. 'We're higher. Who knows?'

The little green LCD screen of the handset blinked when he held it up.

'You're in luck . . .' the young officer said.

Fratelli snatched the thing from him, got through to the control room, demanded to talk to Marrone urgently, persisted through all the refusals.

Finally he was connected.

'How many times do I have to . . .' the captain barked at him.

They listened to his angry voice disappear into the thin country air. A clear night was falling. Plenty of stars and a bright full moon.

'There was a unit of the Red Brigades in Tuscany,' Fratelli broke in. 'I know you have them locked up, Walter. Most, anyway. But did you ever find their weapons store? Their guns? Their ammunition and explosives?'

'What is this . . .?'

'Did you find their armoury? How difficult a question is this?'

A pause, then, 'No. We didn't.'

'Join us at the Efron woman's farm. Near Fiesole. I've something you ought to see.'

One hour later. Teams of Carabinieri in dark blue winter jackets lugged floodlights up the hill. Marrone was directing proceedings from a tent erected on the rim of the indentation where the arms cache had been found. The size of the store astonished even the antiterrorist officers brought in for the event. More were on their way from Rome. From what Fratelli could glean, Chavah Efron and her late husband Ari Greco were the keepers of the last remaining significant weapons cache possessed by the disbanded and largely jailed group of criminals who called themselves the Red Brigades.

Not that anyone was handing out much praise to Fratelli and Luca Cassini for locating them. It was a clear, cold night, heading for frost. The two men stayed in the tent with Julia Wellbeloved, watching Marrone and his officers direct the slow and careful recovery of the weapons, shells and plastic explosives. Another team was searching the house. Julia had asked why. Fratelli shrugged. The birds had flown. There was, he suggested, little of interest to be found in this dilapidated farm on the hills outside Fiesole.

Shortly before six, Marrone marched into the tent and ordered all three of them to return to Florence and report to the *stazione* to give statements in the morning.

'The morning?' Fratelli asked, wide-eyed. 'We're here now, Walter. I have a registration number for the woman's VW van, by the way. I noted it . . .'

'We've got that already,' Marrone snapped. 'I need no more help from you. Go home. Stay out of my way.'

'You don't seem very grateful,' Julia observed. 'I mean honestly, Captain. If it wasn't for Pino and Luca here—'

'And you,' Fratelli added quickly. 'No false modesty, please.'

'I've no need of amateur detectives,' Marrone roared. 'You'd no business being here in the first place. I expressly ordered . . .'

A figure entered by the tent door. They stopped, looked at him in silence.

'Why the angry voices?' Sandro Soderini asked with a smile. 'This is a happy occasion, isn't it?'

'Mr Mayor,' Fratelli said pleasantly, then walked forward and shook Soderini's hand. 'My name is Pino Fratelli. I was passing and stumbled upon our odd discovery. This is a young Carabinieri officer, Luca Cassini. A talented chap. You'll hear more of him.'

'Delighted,' Cassini said with a nod of the head.

'And my English friend—'

'You're a long way from the Uffizi, Julia,' Soderini interrupted. 'Is there meat for your thesis here?'

'Just looking,' she said. 'Was it worth tearing yourself away from the Palazzo Vecchio for this?'

His aristocratic face fell. 'These bastards have been dangling their cowardly threats over us for years. I thought we had most of them dead or in jail.' He glared at Marrone. 'That's what was supposed to happen, wasn't it?'

'The fugitive who cached these weapons is an American,' Marrone said. 'Her name is Chavah Efron. Neither she nor her husband appeared on any of the suspect lists we had from intelligence. We've no reason to believe they were active in any way. Fellow travellers perhaps . . .'

'They were sleepers,' Fratelli said. 'Of course they didn't wave around their flags.'

He looked at Soderini.

'Were there specific threats, Mr Mayor? To you? To your fellow councillors? Like Tornabuoni?'

Soderini's smile became forced and brittle. 'Specific? What do you mean, specific?'

'I mean what it sounds like,' Fratelli replied brusquely. 'Did you receive letters? Phone calls? Warnings? Messages that said do this or we'll . . . I don't know.' A pause. He smiled at the man in the smart suit and raincoat. 'Or we'll kill you.'

'The Red Brigades are history,' Soderini said. 'I'm sure it's as the captain suggests. This was a cache of weapons some timid supporter was storing for a revolution that was never going to arrive.'

'So they didn't kill Tornabuoni?' Fratelli asked outright.

'The gardener killed Tornabuoni, didn't he?' Soderini answered, looking at Marrone for support.

'Yes,' the captain replied.

'And Tornabuoni himself didn't kill Chavah Efron's husband by any chance . . .?'

'Dammit Fratelli!' Marrone yelled. 'That's enough.'

Sandro Soderini took one step towards them. 'Giovanni Tornabuoni was a gentleman,' he said calmly. 'He had his . . . eccentricities. But a man like that has no call to murder anyone. Why would he?'

'So why did we think he did?' Cassini asked with an inquisitive, friendly smile. 'Being a cadet I'd just like to know. To learn from things. I like learning. I've learned a lot these last couple of days . . .'

'We'll find this woman,' the captain declared. 'That's all you need to know.'

'And her friend,' Julia Wellbeloved intervened. 'She wasn't alone.'

'A man,' Cassini added.

'A tall man. Quite heavy,' Fratelli said. 'Judging by the footprints.'

'There's a man with her?' Sandro Soderini murmured.

'This is all in hand,' the captain insisted, then half ushered, half shoved them out into the cold night and bawled at them until they set off down the muddy track back to the farm.

Expelled from the investigation, the case itself – such as it was.

A search for the last and junior member of the Red Brigades, or so Walter Marrone would have it. And an unknown accomplice.

'Why would Tornabuoni kill this woman's husband?' Julia asked when they got to the car.

Luca Cassini mumbled something and marched off towards the farm.

'Always look for the easy answers,' Fratelli said. 'Soderini's right. It's hard to imagine the city arts commissioner as a born and willing murderer.'

'Then . . .?'

'Then he was an unwilling one. People who don't kill out of personality or inclination tend to do so for one reason only. Self-defence. The Greco character hoped to kill him. Tornabuoni defended himself.'

She thought about this. 'So why hide it? Self-defence isn't a crime.'

'Good question,' he noted. Something bothered him.

'Pino? You're thinking.'

'Soderini,' he said. 'The mayor of Florence. Why did he walk up a muddy hillside out in the sticks like this? Any ideas?'

'None.'

'Any observations?'

'Don't be so cryptic, please.'

'I'm not being cryptic. You've met him before. He's fond of you, I'd say, judging from the rather genial and familiar way he greets—'

'Stop it!'

'Didn't you notice anything? Something that perhaps connects him to Tornabuoni?'

Luca Cassini was coming back. He had the black mongrel on a chain and was chatting happily to it.

'You've lost me,' she said.

'Think a couple of steps ahead. Vanni Tornabuoni killed Aristide Greco because Greco attempted to murder him. We must assume Greco was a trained terrorist. These people regarded themselves as soldiers. They weren't amateurs with a gun. Well then . . .?'

'Tornabuoni had a weapon too. He knew he was in trouble. That was why you were asking if Soderini had been warned.'

'Not just that,' he said, opening the doors of the little Fiat.

'Then what?'

'Tell her, Luca,' Fratelli ordered.

'He had a gun on him,' Cassini said, sounding shocked. 'The mayor. Dead obvious. Shoulder holster. Over the right-hand side. Could see it bulging under that fancy raincoat of his.'

'A man like that isn't easily scared,' Fratelli continued. 'Which means, I suspect, he's no idea who or what he's supposed to be frightened of. Only that it's out there.' He glared at the dog. 'What do you intend to do with this animal?'

'Take it to my uncle's. After I drop you two off.' Cassini scratched his head and looked at the tiny car. 'Someone's going to have to sit in the back with him,' Cassini added. 'He's a bit pongy . . .'

'I'll do it,' Fratelli said, and climbed through the tiny door on to the rear seat, watching as the young man persuaded the mongrel to join him.

'Put an arm round him,' Cassini advised. 'He might not like it when we start moving. I had a dog who threw up every time he got in a car . . .'

Then they set off on the slow, winding road back towards the city.

When he got back she'd lit the fire. Slow flames licked over the old logs in the grate. Smoke rose to the chimney sending a damp, dark aroma through the room.

Something on the table. He looked.

Apples and pears, gathered from the trees outside, which were now shedding their leaves for winter. Two plates, two sets of cutlery. All washed.

There were more candles than he ever remembered. His mother never used them without a need. They had no money. She worked in the gardens, sweeping leaves, planting vegetables, digging, fetching, cleaning. The tiny, dank cottage was the reward. A place where an unmarried mother might live, survive, beyond the judgemental stare of the city outside the walls of the Pitti Palace.

'How long do we have?' she asked, taking the bag from his arms, putting it on the table, sifting through the contents.

'Before what?'

'Before they know someone's here?'

They worked the gardens all year round. It was a sprawling estate, now in the hands of the city. Soderini, Tornabuoni when he lived. The Medici's heirs. They coveted it, enjoyed it. Got others to do the work.

'Long enough,' he said.

Two pizzas, plain food. Some ham and *salumi*. Water and a bottle of Chianti already opened, the cork stuffed back into the neck.

Chavah Efron poured two mugs, left his on the table, swigged at hers, tore off a strip of pizza, stuffed it into her mouth with some meat.

He hadn't realized how hungry he was. She looked as if she hadn't eaten in days. They pounced on the food, finished every last morsel, so quickly he offered to go back down the hill and find some more.

'Visibility increases risk,' she said, without looking at him. It sounded as if she were reciting from a manual of some kind.

The fire crackled. The windows began to steam up. Down the hill, through the trees, lights were just visible in the palace.

He got up, drew the tattered curtains, wondered if they'd be thick enough to block out their presence. But he didn't worry too much. His mother had been here for more than four decades; a hermit, a recluse, tolerated for the work she did. The men in the palace scarcely noticed her.

She filled up their mugs again, raised hers, smiled, toasted him.

Cheap Chianti. Harsh, crude. The kind the poor drank, not knowing any better.

Still . . .

He liked the way it blurred the feelings in his head.

Then she pounced on the fruit she'd picked, the last of the apples and pears from the summer.

Picked up the biggest of the apples, green with a rosy tint to the skin. Carved it in two with her knife. Held half up to him, grinning.

'Are you afraid of me?' she asked in her gruff, accented voice.

Her eyes glittered in the candlelight. The wine had done something. That and the memories. Illicit moments here as a child, wondering what it would be like to be a man. Before the Brigata took his innocence from him. Before the Fall . . .

'No,' he said, and took the fruit from her, bit into the soft white flesh.

She finished hers quickly. Then looked at the low bed in the corner, his mattress next to it. Too small for him. Had been for years. Trying to squeeze his long frame on to it had been awkward and uncomfortable. Not that his mother left him any choice.

'I don't believe you,' Chavah Efron whispered, her sparkling eyes on him every moment.

'I can't help that. Tomorrow I can go and steal something. Find some money. Get a car. We can—'

'Tomorrow we've got an appointment. You and me.'

He'd told her where he worked before the Brigata. He was still worried about the way she took that information, seemed to dwell on it.

'We can get out of here. Go south, maybe. Where Ari came from . . . In Calabria no one's ever going to know.'

'First,' she said, 'you'll do as you're told.'

He didn't answer, just poured some more wine. Found his fingers trembling.

'Tonight too,' she added.

A pause.

'Get on the bed, Aldo.'

'I don't . . .'

But she was on him then, her warm damp mouth against his skin. And he was lost.

After the argument at the farm he wouldn't go straight home. So the three of them sat with him in the bar in San Niccolò, Fratelli with a Negroni, Julia with a glass of white wine, Cassini sipping at a Coke and grabbing fists of meat and cheese from the plates that came out of the kitchen.

The dog stayed in the little Fiat but its smell came with them.

Fratelli's mood was black, however much the other two tried to cheer him.

'Well,' Cassini declared after a while. 'I suppose I'd best be going really. Take that mutt up the hill . . .'

'Why do you bother, Luca?' Fratelli snapped. 'What's the animal to you?'

'I bother because if I didn't, no one else would.' Cassini sounded cross. 'You can't just walk away from things. Not in this job. My grandpa never did when he was in the *stazione*. He always said you didn't, Pino. In fact, you were a pain in the arse . . .'

'Yes, yes. So you said!'

'Let's go,' Julia broke in. 'It's been a long day. I'm tired and grubby. And—'

'This is all wrong!'

Fratelli's tumbler of gin and vermouth slammed on the table, spilling drink and peanuts and *pinzimonio* everywhere.

Luca Cassini scratched his short black hair. 'I don't get what you're so bothered about. I mean, I know it's not nice of someone to mess around with those old paintings in the Brancacci. But it's not like killing someone. Or those weapons we found. You can see why Marrone's more interested in—'

'It's not about the paintings in the Brancacci!'

They were getting stares from the woman behind the counter.

Luca Cassini didn't blink. It occurred to Julia that he had engineered this moment rather cleverly.

'I sort of thought that actually, Pino,' he said quietly. 'But since you don't want to tell me what it *is* about, there's not a lot I can do, is there? I know. I'm just the office boy. Walter Marrone doesn't trust me. Neither do you really.'

He paused. Waited. Heard nothing.

'Do you?'

'It's not a question of trust,' Fratelli insisted. 'It's a matter of belief. If nobody listens to a word you say . . .'

'I'm listening. Have been all along. You've put more faith in me than anyone ever did in Ognissanti. But it only goes so far, doesn't it? I'm still the boy—'

'Tell him,' Julia cried. 'For God's sake.'

Silence.

'It's to do with your wife, I imagine,' Cassini prodded. 'I guessed that.'

Fratelli glowered at him. 'People do talk, even to the office boy. You can't stop them. They said you went bonkers years ago when she died. From what I heard . . . can't blame you. But that's not all, is it?'

'Tell him!' Julia said again.

'No,' Fratelli muttered. 'It's not all.'

He got up, walked to the bar, talked pleasantly to the woman there, came back with another round of drinks.

Then started slowly going through the story he'd recounted to a horrified Julia the night before.

She found she couldn't hear this again. So she went outside, opened the little Fiat, took the black mongrel from Fiesole for a walk in the park for a while.

When she returned, there was a man waiting anxiously by the door of the bar, as if frightened to go in. Tall, in his fifties, a down-cast distinguished face beneath a black beret. He was puffing a cigarette and looked familiar.

'I know you,' she said as the mongrel from the farm pulled on the lead.

A dog collar. A face from another context.

'You're the Englishwoman,' he replied, staring into her face. 'Fratelli's friend from the chapel.'

'His lodger. But yes, his friend too, I imagine. Have you cleaned up your paintings?'

He shrugged. 'It was just a lunatic who broke in from the street. Nothing at all. The damage was fixed the day it was done. Washed off for good. I've forgotten about it already.'

Father Bruno. That was the name.

He nodded towards the bar. 'Why won't Fratelli let this go? He's a sick man. I tried to talk to him with his doctor yesterday. He as good as told me to get out of the room.'

'I don't think he regards himself as one of your flock.'

'He grew up in my parish. In my eyes that's exactly what he is.'

'Why are you here?'

'God knows. I don't.'

'I don't have a line to God.'

'Oh, very clever! I thought I'd try one last time to persuade him to behave sensibly again. But looking inside . . .'

Fratelli was talking to Luca Cassini, his face set in the gloomy, determined expression she'd come to know.

'I'm wasting my time, aren't I?'

'You mean he should meekly accept what's happened to him? Stay in bed until . . . one day . . .'

There was an unpleasant cast to the man's face.

'I deal with the dying every week of my life, Signora. Don't talk down to me.'

'I didn't. Who asked you to come? His doctor?'

'I'm the parish priest. Everyone begs me to intercede on behalf of those in trouble. It's my job. My calling. What I do.' He looked even more miserable than Fratelli. 'All I do.'

'Who asked you to come?' she repeated.

'His old captain, of course. Everyone knows Fratelli. Most like him. And we all feel sorry for the man. But what can we do? Every night he's here, taking solace in alcohol . . .'

'He has two Negroni. That's all I've ever seen.'

The priest looked her up and down, as if staring at something of which he disapproved.

'And when he doesn't have pretty company he wants to impress? How much then?'

'I've no idea. Do you see what happens then? Does God tell you?'

He didn't answer.

'Why would Walter Marrone wish . . .?' Julia persisted.

'A vandal broke into the Brancacci and caused a small amount of temporary damage to those paintings of ours. It's been repaired. No one will notice. No one need worry about it. The Carabinieri have better things to occupy their time. This terrible business with Tornabuoni . . .'

'I thought Tornabuoni's murder was supposed to be solved.'

'Marrone told me you were egging him on,' the priest said coldly. 'Do you think that's wise? Do you think it's good for him? To be encouraged to believe he's still a working detective? The best in Florence, or so he thinks? Not a dying man engrossed in his own sorrowful delusions? What business is this of yours?'

She was so taken aback by his sudden vehemence she couldn't think of an answer.

'And who are you anyway?' he snarled. 'A foreigner? Come here for your own amusement. Is Pino Fratelli part of that? Another sight on the Grand Tour? An unexpected discovery for you to take back to England when you pack your bags and leave? Like a picture postcard or a little statue of the Palazzo Vecchio?'

'That's uncalled for.'

'Is it?'

The dog was starting to growl at him.

'The best thing you can do for Fratelli is to persuade him to listen to his doctor and his friends. His parish priest perhaps, too. To accept his fate and learn to make good use of what time remains to him. Not be consumed with these ridiculous fantasies . . .'

'I think you should go and tell him that yourself. If you've got the guts.'

'What's the point?' the priest said, stepping back from the black animal, which was pulling towards his feet. 'He won't listen to me. Or Walter Marrone. Or anyone.'

The grey, ascetic face lit up for a moment.

'Except perhaps you. A stranger. That's the way he is. Always was. Peculiar in the extreme. But I imagine you're having too much fun to do him that service.'

'I will not listen to this.'

'No need. I won't waste my breath on Fratelli any more. Or you.'

He threw the cigarette into the gutter, patted the black beret in an ironic salute, then said, 'Good night.'

And was gone.

The dog stopped growling. Fine rain was starting to fall from somewhere. The sky still looked clear but a little out of focus. Or perhaps it was her eyes.

She was startled by someone taking the mongrel's lead from her hands. Luca Cassini. He looked pale and shocked. Pino Fratelli had now introduced the young man to his secrets and she couldn't stop herself thinking: how much of this is true? How much only real in Fratelli's disordered, dying head?

'I'd best get this little chap tucked up for the night. Out of this bloody city,' Cassini mumbled in a quiet, fractured voice.

She glanced back. Fratelli was still at the table, clutching what looked like a fresh Negroni.

'Did you suspect?' she asked.

'I knew his wife had died. Poor bugger. All that other stuff about . . .'

Luca Cassini looked ready to burst into tears himself.

'What's going on, Julia? What are we supposed to do? Walter Marrone won't have him in the *stazione* after this. Or you. Or me probably. We can't . . . Sit!' He pulled on the lead as the dog struggled. The animal went down on its haunches obediently with one spoken word. 'We can't fix all that for him, can we? Even if it's true.'

She didn't know what to say.

'Is it?' he wondered. 'True? I mean . . . why didn't he tell someone back then?'

'Because he was in a sanatorium. Lost to the world. Would they have listened if he had?'

'I don't know. Maybe. You'd still think he would have said something . . .'

'He thinks the sickness started then. The tumour. He thinks what happened prompted the cancer inside him. Maybe he's right.'

'Maybe,' Cassini agreed, with little conviction.

'Leave it for now,' she said, and touched his arm, tried to smile. 'It's been a long day.'

'How can we leave it? He needs looking after. He can't go on like this. He looks poorly. It's driving him mad.'

'I'll deal with it, Luca. Take the dog to your uncle's. Let's talk tomorrow. And thanks . . .' She was struggling with the words and they should have been so simple. 'Thanks for everything.'

'Didn't do bugger all,' he grumbled, and slunk off, leading the animal to the car.

She went back to Fratelli's table, turned down the offer of another drink.

'It's time to go, Pino. I'm filthy. And tired.'

'The American woman never went inside the Brancacci,' he said. His face was pale, his eyes bloodshot. 'It's unthinkable that damage was her work. She was ten when Chiara died. The man with her. It has to be. I'll make some calls . . .'

'Who to?'

He hesitated, looked a little sheepish.

'I . . . I still have friends. Contacts. Marrone can't freeze me out of this city. I grew up here.'

She said nothing.

'Julia. You see things almost as well as I do.'

'I'm flattered.'

'You should be. For whatever reason, two weeks ago, Aristide Greco went out to kill Vanni Tornabuoni only to find himself the victim. Another man has taken his place by the side of Greco's wife. He – or they – then murdered Tornabuoni. The political classes still fear some kind of retribution. Why else would Soderini be there? Armed too? And Walter Marrone wishes to pretend none of this has happened. That it's all . . .'

His voice fell; his eyes went to the black night beyond the window.

'It's all water under the bridge.'

'There's nothing to say this concerns you or Chiara.'

'Because we haven't seen through the mist yet.'

'I want to leave.'

His mournful eyes peered at her. She got up, picked her bag off the back of the chair and walked outside.

The bus stop was by the river. The rain was steady now but there were still stars. Across the Arno the lights stood dim and yellow in the arches of the Uffizi. The ugly castellated tower of the Palazzo Vecchio rose behind in the Piazza della Signoria, exaggerated and comically grand.

Winter in Florence.

Arrhythmic breathing by her side. A cough that had an apologetic ring to it.

'I'm sorry,' he said simply. 'I just thought . . .'

A shape in the distance along the riverside road. Their bus was bouncing towards them.

'Come,' he said, taking her gently by the arm, leading her to the open door. 'Come, Julia. Let's go home.'

She made him lie in the centre, head on the fusty pillow, ran her hands over his jumper, pulled it off.

His breath was coming in short gasps. His mind was racing, confused. There were things to think about, plans to make. Yet all these sensible ideas seemed not to matter at that moment. He was with her, drowning in the force of Chavah Efron's character, her forceful physical presence.

As always he did as he was told. Lay down on the soft coverlet, not moving a muscle as she reached out and, with lithe, slow fingers, dragged the clothes from him then stripped off her own, touching him gently, laughing all the time.

She rolled one leg over his stomach and straddled him, hair falling against his cheeks, the smell of her everywhere, the fatal scent of woman.

'Don't tell me I'm the first,' she whispered.

'Of course you are,' he wanted to say, but then she had him, held him, moved closer and took him in. Kept him there, not moving. Trapped like this, he felt he might not breathe again.

'I am Chavah . . .' she said, and rocked him, just the once. 'I am the woman here. In this place. With my guns. And . . .' Her pupils narrowed, like an animal, as he watched. Some emotion, a stirring of passion, detached a little of her sense of control. 'When I want something, I get it.'

He was somewhere else. Down the hill, two decades before.

'You with me?'

'*Sì*,' he gasped.

'This is my world and you entered it without asking. My life. Not yours. Not Ari's, not . . .'

She snorted through her nostrils, an animal noise.

It took a minute, maybe even less, and then he grunted like a pig and felt the sharp, sweet stab of release between them.

All the years he'd never known this. And now it seemed such a brief and ordinary thing next to the ordeal that went before.

Still she didn't move. Her hair was in his face, her breath warm and damp against his neck.

'Ari came like that,' she murmured, her voice so close it felt as if she was inside his head. 'When I made him. I could choose.'

He coughed and tried to force his breathing into a familiar rhythm as he stared at the cracks in the ceiling, trying to count them, the way he did as a child.

She wriggled from him, slipped on to his thighs, stayed there, elbow on the creased sheets, green eyes on him, always sharp, always focused.

Her hand came out and stroked his cheek.

'Do you still want to save me, Aldo? The lost woman. Fallen. Needing her man to rescue her.'

'Right and wrong,' he mumbled. 'I know the difference.'

'That's sweet, in a stupid kind of way. Ari wouldn't have done that.' Her face darkened. Her hand moved to his chest. 'Stood up for me.'

'Tornabuoni raped you. Your husband wanted to . . .'

'Tornabuoni was a minnow. As much a plaything as me. Or you. Ari was mad because he felt he'd taken something that belonged to him alone. It wasn't about me. It was about him.'

She shuffled over, kissed him once on the cheek, smiled.

'I don't think you're like that. Tell me again. What day is it?'

'Wednesday.'

'First Thursday of the month. Every month. Ever since . . .' She ran a finger across his brow. 'Ever since when?'

The beginning, he thought. That first day outside the garden.

'Tomorrow was when we were supposed to move,' she said. 'If Ari hadn't let his stupid male arrogance get the better of him.'

'For what?'

She leaned down and whispered hot in his ear. He could smell the wine on her breath, feel her excitement.

'For the reason we're here,' Chavah Efron said as her fingers reached down and played with him again. 'Fire and blood. For all of them . . .'

And then she was on him again; nothing could stop her.

The house was dark, too warm and empty. They stood on the landing, stamping their damp feet. She felt filthy. All there was in her room was a small shower crammed into little more than a closet. The water came in a miserly stream – and that only when it was in the mood.

Fratelli watched. Reading her mind, she thought. He could do that.

'There's a tub in my bathroom, Julia. Please. It's yours. I'm Italian. I'm used to squeezing into little places. The English like their baths. I know.'

She went and got her things, passed him going the other way on the landing, didn't say a word. Went into his bathroom. A white bath, white sink, white tiles, all gleaming; all the bachelor things – a razor, a toothbrush – set on a mirror by the window. Along with a line of medication: four bottles, one pack of tablets. This was the Grassi dragon's work. Keeping everything spotless, making sure he took his pills. And she'd broken into this precise, fenced-off world. Then – the priest had made this plain – encouraged Pino Fratelli in his madness.

Julia ran the taps. Lots of hot water. Some bath salts. Her own soap. She stripped off her muddy clothes, left them in a pile. Washed her hair under the shower tap and got in. And cried.

Cried freely, with a release of emotion she'd not known in a long time. Not even when her brief and stupid marriage was falling apart. Her mother had died ten years ago now. That was the same, perhaps. But then there was no sense of guilt.

And so she refused to analyse this further, simply sitting in Pino Fratelli's gleaming white bathtub, washing off the mud and filth of Fiesole, weeping sporadically, sniffing, wiping at her nose with her arm.

How long? Till the water, cloudy and grey with the dirt, started to turn tepid, then cold. Finally she got out, checked her eyes in the mirror. The pinkness there might be excused by the long day and the heat of the bathroom. She dried herself on his fresh towels, climbed into the rather juvenile but practical blue pyjamas she'd bought from Selfridge's.

Wrapped a towel round her hair. Went back into his living room, feeling her heart pumping. The bath. The day. The heat.

He was in his leather armchair, a long thick dressing gown round him, plaid slippers on his feet. Hairdryer in right hand, blowing his long silver locks. In his left was a book. Another art volume, she saw. On the cover were the paintings of the Brancacci.

She came over and took the book away; sat next to him, half furious, half grieving for an event to come.

'Here,' Fratelli said, turning off the hairdryer. 'I'm done with it. I only let my hair grow long when they threw me out of the Carabinieri. It was a kind of protest. Childish. If I don't dry it, I look an even bigger clown . . .'

Then he brightened, put a finger in the air, and headed off into the tiny kitchen. A few minutes later, with her hair just about done, he returned with two steaming mugs.

'Tea,' he said. 'Earl Grey. I gather you English like it. I bought some when they said I had a visitor coming.'

The musky smell of bergamot. A memory of home. She sipped at it, said nothing.

'Perhaps,' Fratelli said cautiously, 'it would be wise if we reconsidered this arrangement.'

She was protesting immediately.

'No, please,' he insisted. 'Hear me out. I'm aware that I've monopolized your time since you arrived. The reason you came . . . your dissertation. I've distracted you from it and that's unforgivable.'

'You want me to leave?' she asked sullenly.

He emitted a low, wordless grumble. 'You're a very recalcitrant woman sometimes. I never meant to entangle you in this.'

'Oh, no? You've been prodding me all along.'

'It was . . . inadvertent.'

'Like Luca Cassini? You've scooped us up, Pino. Infected us. Now we're as—'

Almost a stumble.

'Say it,' he broke in quickly. 'Now you're mad too.'

'I didn't mean that. What I wanted to say was . . .'

And another stumble.

'Was what?' he wondered.

'You have to leave this. For God's sake. I've seen it eating at you. I don't want to watch any more.'

'Which is why you must go—'

'No! It's why you must stop. Walter Marrone's your friend, isn't he?'

'So I thought.'

'He sent along that priest. To the bar tonight. The one we saw in the chapel.'

Fratelli's brow wrinkled and she regretted this revelation immediately. It had set him thinking again.

'Bruno?'

'He didn't dare come in. I talked to him when I walked the dog. While you told Luca about your wife. They want you to stop this. It's breaking their hearts. Can't you see that?'

'The heart of a priest I barely know? Why didn't he come in and tell me to his face?'

'There you go again! Not listening . . .'

He laughed, raised his mug to her.

'But I am. The priest wants me to stop. The captain of the Carabinieri wants to stop. My doctor. The mayor of Florence . . . that goes without saying.'

Fratelli hesitated, looked at her.

'And now you,' he said in a voice that was close to a whisper.

'If there's nothing you can do . . .'

'There's always something you can do,' he retorted with a sudden vehement conviction. 'Always. Unless you're dead, and I'm not there yet.'

She closed her eyes and felt like weeping again. When she opened them there was guilt written all over his face.

'There. You see. I'm right. You should find new accommodation.'

'So now you're trying to drive me out!'

He wrung his hands, let loose an epithet at the low ceiling.

'I'm asking this for both of us. I don't want to hurt you, Julia. And that's all I'm doing. All I'm capable of. Please. I'll phone the Uffizi in the morning. Find another home for you. Go and see your paintings. Visit San Marco tomorrow. Marvel at its beauty, because it is I think the most lovely place in all this grim city.'

He sipped some more tea, pulled a disgusted face.

'This is not for me. It tastes strange. Like perfume.'

'And Soderini's secret invitation? The Brigata Spendereccia?'

'Forget it. That's my advice. It's doubtless just a little orgy for a bunch of sad middle-aged men who think they run this place. We've had them in Italy since the days of Caesar. We'll doubtless have them for many centuries to come.'

She put her mug on the table. 'It doesn't taste right here,' Julia said. 'I agree. Goodnight.'

He was still in his chair, smiling wanly at her, when she got to her feet.

'I don't want you staying up reading, listening to your records,' she added. 'I'll never get to sleep if I think you're doing that. Off to bed now.'

'Yes, ma'am. Yes!' he said, then strode off to the bedroom, saluting her from the door.

He didn't move like a sick man. Or a middle-aged one, for that matter. He moved easily, with a firm purpose, a deliberate intent. An energy that was vital because he knew its time was finite.

She smiled at him as he closed the door, then stayed where she was, trying, with little success, to analyse her thoughts, her feelings. It was impossible. She couldn't see the way forward for the simplest of reasons: she'd no idea what she wanted that to be. After the marriage, after walking out on the job, she'd found herself in an aimless limbo. The idea of academia had appeared on a whim, one formed by joining her love of intellectual investigation with her admiration for art. It was nothing more than a juvenile daydream, a line on a letter never posted to a Santa Claus who did not exist.

The dissertation would never be written. The basis for it – why art attracted violence – was a fabrication created out of desperation for something to fill the abyss that had opened up in her life. When she was faced with her supposed subject in reality, she'd been fascinated not by its intellectual aspect, but the more pressing and exciting one that Pino Fratelli, in his damaged state of mind, had offered.

A chase. A search for an elusive, hidden truth. The thrill of the hunt. A rush of the blood.

The dour priest had hit the spot. She had encouraged a sick and possibly deluded man for her own purposes. To provide amusement; to keep herself from facing the emptiness all around.

And yet . . .

It had been so wonderful. She'd never felt quite as alive as she had these past few days in a rainy Florence with this damaged and entrancing man, feeling history slip around her like an ancient, damp and musty cloak. Whispering in her ear. Promising revelations in dark corners, surprises that were never to be found in the grey and tedious corners of England she'd always regarded as home.

Julia looked round his tidy, bachelor room, shook her still-damp head, and whispered to herself, 'Why do you always run away?'

Because I'm frightened, she thought. Of myself. Of closeness. Of risk. Everything that Pino Fratelli embraces so readily and with such visible energy.

She walked over to his bedroom door. It was still half open. He was in his double bed, beneath neatly ironed sheets and a coverlet, a lamp by his side. A book in his hands.

'What did I say about reading?' she scolded him.

'Checking up on me now? You're not the Grassi dragon and you never will be. Kindly pack your bags and be gone.'

She came and sat on the bed, watching amused as he shuffled over to the other side as if in fear.

'This isn't right,' he said quickly. 'I'm an old man. Your landlord. You shouldn't be in my room—'

'Listen to me. About tomorrow . . .'

'Leave at your own discretion. I'll refund all the rent you paid—'

'About Soderini's party.'

His face fell. 'Oh, Julia. Please don't . . .'

'I have a suggestion. I want you to consider it. I'll go to the Brigata Spendereccia . . .'

'I should never have asked you.'

'It's an invitation from the mayor of Florence! How can I refuse? If it turns a touch risqué, I'll leave. And if there's something there of use, I can tell you.'

He gave her a baleful stare. 'What's the other half of the deal?'

'Oh, that's easy,' she said. 'Next week you come back to England with me. Just for a few days or so. I told you. My dad's a doctor. There are people in Harley Street . . .'

'I've seen every doctor in Italy!'

'Don't exaggerate.'

'What about the money?'

'Leave that to me . . .'

'But why?'

She started to shut the door, signalling the conversation was at an end. 'Because I want to see what you look like out of here. I want to know if you're right, and a part of the poison is Florence itself. And, if it is . . . In London maybe . . .'

'Go back to your room and forget this nonsense.'

'No. I won't.'

'You're the most stubborn woman I've ever met. Chiara was a compliant angel next to you. Leave me.'

'No!'

Another flurry of Florentine curses that she was glad she didn't quite understand.

'You won't ever want to stop chasing him, will you?'

'Not now,' he admitted. 'Why should I? It's too late.'

'And if you find him?'

'Then Walter can do his job. What do you think? That this is about vengeance? Please . . .'

'I didn't mean that.'

'Then what?'

'What if the truth doesn't just release the poison? What if it takes everything you have?'

He smiled. 'If poison's all that's kept me alive, then I'll die, and deservedly,' he said. 'Which will happen anyway. Unless . . .'

'Unless?'

'Unless something else – a miracle – comes to take its place.'

Julia said nothing for a long minute. 'Do we have an agreement, Pino Fratelli?' she asked finally.

'If you insist, Miss Wellbeloved,' he replied, and his sad eyes never left hers. 'Now goodnight.'

Thursday, 6 November 1986

First thing the following morning, Fratelli got his cordless phone and, from the comfort of his bed, called everyone he could think of. A sleepy Luca Cassini. Two butchers in Sant'Ambrogio market. A retired Carabinieri officer who was none too pleased to be woken after a hard night on the booze.

Finally the priest, Father Bruno, with whom he had a pleasant, brief conversation, acknowledging the wisdom of accepting his fate and one day – not this day, but soon – returning to Carmine,

taking the magic wine and the holy bread once more, setting foot
on the happy road to dying in the arms of the Lord, and with such
acquiescence winning the guarantee of a decent Catholic burial,
eulogy, hymns, blessing and all.

The shroud of a good Florentine waited for him there, and with
it he could climb into the grave contented.

He thanked the man for his concern, could not help but hear the
note of wariness in the priest's voice. Then he fell immediately
asleep for a while, only to be woken at nine by a roaring sound he
knew only too well. When he walked out into the living room, Julia
was having breakfast at the kitchen table. Filling the door was the
large shape of Signora Grassi, blocking out the grey winter light,
demanding answers.

The first Thursday of every month.

She did an extra shift to keep the place clean. He should have
remembered. But lots of things slipped his memory these days.

Julia was in her blue pyjamas. A pot of coffee in front of her.
Two plates. Some toast and butter and jam.

'I slept late and thought you wouldn't mind if I helped myself,'
she said with a sweet smile, holding up a jar of strawberry preserve.

The radio was on, the news dominated by the arms find outside
Fiesole. Few details; only that the Carabinieri were looking for an
American woman in connection with the haul.

'Well, Fratelli?'

Signora Grassi had her hands on her hips, lips pressed together
in an expression that, on another woman, might have passed for a
pout.

'Well what? My guest needed breakfast. Why shouldn't she help
herself?'

A salute, a wry grin from the table, then Julia Wellbeloved got
on with her coffee.

The Grassi dragon rattled her mops and brooms.

'This is my house,' he added bravely. 'I'm grateful for your
assistance, as always. But there's nothing for the confessional here,
I promise . . .'

'I shall return in thirty minutes,' the woman announced. 'By then
I expect you to be dressed and gone. Some of us have work to do.'

'We do,' Fratelli agreed, and smiled as she left.

Coffee at the breakfast table. A pleasant face opposite. He'd
forgotten what it was like.

'You slept well,' he said.

'I did.'

'Me too.'

'You agreed to something last night. You promised. Three Negronis won't stop you . . .'

'You counted. I'm impressed.'

'You do remember?'

'Of course I do.'

'I told you. I can't take it if people lie to me. If they break—'

'I don't lie and a promise is a promise. If this futile visit to London's what you want. But don't go to Soderini's party for my sake, please.'

'I'm not.'

'Then why?'

'For mine. Because I want to. You don't understand. I've led such a trivial life.'

'It doesn't look trivial from where I'm sitting. It looks fresh and full of hope and promise. And adventure.'

'Well, it seems trivial to me.'

He picked up a piece of toast. Spread butter. Jam. Drank some coffee. Felt that if there were a paradise, a place from which the couple in the Brancacci had been expelled, it would be very like this. No need of peacocks and unicorns, of fiery, sword-wielding angels and dire, judgemental threats.

'Then you should go to the Brigata Spendereccia, whatever, wherever it is. And tomorrow I shall pack my bags for London. Which holds the same sense of mystery for me, I might add. Though where the money—'

'I'll call my dad and make some arrangements. We won't get an appointment till Monday at the earliest. There's no need to leave tomorrow. The weekend will do. Whenever's easiest.'

She rose from the chair, picked up her plate and mug. He lacked the intuition to interpret the look in her eyes. Pity? A sense of care? A simple bond of amity?

'And this morning?' Fratelli asked. 'What are you doing?'

'Shopping for a dress, of course. Something suitable for this evening. You?'

A flash of guilt on his face.

'I thought I'd . . . go for a walk.'

'Where?'

'Up the hill,' he said, vaguely waving at the ceiling.

'You won't go near Walter Marrone, will you?'

'Of course not. I'll have a coffee with Luca somewhere if he has the time. Tell him not to dwell on all that stuff I told him last night. Perhaps we could go to San Marco with you.'

The suggestion surprised her. 'Good idea. That should keep the pair of you out of trouble,' she said, then deposited the plate and the mug by the sink and walked to her room.

Pino Fratelli watched her go, thinking.

In twenty minutes the Grassi dragon would be back. He needed to be out of the house. Talking to people. Feeling his way back into the case, the way he should have done days before. Directly.

Morning in the green bowers and lost glades of the Boboli Gardens. The two of them emerged late and lacking in words.

Somewhere in the distance, a high-pitched two-stroke engine whirred. Voices. Men at work. It was close to ten. A bright clear day, though grey-brown clouds were starting to gather against the blue sky, as if to talk about the rain to come.

'They'll find us,' she said, taking his arm, pulling him back into the shadow of the doorway.

The smell of the cottage, damp and smoke from the fire he'd set, was stronger than ever. The workmen were tending to the ornamental gardens a good distance away. Closest to them were the vegetable patches: winter onions, dying artichokes, kale and cabbage. He knew the routine by heart. Some time around eleven, one of the kitchen people would come round looking for something to throw into the inevitable *ribollita* for the staff. Stale bread, green leaves, some cold meat if they had it, onions and garlic. He'd grown up on this pauper's fare and the memory brought its smell to his nostrils as vividly as if his dead mother was reheating the same old pot on the stove, the way she did most days.

'We could run,' he said.

That sounded like a prayer now, uttered into silence, not knowing where it went.

'Tomorrow, Aldo.'

He got what few things he had. Passed her the rest of her clothes. Then hid the weapons and the ammunition. When the gardeners came, they'd think tramps had broken in, spent the night, and fled knowing there'd be a beating if they were found.

The men were stupid. They'd never look behind the log store, thinking to find semiautomatic weapons and bullets there.

'We're here for a reason,' she insisted, touching his arm – not that he minded any more. He was hers. He was fallen. He was one among the grey doomed drones who walked the streets of Florence. 'We have to. Then we're gone.'

'Where?'

She hesitated then. He knew why. She'd never given it a second thought.

'The south. Calabria. It's warm there. And green.'

'Never been,' he said.

'I have. I'm telling you.'

Another voice outside. Nearer.

He picked up what few things he owned and walked outside, found the narrow meandering path back to the broken door in the wall, knew she was following all the way.

Soon they were in San Niccolò, glad to be drinking two hot cups of cappuccino and eating warm *cornetti*.

'Who was this man you told me about?'

'What man?'

His head felt light and unreal. Life was a machine moved by cogs and mechanisms. Something had turned the previous night, as she strained and heaved over him, screeching with her passion, bringing the same animal noises from his throat. Forcing him back with her fist when he tried to turn her, straddle over her, do the same in return.

'The one they burned. The one they hated. Your hero.'

'Savonarola,' he said, remembering the brass plaque outside the Palazzo Vecchio, and how he'd placed Vanni Tornabuoni's head beneath the fist of Perseus, a few short strides away, dead eyes set on the cobblestones where the priest and his two fellow martyrs had died amidst the jeers and crackling flames almost five centuries before.

'He was a good man who saw the world as it was.'

'But who was he, Aldo?'

He looked at the clock. Time to go to work. To the refectory kitchens that the catering company rented from the city for the occasion; the same kitchens that had once fed the awkward friar and his little army.

'I'll show you,' he said.

*   *   *

Sandro Soderini spent most of the morning alone in his office in the Palazzo Vecchio, putting off meetings, refusing calls.

Thinking . . .

Had Vanni Tornabuoni received those same, strangely worded threatening letters? If so, the voluble arts commissioner had never mentioned them, which was strange and out of character. Besides, the language . . .

The bloody antics of the Red Brigades had been headline news for more than a decade. They were revolutionaries, fired by a perverted brand of savage Marxism. Not religious fanatics wishing to warn their victims with the mangled words of a lunatic priest.

Something felt amiss. And then there was the nosy, persistent and sick Carabinieri detective. He knew a little of the man's background from Marrone. But nothing in it explained why he was out in the countryside around Fiesole, chasing what appeared to be the last, fugitive member of a terrorist gang. One most of Italy thought had ceased to exist, shattered by raids and prison sentences that would see an end to the bloodshed and the fear that had dogged politicians and industrialists the length of the nation.

None of this made the mayor of Florence feel happy or secure.

So he picked up the phone and got through to Marrone in Ognissanti, demanded a report on the state of the investigation, into the woman called Chavah Efron and the man thought to be with her.

He got the captain's usual surly grunt, then a perfunctory report: photos distributed, social service records checked. Nothing much found.

'Her VW van was left in a side road in San Niccolò last night. We found some prints there,' Marrone said. 'We're checking them now.'

'You think they're in the city then?'

'It depends how stupid they are,' the Carabinieri officer replied. 'If they have any sense they'll have stolen a car and got out. I've sent people down to the stations to check the bus services. If this woman's a genuine terrorist, she'll know the form. The moment you think your cover's blown, you flee. She'll have the money. Contacts elsewhere . . .'

'I thought,' Soderini said archly, 'we'd dealt with this scum.'

'As did I.'

'Then who would she go to?'

Silence. Then Marrone said, 'I've put extra officers in the Piazza della Signoria. Around the civic buildings elsewhere. All the obvious targets. Given the amount of weapons and explosive they left behind, I doubt they could have taken much with them. They were in a hurry.'

'Guesswork, Captain. We don't pay you for that.'

'What do you want of me?' Marrone asked, a harsh note of temper in his voice.

'Certainty. Knowledge. These people out of the way. For good.'

'I'll do my best. In return I require circumspection on your part. Don't engage in any new public engagements without our prior knowledge. Keep us informed. Be vigilant. This event of yours tonight. I assume it's cancelled.'

Soderini felt the heat rise in his head. 'Because?'

'It's a time to lie low,' Marrone added. 'To stay out of sight. If you—'

'Florence is my city! Don't presume to tell me where to go and what to do.'

'I advise—'

'This is a private engagement of long standing. God knows I've missed enough of them already. We're not cowards. Nor are we parading ourselves in public. You know your duty when it comes to that. Find these two. The American and whoever's with her. Do what you must. If you can save us the expense of a jail term, all the better . . .'

'The way someone dealt with Aristide Greco?'

Soderini was astonished by his tone. 'That seemed an admirable outcome to me. One less dangerous parasite to deal with. Are you going soft in your dotage, Marrone? Do I need someone younger and better to run the Ognissanti *stazione*?'

No answer.

Eventually the gruff and distant voice said, 'Even in Florence, there's a limit to how much shit can be shovelled underneath the cobblestones. The journey from hero to villain can be remarkably short. I thought a professor of history might appreciate that.'

Then the line went dead.

Julia Wellbeloved wandered through the shops in the Via dei Calzaiuoli, gasped at the prices, meandered round the Duomo, found a coffee in a place with a payphone, managed to call England, reversing the charges.

She felt like a teenager again. Stranded somewhere. Stupid and in trouble. Not that she'd done that more than two or three times. Her father seemed more amused than offended and listened carefully as she talked of what she wanted: an appointment with the appropriate consultant in Harley Street the week after. A favour from a friend who'd offer at least an opinion for free, or whatever sum a doctor felt to be a pittance.

That done, she wandered east towards Sant'Ambrogio, finally found a black evening dress in a second-hand shop run by a garrulous, friendly woman with too much make-up and a cigarette dangling permanently from her lower lip.

By then it was noon. Fifteen minutes' walk away was San Marco, the famous convent, now a museum and closed for refurbishment, but not to friends of Sandro Soderini. She slipped into the first cheap café she met, bought a glass of wine and a panino. Wondered where Pino Fratelli was.

Not strolling up the hill. That was for sure.

'You think you can get round me with a bit of bread and some *lampredotto*?'

Noon in the Sant'Ambrogio market. Fratelli and Luca Cassini back at the same stall.

'I was being generous. Trying to say sorry for last night. I never wanted to drag you into my problems. You insisted . . .'

Cassini had been told to steer clear of the *stazione* for a few days until the air cleared and Walter Marrone decided what to do with him. The prospect of being kicked out of the Carabinieri didn't seem to bother him one jot. His father was already talking about a career in one of the leather stores, selling expensive valises to rich foreigners. Not a job he fancied, Fratelli felt, but Luca Cassini was an easy, amenable soul. One who expected little of the world and was grateful mostly for what he got.

'And then what?' the young man asked.

'Then we go to meet Julia in San Marco. You like painting, don't you?'

''Course I do. Don't know a thing about it, mind. Why are we going there?'

'Because she asked for us! Must I always have an ulterior motive?'

'You tell me,' Cassini spluttered.

'Don't talk with your mouth full. Just listen, Luca. Walter Marrone still has no idea who this man is. The one who was hiding with Chavah Efron when we went out to Fiesole yesterday. It says on the radio they've found the van. There'll be prints in it, but you know how long it'll take to match them to anything.'

'They've got a computer now.'

'A decent filing clerk would find us an answer more quickly.'

'This isn't your problem, Pino, is it? Or mine?'

'I've made certain inquiries. Around the market here. To see who's been buying curious food.'

'What's that got to do with that stuff we found in Fiesole?'

'Perhaps nothing. Who knows? The man who attacked the paintings in the Brancacci—'

'Here we go again.'

'There's a link,' Fratelli insisted. 'I'm sure of it.'

Cassini finished his panino, balled up the paper it came in, threw it on the stone market floor.

'Marrone's got a whole team on the case. And some big knobs up from Rome. One mention of the word terrorist and you're knee deep in blokes in black suits and sunglasses on their heads. Funny lot, if you ask me.'

'How do you know this?' Fratelli asked.

'I did report for work this morning, you know. Asked a few questions before they booted me out of the *stazione*. I'm not daft.'

'I never thought you were. And the more we work together, the more I like what I see.'

'I'll give you a discount on a nice handbag then,' Cassini moaned.

'You're not out of the Carabinieri yet. We need a name. I've made inquiries. It'll take a little while. If you could find a way to sneak back into Ognissanti this afternoon . . .'

'More than my life's worth. Captain Marrone stared daggers at me this morning. I was lucky to get out of there with my balls intact, thank you.'

Fratelli shrugged.

'Stop it!' Cassini cried. 'I'm not going back in there.'

'Fine. Your choice. I respect it.'

'Pino . . .'

But Fratelli wasn't listening. Someone was marching down the hall towards him. A big man in white cotton overalls and green boots, covered in blood from chest to fat thighs.

He was grinning and waving a piece of paper in one hand, a long yellow chicken neck, the head still intact, red comb, shiny mustard beak, sinews dripping from the severed end.

'Fratelli!' the butcher roared when he found them. 'I have news!'

The refectory kitchen in San Marco. Blood and flesh beneath the frescoes of the last supper: hungry saints watching a whey-faced Christ. Fish and raw winter vegetables: the dark crinkled leaves of cavolo nero, leeks and carrots, chicory and radicchio. Pontecorvo examined the produce on the table, reading the menu for the night.

Waiting to be told.

That was all he did, and now the orders came from someone new. She was making *puntarelle* by the sink the way he'd instructed, scraping the tall, weed-like chicory plants into pale green strips then dropping them into a bowl full of water and ice cubes to curl. On the counter by the side stood a basin of crushed, salty anchovies and olive oil that would cover them when, finally, that evening, they were served among the antipasti.

It was two in the afternoon. The temporary staff for the catering company that occupied the ground-floor premises – once a refectory for Savonarola's novice monks – had assembled for work. The money was a pittance; experience was, for the thugs who hired them, a boon. So he'd had no difficulty persuading them to take on a new hiring, a strong young woman who'd carry and skivvy and do whatever they wanted.

The company only worked special occasions, one each month more special than the rest. Aldo Pontecorvo had been left to his own devices when it came to that commission. He was a fixture; had been that way for more than two decades when he began as a lowly trainee sous chef waiting on tables, too fearful of his betters to look them in the eye. Now this was his task alone and no one even asked him what the menu would be. The epicurean splendours of the Brigata Spendereccia, which would be only one of the attractions on offer for that evening in the secret hiding place of the Medici, were left to his imagination and slow, patient research among cookery books going back eight centuries and more.

As usual, one week before, he'd spent one morning going through the resources handed down from generations past, in the archive building near Sant'Ambrogio. Then he'd scribbled down the dishes and walked round the busy, colourful market, talking to buyers, assessing what was practical.

They didn't pay him for this. It was a reward of its own. Left to his own devices in the archives, with a tame librarian willing to fetch anything he asked for, Aldo Pontecorvo had, over the years, read some of the most precious documents the city owned. Touched the paper Savonarola had written upon. Run his fingers over the words of Benvenuto Cellini, complaining about the miserly philistines of the Medici court. Felt the bloody history of the city rise from the pages and infect his troubled, wandering mind.

The nobility of the thirteenth and fourteenth centuries possessed tastes as bizarre and outlandish as their heirs of the twentieth. They were no strangers to herbs and spices from the Orient, to obscure meat and fowl, and fanciful *dolci* that mixed sweet with sour, fruit with meat. When he knew what was possible he would place orders for the produce and then, the Sunday before the Brigata meeting, start the preparation: cutting and slicing, setting aside the flesh to marinate, in oil and vinegar, honey and herbs.

Then his landlord threw him out. After that, in the pouring rain and cold, alone, wandering the bleak streets of Oltrarno, the worm of anger and vengeance began to work inside him.

Now he was back in their midst, turning the results of those ancient scribbles from the archives into a banquet to be delivered by van at six that evening, and carefully set up in the secret place where the ceremony took place.

Then he would stay and help serve, as usual. Watch in horror and shame, sometimes, and still be too fearful to flee.

On the long, wooden tables, cracked with age, bleached with centuries of use, ranged bowls of handmade *testaroli* pasta, sage leaves ready to be fried in batter. Doves lay naked on metal platters. Rabbits, flayed and jointed, their kidneys and livers reserved by their side for the sauce. Ugly monkfish split open, their delicate intestines removed to make tripe antipasti. Piglets' feet, as pale and naked as those of children, were tidied in serried lines on trays ready for the oven; alongside them rows of ducks' necks, stuffed with forcemeat and plums, heads and long waxy beaks arranged neatly in a line, as if this were a troop of dead birds saluting to the left. A vast cauldron of soup made from spelt, the grain the Etruscans ate, simmered on the kitchen range. And for the dessert, platters of fruit and circles of *panforte*, not the sweet dessert fed to the tourists, but the original *peposo*, laced with pepper and spices and filled with the piquant minced pork.

And *cibreo*.

A feast for the lords of Florence. The kind they would have gorged on when Dante and Botticelli walked the streets outside. When Savonarola himself sat upstairs in this very building, locked in his plain, ascetic cell, praying for the deliverance of the city from such sinful extravagances, listening to the word of God and then proclaiming it in angry sermons from the pulpit in the Duomo.

There were two minions in the kitchen at that moment. A surly, talentless kitchen hand from Turin, and a silent, miserable woman who came in from Empoli when needed. He ordered the man to turn up the heat on the huge gas grill they used for searing and grilling, then told them both to take their break now, a few minutes earlier than usual, and not to hurry back.

'It's Christmas?' the man from Turin said.

'You want free time or not?' Aldo Pontecorvo retorted.

He joined Chavah, still patiently slicing the vast heads of chicory into the icy water for *puntarelle*.

'Tonight. They're not all bad,' he said. 'Just some of the men. One in particular.'

'You do your part,' she ordered. 'Don't worry about me.'

Still, he hesitated.

'Why did you kill Tornabuoni?' she asked.

No answer. She came close to him, placed her hand, weather-beaten and scarred, on his chest.

'It wasn't for me at all, was it?'

Twenty years before, that night in the dark streets, water everywhere. Time didn't pass. It stayed with you sometimes, clinging to your mind like foul mud. And now it was alive again, starting to move.

Two days before he'd killed a man. That was supposed to be an end to things. Not a beginning.

'This is enough,' he muttered. 'No more.'

'No, Aldo,' she said, taking the lapels of his stained white jacket. 'We do what life makes us. What *they* make us.'

He could smell her breath, sweet from the fruit she'd been picking at in the kitchen. Some slices still stood in her hand. Sharp, hard apple from Trentino, ready to be turned into sugary fritters.

Chavah reached up and placed a slice of the fruit in his mouth, fed it beyond his lips and watched him, stroking his chest as he ate.

*   *   *

San Marco was little to look at from the outside. One more church portico on a piazza, a visitors' entrance by the side. Julia met Fratelli and Luca Cassini at the door, then Fratelli spoke to a caretaker. Soon they were joined by the director of the museum, a harassed-looking individual who introduced himself as Franco Mariani.

He was a nervous man, cadaverous, with thinning brown hair and a gloomy face made more miserable by a drooping walrus moustache and sad, brown eyes. Mid-forties, the standard age for civic dignitaries in Florence it seemed, and dressed in the well-tailored business suit which seemed to be the uniform for senior city officials.

'What's this?' Mariani asked, glaring at Fratelli. 'You're Carabinieri. I recognize you from the past. That break-in. The Palazzo Vecchio said nothing about you.' A pause – bitterness, not regret, on his face. 'Don't you have better things to occupy you on a day like this?'

'This is pleasure, not business,' Fratelli told him. 'Tornabuoni's case is well taken care of . . .'

'Those terrorists—'

'Do not visit shuttered museums, I assure you. Captain Marrone—'

'My appointment's with the woman—'

'Luca and Pino are helping me,' Julia interrupted. 'With the mayor's knowledge and encouragement, I believe.' That took him down a peg. 'We've been following the vandalism in the Brancacci. They have a professional interest.'

Mariani swore and shook his head.

'Three times in twenty years I've seen this. A French fool in the Uffizi, with a hatred for Botticelli. Some mischievous idiot in the Pitti. A man who somehow managed to get a mallet into the Accademia. Paint, ripped canvas, shattered marble. Had they done this to a man or a woman, they would have languished in jail for years. Instead we send them to a comfortable institution, wait while they calm down and then blink innocently as if to say: that was me?'

'You've spoken to these people?' Julia asked.

'Once. The Frenchman.' Mariani frowned, as if trying to remember. 'This was some years ago, in the beginning when, like you, I thought there was something to be learned.'

'And?' Fratelli prompted him.

'He said Simonetta Vespucci – Botticelli's muse, if you recall – reminded him of his girlfriend. Who had recently dumped him.' The director opened his arms wide in despair. 'That was it. Why do we allow such scum through the door in the first place? They've no appreciation. No feeling. No sensitivity. Art is for those who appreciate it, not the masses.'

'How can the masses begin to appreciate what they can't see?' Julia asked, genuinely puzzled.

'And Benvenuto Cellini and his kind were not sensitive men in some respects,' Fratelli noted. 'Julia' – he nodded in her direction – 'would simply like to hear what precautions you intend to take when you reopen San Marco to the public. To learn what you know of those who would harm the treasures in your care.'

'The latter first,' Mariani declared. 'They're lunatics and vandals. Religious maniacs. The insane. How else can you explain it? What is there to comprehend?'

'Soderini said they hated beauty,' Julia told him.

'Which is true. Soderini's an intelligent, learned man. He understands these things intimately, from his own perspective. He will . . .'

Mariani's declaration stuttered to a halt.

'He'll what?' Julia asked.

'Be a better source of guidance on this subject than I,' the man said in a low, hard voice. 'Come. I'll show you what we can do to prevent such damage. It was next to nothing before these present works. It will be next to nothing after. After which, you must leave. We're in no fit state for visitors, nor do I have staff to keep you company.'

'I need a break,' Pontecorvo said, then left the three of them working in the kitchen and walked out into the open courtyard of Savonarola's convent. He felt he could hear the voices of all those dead Dominicans whispering in the shadows as he walked; another sinner on the road, another soul striding towards Purgatory. Briskly, moving at speed in the belief that haste might still his thoughts and fears, he strode to the former hospice building by the cloister. The place was empty. This was November. A dead month for all but the hardiest of visitors, even at the best of times. With most of the complex closed to tourists, only the occasional workmen and civic officials meandered its corridors.

He strode into the hospice and sat in front of the work that dominated the room, Fra Angelico's *Last Judgement*. In the centre stood the tombs of the dead, thrown open by a blue-robed Christ in Judgement, seated on his throne in the sky, surrounded by the Virgin, saints and angels. To the left, the godly and chaste entered the Garden of Eden, hand in hand beneath those same trees and palms and trilling birds that Masolino and Masaccio had painted in the Brancacci. The gate to Heaven, the portal through which Adam and Eve had been expelled in the beginning, was open now, and welcoming. Through it flooded the glorious golden light of God Himself. The worthy entered Paradise to enjoy eternal life and joy. While, on the right, demons and monsters drove vile sinners and the unrepentant to Hell, stabbing them with stakes until they passed through into a subterranean inferno of pain and agony and torture; a pitiless, never-ending torment, where the fallen devoured one another and were in turn torn to pieces by a grim, horned Satan surrounded by the flesh and entrails of his victims.

His eyes strayed upwards, to the ceiling. The cell of Savonarola, where the man had worked alone in fury, documenting the venality of the city with fearful warnings, stood somewhere above.

He'd read those sermons while he was supposed to be searching the state archives for ancient recipes to amuse the Brigata Spendereccia. Sinners were meant to enter the eternal fire. The wicked deserved retribution. Those who did God's work . . .

An image of the horror in the barn in Fiesole came to him. Tornabuoni trying to scream from behind the gag. A bloody corpse, bone and gore.

In the cold chamber of the hospice, Aldo Pontecorvo shivered, trying to force those pictures from his head.

He'd shown Chavah all these places when they'd first arrived that morning. Did she understand? Had she guessed? Why now? After twenty years in purgatory?

Because he couldn't live with himself, with the pain, any more. Not that he could tell her.

So he got up and walked back to the kitchen, checked the work, went back into the convent and headed for the cloister and the stairs to the first-floor dormitories where the brothers had lived in sacred isolation most of their lives.

It was so cold, he half expected to see frost shimmering on the plain columns and arches. There were voices, loud and confident. He stopped and fell immediately into the cloister shadows. Two men: one middle-aged, with an intelligent, acute face and long white hair; the second younger, burly. Big feet, black shoes, broad, aggressive face.

And a woman. Striking, with a long, pale face, fair hair tied back severely so that it exaggerated her high forehead. He was close enough to hear their voices. She was speaking. Italian with a foreign accent.

A voice he'd heard before. His own words came back to him and he felt himself shiver involuntarily.

What are you looking at?

Then that frightened, accented response.

Niente, niente, niente.

He watched this tall, composed and serious Englishwoman.

All acts invited responses. Sins demanded confession or retribution. They began a cycle that only virtue and sacrifice could close.

He slunk back to the kitchen, keeping to the dark side of the cloisters all the way.

His practised eye ranged over the dishes. Most, he was glad to see, were complete. What work remained was menial and easily left to others. Transport was in the hands of the catering company. All seemed organized.

'Chavah,' he said, taking her to one side.

She looked bored. These chores didn't suit her.

'The police are here.'

'How?'

'I don't know. Two nights ago in the square . . . a woman saw me.'

A flash of anger. 'You never told me this.'

It didn't seem important. A stranger's face in the dark.

'We should leave,' he said. 'Right away. You can . . .'

This tense relationship ebbed and flowed. He'd no idea which of them was dominant at that moment.

'I can what?'

'Take some things and go. It's me they want. You've done nothing.'

'We're not done yet.'

'Just go . . .'

She held him then, tightly, refusing to move. There was something so plain and ordinary in her touch, he wondered that he'd avoided this simple intimacy all these years.

'No,' she whispered. 'I won't. And nor shall you.'

The four of them walked up a stone staircase, past scaffolding and sheeting, Mariani striding ahead, talking all the time, of history and the difficulties of preserving it. He stopped at the top and, for all the recent dark events, Julia Wellbeloved found herself smiling with a sudden, warm burst of instant pleasure. She'd read about this place. It was a little out of the centre of the city. One more institution that hid its jewels from prying, public eyes.

Now, with the help of the director's incisive, brisk talk, she recalled the story of the remarkable works of art created here for the benefit of the solitary, ascetic inhabitants alone. In the middle of the fifteenth century, two decades before Savonarola's arrival, the artist brother Fra Angelico had been asked to decorate the forty-three monastic cells that ran along three first-floor corridors of the dormitory surrounding the Sant'Antonino cloister. Here the friars read and thought and prayed, surrounded by frescoes mostly from the hand of the man they knew simply as 'Brother John of Fiesole'.

At the head of the stairs stood the most breathtaking of Angelico's images, a large *Annunciation* of such tender humanity it was impossible not to be moved by its sense of simple and serene joy, its wonder at the miracle of life. A slender, pious Mary sat, head bowed, in an archway next to a beautiful garden, listening carefully to the words of an angel with glorious multicoloured wings telling her she would bear the son of God. There was something so touching, so personal about the painting, that she could only marvel that it came from the hands and imagination of a monk sworn to celibacy and retreat from the venal, living world beyond San Marco's walls.

A sheet of thick plate glass covered the whole of the fresco.

'That's it?' Fratelli asked, going closer to the fresco than the rest. 'That's your protection?'

'What else are we supposed to do?' Mariani asked. 'The work belongs at the head of the stairs. It's the introduction to the dormitories. Would you rather it were lost in the Uffizi?'

'Not at all,' Julia said. 'It's perfect here.'

'Of course,' the director agreed. 'This is its home and always has been.' He glanced at the ceiling. 'We'll have some video cameras up there. In all the entrances. Anywhere someone might get in. There'll be more attendants, sitting around doing nothing all day. The cost of all this' – he shrugged – 'will come from the drones who troop through the door, naturally. But if you ask me . . . can we stop the madmen?'

Mariani's eyes fell on the perfect, calm face of Angelico's Mary.

'No. What if someone were to smuggle a hammer beneath their jacket and attack the glass? Should we search everyone? Art's like life. The safer we make it, the more remote and meaningless it becomes.'

They walked along the corridor. In each of the modest cells was another painting from the life and passion of Christ. Jesus risen from the tomb, telling a prostrate Mary Magdalene, '*Noli Me Tangere*' – do not touch me. Deposed from the cross. As an innocent, naked infant at the Nativity. Then, in a strange, almost surrealistic image, blindfolded and holding a cane and globe, the symbols given him by his tormentors, slapped by unearthly hands, spat at by a disembodied head.

Ropes cordoned off each cell. Anyone might step over them in an instant.

'We'll let people know where they can and cannot go and keep them out as much as we can,' Mariani said. 'They may wander into a few cells that contain lesser works. But . . .' He sighed. 'This is the extent of our precautions. If you have any other suggestions, do please tell us. Paintings are like children. One must love them, protect them, guard them against evil as much as possible. But they live in the real world, our world. One can no more protect them against everything than one can keep the grimmer side of life secret from a son or a daughter. Angelico was a practical man. He would never have expected his work to continue to amaze people here five centuries after his death. There's the miracle. That we have it at all. Besides . . .'

A wry look of amusement broke his scowling features for a moment. 'We fool ourselves if we think a few psychopaths are our greatest enemy. Time, neglect and forces we cannot control wreak more havoc on this city than its inhabitants. Decay, so-called restoration . . .'

He led them to a small annexe at the end of the corridor.

'These were his quarters. A small oratory, a study, a bedroom.'

Mariani guided them to a panoramic painting on the wall. It depicted, he said, Florence at the end of the fifteenth century, not so much changed in the centre from today. The Palazzo Vecchio looked a little more grey and severe, Brunelleschi's dome on the Duomo rather more pristine. The hillside church of San Miniato al Monte was visible to the right behind San Niccolò, unchanged. Through the canvas, the Arno wound beyond city walls, now but remnants, out into verdant countryside and on to the distant peaks of the Tuscan Apennines.

Townsmen and -women wandered around the Piazza della Signoria in the foreground, chattering, bargaining, meandering on horseback. Children played tag. Soldiers flourished their weapons. Only a few

– among them two men carrying bundles of faggots on their backs – seemed to notice the commotion at the centre: a bonfire joined to the Palazzo Vecchio by a wooden walkway, a tree trunk rising in its midst, planks to make a scaffold, a ladder attached to its summit.

Painters of this period often played with the notion of time, she remembered. This represented not a single event but a succession of them, all leading to the same moment. On the steps of the Palazzo Vecchio, three men in white knelt before a makeshift court (the tribunal of judgement, Mariani said), watched by a handful of bystanders from the bare steps of a loggia free of sculpture. At the same time, these three condemned men appeared on the pathway to the fiery stake, held between the arms of burly minders in black, faces hidden beneath sinister, pointed hoods.

Then, finally, in death. Three ragged figures, suspended by nooses, consumed by flames.

'There,' Mariani declared, 'Savonarola built the bonfire of the vanities in which Botticelli and even Michelangelo destroyed their work. If you believe the tourist books, anyway. And died on the same spot himself a few years later. They seized him . . .'

He pointed back towards the way they'd come.

'Right there. By the library. I can show you the very spot. There's a plaque on the wall.'

History.

It was beginning to swirl around her again, making the room swim, filling her head with strange thoughts.

'He can't have hated art that much,' Mariani's brittle, unemotional voice continued. 'He never saw fit to demand the destruction of the frescoes that graced his own home. Nor bar his adoring followers from recording his own image. A hypocrite. Come . . .'

They turned a corner into the tiny room that was, the sign said, Savonarola's private oratory. Mariani pointed out a small portrait on the wall. A tonsured man in a monk's habit, smiling though his head was split open by a vicious, blood-drenched sword.

'Fra Bartolomeo,' the director continued, 'came after Angelico. A more sophisticated man in some ways. A friend and associate of Raphael. But a Savonarola lover . . . have no doubt. This he painted as a memorial to the friar after his death. The city dignitaries might have had his head if they'd known, naturally. So the portrait pretends to be of Peter, not our awkward, fundamentalist monk. It's him though. Without doubt. Follow, please . . .'

They walked on into the next room, Savonarola's own cell.

A new portrait now, close up, frank. From life, it could only be.

Julia Wellbeloved looked at it and found herself unable to move, to think clearly, to speak for a moment.

It was the man from the canvas in the other room, but seen in an entirely different light. Wrapped in a black cloak that might have been a shroud, his face was pale and hairless, his nose and eyes prominent and marked with both pain and some solitary determination.

'It would seem Bartolomeo dashed this off in the brief time after Savonarola was seized and before his execution. Perhaps from memory of a meeting in the Bargello. There's an air of foreboding about it . . .' Mariani came nearer and gazed at the head close up. 'Quite remarkable. I intend to move both these works to somewhere more spacious before long. In some quarters Savonarola is regarded as a martyr. There are those who wish him beatified – not that the Vatican will play ball. The Dominicans, or some at least, wish it. Others regard him as a heretic and a criminal. He died excommunicated and remains so. I'm too timid and too wise to step into a fight between priests. Bartolomeo's portrait was held in private hands for centuries. We only acquired it a few years ago. If it's true to life – and there's no reason to think it's not – I'm glad I never got to meet our severe and judgemental friar. He hated what Florence was in his own time. I doubt he would have approved of what we've become since. Though perhaps we should follow his example, and those of his executioners, and burn our pesky vandals instead . . .'

She couldn't take her eyes off the figure on the wall. The prominent nose, the burning eyes. The sense of an iron will staring death in the face.

Another image rose in her imagination. A dark shape emerging from the shadows of the Loggia dei Lanzi, bag in hand. Moving towards Cellini's *Perseus* . . .

The room dimmed, her legs folded beneath her. Before she knew it, Julia Wellbeloved was on the floor.

When she came to she was downstairs, being placed on a sofa in an office by Luca Cassini's strong arms. Even Mariani looked worried as he scuttled round getting water, offering tea, coffee, *biscotti*.

Fratelli knelt by her side. He looked terribly worried. 'What happened?' he asked.

'I fainted, of course.' She looked at Mariani and said, 'Tea would be nice. It was nothing. I'm not . . .' She felt her legs, her arms. 'Not hurt.'

More nervous now than ever, the director hurried from the room, calling to an unseen secretary somewhere.

'What really happened?' Luca Cassini asked.

'I've seen that face before. The black hood. The long nose. Those cold, dead eyes.'

Fratelli said not a word.

'But you knew that, didn't you, Pino? That's why we came.'

'You had an invitation from the mayor. Not me.'

'You knew.'

'I had an inkling. I didn't want to push you to conclusions.'

'Thank you,' she said, folding her arms.

'It's nothing,' he replied, without the least embarrassment or suggestion of an apology. A tug of the white hair. That distanced, puzzled look. 'A man who thinks of himself as the new Savonarola. A deliverer of judgement to a tainted, corrupt den of sin and iniquity.'

'We're not that bad,' Cassini complained.

'To him you are,' Julia said. 'Who is he?'

Fratelli took a piece of paper out of his pocket. It had bloodstains on it and the printed logo of a Sant'Ambrogio butcher.

'I believe his name is Aldo Pontecorvo. He buys unusual items from the market once a month. Pays cash always. Picked up an order last Saturday, three cockerels among them. Not seen since. No one knows where he works. Where he lives. A quiet, surly man. Big.'

'You've got a name?' Cassini said. 'You know what he looks like?'

'It would seem so, Luca.'

'Oh, crap.'

'What?' Julia asked.

'We're going to Ognissanti, aren't we?'

Cassini sneaked into the *stazione* by the side entrance using his ID. Fratelli and Julia Wellbeloved marched to reception and demanded an audience with Walter Marrone. After close to an hour of argument, and finally being threatened with arrest, Fratelli scribbled out a name and a description on a piece of paper and told the desk officer, 'If you want to find the accomplice of the terrorist Chavah Efron, tell your stubborn captain to look for this man.'

By six o'clock they were back at Fratelli's terrace house in Oltrarno, drinking coffee and talking in his living room. Luca Cassini had not been idle. The *stazione* had been too occupied to eject him, so he'd hung around the corridors picking up what little gossip was going. The general opinion in the office was that in Tornabuoni's gardener they had their murderer, if only he'd do them the courtesy of reaffirming their suspicions. The man had now withdrawn the confession he gave under interrogation. Even so he was due to appear in court the following day. At Fratelli's suggestion the young cop had made inquiries to see if there were any reports of an unusual-looking man wearing a black monk's habit acting suspiciously around the city. His questions had been met with raised eyebrows and a curt answer in the negative. His attempt to search the files for the name Aldo Pontecorvo had led to him being ejected by the records officer. The Romans had taken over the terrorist case and seemed unwilling to allow any locals near. If they had leads, they were keeping the fact quiet.

'Why would anyone report him?' Julia asked.

Fratelli frowned. 'Who knows? You can't get answers without asking questions. There has to be a reason he's doing this. Pontecorvo's a casual worker in the food industry. Thirty-five, forty years old according to my butcher friend. Once a month he buys unusual provisions in quantity, pays cash and never explains what he does with it all. But why should he start killing people now?'

Cassini put his coffee cup on the table and said, 'So we're looking for some bloke who thinks he's this Savonarola nutcase? A mad monk who hated . . . what, exactly?'

'Everything he saw as impure, unclean, corrupt and worldly,' Fratelli replied without the least hesitation. 'Homosexuals. Corrupt city officials. The godless. The sensuous. Men who had affairs and visited prostitutes. Women who wore garish clothes and displayed their bodies.'

'Doesn't exactly narrow it down, does it?' Cassini responded. 'He must hate most of us then.'

'I believe he does.'

'Including himself,' Julia suggested. 'Logically . . .'

'Logically he must!' Fratelli declared with a grin. 'There's an interesting thought. Didn't Savonarola whip himself in times of doubt? I don't remember. Many of his peers, though . . .' He glanced at the shelf, seemed to think about pulling down a book, then decided against it. 'Self-loathing is an interesting idea. Some burning sense of guilt. Perhaps lasting decades. I like that, but it must have a source.

A reason why he should turn murderous two nights ago – not two years or two decades. For that . . . I have no ideas whatsoever.'

He smiled at her. Julia now wore her new clothes from the second-hand shop. A simple black dress, sleeveless and modestly cut at the front, with a string of pearls, a relic of her brief marriage, around her slender neck. The shoes didn't match. Her hair was tied back in the severe way she had adopted for work. When she thought about it, she might have been ready to walk back into her old office and attack a new set of conveyancing documents. It probably wasn't right. But for such a mysterious evening, what was?

'Have I done something wrong?' she asked, worried by the way they were looking at her.

Fratelli tugged at his hair and winced.

'You look a bit scary,' Cassini offered. 'Like a schoolteacher. No offence but . . .'

She sighed then, grumbling, took off the band and shook her fair hair around her shoulders.

'That's a lot better!' the young *carabiniere* cried.

'You're too kind. What am I supposed to learn tonight?'

No answer.

'If this turns into something squalid—' she began.

'You must do what you see fit,' Fratelli cut in. 'You're a guest of the city. A foreigner. A woman who happens to be lodging with a former *maresciallo ordinario* of the Carabinieri. If you choose to walk out of the Brigata Spendereccia, Soderini might be cross, offended – vindictive, even, when it comes to helping your project in the future . . .'

'My project,' she muttered under her breath.

'He'll do nothing to prevent you leaving, Julia. He's no fool.'

Luca Cassini drained his cup. 'Well I grew up here and I never heard of this nonsense. Not till Pino mentioned it. Toffs like Soderini. All them posh people who think they own everything. They love their secrets, if you ask me. Why? I mean . . . they run the bloody place as it is. They've got this city in their tight little fists already. There's nothing left that isn't theirs, my granddad says.'

'And he's a wise and worldly man,' Fratelli added.

'Exactly,' Cassini agreed. 'So what have they got to hide?'

Julia and Fratelli exchanged glances. Luca Cassini was coming out of his shell so quickly, revealing a smart and likeable young man. She hoped Fratelli's use of him wouldn't work to his disadvantage.

A glance at her watch. It was time to go.

'Will someone walk me to the Palazzo Vecchio?' she said. 'I seem to have a date.'

'Two noble escorts into the Florentine night,' Fratelli said grandly, then stood up and offered his arm. He looked well again. Activity suited him. It was hard to believe he was sick at all when she saw him like this.

Cassini fetched her black winter coat, holding it as she shuffled her arms into the sleeves. Then they put on their own heavy jackets for the cold, damp night outside.

'Rain,' Fratelli said. 'Best we get the bus. You wouldn't want to turn up wet.'

They caught it round the corner. Empty again on this dark November evening. They went over the Ponte Santa Trinita. Luca Cassini chattered about football. Fratelli stared out of the window at the full waters of the Arno, glistening under a sickle moon. She thought of that night twenty years before when, finally, he'd struggled to make his way across this same bridge once the floods had retreated, only to find his wife murdered in the house they'd just left. That moment was with him now. She felt sure of it, from the way his eyes wouldn't leave the banks of the river, forever flitting back towards Oltrarno.

The bus bounced as it left the bridge and hit the cobbled road on the far side. Fratelli was scribbling something on his notepad, tongue out of the side of his mouth, an amusing picture of concentration.

'Here,' Fratelli said proudly, passing her a sketch of streets and palaces, and the name of a bar.

'What's this?'

'It's where we meet tonight,' Cassini said. 'Afterwards.'

'I don't know where I'm going! Or what time it finishes.'

Or I walk out, she nearly added.

'None of us can guess the time, Julia,' Fratelli told her. 'But the place.' He patted Cassini on the arm. The young officer grinned like a teenager. 'Luca's got an idea about that.'

'Our uniform lads have been told to stay away from the Pitti Palace,' Cassini added. 'Happens first Thursday of the month. Stay clear. Don't peek.'

Fratelli leaned forward and gazed into her face. 'Any trouble at all and you get up and march straight out of there. This' – he pressed the paper into her hand – 'will take you to a small café I know which stays open all hours. There we will buy you a Negroni and treat you to a professional Carabinieri debriefing.'

He rubbed his gloved hands.

'Motion. Events. Action. This is what our case requires.'

'And if you see someone who looks like that mad monk,' Cassini chipped in, 'best you run a mile.'

She didn't laugh at that, and nor did Pino Fratelli.

Walter Marrone sat alone in his office, staring at the street lamps in the Borgo Ognissanti, feeling miserable and impotent. His dealings with the awkward, enchanting Fratelli had woken memories – unpleasant, unwanted ones. Of a time, two decades almost to the day, when the fragile facade of safety and civilization had been wiped from the city in a few chill, savage hours. The handful of *carabinieri* who'd worked in the *stazione* that night did not emerge from the experience without scars. They saw a side to Florence that had lain hidden beneath the surface, unrecognized, too dark to acknowledge.

And then there was Chiara. He'd watched, powerless, as senior officers turned on the distraught Fratelli demanding answers.

Why had he called no one to the house when he found her body?

What exactly had he seen?

Marrone had tried to intervene when his friend's silent grief – obvious to one who knew him – only spurred the suspicions of those for whom he was a stranger. Or worse, half recognized as a prickly and occasionally arrogant individual in an office where ambition was stifled unless it lay in one direction only: that of satisfying the wishes of the city's powerful elite.

He'd adored Fratelli's wife for her bright intelligence, her beauty and, more than anything, the way she brought a sense of calm rationality to a difficult, occasionally wayward man he admired and regarded as a close and decent friend.

The Ognissanti *stazione* was a good Carabinieri unit, staffed by dedicated men. They worked hard to sift some truth from the grime and muck that filled that little terraced house. Yet, long as they laboured, there was nothing to be found – not in Chiara's wounded body, her torn clothes, the few scraps of evidence, a cigarette butt, a tissue; all discovered in the dank brown silt and slime that filled the doorway and half covered the staircase of Fratelli's modest home.

One new fact only had emerged. Chiara had been attacked, and perhaps died, in the first-floor living room, then left on the stairs. Nothing more.

This was two decades before. Marrone, now captain of the station, was aware his mind ought to be on other things. The callous, brutal murder of a city dignitary, if such a term could be used for Vanni Tornabuoni, a man whose vices were an open secret to his peers, and to the police and Carabinieri with whom he had occasional dealings over his indiscretions. Tornabuoni was a vile, corrupt aristocrat, an arrogant blue blood who, had he come from a different part of the city, would have found his way into the penal system years before, and doubtless landed up in the old Murate Prison where he belonged. The man charged with his murder would be dealt with. Sandro Soderini had made this clear, and what the mayor wanted the mayor got, one way or another.

But justice for Fratelli's wife? That had never happened and never would. There was no easy way of resurrecting these long-dead cases. No new conduit into the past.

Twenty years. It had taken half that time for Fratelli to reveal to Marrone the truth about his birth. How he was snatched from Rome and his parents to be brought up almost as a foundling in Oltrarno with a doting single foster mother. A decade on, the truth about Fratelli's condition became clear too. Then, Marrone had taken it on himself to call his friend into his office and tell him face-to-face that he could no longer work as a *maresciallo ordinario*, or in any other capacity for the Carabinieri.

Fratelli had shouted and screamed to no purpose. The idea was unthinkable. The doctors felt he could suffer a catastrophic collapse at any instant, one that sudden stress might bring on. Marrone had also noticed uncharacteristic lapses in his capacious memory. The man's mind, so sharp and sensitive, would fail without warning, lead him to ask the same question twice in the space of a minute, demand the answer be repeated more than once before it seemed to stick. Then, moments later, he would be normal and fail to understand that anything had been wrong.

There was treatment. Drugs and counselling, principally, since the medical advice suggested the tumour was too far advanced for the surgery and radiotherapy which would have been used had the illness been detected earlier.

The consequences were plain and depressing and both men knew it. So, on that dismal sunny day, Marrone asked for his friend's driving licence and Carabinieri ID card, put them both safely in a drawer, and then the two of them went to Fratelli's favourite bar in San Niccolò and got stinking drunk.

This was not, on reflection, the best thing to do with someone terminally ill. But that was, for Marrone, and perhaps for Fratelli too, the most infuriating aspect of the business of all. This dying man looked, for the most part, fit and well, if prone to the occasional forgetful moment and angry outburst. Until the final collapse occurred, Fratelli could, in theory anyway, function as well as any other officer inside the *stazione*. Better than most, if Marrone were honest.

But if a man couldn't drive a car, how could he act as a *maresciallo ordinario*? Or perform any more mundane functions – something Fratelli offered to do repeatedly? What price for brilliance against that ticking monster hidden beneath his skull?

All this occurred six months before, during a beautiful bright summer. At the time Marrone could not bring himself to believe that, if the doctors were right, he would be attending Pino Fratelli's funeral before another eighteen months was out. And perhaps much sooner than that.

Even then, a troubling thought had nagged him. What if the thing consuming Fratelli from the inside was somehow linked to Chiara's death? Could a man trap poison within his own head and quietly let it grow, year after year? Just as, if he were honest with himself, the city's authorities had allowed the insidious corruption of Sandro Soderini and his acolytes to spread their venomous talons over Florence and all her institutions.

After a while he'd dismissed that idea as fanciful nonsense. Until that morning in his office, when Fratelli had been on the verge of revealing something, egged on by the attractive and intelligent Englishwoman.

Pino Fratelli had a secret, something pricked by events in the Brancacci Chapel; a drop of that inner poison that had started to wake, and perhaps whisper in the ear of the larger monster inside Fratelli's head.

Time, never a friend of his, was surely running out.

Marrone was aware he should never have allowed those two to leave his office without insisting Fratelli say what was on his mind. But, thanks to his own embarrassment and cowardice, that hadn't happened, though he was determined now it would. In the morning, when the gardener was in court and the Tornabuoni case closed as Sandro Soderini wanted.

When talking to his wily friend, however, it was always best to be well informed ahead of the event. This was why, late that afternoon, Walter Marrone had called down to the records department and demanded every file that remained concerning Chiara's murder. The folders, battered manila ones, shouting their neglected age with every fold and tear, sat in front of him, their contents ranged in orderly piles around his desk. Years before, during one of the periodic clear-outs, he'd insisted nothing from the case be archived as long as he was captain of the station. Chiara's death was still as real for him as it was for Fratelli, even if there seemed scant chance that it might be reopened with any great enthusiasm.

Marrone had read every page of the reports. Two decades provided him with an interesting sense of perspective. Looking back, it seemed astonishing that anyone could have considered Fratelli a possible suspect at all. If he'd killed Chiara so viciously, why would he have stayed with her body throughout that long, heartbreaking night? What demons could make a loving husband rape and murder his own wife?

The initial suspicions of the investigating team – which Marrone could observe only from afar, since he was known to the man in the interview room – were based entirely on Fratelli's own condition, one that a more worldly Carabinieri detective, familiar with psychology in a way that was rare in 1966, would have labelled 'catatonic'. Frozen by sorrow. Rigid and silent.

Uncooperative.

An idiot investigator had scribbled that on the page. Fratelli had nothing to offer them. No pointers, no evidence, no ideas. Only his own misery, and there was a surfeit of that in mud-soaked, tragic Florence at the time. So no one noticed or listened.

This was, Marrone felt, a shame. It was clear from a cursory glance at the evidence that such a crime was surely committed through opportunity, by a man, or more than one, seizing Chiara during that strange, dark night. Four days later, the autopsy reports had confirmed that Chiara had died long before Fratelli reached her, in the early hours when he was raging in the *stazione*, struggling to reach her, or bravely fighting his way alongside his colleagues, trying to help the stricken in the flooded streets of Ognissanti.

Only then was Pino Fratelli taken off the suspect list, though it would be a full two weeks before he was able once again to speak in a fashion that could be counted normal.

What had really happened? That was the question the Carabinieri sought to answer so often in their work. A simple task, made difficult by the singular, sly and complex nature of humanity. Scanning the peripheral notes, one seemingly minor fact was new to him, however. According to the records, the pathologist had noted the presence on Chiara's face of a slight smear, one that ran from beneath her lower lips to her upper cheeks. It was light and almost indistinguishable, as if it had been rubbed, perhaps during her attack or possibly by Fratelli himself as he held her or touched her face.

The substance concerned turned out to be scarlet lipstick. The pathologist of the time was a thorough man who had later gone on to greater fame in Rome. Thanks to his persistence, four months after Chiara's death a report had arrived from a lab in Milan identifying the brand. It was expensive and French – not that anyone took much notice, since by then the case was quietly fading from view.

Marrone could never recall Chiara wearing lipstick. Artifice was not in her nature. She was beautiful without make-up. Why bother? If she died in the early hours of the morning, the idea she was wearing it when she was murdered seemed even more improbable.

And now Pino Fratelli was suddenly obsessed with an act of vandalism in the Brancacci Chapel. One that involved a smear of scarlet paint and a naked woman. Sick the man might be. But when the tumour slumbered he was as sharp and quick as ever. A connection had been made, and it was one Marrone might have heard for himself had he not been so abrupt and dismissive.

Then came another idea. One that left him feeling cold and a touch uncertain. He phoned down to the records office and managed to catch the day man before he knocked off from his shift at seven, the time Marrone's own duty was supposed to end.

The civilian seemed more than a little put out by a sudden demand for a routine office document from twenty years before. Marrone was not to be denied. He ordered it to be delivered to his desk immediately.

Ten minutes later, the records officer came in with the desk diary for the week starting Monday, 31 October 1966. The last few pages were blank. No one had had the time to write them up once the flood arrived. It was a miracle the book itself had survived the inundation.

Scanning through these twenty-year-old pages, written by officers
he barely remembered, Marrone found the days before were as
routine as most other weeks in the Ognissanti *stazione*. Domestic
arguments, traffic incidents, minor theft, lost cats, howling dogs,
drunks galore.

Right up till the moment, early on Friday morning, when the
Arno broke its banks. All the regular events were there. One he was
both surprised and appalled to see.

The first Thursday of every month.

The Brigata Spendereccia would have met around seven thirty,
as they did today. And back then they asked for seclusion too. It
was all there in the diary.

'A civic event requiring privacy in the vicinity of the Pitti Palace
will take place this evening. Security will be provided separately
by the organizers. All officers are required to avoid the area and
refer any calls in the vicinity to the relevant authority in the Palazzo
Vecchio.'

What did they do at this odd event? Marrone had his ideas.
Whispers, faint rumours. When he was promoted to captain, with
Soderini's backing, he was invited along once himself. His simple
excuse – he genuinely had another appointment – was met with an
icy stare. The offer was never repeated. Even today, only senior
officers knew of it by name, and that was primarily a lure, a
conspiratorial gag to ensure their silence when needed.

How many of the men around him had accepted Soderini's
summons? Walter Marrone didn't know and didn't want to. Like
all Italian institutions, the Carabinieri comprised multiple layers of
separate, sometimes competing, interests. He had no interest in
freemasonry or other so-called friendly societies. Those dalliances
he would leave to others.

'Go home,' he told Rossi, the grumpy civilian from the records
office. 'I'll keep this. And the rest. Thanks.'

'What's going on here?' the man retorted. 'These things are twenty
years old. There's a murderer out there right now. And here you
buggers are . . .'

'You're paid to file things, not solve them.'

'That gardener never did it. I saw him when he came in. Weakly
little thing. Couldn't chop the head off a mouse.'

'Thank you!' Marrone cried.

Rossi tapped the papers on the desk. 'Twenty years! And you're the second one going through all these dusty files today. What's this damned place coming to?'

Marrone stared at him. He should have guessed. 'You mean the files on Fratelli's wife?' he asked.

'Bah!' Rossi waved him away. 'No, I don't. That daft lad Cassini was rifling through those yesterday – doing Fratelli's bidding, if you ask me. He knew what he was looking for.'

'Did he find it?' Marrone demanded.

'I don't know! You're the captain here. You ask him.'

'And today . . .'

Rossi stamped his fist on the desk diary. 'The kid came in asking about a man. He said Fratelli tried to tell you but you'd kicked him out of the *stazione*.'

The records officer pulled a scribbled note out of his pocket. Showed him the name there: Aldo Pontecorvo.

'Did you find anything?'

The man broke into a sarcastic grin and opened his arms as if to say, 'You're asking me?'

'Did you find anything?' the captain repeated.

He went downstairs and returned with a blue folder that contained a single sheet of paper and a black-and-white mugshot of a surly, pale-faced man aged somewhere under forty.

'One more Oltrarno louse,' the man said. 'Bastard son of a madwoman who used to live in the Boboli Gardens, opening her legs for the staff there from what I can gather.'

'This is it?'

'His mamma died last January. He went a bit mad. Started shouting abuse in Santo Spirito. Stuff about the mayor and his pals.'

Cautioned, the report read. Told to sober up and go home. There was an address and a phone number. He went to the desk and called the place.

He could picture the kind of hovel from the address and the gruff, aggressive tones of the man who answered. A flophouse near Carmine, not far from Pino Fratelli's house.

Pontecorvo had been thrown out the previous Sunday for unpaid rent. He'd been muttering more threats. The man was crazy so no one took much notice any more.

'Just another Oltrarno louse,' the civilian said again when he finished the call. 'You're going to put out a call for something like that?'

'Go home,' Marrone ordered. 'If Cassini or Fratelli come near your office again, tell them they need to speak to me first. Before they see anything.'

'What's that they say about stable doors and bolting horses?'

Marrone got his own coat and called home, telling his wife he would be late for dinner, offering no explanation.

Tonight he had other matters to chase – as, he guessed, did Pino Fratelli.

Two flights of stairs through an empty Palazzo Vecchio. Except for the ghosts. They took Savonarola this way after he was arrested on the threshold of the library in San Marco. A few weeks later he walked down the same steps, defrocked, and was dragged to the stake by hooded men in black to greet the flames and the noose and a grim, public death in the square outside.

Her footsteps echoed against the walls. She tried to push that face from San Marco – bloodless, fixed with a cruel determination – from her head.

The door to Soderini's office was open. His staff gone for the evening. The mayor wore a dark suit with a white carnation in the lapel.

It was hot in the large, ornate room. She took off her coat. Soderini stared at her, the black dress, the pearls. Julia Wellbeloved felt herself being judged, measured, and in other circumstances would have turned straight round and returned to the rainy Florence night.

'Black,' he said in his calm, smooth English. 'Like me. I'm in mourning for poor Tornabuoni. You?'

'We're in Florence,' she said. 'Speak to me in Italian, please.'

He came to stand in front of her. 'You're a very unusual woman.'

She laughed at him. 'You know that, do you?'

'I'm paid to judge people.' He looked her up and down again. 'You never met Tornabuoni. Still, the thought's appreciated. How's this report of yours going, Julia? Have you found time to do your homework while chasing terrorists?'

'We went to Fiesole thinking it was something to do with the Brancacci.'

'And was it?'

'Why not ask Walter Marrone? Is your wife coming?'

A flicker of unexpected emotion ran briefly across his face. 'My wife? You have been busy.'

'I can read the paper. Had to go back a bit. No one speaks of it much.'

'My wife lives in Sicily. Taormina. She rarely returns. It's best that way.' He tidied some papers on the desk, avoiding her eyes. 'She's half-English. Did you read that too? Her family were one of those aristocratic tribes who came here at the beginning of the century, held their noses while Mussolini was in power. Never quite found the time to leave, or sufficient spine to warrant internment like some of their peers.'

'I didn't mean to pry.'

'No?' he said with a sardonic smile. 'In that case why ask? I live a bachelor life. A gentleman with occasional companions when I have the time. This city is my bride if I'm honest. Beautiful, if demanding. I can't complain if a woman feels she's unable to compete. Mariani tells me you took your Carabinieri friends to San Marco with you. Why?'

'For company,' she said with a shrug.

'A crazy detective unfit for work and an idiot junior? This Fratelli—'

'You know him?'

'I know of him,' Soderini said with a scowl. 'A troublemaker. A man who doesn't know his place. That type never fits. This is why his career turned to dust.'

He brushed something from her shoulder. Something that did not perhaps exist.

'He's ill. Retired on medical grounds.'

'He was as good as retired long before that,' Soderini retorted. 'There's a hierarchy here. One works with it or fails. Fratelli—'

'Is ill,' she said again.

'Were these men helpful? Do you have any fresh answers as to why someone might wish to despoil our treasures?'

Julia thought about this and said, 'I think I misread the question. Or asked the wrong one. I thought this was about the paintings somehow. I wanted to believe that. It seemed the natural conclusion. The obvious one.'

'And?' he persisted.

'I'm now inclined to think the problem is more to do with the individuals themselves. What makes them the way they are. A flaw in their history that's affected their character. The painting – art itself – is a catalyst, as it is for the rest of us. A spur. Something that eggs them on, makes them cross a line they always observed before.'

He put a hand to his chin, staring at her. 'There,' Soderini said confidently. 'You have a premise for your paper.'

'Not really. It's a matter for the police, not an academic. I can't invent a reason for their behaviour. Not unless someone finds me a criminal.'

She cocked her head to one side and asked, 'Do you have one for me?'

'Here?' he asked, spreading his hands to indicate the grand office he'd inherited from a line of city burghers and a pope.

'Somewhere. Tornabuoni's murder . . .' she said, almost in a whisper. Her eyes flitted to the back of the room, in the direction of the square outside. 'I was in the piazza that night. I might have seen—'

'What?' Soderini demanded with a sudden urgency.

'Someone who looked the spitting image of Savonarola. Hiding in the Loggia dei Lanzi. A troubled man with a pale, distinctive face and a black cloak. Like that of a monk.'

Soderini took a deep breath and waited for more.

'But then,' she said brightly, 'I visited the Carabinieri station and it was clear I was mistaken. The timing was wrong. They have their culprit.'

She walked forward and touched his arm, quite deliberately.

'Why am I telling you this, Sandro? You know it already.'

'I knew they had a suspect. I'd no idea you were involved. You should have told me straight out.'

'I've told you now,' Julia pointed out.

Soderini picked up her coat and held it. 'In future you'll come to me when you have doubts. Or problems. I need make one phone call only. This investigation of yours will succeed, I'm sure of it. You know what they say about Rome? *Non basta una vita.* One lifetime isn't enough. Florence is smaller than our southern cousin. But Rome is one world. We are many. Give us time.'

She followed him, the same route to the start of the Vasari Corridor she'd taken before.

'Where are we going exactly?' she asked as they began to walk past the long lines of self-portraits.

'I told you. To meet the Brigata Spendereccia.'

'Which is . . .?'

'An evening of food, wine. Pleasurable entertainment. Or so I recall. This job . . .' He looked round the palazzo. 'So many of your questions seem to have little to do with your apparent reason for being here, Julia. Why is that?'

'Because I can't think straight walking down a freezing cold corridor, dressed to the nines, with a man I don't know, going God knows where.'

He looked at her and laughed. So freely she couldn't help but do the same.

'The guidebooks will tell you there are four grottoes in the Boboli Gardens. Secret places of delight for the idle Medici bored by the splendour of the Pitti Palace and the public empire beyond its walls.'

'Grottoes,' she said softly.

'Grottoes! Like the Roman emperors used to have. Splendid, private places, built into the hillside of that sprawling garden behind the Pitti. Reminders of another time. Before the Pope's pronouncements. Before confession and guilt. Windows into a world of the old gods, Pan and his satyrs. Bacchus and his maenads.'

Gardens had never interested her much, nor mythology.

'Four of them?'

'So the guidebooks say.'

Sandro Soderini tapped the side of his nose and winked. Coarse gestures. Ones that made him look like a cheap, jumped-up politician for a moment. A nightclub performer or a charlatan selling tricks.

He wound his arm tightly through hers. 'But guidebooks are for the rabble. You have me now. And I know places the riffraff have never seen. Be grateful. Be attentive. Be . . .'

She waited, and when he didn't go on asked, 'What?'

'Be good.'

The two men wandered back to the café near Fratelli's home, to sip coffee, check their watches, talk carefully under the watchful eye of the Grassi dragon. When she ordered her husband to lug some beer crates outside, then slipped into the kitchen herself, Cassini leaned over and whispered, 'Who's the battle-axe?'

'A very good woman,' Fratelli told him. 'An angel, of sorts.'

'Never seen an angel with a mush on it like that. She'd scare the life out of me on a dark night.'

Fratelli scowled. 'I need to work on your education, Luca. Angels are supposed to scare you sometimes. That's their job. How else are you to do as you're told? Speaking of which . . .' He looked at Cassini, a big, shambling figure inside his winter coat. 'What's your job tonight?'

'Eyes and ears,' Cassini repeated from their earlier conversation. 'We've discussed this already, thank you. I'm not stupid.'

'I know that,' Fratelli lied, trying to recall if they really had talked it through. 'And legs, if needed. I can't run any more.'

'And this too,' Cassini said, balling a fist.

Fratelli groaned.

'If the occasion calls for it,' the young man added quickly.

'If the occasion calls for it you'll get the hell out of there. I'm not having you put your career or your wellbeing on the line. I'll call the *stazione* and let them deal with it.'

'You don't need to look after me, thank you. Besides, the *stazione* have been ordered to steer clear.'

'When Fratelli calls, they come! I'm not looking after you. This is for my sake alone. I don't want to be saddled with the destruction of what few prospects you possess. I do have a conscience, you know.'

Fratelli glowered at the young *carabiniere* and muttered something low and vile.

'No one gives a damn about your conscience,' the Grassi dragon declared, marching into the café, dishcloth in hand, polishing an old-fashioned glass cappuccino cup. 'What about your medication?'

'What about my medication?' he grumbled.

'Have you taken it? The right number? At the right time? The way that charming lady doctor of yours—'

'I've taken my pills! I've visited the lavatory and washed my hands afterwards. My ears are clean, my hair is combed, my under-wear spotless and so neatly ironed the damned undertaker will cut his bill should I fall down dead on the spot and leave you all to clear up the bloody mess! For God's sake, woman, will people simply listen to me for once? And, after that, kindly bless what little time I've left on this earth with some quiet!'

He got what he asked for then. The silence. A shocked one. Fratelli was only aware afterwards, from the ringing of his voice around the walls of the little café, how loud and intemperate he had, in an instant, become.

Signora Grassi's face was a mask of grief and guilt. Her eyes glassy with tears.

'Never mind, eh,' Cassini said gently. 'I'm sure it'll all work out fine.'

Fratelli fought to think straight. Did his head hurt? Was he really angry or just . . . lost?

These moments came from time to time. Not so regularly. Or were they now more common?

Signora Grassi was dabbing at her face with a handkerchief. He found himself racked by a sore sense of guilt.

'I'm so very sorry,' he said, reaching across the counter to take her old and wrinkled hands. 'I'm the most worthless man in the world and do not for one moment deserve your constant, selfless kindness. I reward it with anger and ingratitude and don't even realize it until after this cruelty of mine is over. But why . . .'

His hand flew to his mouth. His eyes pricked. His head whirled and for a moment he felt so unsteady his hands gripped the old wooden counter, fighting to keep himself upright. He couldn't see properly. His head was filled with a sea of hissing tinnitus.

Cassini was there in an instant, saving him with his strong arms, feeding a chair beneath Fratelli's backside, lowering him down into the seat and safety.

A long moment punctuated by nothing but the ticking of the grandfather clock at the end of the bar, beneath the purple football scarves and photos of old Fiorentina football squads.

Then the metallic rhythm of the clock stopped completely and Pino Fratelli felt his heart freeze with a sharp and unexpected fear.

Was this the instant? No. That would be too cruel. He had work to do. Broken circles to close. A few final deeds, some ghosts to be laid, vile spirits exorcized.

Not now.

He'd pray to a god he didn't recognize to escape that. Just for a while. Long enough to know some final peace.

He was sweating; breathing in short, pained gasps.

The beast inside was blind and dead. It would wake at a time of its own choosing, regardless of any exterior consequences.

Then the clock ticked again. Fratelli opened his aching eyes and realized they were all there – Grassi and her henpecked husband, Cassini too – holding a glass of water in front of him.

He took it, sipped shakily.

How long? A second? A minute? An hour? He'd no idea.

The pressure in his head eased. It was not pain, not really.

More a nudge from something alien inside him, wishing to make its presence known, then, once recognized, roll over and return to sleep.

Fratelli looked at the clock. It had barely moved. A minute perhaps. No more.

He finished the water, shrugged off Cassini's arm and, as he did so, said, 'Enough of this. I stood too long at the counter. That's all. I have an important question for you, Luca. What's your job tonight?'

The silence again.

Fratelli leaned forward and gazed into his blank young eyes. 'What is your job?' he repeated.

The young *carabiniere* paused, glancing at the other two in embarrassment. 'I'm your legs, Pino,' he said eventually.

Fratelli could read those looks. 'I asked before, didn't I? That very question.'

'You did,' Grassi's husband told him.

'When?'

The café owner shook his head and said, 'Get yourself home, Pino. To bed. We'll take you. Rest. Sleep for a while.'

'Sleep? Sleep?'

It was November in Florence. A black, wet night. Just like the one twenty years before when the river rose and engulfed the city in its foul, dank waters, letting loose a heartless creature that still lurked in the shadows somewhere, waiting for another moment, a second opportunity.

He'd sent Julia Wellbeloved out there knowing all this, using it to encourage her natural curiosity and sense of decency and justice. So a part of this creature lay within him. Came from him. Perhaps the spur now, the catalyst, was nothing more than the shrieking cries of a dying *maresciallo ordinario* gnawed by the cancer of guilt over his wife's brutal and unexplained murder, willing to sacrifice anything and anyone in order to salve and bury that pain.

'The time?' Fratelli asked, too weak to look at the grandfather clock. Or perhaps too frightened, afraid it might cease its ticking once again.

'It's ten past seven,' the husband told him. 'You looked at the clock just now. Go home.'

'I was making conversation,' Fratelli said, forcing himself to his feet. He straightened his long silver hair as best he could, smoothed down his old creased coat, reached into his pockets and, very slowly, with no small difficulty, pulled on his old and tattered calf leather gloves.

His mind was returning. The signs of distress – that dizziness, the ringing of a million tiny bells, the fringing and lack of focus of his vision – were surely diminishing.

'Luca and I have an appointment,' he said, convincing himself he felt better already for getting upright. No, not better.

Fine.

Good.

Well.

'We have?' Cassini asked.

'Why else do you think I brought you here? You must learn to ask questions. To demand answers. I had to wait until the due hour before I could act. So we took a coffee. Do I make idle decisions? Am I a man who wastes what time we have?'

Cassini looked a bit offended by that.

'Who are we meeting then?' he asked.

Fratelli drew himself up to his full height, which brought him up to Luca Cassini's chin, and said, 'A fat naked midget. Who else on a night like this?'

Outside it was cold and wet. For once he was glad to feel the cold sharp rain on his face.

As they strode through the Vasari Corridor, across the Ponte Vecchio, Soderini spoke all the time: of Florence, of history, of his ancient clan and how it had held power here in varying degrees for six centuries or more.

He possessed the soft, persuasive tone of one of those academics who moved so slickly to a career on TV, filling in the spaces for the ignorant while always managing to remind them there was more to be said, though not for them. Knowledgeable and articulate, acutely intelligent yet adept at explaining complex ideas in simple, rational terms, Soderini's personality was both repellent and magnetic. She could imagine how a man like him might acquire the mayor's chair, even without that aristocratic blood in his veins.

A natural master, seemingly born to rise to the top of any society or milieu he occupied. There was a genuine love there, too, for himself and his surroundings. The paintings on the walls of the Vasari Corridor, the church, the bridge, the river . . . all these things he spoke of as if they and the city itself were a part of him, a fifth limb, a visible, tangible facet of a personality that, through his Florentine blood, spanned the centuries.

Then they entered the final narrow portion of the corridor and she saw the sharp right turn towards the Pitti Palace. The fruitless visit to Vanni Tornabuoni's office seemed an age away. The last few days might have been a week or more. In that time she'd seen Pino Fratelli turn from an eccentric, retired cop into a charismatic and troubled man who interested her greatly; for his character, his damaged nature, and the burning pain he sought, in an absent-minded, haphazard way, to lance.

When she had waited impatiently in Tornabuoni's office two days earlier she'd cursed the absent cultural director, blamed his absence on the arrogance and lousy timekeeping of all the men she'd known. Her brief husband, more than any.

But she was wrong there. Tornabuoni was probably dead already; shot, headed for that terrible revelation in the Loggia dei Lanzi that evening.

By a man who looked like Girolamo Savonarola, perhaps believed himself to be the heir of the troubled and troublesome priest. That was fact, whatever Walter Marrone and the others thought. Fratelli had never doubted it. He'd understood she was right from the beginning, and quietly led her to San Marco and that painting in the hope of proving his hunch without once revealing his game.

She forgave that sly yet necessary trick. Julia Wellbeloved had come to believe she would forgive Pino Fratelli quite a lot.

They came to a halt by a small door in the corner of the corridor junction. Soderini pulled a key out of his pocket, and turned on a light. A winding staircase circled down. He led the way and soon they were outside.

Even in her thick winter coat, Julia Wellbeloved shivered. The air was damp and chill, rank with the smell of mould and vegetation. When her eyes adjusted to the darkness, she saw they had emerged on a slope by the edge of the Boboli Gardens. The palace stood to their right, a vast, dark mass. There were lights at a gate by the public street – a guardhouse, she guessed. To her left, barely illuminated by a few lamps, was an artificial cave built into a strange building encrusted with sculpted vegetation and strange mythical figures. Two marble Roman statues stood on either side. Above the arched roof, embedded in the curious ornamentation, was the Medici coat of arms: six *palle*; spheres set in a shield.

She thought she could hear sounds – music and voices – from the depths of the grotto.

'Is this a good idea?' Julia Wellbeloved asked, half to herself.

'New horizons,' Soderini said, and pushed open the iron grille ahead of them. 'They're always good.'

He stood there, a handsome, confident middle-aged man, illuminated by the yellow lamps in the mouth of the cave. His hand was out, a gesture of open invitation.

'You're coming.'

It wasn't a question.

A sound, or a sense of someone close by, made her glance back towards the distant gate at the palace end of the corridor. A shape shone in the light there, pale and glistening in the rain. It seemed too grotesque to be real.

Then Sandro Soderini took her arm and the Grotta Grande consumed them.

There were three men waiting for them by the side gate of the Pitti Palace, though only two were made of flesh and blood. The third sat squat and glistening in the light evening rain. Luca Cassini laughed at him.

'I remember that fat little clown from when I was little,' he cried.

Fratelli never felt entirely comfortable with the statue of Morgante the bearded dwarf, jester to the court of Cosimo I. Obese and ageing, with a grizzled beard and a hand outstretched to mimic the pose of the great statue of Marcus Aurelius on the Campidoglio in Rome, the clown sat naked on a tortoise spouting water from its beak. The pose was a parody of the Campidoglio masterpiece, a beautiful piece of sculpture with an ugly intent, to mock the physical grotesqueness of the Medici's personal entertainer. There was something obscenely callous about the thing; especially the way the dwarf's genitalia were exposed – not hidden as was the case in an obscure and troubling portrait of Morgante in the Uffizi, naked again, younger though no less deformed, his manhood concealed behind a passing butterfly.

Perhaps it was his Roman blood, but Fratelli loved the original, the statue of the great emperor on his horse, hand outstretched to the empire, noble and, in reality, an interesting and intelligent ruler. The Medici, a lesser breed, would have identified with Marcus Aurelius in their stature as grand dukes of Tuscany, patrons of the arts that made the city the gem of the Renaissance. And here was

their sad little slave, potbellied and hideous, riding not a horse but
a squat tortoise, frozen forever in stone by a wall under a cover of
shrubbery beneath the Vasari Corridor. What a wonderful joke it
must have appeared, for the beholders anyway. Humour was often
attached to cruelty, it seemed, and cruelty troubled Pino Fratelli. It
always had.

'You've never been here since you were a schoolboy?' he asked,
shaking himself out of this sudden and unwanted reverie.

'It's a garden,' Cassini responded, drawing himself up to his
considerable height. 'I don't mind looking at paintings from time
to time. But gardens. I mean, honestly . . .'

He scratched his crewcut. Sometimes he looked more like a
strapping, ingenuous sportsman, not a *carabiniere* at all. 'No offence
but . . . gardens are for old people, aren't they?'

The two men who'd met them by the gate glared at him in silence.

'Sorry, sir,' Cassini added, looking at the taller of them. 'I didn't
mean any offence. I'm sure gardening's all well and good once
you're up for it. If you're a gardener, that is . . .'

'I'm the captain of your Carabinieri *stazione*,' Marrone boomed.
'A place that appears to have lost its sense of discipline.'

'Too loud, too loud,' hushed the man next to him. He wore a
long blue overcoat and a hat with the badge of the Pitti Palace.
Ludovico Ducca was a shadow of the virile young cop who'd helped
Pino Fratelli on that grim day twenty years before. Illness had taken
its toll on his frame and finally ended a modest career with the
Carabinieri. But the city looked after some of their own. Ducca
became a guard for the Pitti Palace, not an onerous task. The moment
Fratelli had realized that had to be the destination for Julia's meeting
with the Brigata Spendereccia, he'd called his old colleague and
arranged for the two of them to meet. Marrone's presence had not
been planned.

'Discipline?' Fratelli added, coming to stand in front of his former
boss. 'That's a bit rich, isn't it? Luca wasn't in the station when
you issued the orders to steer clear of this place. He can't disobey
an instruction he never heard.'

'No, I can't,' Cassini added firmly. 'If anyone had bothered to
tell me . . .'

'Shut up,' Fratelli ordered, then dragged Marrone by the arm and
took him a few steps beyond the obese stone dwarf and the spouting
tortoise.

'Well?' he asked when they were out of earshot of the others.

'Well what?' Marrone retorted. 'Am I answerable to you now?'

'I know why I'm here. It's because you don't want to be.' He turned and waved at the vast spreading gardens stretching up the hill behind them. 'My friend Julia is up there somewhere. At Soderini's blasted party. Which is called, I gather—'

'The Brigata Spendereccia,' Marrone interrupted.

There was a moment of silence, and embarrassment on the part of both men. Marrone for disclosing his secret knowledge; Fratelli for innocently forcing it from his friend.

'Is it an interesting spectacle?' Fratelli asked.

'Do you think for one moment . . .?' Marrone exploded. 'Good God, Pino. If you'd listened to my advice a little over the years you'd be in the position I'm in now. Party to some of the nonsense that goes on in this city, powerless to do a thing to stop it.'

'That's why I ignored you—'

'No it's not,' Marrone cut in savagely. 'You ignored me because you're you.'

'Do you expect me to leave that Englishwoman on her own? At an event you're too timid to police? Is Chavah Efron here too? And a man called Aldo Pontecorvo . . .'

'Am I meant to be psychic? You're the most arrogant and impudent human being . . .' Marrone cried. 'I'm here, aren't I?'

'Yes. Alone. Spare me the insults. Where does this bacchanal of theirs take place? I don't intend to march in there without good reason, but I'll be damned if I'm going to be far away.'

'I don't know! How could I?'

'If one hair on that woman's head comes to harm . . .' Fratelli began, stabbing a gloved finger in the captain's face.

'You sent her there, didn't you?' Marrone's florid face came close to him in the moonlight. 'This was your doing. Not mine. And why?'

Silence.

'Why?' Marrone demanded again.

'I have my reasons,' Fratelli muttered, glancing at the hill. 'Besides, she wanted to go, and I suspect there's no stopping her. Not when she wants something.'

There were lights in curious places. Somewhere to look. To stand and wait.

'I also have my reasons,' Marrone said. 'To do with a friend. A man I've known all my life, loved like a brother, tried to help as much as I can. And still he won't confide in me. Still he runs away, hands on ears, tongue-tied when he should be speaking. When I could help if only . . .'

Fratelli took one step towards the rising incline ahead of them. The lights were becoming clearer. They had a kind of order. Some were close and appeared to be coming from what appeared to be an ornate cave, one of the follies rich men and cardinals built for themselves as amusements, a place he dimly remembered from visits here.

'Do not turn your back on me!' Marrone barked, then, with a strong hand, took Fratelli by the coat collar and dragged him round so that they stood there in the gentle rain, two men in early middle age, staring at each other as if they were squaring up for a street brawl.

'What is this?' Fratelli said, shaking his long white hair. 'Why are you so mad at me?'

He felt weak for a moment again, and recalled how close he'd come to passing out in the Grassi dragon's café. He was stronger now, but not recovered by any means. So he held on to Marrone's outstretched arm, grateful for the support. Then the brief giddiness was gone. Pretty much, anyway. The monster inside him was like an infant. It slept as readily as it woke.

'How did I offend you so badly, Walter?' he asked quietly. 'Truly . . .'

He removed Marrone's hand from his collar and stepped back. 'Sometimes . . . I don't know what I'm saying. Or doing.' He paused then whispered, as if to himself, 'We're in the Boboli Gardens. Somewhere nearby Julia is attending the Brigata Spendereccia with Soderini and his fellows. Perhaps Aldo Pontecorvo, the cook, is present, who certainly committed that strange damage in the Brancacci, and perhaps murdered Tornabuoni too. I care about none of that. Only Julia. She'll leave if she's offended. I've told her so, though she's a good and wise woman and would have worked this out for herself.'

He turned on Marrone.

'Where are your men? You have a suspect. Pontecorvo was there in Fiesole. I guarantee it.'

'I've added him to the list. Be assured of it. But we're snatching at ghosts in the dark. I can't march in there on the basis of your guesswork . . .'

Fratelli looked back towards the gate and the white dwarf glistening in the rain. Cassini and Ducca stood next to the statue, shuffling their big feet. Good men, he thought.

'All my life,' Marrone went on, in a hard, embittered tone that Pino Fratelli did not recognize, 'I looked up to you. Sympathized with you. Covered for you when you went off the rails. All my life . . .'

Fratelli placed a hand on the captain's arm. 'Walter. Now is not the time.'

'When was? When you recovered from Chiara's death and could have talked to me then? Over the years when we worked alongside each other? Drank ourselves stupid when we felt like it? When I told you my secrets? And you kept yours locked inside, as if all the grief in this city belonged to you alone? My God . . .'

'What are you talking about?'

Marrone stepped back and glowered at him. 'Or was it yesterday? When you came to my office with your Englishwoman? What was it she yelled at you? Tell him. Tell him, Pino.'

Fratelli felt cold and tired. 'This is a stupid argument about nothing,' he said. 'You're here. We both know why. To make sure Soderini's little party doesn't get out of hand. I'd advise you bring more men . . .'

'I *know*!' Marrone roared.

The angry words rang out in the black, cold night and echoed off the rusticated stone of the ugly, hulking palace by their side.

'I know,' Marrone repeated, more gently.

Fratelli felt another headache coming on. A Negroni would have killed it. The gin and the vermouth. A plate of *finocchiona*. Five minutes with Julia, bandying clever chitchat across the table.

'Know what?' Fratelli asked, and regretted the words the moment they'd passed his lips.

Marrone came close and peered into his face. 'I read the files from twenty years ago this evening. Every last one of them.' He sighed. 'I should have done it long before. I thought it wisest not to. I'd hoped you'd buried her. My prurient interest seemed an imposition. A pointless one. Now I know—'

'Know *what*?' Fratelli screamed at him.

A moment of hesitation, then Marrone said, 'I know something was smeared on Chiara's face too. Just like Eve in the Brancacci. By the man who killed her. I know that twenty years ago it was an expensive French lipstick, of a kind she'd never have worn.'

'It was?' Fratelli asked, suddenly calm and interested. 'You're sure?'

'French. Chanel. There was a forensic report came in three, four months afterwards. We wouldn't let you near the files, would we?'

'No.' Fratelli put a hand to his chin. 'French lipstick, twenty years ago. The blood of a slaughtered rooster, perhaps killed for Soderini's private feast tonight. That's quite a contrast, don't you think?'

The *carabiniere* in Marrone surfaced. 'You can link this to the Brigata somehow?' he asked.

Fratelli shrugged. 'If I'd had access to those papers, who knows? We might not be here tonight. And Vanni Tornabuoni—'

'In the circumstances,' Marrone interrupted, 'we had no choice. How could we allow a man to investigate the murder of his own wife?'

Fratelli looked at him and said nothing.

'The lipstick—' Marrone continued.

'It was smeared on Chiara's face like a frown,' Fratelli cut in. He shrugged. 'As you said. Just like the Brancacci two days ago. I'm sorry. I would have told you yesterday but you seemed to think you had your man. Also, I had the impression you couldn't wait to get me out of there. I'm an embarrassment, Walter. No, no. Don't object. I *am* an embarrassment. I know this better than you.'

'You could have told me. Bella and I loved Chiara too. You owed us that.'

Evenings out in the city eating cheap pizza, drinking red wine. Fratelli with Chiara, Marrone with his charming, too-loud Neapolitan wife. She'd left him for a lawyer ten years before but they stayed on good terms. Marrone proved a fine father to their twins, even though the lawyer was a crooked villain with a poor reputation in the city. Four lives tied together by amity and love two decades before, now irrevocably severed by time.

'Why didn't you tell me?'

'Because I was broken. I didn't know what was real and what was part of the nightmare. I felt my world had disappeared and something bleak and dark and evil had taken its place. Then, later . . . You had problems of your own.' His hand went to Marrone's shoulder. 'Was I wrong?'

'Yes,' the captain replied in a curt whisper.

Fratelli found himself stifling – successfully for once – a rising sense of anger.

'When I woke up I was in that sanatorium. And you were visiting every day, with chocolates and smuggled bottles of booze. I was fighting to find a little of who I was. To understand Chiara was gone from me. Besides, neither of us wanted to talk much, did we? Not then.'

'Perhaps not,' the man next to him agreed.

'Is there more?' Fratelli asked.

'You know there is. You asked Cassini . . .' He nodded back towards the gate. 'You told him to check the file. You suspected it was there.' The captain laughed, a short, dry sound. 'You always were one step ahead of everyone else, weren't you? And as usual you never thought to mention it.'

'Would you have listened?'

'It would have pained me. Not as much as you, of course. But it would have hurt. And I would have listened,' Marrone insisted. 'How could I not?'

'Then what is it I know?' Fratelli asked.

'That the night Chiara went missing there was a Brigata meeting. Our men back then were told to avoid it. Just as they are now, two decades on. Who was there . . . we've no information . . .'

'Soderini and Tornabuoni,' Fratelli told him. 'Along with half their peers. Haven't you noticed the governance of this city is handed down from generation to generation? Slowly, with a pretence of fairness. But we're theirs, Walter, and they know it. As do we.'

Marrone sighed and stuffed his hands deep into the pockets of his coat.

'I've never turned my back on a crime in this city,' he said. 'Nor would I. Whoever was the perpetrator—'

'Oh, please!' Fratelli complained. 'We're too long in the tooth to mince words with one another. If a villain presents himself . . . of course not. But do you look?' He waved an arm around the vast gardens ahead of them. 'Or do you hide when they order it? We both know the answer. This is how the world works. Ours, anyway. Soderini and his acolytes were council men twenty years ago. I checked. The Brigata's a secret, private civic institution. I have no proof, no piece of paper to say it. Do you think they keep an attendance book? But they were there. I'm sure of it . . .'

'If you're sure, you're sure.'

Fratelli shook his head. 'There's a worm in this dark place. There always has been. Perhaps it's a part of us, a part we seek to dismiss, to ignore and pretend it doesn't exist. Unless you're one of them.'

The vast stone bulk of the Pitti Palace, a hideous fortress brimming with gorgeous treasures, loomed over them, casting a shadow beneath the sickle moon. The heavy downpour of early evening was turning to light drizzle. This wasn't twenty years before, when the heavens had turned on the city in constant, howling blasts.

'Perhaps we're the fools,' he whispered. 'The deceivers. Blind to what we really are.'

The taller man came forward and held Pino Fratelli in a tight bear hug. Then he whispered in his ear, 'Lead and I will follow. But remember this . . .' Marrone let go, stood back, shook a finger at him. 'We're equal, and that's the way it'll stay! No more sly secrets. No more of your trademark trickery. You're a cunning old fox and I've always followed like a willing ignoramus. But please. Together now, Pino. Bring your friend the dullard along with you. This is an unfinished funeral for me as well.'

Fratelli shook his head. His eyes felt moist for some reason and his throat hurt.

'Pontecorvo would have been seventeen that night,' Marrone added. 'He lived with his mother in a hovel here. Close enough to your house.'

'Seventeen?' Fratelli muttered. 'Not much more than a child . . .'

'We pulled him in for unruly behaviour in January when his mother died,' the captain went on. 'Last Sunday he was thrown out of his lodgings over debts. He was ranting, bellowing threats against all and sundry. There's your catalyst. You always want one, don't you?'

It had to be said.

'There's a man in his grand office in the Palazzo Vecchio who thinks he owns you, Walter. Along with every other brick and cobblestone in Florence. I'm just a dying, failed *maresciallo ordinario*. You've a career and a reputation. You could give me your weapon and leave this to me. I've not got a damned thing to lose.'

'Let me worry about that,' Marrone told him. The captain glanced back at the gate. 'We've got Ducca, who's not fit for much, if I'm honest. And one mindless young cadet . . .'

'Don't speak of Luca that way. He's a fine young man who deserves better.'

Marrone cast his head to one side and frowned.

'And they're all we've got,' Fratelli added.

'Good,' Marrone said, then rubbed his hands and grinned. It

occurred to Fratelli he hadn't seen that happy expression in a long time.

Julia Wellbeloved found herself in a place so curious she had to unwind her arm from Sandro Soderini's and stand in the middle of the Grotta Grande, wide-eyed and lost for words. A gently curving artificial structure now held them like a monster's mouth enfolding its victims, ready to swallow. The fantastical cavern was a riot of decoration, a rich lunatic's junk room crammed to the gills with the dreams of several warped imaginations. The walls were covered in shaped mortar and stalactites festooned with shells and pebbles and hunks of quartz. When these encrustations retreated, the gaps were filled by frescoes of Arcadian landscapes, paintings of strange, exotic creatures, leopards and monkeys, goats and mountain bear. As her eyes adjusted to the half-dark, she could see – emerging among the flamboyant mortar half-formed figures there – satyrs and leering shepherds, fantastic anthropomorphic creatures chasing capering nymphs.

She followed him through the interior arch and entered a tiny chamber dominated by a single statue: a muscular, naked man abducting a beautiful, protesting woman. The fingers of this virile attacker bit into his victim's flesh in a cruel and physical way that reminded her of Bernini. This was too good a work to hide in the darkness beneath the hill of the Boboli Gardens.

'Any ideas?' Soderini asked.

'About what?'

'About the statue, of course. You said you studied art. Let's have a little proof.'

'Is this a game?' she asked testily.

'Most things are. Indulge me.'

Shaking her head, amused by this man in spite of herself, she checked the paintings on the walls in this tiny antechamber, her mind straying to the lights in the room beyond, and the rising sound of company somewhere close by, yet hidden.

Classical scenes. Warfare. Rape and pillage. The subject she saw everywhere in Florence; on the ceilings of the Palazzo Vecchio, on the walls of the Uffizi. Old legends, great fairy stories that enchanted the aristocrats of the Renaissance, many of whom wished to trace their lineage back to the ancients.

She walked round the smooth and delicately sculpted marble,

touched the man's strong thigh, the woman's solid arm, looked at her lovely face, turned away from her abductor, yet half smiling in the alluring way that certain men seemed to feel might happen in circumstances such as this.

Rape in classical times always had a touch of beauty, of the spiritual, about it. Men were there to dominate and subjugate, women to be their subjects. That was the way of the world.

'I suppose you think she was asking for it?' she said, turning on Soderini.

'Who was?'

'Helen of Troy,' she guessed. 'This' – she slapped the male statue's thighs – 'is Theseus.'

Soderini nodded, impressed. 'Very good. And this?' he asked, gesturing at the final room.

She strode through into the last of the three chambers. It was taller than the others with a circular window at the top. The glass there was grubby. Through it the weak rays of the moon fell upon a single pale statue in a fountain set at the centre. Vicious horned satyrs clung to the edge beneath the feet of the lovely woman depicted above them, their cruel faces set in expressions of lust and hate.

Hand across her breasts, placid face staring down at humanity. The pose was close to that of Botticelli's depiction of Venus, new-born, emerging from a scallop shell, brought into being when the Titan cut off the testicles of his own father, the primordial god Uranus, and flung them into the bright blue waters of the Mediterranean.

A sudden keen memory from the Palazzo Vecchio. The quarters of Cosimo I, the man who created this labyrinth of underground temples. A vast ceiling painting of the moment of her creation: the vengeful son taking a scythe to the loins of his prone and grizzled father.

A canvas by whom?

She felt the smothering weight of Florentine history begin to bear down on her, linking the living to the dead, the past to the present in a constant, circling nexus as real and as heavy as the stones of the city itself.

By Vasari, who else? The man who built the corridor all the way from the fortress on the other side of the river to this very spot, and designed, with Buontalenti, the interior cave in which the Medici worshipped other gods. A willing slave to the feverish imagination of his masters.

'They practised alchemy here,' Soderini said.

'I thought they burned people for that,' she said without thinking.

'No. In Florence they burned people for disobedience. Here . . .' His hand gripped the head of the nearest satyr, which was clinging to the bowl beneath Venus, eyeing the beautiful woman above it with a naked hunger. 'They tried to turn base metal into gold. Not because they needed it, of course. But to unlock the secrets of eternal life. To reverse what lesser men would call the laws of nature.'

'They failed, Sandro,' she said.

'But they tried, Julia.'

The sounds of revelry were closer, yet just as elusive in their source. Soderini marched to the furthest wall and stared at a hideous face that grinned at them from the mortar. Dusty, probably terracotta, she thought, it resembled that of a man turning into something else. A creature of the sea, half flesh, half seaweed. The muffled sounds were coming from beyond.

'The books will tell you there are three chambers in the Grotta Grande,' Soderini said.

He found a handle on the grim face on the wall, pulled, and the masonry began to move.

'The books lie.'

Voices and music. Then a sudden wave of heat.

The caves were nothing more than fanciful decorated rooms set inside a series of small, interlinked buildings attached to the lower side of the Boboli hill, covered in part with earth, then decorated and made to look real, natural.

A small reservoir was created above the complex. It provided sufficient pressure to power the fountains inside, a sink in the kitchen and a tiny washroom. In summer, hidden shafts were opened to allow in fresh air. In winter, gas heaters brought a stifling, damp heat to the final, secret cavern where they met and dined. A narrow lane at the rear allowed food and other goods to be brought in without spoiling the theatrical illusion at the front.

'You know this place,' Chavah Efron said. 'What next?'

They stood outside by a catering van. She had the bag from Fiesole heavy in her hand.

'We serve them,' he said.

Then one more death and we flee. Take what money we can steal, walk to Santa Maria Novella and catch the first train south – to

Rome, to Naples; to somewhere warm with the promise of sun and a different life.

No more seedy assignations beneath the Boboli earth. Twelve times a year. Two hundred and forty Brigate in all. He'd worked every one, as skivvy and waiter; then, latterly, following the butcher Bertorelli's incarceration, as master of the kitchen in San Marco. The only source of a pitiful income, as his solitary mother grew meaner and madder with the years, relying on him to do everything until the very end.

And all the time the grotto lived in his head like a disease, as it had since that distant night of the flood.

Drink this now, boy, and everything will be fine.

They'd lied to him then, for their own purposes. In the intervening years they would lie to many others, often in his presence, as if he didn't exist. So he'd stood and watched, a craven figure, half hidden in the shadows, feeling the atmosphere change, the innocent and the cowardly depart, the hardened figures in the gang grow drunk and bitter as the evening turned from louche carousing to riot to debauchery then worse. When the screaming started he stayed there too, watching those who had taken his place, knowing he was as much use to them as any of the stone satyrs leering from Vasari's hideous mortar.

Afterwards came that siren, wheedling voice. A word in the ear. A rank, breathy introduction with an offer. A job, a threat, a simple promise: be silent and await your reward. He saw them now, faces at the back of photos in museums and institutions. Mostly women, but not always. Tornabuoni, a man who would consume anything, saw to that.

This was about submission as much as rape. They would be made tame and timid, loyalty bought through a small gift or preferment, the memory of their loss cemented in place by an inner sense of shame he understood only too well. These were the hierarchies, made up of the bones and corpses of centuries, upon which Florence – his city, as much as Tornabuoni's or Soderini's – was built. A man like Savonarola, retrieved from those lost ashes scattered on the Arno from the Ponte Vecchio, would recognize it in an instant, and shriek his curses into their ears, all of them, high and low.

A month ago he'd watched, more closely than ever, not knowing why. There was something about the victim they picked this time. Someone, a local, infrequent visitor one of the kitchen hands said, had seen the girl performing at a private function in the city. Brought her along, paid for her to wear her Egyptian costume, a bikini with a flimsy golden skirt barely covering her hips, a top just as skimpy, a jewelled headband, a transparent shawl. Then, after the dinner, she'd danced for them again, a more lurid and sensual performance. Twelve men, three women guests. When the direction of the evening became obvious, the women left, then most of the men. They'd seen Chavah Efron, the dancing girl brought in to shake and tremble her naked thighs and hips in their faces, lean down and show them her breasts as they slavered over their cups, eyes glazed and full of heat.

The rest knew what was coming.

Drink this now, boy, and everything will be fine.

That was the biggest lie of all. Just two of them took her, threw her screaming into the shadows, did whatever they wanted. The rest retreated and it was always like this. Always them. The same pair from twenty years ago, assailing her as once they'd assailed him.

'What would you have done?' he asked. 'You and Ari?'

Chavah Efron stood there, a small, muscular determined woman, and said, 'Killed them all. That beast Tornabuoni first . . .'

'I dealt with him,' he said.

'You cut off the snake, not the head . . .'

'The head goes on forever,' he whispered.

The head is us, he thought. This city, running through our veins as the Arno runs through it, in a muddy, swirling flood.

She had him by the collar, so close he could smell the sweetness of her breath. 'If you lack the courage, why are we here?'

'To find the last one . . .' he began.

'They're all the same. Can't you see? All . . .'

'We could go south . . .'

She laughed and then he knew. This was a dream, had been from the moment of his birth, would be till the end. They were living through the Anni di Piombo, the Years of Lead. A time of bombs and bullets, from left and right, Cagliari to Milan; blood and chaos throughout an Italy shrieking beneath the mass of its own corruption.

A noise. A quick movement of her foot. She kicked the flap of the bag open, and as she did so he saw again the weapons hidden there, metal shining in the half-light.

I shall spill flood waters upon the earth. You shall know them, and in them shall be your blood.

The flood did not recede. It ran through you, stormed greedily down your screaming mouth, lurked within your heart, craving justice.

'The first,' she said, 'is yours.' Then Chavah Efron picked up the bag, reached for the weapons inside and offered him the first to come to hand.

Franco Mariani, the man from San Marco, stood near the entrance, a little drunk, his walrus moustache now drooping more than ever. Julia soon realized she was the only woman, the idle focus for the attention of a dozen men in all, every one of them middle-aged, dressed in a dark suit and downcast in mood – even Soderini now, it seemed. This chamber was perfectly circular, with a door in darkness at the rear through which a couple of waitresses were emerging bearing drinks.

The walls here were frescoed, with none of the mortared stalagmites and encrustations of the previous rooms. Instead they offered a panorama of a riotous Arcadian age: battling warriors, screaming women, rampant satyrs, lust and violence, passion and a searing animal thirst for life. The contortions of naked skin, of grin and grimace, death cry and lustful croak, travelled around the circular space, all pointing to a focal point, back behind her, above the secret door through which she'd entered.

She sought the centre of this tumultuous, rolling fray; found it finally. Above the dark arch which had led them past the figure of Helen's abduction, past the statue of Venus and her stone satyrs, was a large fresco that depicted a naked couple wrapped in each other's arms, on the point of coupling ecstatically in an artificial pose, upright, locked together against a tree of orange fruit. This was Masaccio's stricken couple, the newly fallen Adam and Eve, stumbling into the world that awaited them. The real world. That of Florence; of Sandro Soderini, his ancestors and his heirs.

Gone was the shame, gone the despair. Their nakedness was displayed openly. Their beautiful faces were wreathed in anticipation, not coarsened, as they appeared in the chapel, but made more beautiful by this open acceptance of who and what they were.

It was Eve's mouth that drew Julia's attention above all else. The lips were full and carmine, raised in an ecstatic grin that was the mirror image of the gory smear she'd seen defiling the calm, pure face of Masolino's Eve on the column opposite in the Brancacci.

The couple above the tiny door looked ready to consume each

other. She took in the careful, exact detail of their perfect, powerful
bodies, all the physical facts that artists of this time were supposed
to ignore: hair and flesh meant to be hidden or carefully ignored
by the Renaissance artist's brush. In Vasari's hidden cavern, beneath
the earth of the Boboli Gardens, all was revealed, displayed proudly
for the voyeuristic audience below.

Soderini eyed the circle of tables set for dinner, then raised his
glass to her. Soon they would sit down and the meal begin.

'I told you, Julia. This is our secret. Yours now, too.'

Briefly, for no more than a second, there was a face at the door.
A tall man, with a pale and bloodless look, beaked nose, beady
raptor eyes full of hate and misery, gleaming skull.

She felt as faint and weak as she had in San Marco, tried to
steady herself on Soderini's arm. When she looked again, the shape
at the door had vanished.

'Are you all right?' Soderini asked.

'Never better,' she murmured automatically.

There was a waitress with them. A striking young woman with
dark hair and an interesting, engaged face.

'Is everyone here?' she asked. 'Is it time to start?'

Soderini glanced around the room. 'They're here,' he said.

The woman smiled and left. The face hadn't reappeared. It was
a trick of the light, her imagination feasting on the atmosphere and
the half-seen faces in the shadows. That was all.

Luca Cassini pushed at the iron gates on the Grotta Grande. The
sound of voices was muffled and subtle. But it was there, and so
was the Brigata Spendereccia, with Julia Wellbeloved among them.

'I can get in,' Cassini said. He tested the ironwork again. 'Kick
it down if you want. But . . .'

'But what?' Fratelli asked.

'What if it's just a party? Bunch of men getting plastered with
a bit of pretty company. I mean . . . if Julia's in trouble, no problem.
But what if it's . . . innocent?'

'Do innocents scurry beneath the earth to have their fun?' Fratelli
asked, watching the way Marrone and Ducca stared at the damp
ground, shuffling their feet. 'Tell me truthfully, Walter. What's
happened here over the years?'

Marrone took a deep, pained breath. 'Nothing. No complaints.
No tearful women racing to the *stazione*. Nothing . . .'

'Because?' Fratelli demanded.

'Because they get something to keep their mouths shut,' Ludovico Ducca said. 'People talk. I've heard them.'

'Heard what?' Cassini asked.

'They get the nod. Stepping on the "up" escalator for no good reason. Women mainly. Not always. Oh, please. You've never noticed? Not seen someone turn up one Monday morning, fresh desk, new chair? Nice comfy job in the office. A seat on the council. A place on one of those well-paid committees. And you ask yourself: where the hell did they come from? How come they got that, not me?' He grimaced. 'Boy or girl. Vanni Tornabuoni . . .'

He glanced back at the grim shape of the palace behind them.

'I found a lad in his office one morning. Naked, shivering. Covered in scratches. Scared witless. Orphan from one of the charities. God knows what that animal got up to.'

'You could have told me!' Marrone complained.

'Then we'd both be out of a job. You know what that kid was doing when I saw him next?'

Ducca leaned over and winked at Walter Marrone in the moon-light. 'Sitting on a horse outside the Palazzo Vecchio. Blue cap. Pretty uniform. Municipal police officer, telling off tourists for dropping litter. I've seen it happen in your own *stazione*. And so have you. So would Pino here, if he wasn't so damned blinkered he thinks the only bad in the world lies out there . . .'

Ludovico Ducca waved his arm towards the outline of the palace and the lights of Oltrarno beyond.

'It's there that bothers me right now,' Fratelli cried, jerking his thumb at the Grotta Grande.

'Do you lot want me to break down these bloody gates or not?' Luca Cassini demanded.

'Can you open it . . . gently?' Fratelli asked.

Cassini placed his strong right shoulder to the metalwork, dug his feet into the damp gravel and pushed.

Nothing.

Fratelli joined him, putting his weight against the gate. A moment later Marrone was there too, and then Ludovico Ducca.

It wasn't gentle. Certainly not quiet. When the lock on the gate finally gave, it did so with a high-pitched crack that rang around the mortared walls of the grotto like a gunshot. All four men fell through, stumbling forwards with its collapse. The grating held briefly in their hands, then through its own bulk and momentum detached itself and crashed down on the first low circular marble fountain near the entrance, shattering the rim, dispatching shards of stone into the darkness.

When the ringing of the metal subsided, they went inside the Grotta Grande. A hubbub of distant voices drifted to them from somewhere ahead in the dark.

Then something unmistakable broke the indecipherable babble.

A scream.

Soderini watched the two walk through the door, saw what they were carrying, thought for a moment and stepped back into the shadows. There he felt for the small black handgun he'd kept with him ever since the strange, threatening messages began to appear. He was out of sight in the small, overheated cavern. The crowd had gone quiet the moment the pair emerged – the woman shouting, the man behind her silent and sullen.

Tall, bald, imposing, in the food-spattered uniform of a chef. Vaguely familiar, Soderini thought. A Brigata minion, a permanent fixture. The woman was the waitress. Her eyes sparkled with anticipation.

He looked around. Julia Wellbeloved was nowhere to be seen. Mariani stood at the front, shouting and waving his arms like the pompous buffoon he was.

'What is this noise?' he bellowed. 'Be gone! You disturb the evening . . .'

The idiotic rant went on. Soderini didn't listen. Instead he caught the glint in the woman's eye and retreated further into the darkness, slipping the handgun by his side. There was no clear shot for him, not through the forest of bodies ahead; a dozen men in suits, civil servants and businessmen, hangers-on and Florentine arrivistes, milling around this angry, strange couple.

Many things happened in these caves and never found their way out into the light of day. Perhaps they thought this was one more show, another theatrical performance to amuse the satyrs frozen in the walls: two figures like comical, avenging chefs, marching from the kitchen, looking for someone. That was clear.

The man had a pistol low in his right hand, the woman some kind of larger semiautomatic.

What was a small handgun against a weapon like that? Soderini, a practical, careful man, knew the answer.

A hole in the wall of the final chamber, a secret door crammed with flailing bodies, men in suits, drunk and fearful, trying to squeeze their way through.

Fratelli's head felt strange. The closeness of the caverns, the heat, the noise, the damp and noxious air . . . all these things conspired to bewilder him, to fill his fevered mind with fear and uncertainty.

It happens soon, he thought. And there are still such matters to be dealt with.

Julia was here. He'd sent her into the presence of the man who'd murdered Vanni Tornabuoni; someone who was there that distant, dismal night of the flood when Florence succumbed to the cold embrace of the river and Chiara died on the staircase of their house not far from the tragic couple in the Brancacci.

The painful round of self-hate was interrupted. From somewhere came the low rattle of a weapon and the shrill sound of a human scream.

Bodies poured towards him, scattering tables along the way. The mass seemed impenetrable, the panic a human flood; a relentless, inevitable tide, impossible to hold back.

Fratelli found himself praying for a weapon, anything to smash a way through this screaming mob. Finally Luca Cassini drove past, bellowing, using his fists and elbows, his massive strength and size to get through.

The mechanical chatter of gunfire – a quick, heartless burst – broke the din again, but Cassini was beneath the entry arch by that time, dragging Fratelli behind him as they squeezed their way through the narrow gap in the wall.

More light, the smell of food and drink, the sharp and brittle tang of fear. Fratelli felt his foot catch on something – a rock, a fleeing reveller from the disastrous Brigata, he never knew. Cassini's hand left him and all he saw was a forest of limbs, trampling, stumbling. Head down, white hair flying around him, he wondered if this was where the long and fruitless journey ended, in a smashed skull on the rock floor, his life, his ambitions eking out as nothing but the dreams of an impotent old fool.

Then another hand came out and took hold of his jacket, jerked him into the corner, the shadows, a place of momentary safety.

Pino Fratelli found himself looking into the face of Sandro Soderini. The mayor had his back to the wall, a small handgun in his right hand, his hawkish eyes flashing between the man before him and the room. Fratelli followed the line of his gaze. The banqueting tables were thrown to the floor, dishes and drink and food scattered across the stones. At the centre, scattered like a cast-off toy, a body, bloodied face upright. The museum official, Mariani.

Luca Cassini was fighting to reach the two figures with the weapons, Marrone and Ludovico Ducca behind, trying to drag him back, speaking words of warning, of sense. Fratelli felt his skin grow cold as he recalled the way Luca had smirked when they'd first met and showed him that massive balled fist.

Bit of a fight? I'm your man.

Not now, Fratelli said to himself.

Not with Savonarola's double marching through the tables, staring at Cassini as if he were a lunatic, barking, 'Where is he? Where is he?'

'Get back, Luca,' Fratelli shouted at Cassini, who took not a moment's notice.

Instead the young officer waved his arm ahead and yelled, 'Put that weapon down, will you?' As plainly as if he were dealing with a drunk in the street. Then, at the woman, Cassini bawled, 'And you. I've got your dog, you know. There's going to be more *cara-binieri* in here in a moment than you two have seen in a lifetime. Put those bloody guns down, I say . . .'

Crazed, fixated, Pontecorvo hunted for a single victim among the mob.

Soderini stayed in the shadows, didn't protest when Fratelli reached out and demanded the gun. Holding it down by his side, out of sight, he then stepped out into the waxy yellow candlelight.

I'm a dead man, he thought. What does it matter where and when?

'Where is he?' Pontecorvo yelled.

'In custody,' Fratelli declared as he strode boldly into the room to confront them. 'This nonsense is at an end, Aldo. And so, please, is your anger. Righteous or not.'

The museum man was gone, no doubt about it. It was a miracle he was alone. This wasn't slaughter for slaughter's sake. Not yet.

'He's in our custody.' Fratelli smiled and held out his free hand, keeping the gun hidden by his side in his left. 'As you must be now. You . . .' He nodded at the lean, pale figure behind her. 'And your friend. Put down the weapons. Come with us. Tell us what you know. We have as many questions for these people as you. Help us and we will find you justice . . .'

'Find what?'

It was the woman, and her voice possessed a cold and stony vehemence. She raised the ugly black weapon in his direction.

'Find justice,' Fratelli said more loudly. 'For you. For all of us.' He kept his eyes on the man and it occurred to him that the handgun in those long, powerful arms looked utterly out of place, as if he had no idea how best to use it.

A cook. Someone familiar with knives and the butchery of meat. Vanni Tornabuoni's severed head was his. The bloody corpse of Mariani hers.

Pino Fratelli watched him carefully as he said, 'Twenty years ago my wife died on the steps of our house in Oltrarno, not far from here. Raped and murdered.' His eyes never left those pale, grim features. 'Left with a scarlet frown of lipstick.'

The pale and featureless face broke in a howl of wordless grief and terror.

'Talk to me,' Fratelli demanded, keeping the weapon down in his left hand, walking forward, furious, his head full of heat and pressure and so many urgent questions. 'Tell me why.'

The woman was the crazier. No grief, no agony on her face. Only anger and insanity, and a growing sense of puzzlement. She was turning towards the man behind her.

'What did you do?' Pino Fratelli asked as his head began to swim.

Twenty years before and the memory of that night was still turning, screaming in his head.

In the darkness of the cave where it began came a picture: their make-up on his face, lipstick too, the same as he had in his pocket. Drugs and drink. And something else. A virus that lived inside his blood, a wriggling, screaming memory.

'Filth!' his mother said when he ran shrieking to her, slamming the door in his face, leaving him alone. A bastard child, stranded by the grim cruel thing called fate.

Lost, unable to think, he'd staggered down the road, following the pair of men ahead. In a narrow street near Carmine, an open door. A woman beckoning them in. The rising tide of mud and filth around them. He watched, he followed, hid in the downstairs room amidst the washing and the junk.

Listened to the sounds from above and felt the hellish grotto had followed him all the way across Oltrarno into this modest little house.

Two decades on, and Aldo Pontecorvo thought of the church of Carmine, the place his mother dragged him every Sunday, to confess his sins, never hers. To pinch him when he stared at the naked women on the columns.

Which were you?

That was one question. Another . . .

The creature behind the tree. The beautiful, blonde head atop the curving body of a serpent, as sinuous and deadly as the long, wide wave he'd seen rising out of the muddy waters of the Arno.

Who, in truth, was she?

The answers had been there all along. He had simply wished to avoid them. And had done so, since when the lights had failed and the waters receded a little, he'd stumbled out of that dread house, gone home, let his mother beat him, knowing all the time he was changed forever just as surely as the angel's bitter, violent fury had transformed the fleeing couple as they were driven from the Gates of Paradise.

Two decades to see a chance of salvation. It was with him now in the sweaty, confused interior of the cavern, leering satyrs watching from the crumbling walls.

The woman who'd seduced him. The white-haired man he'd followed from afar for years. A serious, talented detective. Though not wise enough to save his wife.

He watched as the woman turned towards Fratelli, weapon rising in her hand. She'd killed the first man she'd seen, a drone who always left the Brigata early. Would murder them all. That was her intent all along. The hunger was in her blood, unstoppable, and always had been.

'What . . .?' Fratelli began.

Now the detective stood in front of him, oblivious to the woman with her weapon and her rage.

The *carabiniere* had a gun. That was to be expected, though he didn't seem ready to use it. Not yet.

'I will show you . . .' Pontecorvo began.

But saying it brought back the dread pictures, robbed his throat of the words.

'Show me what?' the man demanded.

There were no easy beginnings, no simple answers, and what responses there were lay buried deep, hidden beneath the stultifying layers of time and hurtful memories.

'Enough,' Chavah screamed, turning, flecks of spittle flying from her furious lips, the weapon tight in her strong, bronzed arms.

Fratelli took one step forward. A mistake.

Aldo Pontecorvo watched her start to move and, as she did, he placed the handgun from the Fiesole farmhouse close to the back of her head and pulled the trigger.

The second shot he'd ever fired. The second death after Tornabuoni's.

A scream in the miasmic, close cavern air, and a small, taut body tumbling, arms flailing, towards the suited corpse upon the floor.

Three more shells fired wildly around him as Pontecorvo stumbled backwards, making his way by the dim light of the wan candles. He fell upon the ancient fountain at the rear and, with all his strength, heaved at the central statue there, toppling it, sending the marble figures crashing to the floor.

The weight and pressure in the hillside cistern was released at that moment, as the Arno had been twenty years before. Chill water gushed out of the shattered mouth. Voices bellowed and shrieked behind him.

He pushed through the torrent, raced out into the cold open air, found the first van at the back of the cavern. Behind him he could hear the freed waters gushing wildly from the shattered fountain. The flood was here again.

A lunge for the driver's door, someone in the way, not moving.

The memory came quickly. The Loggia dei Lanzi on another damp, dark night; Vanni Tornabuoni's head in his sack bag, a boatman's hook to hand, waiting on the moment.

She wore a black evening dress with pearls around her smooth, white throat. Her hair was silver in the moonlight, her eyes intelligent, as indignant as scared.

Shrewd enough to flee the cavern once Chavah walked in and shook that rifle at them. To hide somewhere she must have thought as safe a place as any.

'Who are you?' he began.

'No one,' she answered in that same English accent he remembered. 'Let me go.'

What are you looking at? Niente, niente, niente.

The same answer, the same lie.

He thrust her through the door, forced her into the driver's seat. A face more serene than Chavah Efron's. Not so far from that of the first beautiful Eve on the Brancacci wall.

'Drive,' he ordered, raising his pistol to her face. 'Where I want to go. Drive. Or I shoot you now.'

Luca Cassini was there first, so quickly he managed to bang on the door of the van as it struggled along the lane towards Oltrarno. Moments after, he was leaping into a second vehicle, screaming at them to get in.

Marrone made it into the rear. Fratelli, in the passenger seat, watching Cassini struggle with the ignition, heard an unexpected voice.

'This isn't a place for you,' the captain said.

'I'll decide that,' Soderini replied, scrambling in beside him.

Cassini managed to bring the engine to life. And then they lurched off down the passageway.

It was narrow and winding, but not so much that Fratelli expected to see Pontecorvo's van ahead. There it was, anyway, on the main road from the Ponte Vecchio, slowly heading for a side-street corner, back into the warren of houses and alleys that stretched along the river.

'Where on earth's he going, Pino?' Cassini asked. 'You're always full of ideas.'

Fratelli barely heard. His blood was racing, veins pulsing in his temples. He was glad of the seat, that he could hold on to the door with his hand as Luca Cassini chased after the fugitive Pontecorvo. The monster was stirring, choosing its time, as he always knew it would.

'Pino!' Cassini said, fighting with the wheel as he shook Fratelli's arm. 'Are you OK?'

'He's taking Julia back,' Fratelli said in a quiet, weary voice.

'Back where?'

'To Chiara . . .'

Cassini swore. The van ahead had lurched off to the right, was tearing down a single cobbled lane. Away from Fratelli's terraced house.

'Any other ideas?' the young officer asked.

Fratelli was about to speak when his shoulder shook violently.

'My gun,' Soderini ordered, and a hand appeared.

'Carmine,' Fratelli muttered, ignoring the man behind. In his head he could see the figures on the wall: two peaceful and beatific, two in agony. It might have been Chiara's face for Eve. Or Julia's. He was no longer sure.

'My gun!'

Fratelli turned, pistol in hand, aimed it gently in the mayor's direction.

The van slowed down. There was silence in the dark interior.

Silence even from Sandro Soderini, wild-eyed and furious as he stared down the man in front of him.

'This is mine,' Fratelli said as they approached the low church steps and saw a tall figure fly out of the door, dragging Julia with him. 'And so is he.'

The Brancacci in moonlight. A naked couple frescoed forever on the pillars.

Fratelli took three difficult steps forward, listened. The hissing sea of tinnitus was starting in his head. His mind couldn't focus. And still he had Soderini's gun tight in his right hand, clutched to his waist.

Voices in the shadows, among the still and watchful crowds on the walls.

A man's wild chattering. Julia's quiet tones.

Trying to reassure him. To say . . .

Calm down. Be reasonable. All this will end. And end well.

Such an English response. So civilized and in this of all places, the sacred, ancient corner of Oltrarno where humanity's dawdling trek out of the Dark Ages was supposed to begin.

A burst of dim light. A handful of the bulbs in Carmine's interior began to come to life.

Marrone was talking frantically into his radio. Luca Cassini came and placed his burly frame in front, the way he always would. And Sandro Soderini . . .

The briefest of glances around revealed nothing.

'You stay out of this, Pino,' Cassini said as Fratelli walked on.

He saw them now. The tall, miserable figure of Aldo Pontecorvo, in the centre of the chapel; Julia in his arms, a gun to her throat.

She didn't look so scared. More angry, Fratelli thought.

'Keep back!' the young *carabiniere* yelled and tried to hold him.

Fratelli raised Soderini's weapon to the ceiling, loosed off a shell. Listened to the shot boom around the nave.

'I don't wish to hurt you, Luca,' he said, elbowing the young cop aside. 'So kindly keep out of my way.'

No sheets or scaffolding any more. The restorers' work almost done. No bloody smears from a cockerel's neck; no dust of the ages or stains from that terrible inundation two decades before.

This was a world, a universe, in miniature. The eternal couple either side, beckoning the congregation into a sea of humanity; behind them faces speaking another old story, that of Saint Peter, played out on frescoed walls.

Fratelli could remember his mother – the only true mother he could accurately picture – telling him those stories. Peter healing the cripple, raising the dead Tabitha and the son of Theophilus. Curing the sick with his shadow. Arguing with the magician Simon Magus in front of the cruel emperor Nero. Finally crucified upside down in front of a set of medieval walls that might have been the Porta San Frediano a few footsteps beyond the door.

And all the while the world watched; ordinary men, ordinary faces, Florentines through and through, peering from the brushstrokes left by Masaccio, Masalino and Filippino Lippi half a millennium before.

Pontecorvo and Julia seemed to be part of this visual narrative, distantly observed from the vaulted ceiling by a flock of curious angels and a Virgin, enthroned on high.

His mother's dead voice whispered in his ear, the words he'd first heard forty years before.

'We're all part of this story, Pino. We always will be.'

Not me, he thought. I didn't believe that then. I don't now. We're what we make of ourselves, not the product of another's imagination.

The man in front of him stood still, waiting it seemed, Julia firm in his grip.

Fratelli stepped forward, struggling to keep his balance. His head was ringing with sounds, voices, memories. It was a struggle to raise the gun ahead of him, to say in a shaking voice, 'Let her go, Aldo. For God's sake, no more blood.'

A booming, hollow sound, like wood exploding. The main doors to Carmine thrown open. The shouts of men. Carabinieri, Fratelli didn't doubt it.

'You let your wife go!' Pontecorvo cried. 'What about her blood? Who are you to speak?'

'Pino,' Julia said. 'Don't come closer. Don't . . .'

Fratelli raised the gun again, loosed a second shell into the ceiling, felt fresco and plaster fall around him like hard rain.

For a moment his vision blurred, went black. He could hear his own breathing. Feel the blood racing through his veins.

When his sight came back, he was aware of something else. Behind Pontecorvo and Julia a figure in black, hunched in the corner. Couldn't see who. Anyone might have dashed through the shadows of Carmine, got into that place unnoticed.

Men behind, low voices. Marrone issuing orders. The metallic snap of weapons being prepared.

The black shape shot out of the corner, arm raised, silver blade glinting, fell on Aldo Pontecorvo's back, stabbing, shrieking, flailing at the tall man's back.

A howl of agony and shock. Julia slipped free. Fratelli seized her arm as she fell forward, dragged her forcefully into his arms. Then the two of them fell to the wall, against the faces of dead Florentine nobles, locked together, breathing in anxious gasps.

Two shapes on the floor, entwined like one. An arm rising, falling, a long knife smeared in blood.

Marrone was there, Cassini too, yelling, swearing.

Pino Fratelli wasn't holding Julia any more. She was holding him. Something in her eyes . . . Fratelli was unable to find the words to frame the question.

A final scream and the black shape rose from the chapel floor. Aldo Pontecorvo lay on the tiles, face up, eyes glassy, mouth open, blood on his neck, blood everywhere.

A breathless man climbed to his feet and stood over him, dagger in hand.

'Bruno?' Sandro Soderini said, walking through the crowd of *carabinieri*, into the chapel's heart.

Marrone followed, eyeing the priest and the weapon in his hand. Luca Cassini too, bending down on the floor to check the still figure there.

He didn't look up when he said, 'Well, this one's gone. That's for sure.'

All eyes on the parish priest of Santa Maria del Carmine. Father Bruno Lazzaro. A man Fratelli had known since childhood.

'I heard a noise.' His wild eyes ranging the chamber. 'While I was in here working. This . . .' His hand gestured to the dread shape on the ground. 'This animal had a woman with him. A weapon. I had to act. It wasn't . . .'

Julia's arms left him. Fratelli clung to the wall, head clearing at that point. Mind focusing.

'He told me, Priest!' she said without the least hesitation, pointing back towards the column with the fallen couple. Then, more quietly, as Bruno Lazzaro glared at her, 'He told me. The cockerel was for Tornabuoni. The shape above the snake . . .'

Her hand swept the fresco. Julia Wellbeloved glanced at Fratelli.

'It was a dog collar, Pino. Not a halo.'

Fratelli closed his eyes and wanted to laugh.

'He thought Lazzaro would be at the Brigata tonight,' she went on. 'And when he wasn't, he came for him here. For you. Because—'

'What are these lies?' the man in black bellowed, raising the knife.

Cassini was on him like a shot, forcing the blade from his hand with a wrench of the wrist and a simple, 'I'll have that, thank you.'

Julia circled the priest. 'You and Tornabuoni raped her. Then you murdered her.'

'No!'

'Both of you, while Aldo Pontecorvo, a frightened, broken child, someone you'd used already, listened. Watched. And when you'd fled and he could think of nothing else, he painted that dismal frown on her dead lips.'

She went quiet, for Fratelli's sake. No need. He could picture this already, every moment, each step along the grim and bloody way.

With a nod he walked into the centre of the chapel, looked at the priest, beckoned with his gloved hand, the gun still in it and said, 'More.'

'These are lies!' Lazzaro cried. 'I saw nothing.'

Fratelli raised the weapon to the priest's head. No one moved. No one spoke.

'It wasn't me, Pino! Chiara called us in from the street. Tornabuoni . . . my back was turned. I was downstairs. She said there was a little dinghy you used for fishing. I went looking for it.'

A gesture as if from the pulpit, then hands to his face, despair and sorrow.

'When I came back that beast—'

'He told me,' Julia cut in. 'Everything he'd never dared before. He heard her screams.'

'No!'

She walked forward, stood next to Fratelli to face the priest directly. 'Then, on the staircase, you held Chiara's arms while Tornabuoni throttled her.' A stabbing finger in his face. 'You!'

'And you'd believe this filth?' Lazzaro asked, and fetched a kick at the slashed corpse by his feet. 'You trust his word over a man of God?'

'But God wasn't there, Bruno,' Fratelli said calmly. 'Not on that long and miserable night just when you needed him. He'd left you on your own. Hadn't he?'

Fratelli took one step closer, passed the weapon to Cassini, looked at the man in black and waited.

So many faces on them at that moment. Marrone's men and Soderini. Julia. The young *carabiniere* Pino Fratelli had so come to admire. And the stern, judgemental citizens, given a kind of immortality by the brushes of artists long dead.

A cruel scowl crossed the priest's face. He surveyed them all. 'You pompous, craven asses. You sin like animals and pass the guilt to me.' He stabbed his chest with a bloody hand. 'It was the end of the world.'

Cassini had got a pair of handcuffs from somewhere and was unwinding them.

'The end of the world,' Bruno Lazzaro murmured. 'Am I owed nothing? No pleasure? No company?'

The young *carabiniere* took his hands, slapped the cuffs on his wrists.

'This is what you're owed, chum. And the rest to come. Pino?'

Fratelli's head felt as if it was clearing. He wondered what might replace the terrors and fears and fury that had festered there so long.

Then something new began to rise inside him, cold and roaring, as big as the world, as determined and inevitable as death itself.

The flood. It was here now. In truth it had never gone away.

The bright and vivid colours around him lost their lustre. Not long after, his limbs failed too. Pino Fratelli felt himself falling towards Carmine's hard cold stones and the fast-approaching dark.

December 1986

Snow beyond the windows of the private room. Bare trees in the distance. A city turning white beneath the blizzard. Foreign voices in the corridor outside.

This is not home, Pino Fratelli thought. This is not a place to die.

He lay on the hard hospital bed feeling drowsy from the drugs and the disease. The doctors and nurses had left them for this brief moment before the theatre. Now Julia Wellbeloved and Luca Cassini sat on either side of him; Julia on his right, squeezing the hand that still had a little feeling, Luca making small talk.

Whatever happened now, this last month had been filled with something he'd missed for many a year. Something he'd excluded from his life – deliberately, spitefully almost. A sense of friendship, of family. An unexpected and ridiculous form of love.

'You get in there and get that operation done,' Cassini said, repeating an admonition he'd uttered only a few minutes before.

'That is the general idea, I believe,' Fratelli replied with an exasperated sigh.

'The food here . . . Ugh.'

'No *lampredotto*, Luca,' Julia noted in her beautifully accented Italian. 'No *lardo* or *trippa*, no *finocchiona*, no glass of Negroni—'

'Stop this!' Fratelli cried. 'Stop it now.'

He knew her game. She was as cunning as a vixen. Wave a carrot on a stick. Hope the donkey will smile and follow out of interest. But the donkey was ill. Beyond hope, or so Ambra Neri believed. Julia's father, a doctor too, one with connections to specialists in London, had found a surgeon who felt there was a chance, however slender. He seemed willing to – in the man's own cheery words – 'give it a whirl'.

'We have pies, Luca,' Julia went on. 'You like pies?'

'Oh,' he said with enthusiasm, 'I like pies. Who doesn't like pies?'

'Shut up about food, will you?' Fratelli begged. 'I will ask one more time only and on this occasion I demand an answer. How for the love of God can I pay for all this?'

They looked at one another in silence.

'Answers,' Fratelli demanded.

'Sandro Soderini,' she said. 'He insisted when he heard.'

Luca Cassini was chuckling so much that his big shoulders were heaving.

'Soderini?' Fratelli asked.

'You don't have a monopoly on guilt, you know,' Cassini told him. 'He was dead cut up about what happened. Wasn't he, Julia?'

'You got it out of him,' Fratelli said, jabbing a finger at her.

She nodded. 'Sandro's rich. He's got enough trouble on his plate as it is. True, the bad Brigata . . . Tornabuoni's orgies . . . happened when he wasn't around.'

And were there bargains? He didn't ask. A stupid part of him was jealous. He knew how Soderini looked at her. Knew too that she found this amusing. Perhaps even flattering.

'He was an accomplice to this nightmare,' Fratelli declared.

'I don't think so.' She stroked his hot brow and he barely felt it. 'Really. He rarely went. From what Walter's gathered, most of them absented themselves when it got . . . sleazy.'

'Sleazy?' Cassini asked. 'Bit more than sleazy, if you ask me.'

'Sandro thought it was just a bit of naughty fun. He's such a sad old playboy. Really. That's all. And now he's got the press on his back asking awkward questions.'

'So I'm part of his rehabilitation, am I?'

She smiled, shrugged.

'He doesn't want anyone to know he's paying for this. Even you.' A shrug, an Italian gesture; one perhaps she'd learned from him. 'I warned Sandro you'd get it out of me. You're good at that.'

Fratelli grunted a quiet curse. His left hand went to his head, felt the rough, shorn scalp there.

'Now you're indulging me. They cut my hair. My hair! My long and beautiful mane.'

'Good thing too,' Cassini told him. 'Too bloody long, it was. The captain would kick my arse if I showed up to work like that.'

Walter Marrone had accepted Cassini back into the Carabinieri with eager, open arms. Luca was no longer the *stazione* idiot, the unwanted boy.

Fratelli asked himself: was that why he took to this callow, monosyllabic but utterly charming young man from the start? Not just his transparent, dogged honesty, but the fact that he was, in a way, an orphan too? Was he drawn to the lost and the abandoned? If so, why had he not come across the damaged and dangerous Aldo Pontecorvo, a solitary, crazed pawn in someone else's plans, a victim who had lived only a few streets away from his own home in Oltrarno?

'You care too much,' he said out loud.

'Who does?' Julia asked.

'I do. You told me that once. Didn't you? You can't care for everyone. You said that. I'm sure. Or maybe I dreamt it.'

She went back to squeezing his hand in her gentle fingers. He could feel a little of the warmth. Not much.

'You're babbling, Pino,' Cassini interrupted. He nodded towards the door. 'Get that head of yours in there and come out fixed.'

I will, one way or another, Fratelli thought.

The notion of death didn't bother him much. He'd lived with it for too long to care. But the idea he'd never see Julia Wellbeloved again . . . that he'd never know how Luca Cassini fared in the ranks of Marrone's Carabinieri. All this was unthinkable.

'I should go,' he said. 'Time to . . . *give it a whirl*. Tell them. I'm not afraid.' He smiled. 'Well, a little.' His good hand went to his shaved head again. 'My hair . . .'

'Your hair will grow again,' she told him. 'You'll wake up feeling dreadful. And then . . .' She shrugged and brushed her fingers across his cheek. 'Then you'll feel better. Before long you'll be back in Oltrarno. Sitting in your little bar in San Niccolò. Drinking a Negroni. Picking at a plate of *salumi*.'

'What doesn't kill you makes you stronger,' Luca Cassini said very sagely.

Both of them stared at him.

'Who told you that?' Fratelli asked.

'You did, Pino.' The young *carabiniere* scratched his short black hair. 'Didn't you?'

'My God,' Fratelli groaned, 'if Luca Cassini is quoting Nietzsche at me, this world is surely too interesting to leave. Call the nurses, Julia. Have them stab me with their needles and place a mask over my face. Let's get this done with.'

'Three cheers for that,' said the young *carabiniere*, then winked and left them alone.

*   *   *

White shapes around him. A line in the arm. Soon they'd wheel him from this private room into the theatre.

'What is it?' he asked.

Her fingertips traced the place on his head where they'd drawn their marks – the guides for the incisions and the saw to come.

'You told me all this came from some poison inside. From the time they took you from your parents in Rome. Or when Chiara died. From the flood. That it was a monster waiting inside, wondering when to wake.'

'I talk drivel sometimes. Haven't you noticed?'

There were tears in her eyes and he hated to see that.

'Is it gone, Pino?'

'I want to go to Rome. The Ponte Sant'Angelo. I ought to tell the stone angel I've no need of the name Ariel Montefiore. They can use it for another. Pino Fratelli will do. Perhaps I can show you those tortoises in the fountain. And . . .'

So many things unsaid, undone. Sitting in a quiet cabin in the Bardini Gardens above San Niccolò, drinking in the view of the city with its churches and belfries, its domes and towers. Ambling along the verdant lanes of Bellosguardo. Omissions unnoticed until they seemed out of reach.

'Is it gone?' she asked again.

The nurse was at the door. The surgeon stood by her side, tapping his watch.

Pino Fratelli shook his head. 'Why ask such a question, Julia? You killed it, didn't you? And now your friend will remove its corpse.'

With that Julia Wellbeloved rose from her chair, bent over, kissed him on both cheeks. Her hair fell all around him. Her fragrance filled his aching head. The nurse had a hypodermic and gently fed its contents into his arm.

The flood came for him then, cold and roaring and relentless. Dismal past and hopeful present locked together as one, mingling into the unknown nothingness called future.